A MOTIVE FOR MURDER

Before I pulled away from the curb, Liz ran after me. "Hey, I did just think of something that could be important. I don't know why I didn't think of it before. I guess it's because we were talking about the Teen Center."

"What is it?"

"A few months back, Brody had been doing private counseling for a mystery kid outside of the Teen Center. He had to keep his identity secret. I thought it sounded kind of fishy, but we aren't together anymore so it was really none of my business. Then one day he confided in me that he regretted getting involved in it. He was under a lot of pressure from the boy's family, and he was really nervous about the whole thing."

"Do you know what kind of pressure?"

"I don't know anything more than I told you. He wanted to keep me and Christina out of it. He only told me in case something happened to him. And it looks like something did . . ."

Books by Libby Klein

CLASS REUNIONS ARE MURDER

MIDNIGHT SNACKS ARE MURDER

Published by Kensington Publishing Corporation

Midnight Snacks Are Murder

Libby Klein

KENSINGTON BOOKS
KENSINGTON PUBLISHING CORP.
http://www.kensingtonbooks.com

KENSINGTON BOOKS are published by

Kensington Publishing Corp.
119 West 40th Street
New York, NY 10018

All Kensington titles, imprints, and distributed lines are available at special quantity discounts for bulk purchases for sales promotion, premiums, fund-raising, educational, or institutional use.

Special book excerpts or customized printings can also be created to fit specific needs. For details, write or phone the office of the Kensington Sales Manager: Attn.: Sales Department. Kensington Publishing Corp., 119 West 40th Street, New York, NY 10018. Phone: 1-800-221-2647.

Kensington and the K logo Reg. U.S. Pat. & TM Off.

First Printing: August 2018
ISBN-13: 978-1-4967-1305-6
ISBN-10: 1-4967-1305-2

eISBN-13: 978-1-4967-1306-3
eISBN-10: 1-4967-1306-0

10 9 8 7 6 5 4 3 2 1

Printed in the United States of America

Chapter 1

Mischief and Mayhem were running amuck in South Jersey. Mischief, or as I called her, Aunt Ginny, was on the warpath flanked by her first in command, Mayhem, also known as my black smoke Persian, Figaro the instigator. Today their battleground was the kitchen and the enemy was knee deep in the hoopla installing pearl-gray cabinets and black-and-silver granite countertops.

Aunt Ginny barked out orders like Patton leading the Allied forces through France. "If any one of you puts so much as a single scratch on my Romba cuckoo clock, there will be hell to pay! My first husband, Lovell, brought that home from Germany in 1945. It's survived three wars, a fire, and Hurricane Sandy. I'll be darned if it's going down because of a slipshod kitchen remodel."

I'd been stranded in Cape May with my eighty-ish great aunt ever since I was lured up here to attend my twenty-fifth high school reunion a few weeks ago, and was voted most likely to kill a cheerleader. I'd never wanted to return to the birthplace of my most painful memories, but I'd come to accept that Cape May had a certain charm. One that I'd call "better than a sharp stick in the eye." I'd been away long enough to forget that Aunt Ginny teetered on the edge of crazy. Now it was my job to look after this rickety old rattletrap . . . and the house. With two redheads under the same roof, and one of them having just bought a wakeboard on xtremesports4seniors.com, I think twenty years in the women's prison would have been easier.

We'd been undergoing a major refurbishment to transform the Queen Anne Victorian into a quaint, beachy bed-and-breakfast so I'd have a way to support Aunt Ginny and she could keep her independence. A new roof had been laid, the porch and swing had been repaired, and the entire outside of the house had been freshly painted in Easter-egg shades of butter yellow, baby pink, and lavender. A wooden shingle hung in the front yard proclaiming us the Butterfly House B & B, punctuated with a giant blue-and-black butterfly. I'd gotten the local radio station to run a call-in contest giving away passes to our special Fall Fling Event. The free weekend got me some generosity points, and sent me four sets of guests to be my guinea pigs. There was still a long list of projects to be completed before we officially launched our grand opening, not the least of which was to find ways to keep Aunt Ginny and Figaro from scaring off the clientele.

I ran upstairs with my checklist to the guest bedroom we'd named the Swallowtail Suite and inspected the work. "Smitty!" A little man with a perfectly round bald head like a crystal garden globe, and deep-set cow eyes danced into the room.

"What's up, boss?"

"Smitty, why is this room painted Island Pool? It's supposed to be Buttercream. Island Pool was for the Adonis Blue Suite. It matches the king-size duvet in that room."

Smitty returned a blank expression.

"It's a theme."

Smitty scratched his head.

"We've talked about it at length."

Smitty grunted and pulled a folded checklist out of his paint-smeared overalls. He frowned and looked up into my eyes. "I can fix that." Then he gave me a Benny Hill backhanded salute and a "whoop whoop whoop" from the Three Stooges and shimmied backwards out of the room.

I sighed. Itty Bitty Smitty, as everyone called him, was my general contractor. He was highly recommended by Handyman Haven and I now suspected he either had dirt on the owner or they sent him to me in a self-survival effort to get him off their referral list. He was the only handyman within my budget who was available on short notice. I was starting to see why.

I heard a crash on the first floor and Figaro slinked up the stairs and sat at my feet. "What did you do?" He licked his paw and gave me an innocent look before wiping it on his ear. I ran down the stairs to the kitchen to see workmen cleaning up a stack of broken stone tiles that were left over from laying the new kitchen floor.

"No problem, ma'am. Julio knocked the slate over while backing up to install the new cooler. Everything is a-okay."

The new cooler was a seventy-two-inch, triple-door, brushed-nickel refrigerator and freezer that had cost as much as a small car. I bet you could fit forty-seven turkeys in there. If we ever lost the house we could move into the freezer side and sublet the fridge space to another family. I'd spent a fortune on this bed-and-breakfast gamble, and Aunt Ginny and I had nothing to fall back on if it failed. My mother-in-law had invested just enough into the venture to keep her strings attached so she could yank on me whenever she wanted. I doubted Georgina would approve of our new apricot kitchen or my splurge purchase of a BlueStar Infused Copper range with double ovens. When Georgina makes a big purchase it's a wise investment. When I do it, apparently it's superfluous. Between the bed-and-breakfast baking, and my daily delivery of gluten-free muffins to La Dolce Vita coffee shop, the 1970s avocado-green General Electric model had to be replaced. I was afraid it would explode if I ran it for more than two hours at a time.

I reached into a box I'd brought with me yesterday when I'd officially moved out of the home my late husband and I had shared for more than twenty years in Waterford. It was a painful move, and with it, part of my life—the part with John—was really over. But I had promised him I would live and be happy. I'd had no idea how difficult that promise would be to keep when I made it.

"Come here, baby. Let mama set you up." I pulled out my prized powder-pink Italian espresso machine and lovingly placed it on the new countertop, polishing the chrome. If John could see us now. Thinking of him made my heart grip in my chest. Each passing day got a little better, but sometimes it still hurt enough to take my breath away. I missed him terribly.

Smitty appeared beside me. "Are we on target to have the kitchen painted by Thursday?" I asked him. "I have four sets of guests arriving Friday afternoon for a complimentary practice run. Those initial reviews could have a powerful impact on business going forward, so I need them to be stellar."

"Absolutely. You can count on me, boss."

There was a crash from the dining room, followed by Aunt Ginny's yell, "Smitty!"

Smitty grunted and said, "I can fix that," then ran out to inspect the damage.

Stress like this was why I had Señor Ramone's Tacos and Tater Tots on speed dial in Virginia. I looked around the kitchen. It was coming together. This time tomorrow I'd be up to my elbows in blueberries and almond meal, coconut flour, maple syrup, and Tahitian vanilla beans. I added parchment paper and muffin liners to my growing shopping list for the chef supply warehouse, along with commercial muffin tins, sheet pans, and a twelve-shelf baker's cooling rack.

I was just about to take my espresso machine for her inaugural run in her new digs when Smitty tore in on his cell phone.

"We have an emergency."

"This isn't another out-of-marshmallow-fluff kind of emergency like last week, is it?"

"The BlueStar is on backorder."

I could feel the panic rising. "No no no! It can't be, Smitty."

Aunt Ginny entered the kitchen, her *I Love Lucy* dyed hair piled up in a beehive on top of her head, and dressed in what looked like pale blue pajamas with a white dragon print on the sleeve. "What's on back-order?"

Smitty turned to her. "The range."

Aunt Ginny whistled and shook her head. "I can't take anymore. I'm strung up tighter than a new fiddle. I'm going to karate to relax."

"Please don't crane-kick Jimmy Kapps today. You already have two strikes."

"He knew what he was getting into when he signed up for the class."

"He's twelve."

"How else is he gonna learn?"

I had a better chance of teaching a badger to ride a bike than winning an argument with Aunt Ginny. "I'll see you for dinner tonight. Which now that I think about it will have to be salads or takeout, since we don't have an oven." I narrowed my eyes at Smitty. "How can I run a bed-and-breakfast if I can't make breakfast, Smitty?"

Smitty covered the mouthpiece to his phone and shrugged. "Cereal?"

"I really don't think we want to make a name for ourselves for being the Cap'n Crunch bed-and-breakfast."

My cell phone vibrated and I saw a text from Giampaolo, the owner of the espresso bar. I'd been ducking him since he laid that sizzling kiss on me. Of course, that didn't stop me from daydreaming about him.

I had three men in my life. Tim, my high school sweetheart. I'd never really gotten over him. Then there was John, who knocked me up in college. His family came from money and mine came from crazy, so naturally a shotgun wedding was in order. And finally, Giampaolo, or Gia for short. The sexy Italian barista befriended me during my captivity when I was maliciously and unfairly under investigation by a vindictive blond police officer. But that's another story. I turned into a pool of melted chocolate whenever Gia was around and I'm pretty sure he could tell.

My head was clogged with murky thoughts of men and moving on, and I had to wade through them to read Gia's text. It said he had something important to discuss with me and could I come over this afternoon to do it in person. Before I could tap out so much as a smiley face, there was another crash by the front door, followed by Aunt Ginny crying out in pain.

My heart lurched and I ran to the foyer with a prayer that she was okay. Figaro galloped past me to be the first on the scene. Aunt Ginny's tiny frame lay on the parquet wood floor in a heap. I ran to her side and yelled to anyone listening, "Call an ambulance!"

Chapter 2

"Poppy Blossom, don't you dare call an ambulance or I will flame your heinie." Aunt Ginny groaned and shifted herself upright. "I lost my balance, that's all. I haven't been sleeping, with all this rigmarole in my house. I'm just petered out."

"Falling is not a small thing, Aunt Ginny, especially at your age."

Aunt Ginny scowled and gave me a sideways look.

"Well, it's not. And I think we need to get you checked out to make sure you didn't break anything."

"But Master Kim—"

"Will have to smash boards without you."

I had Smitty scoop her into my Toyota Corolla and belt her in. She made him run back into the house twice before we could leave. Once to get her pocketbook, and the other time to fetch her Pretty in Pink lipstick from the hall bathroom counter.

We started out toward Cape Urgent Care, but Aunt Ginny howled and hollered that only her doctor knew her and was qualified to diagnose her. He'd been her family physician since I was in ponytails, and at her age she should have a say in her medical treatment. For me not to acquiesce to her demands was nothing short of elder abuse. She pitched such a fit that I bypassed Urgent Care and drove straight to Dr. Weingarten's. I was tempted to drop her off at the door and return to collect her at the end of the day, but then she grabbed her chest and said she couldn't breathe, and I immediately repented of my momentary impatience.

The North Cape May office was a converted two-story Victorian Provincial with blue shingles and a sign out front that said CAPE MEDICAL ASSOCIATES. The waiting room was set up in the original front parlor. The odors of cabbage and Bengay permeated the atmosphere. It was currently filled with yellow-flowered sofas and blue-haired old ladies, many of whom didn't actually have appointments. They were here to drink the free coffee and sit in the waiting room playing a few rounds of Where Does It Hurt, or Who Has the Scariest Looking Mole?

I signed Aunt Ginny in at the front desk and filled the nurse in about her episode. She said they would get Aunt Ginny back right away. Not ten minutes later, a young woman in pink scrubs with the phrase *Nurses Do It in Harmony* embroidered over the front pocket came to fetch the crabby patient.

Aunt Ginny narrowed her eyes and grimaced at the nurse. "Where's Yolanda?"

The girl gave Aunt Ginny a pleasant smile. "Yolanda had her baby. I'm Tracy. I'll be filling in while she's on maternity leave."

Aunt Ginny stood, reluctantly. "When was the baby born?"

"Last Thursday in the middle of the night."

"Darn. I had Sunday morning in the pool."

As Tracy led Aunt Ginny through to the patient rooms, Aunt Ginny cross-examined her. "What kind of nursing degree do you have? What kind of grades did you get? I don't want to be treated by a nurse who got Cs. Why didn't you go all the way to become a doctor?"

I sent up a silent prayer for Nurse Tracy. I sat in the waiting room too upset and distracted to read the much pawed-over issues of *People*. I didn't know what I would do if I lost Aunt Ginny. We'd gone through a lot together. I'd fully expected her to be honored by Al Roker and the Smucker's jelly people one day. Sass and stubbornness were all that was holding her together, and they don't have a pill for that yet if it fails. She had been good to me my whole life. My mother dumped me on her doorstep when I was a kid. She had raised me, and I repaid her with a hasty exodus the moment the ink was dry on my high school diploma. If I could take it all back for a few more years with her, I would do it in a blink. Now I was responsible for her well-being. I was going to be sure to take better care of her from now on. I wiped a tear off my cheek.

Twenty minutes later, Aunt Ginny sashayed into the waiting room looking like she'd just won first place at the Senior Center Tapioca Cook-off. She waved at friends across the waiting room. "Hammish, how's the bursitis? Carol gets extra points if that rash has spread."

Nurse Tracy handed me Aunt Ginny's discharge papers. "She's suffering from anxiety and sleep deprivation. The doctor is giving her two prescriptions and she needs to relax and avoid stress as much as possible." She pointed to the papers in my hand. "She has one for her nerves and one to help her sleep."

"That's it? She doesn't need a CAT scan or anything?"

Aunt Ginny smiled at Nurse Tracy and jabbed me in the side with her elbow.

Nurse Tracy smiled back. "Nope. If she doesn't improve in a few days the doctor may order some further tests, but for now she's free to go about her regular routine."

I wondered what Nurse Tracy would say if she knew Aunt Ginny's regular routine included rollerblading on the boardwalk and Krav Maga classes. It was unusual for Aunt Ginny to fall victim to so much stress. Usually she was just a carrier.

We made a quick stop at the pharmacy to fill the prescriptions. We arrived home two hours later, loaded down with Aunt Ginny's shampoo, conditioner, a jar of Oil of Olay, a tub of Noxzema, two packs of Halls cough drops, a tube of ChapStick, a box of Turtles candy, Maybelline's entire Dazzling Disco collection of eyeshadow, blush, and lipstick, a pair of flip-flops from the dollar bin, silver glitter nail polish, emery boards, and the drugs. I was considering taking one of her antianxiety pills for my efforts.

I opened the front door and was rolled over by an eerie calm. There were no saws or electric drills. No workmen hollering in Spanish to each other. No *nyuck-nyuck-nyucks* from Itty Bitty Smitty. Just deafening silence. The temperature had dropped, but it was warmer outside than in the foyer. Figaro was sitting on the third step with his ears flattened against his head, swishing his tail to a menacing beat.

Aunt Ginny was frozen in place. "I don't like this."

I took a step into the house and noticed all the workmen sitting on the couch in a line in the library, hands on knees, looking straight ahead. Smitty was perched on the end wearing a scowl. They looked like little boys caught smoking in the bathroom by the principal.

I approached Smitty, their commander in chief. "What's going on? Why is no one working?"

Smitty rolled his eyes and nudged his head toward something behind me. A pair of icy hands came around to cover my eyes and a shrill voice said, "Guess who?"

Chapter 3

I felt my chest tighten and my breath came in short bursts. *Please just let me be having a stroke.*

Five feet four inches of brunette wickedness packed in a vintage pink Coco Chanel suit stood in front of me.

"Georgina. What a surprise." *Much like the way that iceberg was a surprise to the* Titanic.

"I came to check on my investment and see how the house was coming along."

Oh, sweet Jesus.

Aunt Ginny took a seat in the wingback chair in front of the fireplace. Figaro jumped up on her lap but kept his eyes on Georgina, as if waiting for her to turn back to her natural state as Queen of the Underworld when the sun set.

Georgina marched in front of the workmen like she was looking at a prison lineup. "And thank God, I found these"—she waved her hand in dismissal at the workers—"men about to install the world's largest refrigerator in that tiny kitchen. I knew there must be some mistake. I mean really, Poppy, why do you need a refrigerator that monstrous? You're not holding retreats at the Ritz-Carlton."

"The refri—" I started, but Georgina cut me off.

"And this little fellow . . ." She pointed a perfectly manicured pink fingernail at Smitty. "What was your name again? Smutty, or something?"

Smitty rolled his eyes and grunted.

"Anyway, I found him right in the thick of it, directing them to hook it up."

"Georgina!" My voice came out brusquer than I had intended, so I tried it again, softer. "Georgina, you didn't have to come all the way up here to check on things. I could have sent you a report."

"Nonsense. You know you've never undertaken a project of this magnitude before. What kind of business partner would I be if I left you to lose all our investment money guided by your lack of experience? It's like I told my dear late Phillip, we're partners. You shouldn't do anything without my valuable oversight."

Yeah, I was pretty sure that was what killed him.

The workmen shifted uncomfortably in their seats. Smitty made the sign of the cross.

"We're not launching a hospital wing; we're opening a bed-and-breakfast. Who do you think oversaw all the house repairs for the past twenty years?"

"Well now, you're just making my point for me."

My cell phone buzzed in my back pocket. *Oh, thank God, please be a telemarketer.* I reviewed the alert. It was my calendar alarm reminding me about my appointment with Gia. Followed by another alert to put on Spanx.

"So, I see your cell phone isn't lost after all."

"I didn't tell you it was lost."

"No. You just never answer it when I need you."

Only a fool answers the phone when death comes a-calling. Georgina put her hands on her hips and jutted her chin out. "What? You don't have a smart response for that?"

"Not one I can say out loud."

Georgina narrowed her eyes and squeezed her lips together.

"I have a meeting I have to get to." *And a gorgeous Italian to try to control myself around.* I turned to the workmen. "Guys, you can get back to work. The refrigerator is fine. Georgina, everything is under control. I'll send you some pictures and flow charts by Friday. Have a safe trip back to Waterford." The workmen hotfooted it out of the library. I snatched up my purse and held it in front of me like a shield.

Georgina trilled an imperious laugh. "Poppy, don't be ridiculous. I'm not going home. I'm here for a few weeks to help you launch the business."

Dear God, what have I done to deserve this?

Smitty grunted. Aunt Ginny took a pill. Figaro hacked up a fur ball. Being holed up in here with Georgina criticizing my every move. *If I killed her now, I would be out in time to collect social security.*

Chapter 4

The smell of freshly roasted espresso beans greeted me in the rear parking lot as I pulled into La Dolce Vita's loading zone at the Washington Street Mall. He was waiting for me. Leaning seductively against the doorjamb, all six foot two of Italian sexy. My face grew warm and I began to tingle. Dressed in a sharp white dress shirt with navy pinstripes tucked into dark slacks, his arms were crossed over his chest beneath a confident smile. One eyebrow cocked when we made visual contact and I felt the heat rise to my face.

"*Bella*, I miss you. You have been avoiding me." His deep voice poured honey all over me.

"What?" I gushed. "No, I haven't. Don't be silly. Why would anyone want to avoid you? I sure wouldn't." *Oh God. Shut up, Poppy, shut up!*

He leaned in close and studied my eyes. The intensity of his gaze unnerved me. He smelled so good. A combination of vanilla, cedarwood, and coffee. "Was it the kiss?"

My heart was galloping the Kentucky Derby, but all I could think about were his lips on mine and how I wanted to feel them again. "Wh-what? N-no. Not the kiss."

He reached up and tucked a wild strand of hair behind my ear. "You don't like me?"

I stared into his eyes and my neck and shoulders went loose and giggly. My words came out breathy and uneven. "No . . . I . . . I like you."

He leaned in close to my face and I closed my eyes. I felt his lips graze my forehead. My eyes fluttered open and a moment passed between us where his eyes judged my response to him. He smiled warmly. "Good. I like you too." My knees went gooey. "Come. I will make you a coconut latte and we'll talk of plans."

Oooh. Plans for what? I need to lose at least thirty pounds before I'll allow myself to get naked in the daylight. Wait. What are we talking about?

We went through the back kitchen to the caramel-and-chocolate-colored dining room, where creamy coffee-tone leather bar stools lined up at the walnut espresso bar.

"You've been dropping off the muffins and leaving so quickly I've hardly had any time with you. I thought maybe there was someone else."

"Someone else?" The image of Tim flashed in my mind with a burst of shame.

Gia was watching me closely. His smile never left his face, but there was anxiety behind his eyes that belied some of his confidence. "Is there?"

I took a deep breath. "Well. No. I mean maybe. I'm not sure."

Gia nodded and warmed a pitcher of coconut and almond milk. "Mm-hmm."

"I have sort of reconnected with an old boyfriend."

He nodded but never broke eye contact. "Okay."

"I was supposed to marry him twenty years ago, but my cheating on him and the resulting pregnancy kind of threw a kink into those plans." I paused to let that sink in. I waited for signs of disappointment or disgust to roll over Gia's expression.

Gia cocked his head and a slow smile spread across his face. "*Bella*, you have a child?" He placed the finished latte in front of me.

"Oh no! No. I-I lost the baby. I couldn't have them after that."

His face paled. He came around the counter and wrapped me in his arms. I tried to be cool and keep it together, but I ended up with tears running down his pinstripes. He pulled me closer and I gave in to his embrace.

"I am so sorry for your loss. I don't know what I would do without my son. Henry is such a big part of my life. I know he isn't the same for you, but he does adore you. If you ever want to spend time with him, you just need to say the word."

My heart swelled in my chest for this beautiful, generous man. If only our timing wasn't so off. I dried my eyes on a paper napkin. "Thank you. I would love that."

Gia's sister Karla came in from the back with her long dark hair tied up in a topknot, and wrapped an apron around her tiny waist. Dressed in a red leather miniskirt and red stiletto boots, she belonged on the cover of Italian *Vogue* rather than the business end of a frothing wand. Looking at Karla was like looking in a mirror. At a fun house. After cataract surgery.

She looked from me to Gia and shook her head. Gia sent her off to get a new bottle of white chocolate syrup from the storage room and sat on the bar stool next to me.

"So. This boyfriend. You are serious?"

I took a sip of my latte. "What? Oh no. We've only

been out a couple of times. He's very busy running his restaurant."

Gia cocked his head to the side. "You have an understanding?"

"About what?"

"You are exclusive?"

"With Tim? We've never talked about it. I'm not even sure we're actually dating. I just feel really ashamed like I'm cheating on him again because I keep thinking about kissing you."

What did I just say? Oh no no no no! I flicked my eyes up to Gia's to see if maybe luck was on my side and he didn't catch that. Nope. Judging from his Cheshire-cat grin, I'd say he heard me. I'd seen that look in his eyes before, and I never quite knew what he was up to.

Karla swiveled back into the room with the syrup.

Gia spun my bar stool to face him. "If you haven't discussed being exclusive, then there is no problem." He raised an eyebrow and smiled. "You can tell the high school boyfriend you are keeping your options open and he should too."

Karla snorted. "Oh yeah, that'll work."

Gia threw her a scowl that she matched for him. Then he turned a much softer expression to me. "Let's talk about your deliveries. The gluten-free muffins are selling faster than we can stock them. The Celiac Support Group keeps asking what else I have that's gluten-free. Do you think you could come up with some afternoon and evening treats?"

"I could try some gluten-free cookies, and brownies would be very easy."

"That sounds great. What do you think about those different-colored fancy French cookies that look like . . ." He trailed off and said something in Italian to Karla.

She responded, "Pretentious whoopie pies?"

"*Sì.* Can you make them?"

"Macarons?"

"Yes, those. I see those popping up in coffee shops in New York. Do you think they could be made gluten-free?"

"I can check. I must warn you though. We're having a bit of a snafu with the oven situation."

"What is *sna-foo*?"

Oh Lord, he was so cute when he didn't know American slang. "Snafu means . . . Well, the technical term isn't important. It means my oven is on backorder and I can't do any baking until it comes in."

He thought about that for a minute. "No problem. You can do the baking in Momma's kitchen in the mornings. The restaurant is only open for dinner in the off-season, so the prep staff comes in late."

Gia's mother owned Mia Famiglia, the Italian eatery across the stone courtyard on the Washington Street Mall.

Karla snorted ominously and said something sarcastic sounding in Italian. Gia responded to her, also in Italian.

They got into a passionate debate, hollering in each other's faces in rapid-fire Italian. Then Karla shook her head and laughed. Gia turned his attention back to me.

"Don't worry, *bella*, I will get you everything you need, just give me a list." He kissed me on the forehead and I tried not to let my disappointment show that the kiss wasn't a couple inches further south. "And now you will get to know Momma." Gia beamed a huge smile.

Meeting Gia's mother. I bet she's delightful. Like in those

Olive Garden commercials. If she's half as sweet as Gia, I'm sure I'll love her.

Karla had an evil glint in her eye and whistled the tune to a death march.

I swallowed hard. "What's that for?"

"You'll see."

Chapter 5

I woke up on the edge of the mattress with Figaro planted in the small of my back. I don't know how eleven pounds of fur can command so much space. I went about my morning routine while two orange eyes watched closely for any signs of a can opener in my hand. I was down another pound thanks to the Paleo changes Dr. Melinda had prescribed a few weeks ago. Or as I called it, the Pal-e-NO diet. As in no grain, no dairy, no sugar, and no happiness.

I went through my yoga with a firebird flow, and planned my day ahead. I was committed to be at Mia Famiglia in an hour so Momma could give me a kitchen tour and I could begin working on some Paleo desserts I had planned for the coffee shop. I really wanted Gia's mother to like me. Karla had totally psyched me out yesterday, and I nearly called the whole thing off. I tried to relax in corpse pose, but a sense of impending doom curled around my neck like a noose.

I showered and put some mousse in my hair. It was a valiant effort, but it rarely ever delivered on the promise it made in the ads, to give me supermodel tresses. Still, I kept hoping that one day it would be magic and my red hair would look more like Debra Messing and less like Little Orphan Annie. I gave my hair a quick blow dry and applied some makeup, and dressed in skinny jeans—a term here which is very relative—and a gray T-shirt layered with a pink flannel covered in cat hair.

Figaro tried to assassinate me several times while going down the steps to the kitchen, where Aunt Ginny was putting the finishing berries on our Paleo granola parfaits—coconut yogurt, strawberries, and toasted almonds.

I grabbed a lint roller and removed some of the evidence of Figaro from my clothes. The rest of it had woven itself into the fabric permanently. "You look bright and chipper today. You must have gotten some sleep last night."

"I feel purty good. Those pills the doctor gave me must have done the trick."

I looked around the kitchen wall into the hall and foyer. "Have you seen Georgina today?" I whispered.

Aunt Ginny grimaced. "She left early this morning."

"Left as in to go home?" I asked hopefully.

"Queen Georgie didn't tell me."

Smitty peeked around the other corner from the dining room. "Is it safe?"

"I think so."

He crept into the room and looked as nervous as the dog catcher's cat. "She was waiting for me on the porch this morning to give me a list of chores."

I looked at Smitty's list. It was full of oiling hinges and un-sticking windows. "I'd rather you get the kitchen painted today so we can be ready for the weekend."

Smitty saluted. "You got it, boss. I'll start it this morning."

A familiar click-clacking of stilettos came in the front door and started down the hall. We all held our breath.

Georgina assaulted the room with a giant pink box. "I thought I would get Dunkin' Donuts for everyone. That won't bother you on your diet, will it, Poppy?"

She took out a pink frosted pillow and my shoulder was hit by rainbow sprinkle shrapnel. I took a deep breath and counted to ten. Aunt Ginny took a step backwards and reached for her anxiety pills.

"Of course not. I'm leaving soon anyway." I rammed my spoon in my Paleo parfait. I imagined schmearing Georgina's face with a Boston Kreme.

Smitty sidestepped toward Georgina and took the box while watching me. "I'll take these out onto the screened porch for the guys. They're installing the new windows today."

I gave him a grateful smile.

Georgina dabbed at pink icing on the corner of her mouth. "I'll be out in a few minutes to inspect your work, Sooty."

"Oh goody." Smitty rolled his eyes for me before the door closed behind him.

Georgina ignored the irritated silence in the room and went on as if nothing had happened. "You'll never believe what I heard out at your mailbox."

Aunt Ginny didn't look up from her parfait. "You're probably right."

"One of your neighbors was robbed."

I prepared my espresso machine to pull a shot. "Oh no. Who?"

"Clara . . . something."

"Curly white hair? Glasses? Looks like Mrs. Claus?"

Georgina pointed at me. "That's the one."

"Oh, poor Mrs. Pritchard. What happened?"

"Someone broke in last night and stole some kitschy salt and pepper shakers and a big piece of cinnamon Bundt cake. I can't imagine why anyone would want either one."

I put stevia and a little almond milk in the creamy espresso. "That's a pretty random list. Are you sure you heard her right?"

"I'm positive. That's what all your neighbors are talking about."

"They didn't take anything else?"

"Poppy, the woman looks to be a hundred years old. She probably misplaced the shakers and ate the cake herself."

Aunt Ginny put a mug of water in the microwave to make herself a cup of tea. "We should make her a little consolation cake."

"Oh, that would be a nice gesture. Let her know we're here for her."

"What's a consolation cake?" Georgina asked.

Aunt Ginny got her tea down from the cabinet. "Just what it sounds like. We make her a cake."

"It's something neighbors do to support each other in times of distress. It's an act of friendship," I added.

Georgina managed to look down on me from below. "Are you sure that's a real thing? No one has ever made me a consolation cake."

I handed Aunt Ginny a tea strainer. "I can't imagine why not."

Aunt Ginny added, "Yes, that *is* a mystery."

The microwave dinged, and Georgina took out Aunt Ginny's mug and made a cup of tea for herself. "Are you sure this is a safe neighborhood, Poppy?"

I downed my espresso to keep myself from saying something to Georgina that a lady should never say.

Aunt Ginny let out a deep sigh that was heard through the sound of sawing coming from the porch.

"Of course it's safe. Where do you think we are, the Middle East? This is Cape May."

Aunt Ginny glared at Georgina, yanked another mug out of the cabinet and filled it with water.

Georgina stirred a spoonful of sugar into her steaming cup. "I don't feel safe here. Houses are being broken into. What if there are ruffians in the neighborhood?"

"Ruffians? You think the Mob is here targeting ornamental kitchen bric-a-brac?"

"Don't laugh at me. Maybe you should just finish the house, put it on the market, and come home to Virginia."

"And leave Aunt Ginny here? Alone?"

"Ginny would probably enjoy one of those retirement homes they're building now, wouldn't you, Ginny?"

"Oh Georgina. No . . ."

Aunt Ginny reached for her anxiety pills and took two.

Figaro knocked his water bowl over and Georgina slipped in it and almost went down. I swear I could see him smiling.

Chapter 6

Before heading out to Mia Famiglia, I stopped in to check on Mrs. Pritchard to see how she was faring after her home was violated. She seemed to have thrown together an impromptu garden party in honor of the occasion.

"I just can't believe someone was wandering around my house eating my cake in the middle of the night." All the old ladies on the street were huddled together in Mrs. Pritchard's living room, drinking coffee from bone china. Their cheeks were pink with excitement as they sat forward on the settee, greedy to drink in every detail. From my metal folding chair in the overflow section, I tried balancing my cup and saucer on my knee while holding a small plate with a Danish that Nell Belanger had thrust upon me. As I'm greatly lacking in balance and coordination skills, this took most of my concentration.

Mrs. Pritchard was putting on a full production of the retelling. "I'm just afraid the thief will be back. Thieves always return to the scene of the crime. Don't they, Poppy?"

"Um . . . I think I may have heard that . . . somewhere. Or maybe that was arsonists?"

I trailed off when I saw my Danish sliding dangerously close to the edge of my plate. Mrs. Pritchard was too rapt in her audience to give me much notice.

"Of course, the police were here early this morning, but they don't have much hope for recovering my vintage Porky and Petunia." She shook her head sadly.

All the ladies tut-tutted in sympathy.

Mrs. Colazzo passed me a napkin down the line of sympathizers. "The quality of cops in this town has really gone downhill since Ira Schlessinger was captain. Do you remember him, Poppy?"

"Ah, I don't think so."

"No, of course you don't, you were a baby," Mrs. Colazzo continued. "But he kept those men in line. There would have been none of this funny business like what happened to you a few weeks ago. You remember that?"

"My false arrest? Yes, I remember that vividly."

"And Ira would have had those salt and pepper shakers back by the end of the day, you mark my words."

Mrs. Pritchard clutched her chest. "Oh, Porky and Petunia. You won't find those at Sears. They were a collector's set. And the mess. Oh, you've never seen such a thing. The perpetrator cut my Bundt cake into ten pieces and ate every other piece."

All the biddies gasped in horror.

"What was left fell like dominoes. Such a waste of a beautiful Bundt."

Mrs. Rosenberg asked the question on everyone's mind. "Did they leave crumbs?" It was the only crime worse than the theft.

Mrs. Pritchard clutched her heart for strength. "A line from the table all the way off the porch."

"No!"

Mrs. Colazzo had to fan herself to keep from swooning.

I tried to brush the crumbs on my lap back onto my plate before the ladies noticed.

"Poppy, honey, you're a woman of the world."

I choked on my coffee and spilled a little on my skinny jeans. "Um . . ."

"Would you please keep an eye out for Porky and Petunia on the black market for me, in case they surface?"

I didn't have the heart to tell her that I didn't have black market connections, she looked so hopeful. "I will try."

Mrs. Pritchard and all the ladies heaved a sigh of relief.

I was running late for Mia Famiglia, so I said my goodbyes and told Mrs. Pritchard I would check in on her later.

When I arrived at the restaurant I was ushered to the kitchen, where Momma Larusso was waiting for me. And by waiting, I mean scowling and muttering in Italian while angrily stuffing manicotti shells with spinach and ricotta. I gave her a smile and tried to apologize, but she jabbed at the clock on the wall and said, "Bah!"

Momma was about four feet ten, and as big around. She had salt-and-pepper hair tied up in a giant bun. She would look just like Aunt Bea in a flowered dress and apron, if Aunt Bea were on a killing spree.

She waved me around, speaking quickly in Italian, and I tried to keep up. The room was something off a *Hell's Kitchen* set. I felt myself come alive on a wave of excitement breaking on the shores of regret. *This could have been mine. Instead I let myself be bullied into business school. And that turned out so well . . .*

Along one wall was a bank of stainless steel cabinets

where vegetables and salads were readied. The center
of the room was a block of stations for roasting, grilling,
frying, and sautéing. The opposite wall would have
been my domain in another life: a stainless steel workstation with a Hobart mixer and a Vulcan double
convection oven for the pastry chef. I ran my hand over
the commercial stand mixer and imagined all the breads
and cakes I would have made. I was going to make a
name for myself for my genius use of unusual combina-
tions and delicate sugar art.

The dream evaporated into reality as Momma shoved
an apron into my hands and pushed me toward the hand-
wash sink before going back to her manicotti.

Over the next hour I whipped up three different
batches of muffins. Gluten-free blueberry buttermilk,
chocolate orange, and Paleo banana walnut. I made
Mrs. Pritchard a little banana cake from some of the
muffin batter—something for her next performance
with the neighborhood biddy club. Then I started on
the desserts. I had a gluten-free brownie recipe that I
tweaked to be Paleo by substituting tapioca starch for
cornstarch and honey for sugar. I added a shot of
espresso and a pinch of cayenne pepper to deepen the
chocolate, then a couple handfuls of dairy-free chocolate chips. Next, I made a batch of gluten-free chocolate
chip blondies, adding a scraped Tahitian vanilla bean.
Every now and then Momma would come look over
my shoulder, then look at me and say, something-
something, "*trocco truppo Viola.*"

"I'm sorry, my Italian is very rusty. Do you speak
English?"

Momma fired on me in Italian with her hands waving
around. Either my hair was sprouting dragons or I

could take that as a no on the English. I nodded a lot and tried to look friendly.

"Something smells yummy." Gia's voice carried through the kitchen. I was suddenly very warm, and it wasn't from the ovens. He went straight to his mother, who was now all sweetness and light, and gave her a bear hug. She cooed over him and had him taste a bite of this and a spoon of that. She patted his belly and smushed his mouth in her hands.

He crossed the kitchen to give me a more intimate hug.

"How's it going?" he whispered.

"Fine, I think." I glanced over at Momma.

She narrowed her eyes and gave me a look that made me swallow hard. Then she picked up a rolling pin and slammed it into a ball of dough repeatedly.

Momma muttered something I couldn't understand. Gia laughed.

I whispered, "Doesn't your mother speak English?"

"She speaks some. When it suits her."

"What is she saying?"

"Viola. Has she been calling you Violet all day?"

He told his mother in Italian that my name was Poppy. That much I understood. Momma gave me the stink eye. I understood that too. She looked back at Gia and rambled something while waving her hands at me in dismissal. Gia didn't seem to pay her any attention.

I took the brownies out of the oven and set them on the rack to cool. Gia took a deep sniff. "Mmmmm." Then he looked into my eyes and said, "Delicious."

Breathe, Poppy. Just breathe.

He picked up a fork and took a step toward me, never breaking eye contact. I swallowed hard. He dipped his fork in the corner of the brownie pan and took a bite.

He chewed slowly and closed his eyes. When he swallowed he looked at me and said, "Wow. You're amazing."

"I love you." Okay I didn't really say that. What I said was, "I'm glad you like them."

"They are fantastic." He leaned in to kiss my forehead, but Momma yelled something and he turned to see what she wanted. "Hold on. Momma needs me to get something down for her."

I think Momma just wanted to get her baby away from Viola. I cleaned up my workstation and cut both pans into bars. I calculated the cost point of each item for him to determine his selling price and wrote it on index cards.

"Do you want to come over and have coffee with me while I put these out?"

I wanted to more than anything, but my cell phone went off and I saw that it was a text from Smitty.

911 kitchen situation. Need you.

I sighed. "I can't. There's a problem at home. Can we do it tomorrow?"

He smiled. "I can't wait. You go. I'll take care of this." He gestured to the baked goods.

"Thank you." Before I could stop myself, I reached up and kissed him on the cheek.

When I pulled away he grabbed my hand and pulled me into him. He leaned down and his lips touched mine and sent sparks down to my ankles.

Momma growled like a bear. She picked lids off of two pots and smashed them into each other like giant saucy cymbals.

I had to get the heck out of there before I was on tonight's menu with the tortellini.

* * *

I returned home to a flurry of panic with the work-men. Georgina sat sedately at the kitchen table drinking a cup of tea.

"What's going on?"

Smitty came over and took his hat off and rubbed his bald head. "I don't know what happened. I checked it myself."

"Checked what?"

"The color."

"Color of what?"

"Come see for yourself."

Smitty led me to the mudroom he had been using as a staging area. There were four cans of satin finish paint. He removed the lid from one.

"What's that for?"

"The kitchen."

I narrowed my eyes. "The kitchen is supposed to be a pale shade of apricot. That looks like thunderclouds and misery."

He grimaced and gave me a pointed look. "I bought four cans of Peaches n' Cream yesterday and checked each one. This is not what I bought."

I checked the sticker on the can. "These are dated this morning. What happened to the peach?"

Smitty and I looked at each other, then we both looked at Georgina.

Georgina calmly took a sip of her tea and gave us a sedate smile.

I counted to ten. "Georgina. Where is my paint?"

Georgina shrugged. "Paint fairy?"

Smitty grunted. I imagined myself flying across the room and hitting Georgina in the head with a sheet pan.

Georgina shrugged innocently. "I think someone did you a favor. Pink is so gauche. You would have regretted it. Gunmetal gray is very in right now. You will have a much better resale value."

I had to send myself to a time-out. I flicked the switch to the hall light to turn it off, but the kitchen light came on. I flicked the kitchen switch and the hall light turned off.

Smitty grunted. "I can fix that."

I needed to lie down. "That paint is the color of sadness. It makes me tired. Return it and get my Peaches n' Cream back. It's probably still sitting at the paint counter."

Smitty gave me a Three Stooges hand wave from his face to mine. "Nyaaaah. Whoop whoop whoop." Then he saluted and left the room.

We had two days till our first guests arrived, and either Smitty, Georgina, or Aunt Ginny was sure to kill me before I got through it.

Chapter 7

Thursday morning dawned bright and crabby. The shrill call of the wild pygmy tyrant competed with the primal grunting of the common bull dog as Georgina and Smitty argued over whether the guest rooms should be named or numbered. Figaro was hunkered down in the corner where he could keep his eye on the bedroom door. I had been hiding in my room as long as possible, but I had to get my day started. With a deep breath and one last look at Fig, I yanked the bedroom door open and jumped into the fracas.

"Poppy, tell Smooty here that I'm right and numbering the rooms would add a touch of class. That's how they do it at the Waldorf."

"Poppy has already instructed me to hang these painted plaques on each room to match the butterflies."

I ran past them and down the stairs. "Smitty's right. Leave him alone, Georgina."

I could hear the "Humph" from the foyer, followed by Smitty's "Oh, wise guy!" and then Georgina's "Stop doing that."

Aunt Ginny was in the kitchen grinding espresso

beans. She had a pair of hot-pink earbuds shoved in her ears. The other end of the cord dangled down by her knees. We looked at each other and shook our heads.

I grabbed two espresso cups and the stevia while Aunt Ginny pulled a shot. "How did you sleep?"

She pulled out the earbuds. "Like a teenager. Oblivious to the world."

I smiled and looked around the kitchen. Smitty finished the painting yesterday and the room was Peaches n' Cream beautiful. The only thing missing was my copper range. I needed to see what I could do about speeding up the delivery. I had to get out from under Italian-momma-glowering as soon as possible.

"More neighbors were robbed last night." Aunt Ginny handed me my espresso and we clinked glasses before downing our liquid happiness.

"Who?"

"Mr. and Mrs. Sheinberg. Someone snuck in last night and stole her rooster pot holder."

"Aww. That's been sitting on her radiator since I was seven. Did they take anything else?"

"A piece of apple pie."

"How does she know Mr. Sheinberg didn't just eat the pie?"

"She said a hunk was missing like it was ripped out by a bear claw, and a line of crumbs led to the door."

"Do you think maybe we have some neighborhood kids playing pranks?"

Aunt Ginny shrugged.

The sounds of Georgina clicky-clacking down the hallway put us both on high alert.

"Poppy, good I found you."

"I'm not changing the room signs, Georgina."

"What? Oh, don't be silly. I don't care about that. I wanted to tell you that I had to fire the cleaning girl this morning."

"What! Why?"

Aunt Ginny rubbed her forehead and sat down at the banquette. "She looked like she would steal from you."

"Are you serious?"

"You can't be too careful. Especially with this being a bad neighborhood."

"This is not a bad neighborhood. And Martina came with good references."

"You know more of your neighbors were robbed last night. That now classifies as a spree."

A pain started throbbing along my shoulder blade. I took a deep breath and tried to calm down. "Georgina. This is the off-season. It's very difficult to find chamber-maids who want to work over the winter. Most places hire girls from Eastern Europe just for the summer. I have four couples arriving tomorrow. Now who will clean the guest rooms?"

Georgina didn't look concerned in the least. "Well, I have no idea. I usually just call the service and they send someone over."

Aunt Ginny and I looked at each other. Figaro walked into the room, saw Georgina, and turned around and walked back out.

I sighed. "I have to go. I'm making some gluten-free pie bars for the coffee shop today."

Aunt Ginny grinned. "That boy is very sneaky to get you there every day like this."

I stopped. "What do you mean?"

Georgina stood ramrod straight. "What boy?"

Aunt Ginny quirked an eyebrow. "You know what I

mean. He likes you, so he found a way to keep you near him."

I felt myself blush.

Georgina stepped to the banquette. "What boy, Ginny?"

Aunt Ginny ignored her. "Have you told Tim yet?"

"There's nothing to tell. But I guess I will today when we go shopping at the chef supply warehouse."

Georgina was all business. "What boy? And who is this Tim? You aren't dating, are you, Poppy?"

"What? No, not really."

"I should hope not. Who are these men and do they know you are a grieving widow?"

"Nothing is happening."

"Nothing should be happening."

Aunt Ginny snorted. "She's been a grieving widow for almost a year. It's time she started having some fun."

Georgina narrowed her eyes at Aunt Ginny. "I hardly think nine months constitutes *almost a year*."

Yikes. I had to get out of here before these two grizzlies ripped each other apart like I was the last spring salmon.

I grabbed my bag of ingredients and my purse and snuck out the front door. I ran into Mrs. Colazzo and Mrs. Sheinberg down at the mailbox.

"Oh, Poppy, honey, did you hear?"

"I did, Mrs. Sheinberg. I'm so sorry about Mr. Strut n' Stuff."

"Thank you, bubala. But I'm talking about Helen here."

I looked at Mrs. Colazzo, who was wearing a yellow flowered housecoat and pink fuzzy slippers and wringing her hands. "Oh no. What happened?"

"They got my glass frog figurines and ate the dozen

snickerdoodles I had made for Mary Alice's visit this afternoon."

"They ate a hunk of pie and a dozen cookies?"

"Well, not a whole dozen, no. They took one bite out of each cookie and left the rest of the cookie on the counter."

"Good Lord."

"We're discussing starting a Neighborhood Watch program," Mrs. Sheinberg said.

"And maybe a Weight Watchers meeting," Mrs. Colazzo added.

Mrs. Sheinberg grabbed my arm. "Do you think I should call around to the local pawn shops? Or is it too soon for the thief to have fenced the loot?"

"Well, I'm not sure the pawn shop would be so quick to buy your unique set of items. They might seem too . . . personal."

"You're right, honey. They would give them a cooling-off time."

Mrs. Colazzo piped in, "No, no. It's no good. Everything is done by computer nowadays. There's that new site, eBay they call it. I bet if our stuff is being unloaded, it will be there. What do you think, Poppy?"

"Actually, I don't know if you can find your exact items, but I bet you can replace them on eBay."

Mrs. Colazzo smacked Mrs. Sheinberg on the shoulder. "Told ya."

"Bubula"—Mrs. Sheinberg grabbed my arm again—"promise me that if you come across any shady characters selling glass frogs or a stuffed rooster in a back alley . . ."

Mrs. Colazzo interrupted her, "Or out of a white van."

"Yeah, or a white van. Promise me you'll be sure to report it, okay, honey?"

I held up a Girl Scout honor salute. "I promise."

While Cape May's Thelma and Louise trotted off to discover they would need the Internet in order to get on eBay, I wondered about getting an alarm system installed. I would have to put it on the list and tell Smitty to make it a priority.

Chapter 8

I rushed into the kitchen at Mia Famiglia, ready for another day of passive aggression and open disappointment. Momma Larusso didn't address me when I came in. She met my eyes, twisted her mouth into a frown, and went back to stirring her sauce. *So much for her only using her kitchen at night.*

The Cape May weather was brisk and the leaves were changing, so everyone was looking for fall flavors. Since the market was probably saturated with everything pumpkin spice, I wanted to offer something different but still warm and cozy. Gluten-free honey maple pecan shortbread. But first I had to make another batch of muffins. Gia had texted me that the blueberry sold out and they were running low on the other two flavors. Today I was making pistachio. I added a little orange zest, some toasted pistachios, and a couple drops of sweet almond oil. I was so into my baking that I forgot about Momma Larusso until she snuck up on me.

She asked something in Italian and I caught the words *olio di mandorle.*

"*Olio?* You want to know why I'm adding almond oil?"

Momma nodded while looking at the muffin batter.

"Sweet almond heightens the pistachio flavor. Makes it more pistachio-y."

She looked like I'd just said I was adding grasshoppers, and she wasn't convinced that was a great idea. I hoped nothing was twisted in translation. She dipped a spoon in my batter and tasted it. She didn't comment, but shuffled her raised eyebrows back to her side of the kitchen.

I had the muffins and pecan shortbread on the cooling rack and was about to take the pistachio muffins out of the oven when my cell phone buzzed. I had an email from one of the couples who was due to arrive tomorrow afternoon. The Reynolds were confirming their cancellation? In a panic, I tore through the email train to see what could have gone wrong. They said they received my message and were disappointed, but they would love to visit when we worked everything out.

What the—? No. She couldn't have. Could she?

I took the muffins out to cool and cleaned up my workstation at top speed. Another email came in, this one not so accommodating. It seemed the Blairs were looking forward to their weekend away and already had a babysitter, so I had ruined their lives by canceling the free promotional trip I had offered in order to give the B and B a practice run. I had to get home immediately.

I scrawled a note to Gia about another emergency— *geez, no wonder he thinks I've been ducking him*—set aside a pistachio muffin for Momma, and waved goodbye. Momma waved goodbye back to me. It was a very disgruntled-looking wave and may have meant something naughty in Italian, but I didn't have time to think about it. Georgina was busy destroying my business and I hadn't even gotten it off the ground.

* * *

"Georgina!" *Get in here with your flying monkeys!*

Georgina floated into the foyer looking just as calm and relaxed as if she was having a spa day and not creating a bed-and-breakfast bloodbath. "What's the matter?"

I tried to calm down until I got all the facts. "Georgina, did you cancel my guest reservations?"

Georgina spoke to me like I was a five-year-old asking how many nights till Christmas. "Only three of them. I still have one couple to get ahold of. They aren't answering their phones."

I saw red. "Why . . . How . . . Don't . . ." I took a deep breath but it didn't help. I needed a shot of something stronger. Like hot fudge.

"I don't know what you're so upset about. I'm only trying to help you. You aren't ready for guests, and these aren't even paying guests."

"They can still leave negative reviews and destroy our reputation."

I had to do damage control and fast. I went to my apartment upstairs and got on my laptop. Figaro followed me to sit next to the keyboard with his butt blocking half of my screen. I gave him a half pet, half push to the side, but he still managed to ooze back into my way.

I looked up the reservations and called each of the guests Georgina had canceled. I reassured them that we were in fact ready for them and looking forward to their visit. Ignore the previous phone call, it was from a deranged lunatic. The Blairs had already canceled their babysitter and there was no way to redeem myself with them. I offered them another free weekend any time of their choosing. They said they would think about it, and hung up on me mid-apology.

It was just as well that they weren't coming. Georgina had set up her command post in my best suite, and now I didn't have to give her my bed and sleep on the couch in Aunt Ginny's sitting room.

I looked at the time. I was meeting Tim in less than an hour at the chef supply warehouse he'd recommended. The time had come to swallow my insecurity and have a heart-to-fragile-heart talk with him.

Was Aunt Ginny right? Did I need to tell Tim about Gia? I mean, it's not like anything was really going on between us. Tim and I had a couple of awkward dates—outings, really—not dates. Of course, there was that kiss goodbye. The hairs on my arms stood up when I thought about it.

But then there was also that kiss with Gia. I was still trying to sort through my emotions—okay, guilt. Gia was amazing, sensitive, gentle, and ohmygod was he hot! So hot that most of the time I was sure I was imagining his interest in me. I had heard about men who like hefty women, but I thought it was an urban legend.

Tim, on the other hand, already had a piece of my heart. Who knows what might have been if things had turned out differently twenty-some years ago.

And then there was John. He may be gone from this earth, but he was very much alive in my heart. Starting any new relationship made me feel like I was cheating on John, and that was a feeling I had lived with for far too long after I wrecked things when I cheated on Tim in college. Was I really this girl who couldn't be faithful? As soon as I'd reconnected with Tim, I was kissing another man. I didn't think our relationship could handle another betrayal, even if this time there was no pretense of commitment. No, Aunt Ginny was right. I would have to lay all my cards on the table and see who was left standing when I was done. With my luck, it would be just me and Fig to the end, ride or die.

Figaro flopped over and typed yyyyyyyyyyyyyyyyyyyyyy on my keyboard. Thanks, that's helpful.

Chapter 9

I took the Garden State Parkway up to Stone Harbor, heading for the Master Chef Warehouse. The food service supply center was in an industrial park surrounded by other large, unmarked warehouses. The sand-colored building was the size of a Walmart Supercenter, but there were no windows and only one set of dark glass double doors. I parked next to Tim's Kia and went inside.

The enormous room was poorly lit, with rows and rows of shelving units filled to the brim with stockpots and sheet pans and chafing dishes and industrial-size containers of mayonnaise and cooking oil. Sur La Table this was not.

Tim came around the corner carrying a large bag of Styrofoam takeout containers. He was tanned and tall with broad shoulders and slim hips, his blond hair in that shaggy beach-bum style that hadn't changed since high school. His chin was covered in light stubble. He was scruffy-sexy. Is that a thing?

"Hey, you made it." He gave me a big smile and leaned

down to kiss me, but we were interrupted before he could make contact.

"Hi-yee!"

Oh goody. Gigi the perky and annoying is here. Gigi was Tim's chef "friend" and mentee. In her late twenties, the cute little blonde had a cute little restaurant in West Cape May, Le Bon Gigi, and the uncanny ability to pop up every time Tim and I tried to get close. I might hate her.

"Surprise!" Gigi raised both hands in the air.

Tim stepped back to include Gigi in our circle, like it was some kind of creepy threesome. "Look who came to help."

"Yeah, I can see that."

"I told Gigi we were coming here today to get you set up with some baking supplies and it turns out that she needed a new silicone mat so she tagged along."

Gigi flashed me a smile. "It was so lucky for me that you were coming today."

"Yes, how lucky," I said flatly. Gigi wasn't fooling me for a minute. *Ever heard of Amazon, Gigi?*

The three of us walked up and down the aisles, looking at the baking and pastry paraphernalia and the professional stand mixers. My every instinct for what I needed was apparently wrong, according to Chef Gigi.

"Not those pans, you want a wire rim for a convection oven. Are you sure you want disposable pastry bags? You could just wash the canvas ones. Chicago Metal makes a better jumbo muffin pan than that brand, if you care about quality."

I resisted the urge to fwack her with a spatula and grabbed a large whisk and dropped it in my basket.

"Do you want a ball whisk or a French whisk?"

"Does it make that big a difference?"

Gigi's hands flew to her hips and she tapped one foot

impatiently. "It depends on whether you're whipping cream or making a béarnaise."

Tim put his arm around my shoulders and laughed softly. "Geeg is very passionate about her tools."

"I gathered that."

Gigi picked up a pastry wheel and spun it with her thumb while keeping an eagle eye on Tim's hand on my shoulder. "Hey, I'm just here to be of assistance."

Are you, Gigi? Are you?

Gigi and Tim got immersed in a conversation about baking a fish in a paper bag versus a salt crust, and I snuck off to finish getting my supplies. I spoke with the shop manager about macarons and he chose some pastry tips with large holes for me to try. He also helped me pick a copper saucepan for making caramel, and he put back the roll of parchment paper that Gigi had picked out and swapped it for the box of individual sheets that I had originally wanted. I decided that he was my new best friend. I ordered a twenty-shelf baker's rack to be delivered next week and checked out just as Tim and Gigi caught up with me.

Tim gave me a smile. "Sorry we chef'd out there for a minute."

Gigi linked arms with Tim. "You know how we chefs can be when we're discussing new recipes."

I looked her in the eye. "I'm pretty sure I see how it is."

Gigi had the decency to blush.

My cell phone buzzed, and I saw a text from Georgina:

When are you coming home!
Tablecloth emergency! 911!

I texted back:

What are you talking about?

I could hear the condescension in her text:

Wrong shade of oatmeal!
THEY WILL CLASH WITH EVERYTHING HOW
DO I TURN CAPITAL LETTERS OFF?

How many shades of oatmeal could there possibly be?

AND SMUTTY HUNG THE WINDOWS
BACKWARDS SO THE LOCKS ARE ON THE
OUTSIDE!

Followed by a text from Smitty:

I can fix that!

I sighed.

Tim raised an eyebrow, "Everything okay?"

"I have to go. Georgina is . . . being Georgina."

Tim unwound Gigi's arm from his and took my bags. "Thanks for coming with us today, Geeg. It was totally cool of you to help."

Gigi turned adoring eyes on Tim. "Oh yeah, anytime. Day or night. I'll be there."

Oh, good Lord.

We said our goodbyes to Gigi, and Tim walked me to my car.

"Hey, I'm sorry if Geeg turned it on a little too bossy. She's a total gearhead with tools, but she loves to help."

I hugged my victory box of parchment to my chest. "It's fine. It was nice of her to offer suggestions."

Tim leaned down and kissed me and I forgot where we were for a minute.

"By-eee!"

Oh, for the love of God!

"Bye, Gigi!" I put my hand on Tim's chest and he smiled. "Hey, can I talk to you for a minute?"

He put my shopping bags in the trunk of my car. "Yeah. What's up?"

"Um—" My mouth went dry and I suddenly felt like I wanted to melt into the parking lot. "Well, I was just wondering, you know, if we, maybe . . ."

Tim laughed, "What? Spit it out, crazy."

"Um, are we serious here?"

"Serious about what?" He smiled.

"What I'm saying is, are we officially dating or anything?"

Tim leaned into me and raised his eyebrows. "I thought we were just getting to know each other again. Weren't you the one who thought too much time had passed for us to jump back into a relationship, and we needed to get to know who we are as adults?"

My heart sped up and my breath caught in my chest. "That's very reasonable. It doesn't sound like me at all."

He touched a lock of my hair on the side of my face. "Then why do you ask?"

"Huh, oh, uh. There is this guy, a friend, who wanted to know."

Tim's expression lost all its flirtiness and he cut his eyes to the side, taking that in. He was very calm, but his shoulders showed a tension that wasn't in his voice. "Who is this friend?"

"He owns a coffee shop on the mall. I met him when I was getting ready for the reunion. He's been very nice to me."

Tim was listening closely and nodding.

"He's who I've been making the muffins for. He's selling them in his shop."

"Has he asked you out?"

It was my turn to blush. "Well, something like that. But I told him that I wasn't sure what was between us yet, so I wasn't free."

Tim nodded some more. "Hmmm. Well, we don't have any kind of commitment between us. So, it's cool."

"It is?"

"Yeah, man, I'm cool. We're both adults. I think we should keep it light for now and just see where it goes."

I was a little disappointed. "Oh, okay."

But then he pulled me to him and kissed me with a passion that left me totally confused. When he let me go he walked over to his car.

"I'll call you later and we'll set up a date, if you're free."

I smiled. "That would be nice."

"Yeah. We'll just keep dating each other while we see other people." He gave me a big smile, then got in his Kia and drove away. Gigi pulled out from around the corner right behind him.

Wait! What did he mean we're seeing other people?! Has he been dating other people? What just happened?

Chapter 10

The day for our practice launch had arrived. I lay in bed and went over my checklist one more time. *The guest rooms are clean. Do the bathrooms all have clean towels? I'd better check. And I need to run the fan in the Emperor Suite to dry the paint, since Georgina had Smitty put another coat on the walls last night.* She insisted the purple paint was streaky. Smitty said that it was easier to just do the work than to argue with her. Boy, didn't I know that. The kitchen was finished, sans oven. I had muffins I'd made yesterday at Momma's and baked oatmeal, which I could warm up for tomorrow's breakfast. Thank God you could make bacon in the microwave. Yes, everything was under control. I got this.

I got up and did a warrior sequence for my yoga flow while being openly critiqued by Fig. Then I showered and dressed and we went down the back staircase to make power smoothies for breakfast.

What the—? I stood in the kitchen doorway, too stunned to move. The scene of carnage that was set before me left me speechless, and I struggled to take it all in. Someone had come into my home, in the middle of the night, and smashed every single one of the muffins

I had made for the guests' breakfast tomorrow. Crumbs were scattered all over the kitchen like it had rained lemon poppy-seed streusel.

I narrowed my eyes at Figaro. "Did you do this?"

He flopped over on his side.

Aunt Ginny opened her bedroom door and froze in her tracks. "Sweet Mary, Joseph, and baby Jesus. What did you do?"

"I didn't do this." Then realization dawned on me. "I think we've been hit by the neighborhood robber. Don't touch anything, but look to see if anything is missing."

Aunt Ginny went back into her bedroom while I searched the kitchen. Microwave, espresso machine, pot holders, salt and pepper shakers—check. Then my heart deflated as I realized my brand-new, very expensive, copper saucier was missing. I felt sick to my stomach. I called the police to report the crime and they said they were sending an officer over.

A waft of Hermès perfume floated into the room with Georgina close behind. "Good mor . . . What on earth? Did the cat do all this?"

Figaro sat up and flicked his tail at Georgina.

Aunt Ginny returned to the kitchen. "I don't think I'm missing anything in there. I'll start checking the rest of the house."

I passed Georgina and headed into the sunroom. "We've been robbed."

Georgina took off running up the stairs to her bedroom.

Aunt Ginny muttered as she went by, "No thanks, I'll check this room by myself. You just worry about your own things."

We looked around but everything else seemed to be

in order, so Aunt Ginny and I met in the library to wait for the officer.

Aunt Ginny sat on the edge of the wing chair and wrung her hands in her butter-yellow twinset. "I don't like this. I don't like this one bit. To think, a stranger was roaming around the house while we were sleeping. I've got the heebie-jeebies."

I patted her on the shoulder. "I know, I feel violated too."

"And we were just lying in our beds. Anything could have happened. What if it had been an axe murderer?"

I sat down across from her. "I've been thinking about it, and I wonder if we're dealing with some kids playing pranks."

"Kids?"

"Think about it. What have they been taking? Knick-knacks, cookies, muffins. They're making more of a mess than anything. It's not exactly grand larceny, it's more like . . . grand snackery."

"That fancy pan of yours cost a lot more than some kitschy salt and pepper shakers."

"True. But I doubt kids would know that. They probably just thought it was a run-of-the-mill saucepan."

"Well, if I find the little heathens I'm going to take my flyswatter to their backsides."

Georgina came flying into the room, her face pale as a sack of flour. "Call the cops! My diamond bracelet is missing!"

I eyed her speculatively. "Are you sure? Did you look everywhere?"

Georgina gave me an icy scowl. "Of course I'm sure, Poppy. Don't you think I'd remember where I put a ten-thousand-dollar diamond tennis bracelet?"

"It's just that the thief hasn't taken anything of value before now, so it seems improbable that they passed up the television and my laptop and crept up to your room while you were sleeping and took your bracelet."

Georgina huffed and looked at me like I had an alien sitting on my head. She opened her mouth for a quick retort. Thank heavens we were interrupted by a knock on the door.

"That must be the police." I opened it to find Officer Legally Blonde, Miss Amber Fenton, on my front porch. *Oh great.* Amber and I go way back. Back to a few weeks ago when she tried to put me away for a murder I didn't commit. Back even further to high school, where she and her evil cheerleader cohorts made my life miserable every day from homeroom to closing bell. Apparently, she hates me as much as I hate her, although my reasons are justifiable, and I find her reasons preposterous.

Amber walked in and pulled out her notebook. "McAllister. I'm not happy about this any more than you are, but you called to report a robbery and I'm the unlucky cop assigned to this case."

Smitty arrived in his tired blue pickup and parked behind Amber's cruiser. He hopped out and ran up the porch steps, jamming his hat down on his shiny head. "What's going on? Is everyone okay?"

Georgina shot her arm out and pointed at Smitty. "There's your thief! Check his pockets!"

"Woman! You're batty! I'm not a thief, I'm a handyman."

Amber raised both hands as if to push back the crazy. "Calm down, everyone. One at a time, tell me what's going on."

I led Amber to the kitchen with Aunt Ginny, Georgina, Smitty, and Figaro trailing behind us like a pathetic parade. I showed her the mess and told her about the missing copper saucepan.

Georgina pushed herself to the front of the line. "My diamond tennis bracelet is also missing and I bet this little Curly Stooge here took it."

Smitty shot back, "I've been working in this house for over a month. Why would I steal something now?"

Georgina put her hands on her hips. "Probably because there was nothing worth stealing before."

I was speechless for the second time that day. Figaro stopped mid-bath to glare at Georgina over his raised back foot. Aunt Ginny took a pill. Amber scribbled in her notebook.

"Are we sure about the diamond bracelet? Because that bumps this up to a whole new level, and I'd have to file a different report."

We all turned eyes on Georgina.

"Well, I'll double-check," she said, "but it wasn't where I left it inside the Bible in the nightstand."

Amber made a note in her book. "Has anyone else been in the house unsupervised?"

Georgina was the first to answer. "The cleaning girl. I knew she looked shifty."

"She did not look shifty, Georgina. Good Lord!"

"I'll look into her, but it's most likely a dead end. Your house was hit with the same MO as several of your neighbors. The perp breaks in in the middle of the night, eats some snacks that have been left out, takes something insignificant, and leaves without a trace. The newspaper is calling him the *yummy bandit*. Of course, the missing diamond bracelet does up the ante considerably. I see a security system panel by the front door. Is that working?"

Smitty shrugged. "It was working when I left yesterday. I tested it myself."

"I set it last night when I went to bed," I added.

Georgina took a step back and wouldn't look anyone in the eye. She cleared her throat. "It was making a funny beeping noise. I thought Snotty here installed it wrong, so I turned it off."

Smitty grunted.

Amber slapped her notebook shut. "I have everything I need here. I'll ask the neighbors if anyone saw anything last night. If I learn anything new, I'll let you know. "

I showed Officer Amber out, got Smitty to working on the security system, and Aunt Ginny and Figaro set up in the sunroom to watch *The Price Is Right*. Georgina went off to kick puppies or terrorize villagers—whatever it is that she does when she's not making us miserable. I had to clean up the aftermath in the kitchen. Throughout the morning, neighbors popped in to check on us and bring us consolation cakes. I sent them to the sunroom, where Aunt Ginny could regale them with a play-by-play of our calamity.

It was early afternoon and I had to convince Momma to let me use her restaurant kitchen late in the day to make replacement muffins. With just under four hours until the guests arrived, the house had become a crime scene. We had no muffins, no oven, and no cleaning service. We were, however, neck deep in hysteria.

Chapter 11

Two hours and one batch of Morning Glory Muffins later, I arrived home to find the Panjuans had arrived early, and Georgina was punishing them by making them sit in the parlor and wait. I apologized for Georgina, as much as one can do that, and introduced myself. I took their bags, and then showed them to their room for the weekend. Every guest that arrived got a tour of the house, including the breakfast area on the sun porch, overlooking Mrs. Pritchard's award-winning rose garden next door, a map of the historical district, along with recommendations for restaurants and activity highlights like horse-drawn carriage tours and pottery classes.

They were all very excited to be here, and why wouldn't they be—it was free—except for the Nelsons.

"There's no Jacuzzi tub in the bathroom?"

"No, it's an original antique claw-foot tub."

Sniff. "Don't you have DVD players in the rooms?"

"No, but there is so much to do outside with the boardwalk and the tours and the shopping."

Sniff. "I thought you'd be closer to the beach, but it's a block away. We have to cross the road."

"Cape May doesn't have any bed-and-breakfasts right on the beach. Everyone is on this side of Beach Avenue."

Sniff.

The sniff of disdain was really starting to irk me. It was like that no matter what I showed them. Even the complimentary lemonade and blueberry madeleines couldn't put a smile on their faces. Eventually I had to call it and left them to make their own plans for entertainment.

I'd been having a day. What I needed right then was a latte. I left Aunt Ginny in charge and called Sawyer, my best friend since the fifth grade, and asked her to meet me at Gia's. I parked in the back at the service entrance, and went in through the kitchen. Gia was waiting on a couple of college kids and didn't notice me, but Henry was sitting at the bar when I came through and he launched himself at me.

"Poppy!"

"Hey, sweets, how's my favorite five-year-old?"

"Daddy says I can't watch the jungle movie because I will have nightmares."

"Well, your daddy is very smart, so I would listen to him."

Henry's face and shoulders drooped. I must have been his plan B.

"But, I know another jungle movie from a long time ago that I bet you would like."

"Does it have monkeys in it?"

"Monkeys that sing and dance and get into all kinds of trouble."

"I'm in!"

"Let's make sure it's okay with Daddy, and I'll bring it over."

"Okay!" Henry jumped down and did a couple of

spins of celebration before Karla came in to take him home. "Bye, Poppy! See you tomorrow!"

"Bye, Henry."

Gia finished with his customers and came over to flirt with me, I mean take my order. "Ciao, *bella*." He took my hands in his and kissed them.

I tried unsuccessfully to stifle a giggle. "Hey you. I'm meeting Sawyer for coffee. I thought she would have been here by now."

"Why don't you go sit in the front and wait, and I'll bring you a latte."

"How much do I owe you?"

Gia rolled his eyes. "Your money is no good here. Now go sit."

I waited for twenty minutes and Sawyer never showed. I finally got a text that said, Sorry. Something came up. Please forgive me.

The coffee shop quieted down to the lull between lunch and dinner, so Gia sat to join me. "What happened to Sawyer?"

I showed him the text.

"Hmm."

"That's not like her," I said. "I wonder what's going on."

"I'm sure it's nothing to worry about."

Gia and I sat and talked for a few minutes, enjoying each other's company. I would have loved to stay longer, but I had to get back to the bed-and-breakfast in case I was needed to put out any fires. Fires that I suspected Georgina may have lit. I didn't want to leave when he kissed me goodbye, but I managed with effort to peel myself away.

I returned home to find the complimentary bottle of brandy empty, the tray of cookies for afternoon tea had disappeared, and all the board games had been taken out of the library and left strewn about the front parlor as if Goldilocks had tried out each one and found none to her liking.

Sheesh! I was only gone an hour.

I made a couple of dinner reservations and booked a carriage tour, and chatted with guests as they came and went. But the height of excitement happened around eight p.m.

"I saw it! I saw it!" Mrs. Panjuan came running through the front door and down the foyer, her arms waving wildly around her head like beige tentacles. Her face flushed, she gasped for breath. "Just like you said, I saw her through the third-story window."

Other guests came rushing in from their rocking chairs and down the stairs from their rooms.

Sniff. "What's going on?" Mrs. Nelson held her complimentary robe tight around her middle.

Mrs. Panjuan barreled past all of us and up to Aunt Ginny. "I saw her, just like you said. Poor little Alice Mosby."

I muttered under my breath to Aunt Ginny, "What. Did. You. Do?"

Aunt Ginny ignored me and patted Mrs. Panjuan's hand in hers. "Did you now?"

Mrs. Panjuan bobbled her head around, joined now by Mr. Panjuan. "Right through the curtain, looking at me. She was wearing the blue dress. Poor little dear."

Mr. Panjuan looked back toward the front door. "I couldn't see her. All I saw was the curtain moving."

Mrs. Panjuan patted Mr. Panjuan on the shoulder. "Let's try again tomorrow morning. Maybe you'll see her then." She turned back to Aunt Ginny. "Could we take the Ghost Tour again tomorrow?"

Aunt Ginny cut her eyes ever so slyly my way. "Of

course. You must be very fortunate. Not many people have spied her over the years. If you're very quiet in your room, you might hear her singing 'Frère Jacques' to herself."

"I'm going to go listen." Mrs. Panjuan started up the stairs, gushing to her husband. "That was the best twenty dollars I've ever spent."

Now all the guests wanted a chance to spot poor little Alice Mosby in the blue dress. So I spent the evening giving a tour that we didn't offer, to see a ghost that we don't have.

I was on the second floor giving the Nelsons their tour when I overheard Aunt Ginny making *oooooooo* sounds from the attic. Sigh. *What have I gotten myself into?*

Four tours and one scolding to a very sneaky senior citizen later, finally everyone was tucked in for the night. It had been a long day and I was ready for a hot bath. I was just about to set the alarm system when I was surprised to hear someone knocking at the door.

"Mr. Winston, hi."

Mr. Winston was my neighbor from across the street. He was a little younger than Aunt Ginny, but more rumpled. The widower was sporting a bushy head of hair in the shade of Miss Clairol's black licorice, and a bushy mustache in the shade of Mother Nature's old-man glacier white. He reminded me of Pepé Le Pew, if Pepé wore wrinkled khakis and an Argyle sweater.

"Ho there, Poppy, how's the remodel coming along?"

"It's good. We're making real progress."

"An egret? Has it nested?"

"Um, no, Mr. Winston. IT'S GOING WELL." Mr. Winston was so hard of hearing I could sometimes overhear his phone conversations through my bedroom window.

"It's stuck in the well? I'd call animal control for that."

I smiled and nodded. "Thank you, Mr. Winston. Would you like to come in?"

"No, no. I don't want to impose. I was just wondering if Ginny was finished with my *TV Guide*?"

"Your *TV Guide*?"

"Yes, she borrowed it late last night."

"Last night?"

"No, not a knife, it's a magazine."

"Are you sure she came over?"

"Yes, she came over. We ate some fried chicken and she borrowed my *TV Guide*. Then she went home. All in all, I'd say a lovely visit."

I was having trouble getting through to Mr. Winston, but I knew that Aunt Ginny had taken her meds and gone to bed right after dinner last night. She'd been exhausted. I had a sudden sick feeling in the pit of my stomach. "Mr. Winston."

"Eh?"

I tapped on my wrist. "WHAT TIME WAS SHE THERE?"

He thought for a minute. "Oh, I guess about half past one. I was just up watching an old Dick Van Dyke movie and the light was on. It was a strange hour for visitin', but Ginny's always welcome."

Oh. My. God.

"I'm sorry, I haven't seen your *TV Guide*, but if I find it I'll bring it over."

Mr. Winston smiled and nodded the way people who can't really hear you do when they're faking it.

I waved goodbye and shut the door. My hands were shaking. I had only had this sense of dread a couple of times in my life. Once when we were about to get John's diagnosis, once when I found the cheerleader's body, and now this was the third. The house was at a dead calm, as if we were floating in the eye of a hurricane, but I felt like spiders were crawling up my arms.

Oh, Aunt Ginny. What have you done?

Chapter 12

I feared that Aunt Ginny may have developed a new nighttime routine. The only way to know for sure was to catch her in the act. I turned out all the lights and spun a wingback chair around in the parlor to face the front door. Then I waited. The first couple of hours dragged on with only the occasional squeak from the floorboards above me. I'd been up since six, I was exhausted, and I was struggling to keep my eyes open.

Then, around one a.m., she surfaced. The sight of Aunt Ginny wandering around the front foyer sent a shot of adrenaline through me and I was instantly awake. She'd changed out of her nightgown and was now wearing a lilac pantsuit. She stopped in the foyer, looked into the library for a few seconds, then turned the handle on the front door and went outside.

I stayed quietly behind her as she made her way down the steps, around the sidewalk, and across the street to Nell Belanger's white clapboard farmhouse with red shutters. First, she opened the mailbox, then she weeded the garden. She moved a ceramic rabbit statue and repositioned it under an azalea bush. Then, I watched in amazement as she looked under the welcome mat, picked up a key, and let herself into the house.

I followed her to the kitchen, where she proceeded to make herself a peanut butter and jelly sandwich on pumpernickel bread in the dark. Aunt Ginny seemed normal except for an eerie, drugged-like quality to her eyes. Every once in a while, she'd mutter something unintelligible, like someone was with her.

Nell appeared in the kitchen wearing a long flannel nightgown, her gray hair up in pink curlers and a Louisville Slugger she called "The Enforcer" hefted over her shoulder. She took one look at Aunt Ginny, furrowed her eyebrows, and cocked her head to the side.

I whispered, "She's sleepwalking."

Nell put the bat down and whispered back, "More like sleep ransacking."

We continued to watch Aunt Ginny, who calmly ate half a sandwich, put nothing away, then poked holes in the rest of the pieces of bread.

"I'm so sorry, Nell, I'll repay whatever she damages."

Nell was, thankfully, more amused than irritated. "Don't worry about it. I've had plenty of Ginny's goodies over the years. No harm done."

We made space in the hallway as Aunt Ginny came through. She made her way into the living room and toward the coffee table, where she picked up a painted donkey statue that doubled as a lighter and walked out the door.

Nell gasped. "I just brought that home from Argentina."

"I'll get it back to you, I promise."

I followed Aunt Ginny back down the street and over to Mr. Murillo's house. She was really covering some ground. She felt around the ground like she was looking for something. Then she knocked twice on the newel post and a little door opened to reveal a house key. She let herself into the house and I prayed that Mr. and Mrs. Murillo didn't sleep in the nude.

Aunt Ginny did a lap around the living room. First, she straightened a couple pictures, then she tilted a couple of others. She paused for a moment and cocked her head to the side, like she was listening to someone. To which she replied, "Squirrels." Then she scooped up a handful of chocolates from a crystal candy dish, ate the candy, then pocketed the dish. I quickly scrawled an apology to the Murillos, promising to explain everything later.

On her way out she paused, then unscrewed the light bulb from the porch light, stuck it in a pot of mums, and quietly shut the door.

She turned and headed back for home, stopping long enough to take Mr. Winston's ugly little garden gnome and throw it behind the boxwood. She let herself back into the house like it was just a normal day and she'd been out to lunch. I squeezed in behind her before she turned off the porch light, locked the door, and headed down the hall.

Where has she been keeping all this stuff? How did I not know what she'd been up to? She hasn't had much appetite in the mornings, but I thought she was just tired of the Paleo diet I'd forced her to do with me. I can't believe she hasn't gotten sick from all the midnight snacking.

I followed Aunt Ginny into the kitchen. She opened the door to the storage room and went inside. The room was full of shelves stocked with canned goods and jars of homemade preserves. It was also the room that hid the servants' stairs that I used to go up to the third floor. She went to the far corner and lifted a trapdoor.

I sucked in a sharp breath, and she froze for a

moment. Then she placed the pilfered items in the hole. After closing the trap, she left the little room and I watched her go to her bedroom and shut the door.

I turned on the light and went over to the trapdoor. *How did I not know that was there?* I lifted up the door and sure enough, there was her stash of loot. In addition to what she had just deposited, there was Mrs. Sheinberg's rooster pot holder, Mrs. Pritchard's Porky and Petunia salt and pepper shaker set, Mr. Winston's *TV Guide*, Mrs. Colazzo's glass frog figurines, and my copper sauce pan. There was also a hairbrush and a set of false teeth.

Ok, I don't even want to know where she got that. Oh, Aunt Ginny. This will not go well in the morning. What am I going to do with you?

Chapter 13

"I hardly think the blue flashing lights are necessary." I let Amber in for the second day in a row, this time to receive a confession.

"It's standard operating procedure when working a crime scene." Her police radio crackled and she turned the volume down.

I led her to the kitchen, where Aunt Ginny sat hang-dogging over a cup of coffee. Figaro perched on the edge of the table like a buzzard, in between Aunt Ginny and Amber, knowing he's not allowed up there, as if he were saying *You'll have to go through me first.* I reached for a can of tuna and his resolve evaporated like summer rain on blacktop, and he abandoned Aunt Ginny in favor of filling his stomach.

Amber sat down and took off her police-issue sunglasses. "Hello, Mrs. Frankowski."

Aunt Ginny stared at her coffee cup. "Hi."

"You want to tell me what happened?"

"Well, apparently I've gone crazy and been robbing the neighbors in my sleep."

The corner of Amber's mouth twitched briefly, but

she got it under control. "Do you remember anything about the past few nights?"

"No. I took my sleeping pill and my anxiety medication and went to bed early. I don't even remember dreaming."

"What medications are you taking?"

I handed Amber Aunt Ginny's pills. "Her doctor prescribed them a few days ago because she was riled up more than usual with the house remodel."

Aunt Ginny gave me a sour look. "What do you mean *more than usual?*"

Amber turned to me with mock innocence. "What *do* you mean by that, Ms. McAllister?" She lifted her eyebrows ever so subtly in challenge.

"I think that's rather obvious."

Amber smiled, "Have you ever been sleepwalking before, Mrs. Frankowski?"

"Not that I know of."

"We have a doctor's appointment today to discuss Aunt Ginny's . . . side effects," I said.

We were interrupted by Georgina bringing the Nelsons through on an unsanctioned house tour. "And this is the kitchen, completely updated with new cabinets and granite countertops. You'll have to excuse the color, I think there was a mix-up at the paint store." She pointed to the spot reserved for the new range. "And that is where . . . something goes. A stove, I think. Anyhoo." And then, as if noticing us for the first time, "Oh, and look, the local law enforcement busting up a neighborhood crime ring."

Aunt Ginny leapt to her feet with her fists balled. I grabbed her elbow and dragged her right back down again. "Uh-uh."

Aunt Ginny grunted. The Nelsons didn't notice. They were far more interested in scowling at my copper light fixtures. Mrs. Nelson sniffed as her lip curled up on one side and she looked around the room with practiced distaste. Mr. Nelson pointed at the new refrigerator. "But these aren't period fixtures at all. I thought this was an authentic Victorian manor house."

I bit my tongue to keep from responding, *No, I'm sorry, this house is a replica we bought off of reproductions.com last month.* "The kitchen has been updated, and isn't part of the house tour."

Georgina picked up a dish towel and draped it over my espresso machine, then breezed them through the door. "Look at our seventeenth-century sideboard that has a place of honor in the period dining room."

Amber waited for the Nelsons to clear the kitchen. "Can you show me where the items were found?"

I gestured to the servants' staircase. "This way to the lair."

I showed her the trapdoor. Amber smiled and shook her head slightly before pulling out her cell phone to snap a couple pictures. "What was this used for . . . originally?"

Aunt Ginny leaned against a shelf covered in jars full of green beans and peaches. "It's a liquor hidey-hole."

I looked down into the compartment again. "A what?"

"From the days of Prohibition. My grandfather made it to hide his whiskey and gin."

Amber scrawled some notes in her flip book. "Well, how about that. So, the only item unaccounted for is the diamond bracelet."

"I really think that's an unrelated issue," I said. "I'm sure it will turn up on its own."

"Let's give it a few days. By then I'll have to follow up with the victim."

Aunt Ginny grunted.

"I'm having my handyman install a motion sensor in

the foyer just in case there are lingering effects from the medication."

Aunt Ginny grunted again.

Amber slapped her flip book shut. "Okay. And you're going to return all the items to the neighbors today, you said?"

"As soon as my guests check out later this morning, although I don't know who the dentures belong to."

Amber opened her flip book and reviewed her notes. "Solomon Sheinberg reported the teeth disappeared out of the glass he keeps on his bedside table while he sleeps. Mrs. Sheinberg insisted he imagined the whole thing, and he probably left them at the library."

"Why would he take them out at the library?"

"I didn't ask."

"Well, I'll make sure everything is returned and I'll explain the bizarre circumstances. I doubt anyone will want to press charges when they understand what happened."

Aunt Ginny sighed and left the room.

"Poor thing. Looks like her life has been turned upside down since you crashed here," Amber said.

"What is that supposed to mean?" I bristled.

"Face it, McAllister, drama follows you wherever you go. You must be doing something to cause it."

"Why don't you just stick to police work and stop trying to psychoanalyze me."

"Truth hurts, don't it. Just so you know, I'll be following up with the neighbors. If you don't return those items today, you'll be an accessory after the fact."

I slammed the door behind Amber, and my cell phone buzzed. It was Tim.

"Hey you."

"Hey, gorgeous. What are you up to?"

"Involved in a crime, giving a statement to the police, the usual."

He laughed. "Well, this I have to hear. How about dinner Tuesday night?"

"Sure, that sounds great."

After I hung up with Tim, Aunt Ginny returned and handed me a bag full of her ill-gotten plunder. Her shoulders heaved in a deep sigh. "I'm going to go hand-cuff myself to the bed now."

"See, you're already making jokes about it," I encouraged. "You need me to get Amber's handcuffs?"

From over her shoulder she called, "No, I have some."

Oh man. I'll have to check on that later. I pulled up my britches, metaphorically speaking, and set out for a long morning apologizing to the neighbors. *I wonder if Mrs. Sheinberg has any of that pie left, to go with this crow?*

Chapter 14

"They're calling her the Snack Bandit." I tossed yesterday's issue of the *Cape May Star* into the kitchen trash and dumped a pile of coffee grounds on top of it. Sawyer had come over for some coffee and commiseration. It's like tea and sympathy but with gluten-free cinnamon buns.

Sawyer shook her head and picked up her mug. "I can't believe it's on the front page. It was just a few neighbors. How'd the reporter even find out?"

"Someone must have called them. I just can't figure out who. Everyone was so understanding when I returned their trinkets. Mr. Winston didn't even realize Aunt Ginny had been asleep the whole time. He thought she was flirting with him."

"Phew-ee." Sawyer breathed out. "She'll be madder than a hornet if she finds out it's public knowledge."

"Why do you think I'm hiding the paper."

"What did the doctor say?"

"Apparently, it's not uncommon for people to sleep-walk under the influence of these particular drugs, and Aunt Ginny was taking two of them."

"But with this level of competence? I mean getting dressed? Making sandwiches?"

"Dr. Weingarten said people have been known to shave, drive to work, even go shopping. The part of your mind that is supposed to stop you from moving when you're dreaming doesn't kick in, so you act out your dreams. Anything you can do awake, you can do while sleepwalking, you just don't have the best judgment."

"So, Aunt Ginny dreams about eating, and robbing the neighbors?"

"When she's on drugs she does."

"That must have been humiliating for her, poor dear."

"She was so embarrassed. But the office was very supportive. Her new nurse held her hand and stayed by her side for the entire visit. That helped a lot."

"How'd she do last night without the sleeping pills?"

"She had a good night. I took her to see Dr. Melinda for some alternative medicine Saturday afternoon. She gave her some antianxiety spray made from essential oils, and some valerian to help her sleep without the side effect of terrorizing the neighborhood."

The front door opened and shut. We heard a flop as Figaro greeted Aunt Ginny. "Get up, you crazy fool, it's me."

Sawyer and I exchanged nervous looks, but our wonder was quickly replaced with another emotion, shock. Aunt Ginny came around the corner sporting a bright new purple hairdo. Sawyer, who has zero poker face, sat with her mouth hanging open wide enough to stuff a navel orange in it.

Aunt Ginny threw her pocketbook down on the island, took a coffee mug out of the cabinet and slammed it shut. Then poured herself a cup of coffee. She yanked open a drawer and extracted a tiny bottle of very non-Paleo Irish whiskey and poured it into her coffee.

"Sooo . . . How'd the hair appointment go?" *Hey, I may as well ask. For all I know purple is what she was going for.*

Aunt Ginny threw me a look of scorn and irritation. *Okay, I guess not.* "Sawyer, close your mouth."

Sawyer's mouth snapped shut.

"I'm a laughingstock." Aunt Ginny took a large gulp of coffee.

Sawyer cocked her head to one side and asked, "Beeeecause of the haaair?"

Aunt Ginny's hand flew up to her purple 'do. "Meh! That's another disaster. Last time I get my hair done at Vo-Tech Beauty School. Some of those students need to drop out."

My eyes cut to the trash can and the buried newspaper. "What then?"

"It's all over town that I robbed the neighbors while sleepwalking."

"No." Sawyer and I did our best to feign surprise.

"Do you know they're calling me the Goody Bandit?"

I said, "No," while Sawyer the Quick said, "Snack Bandit."

I gave Sawyer a pointed look and she blushed. Aunt Ginny looked from one of us to the other and took a slug of her coffee.

The doorbell rang and there was another flop from the front foyer.

"That cat is going to give himself brain damage one of these days." Aunt Ginny sighed.

I answered the door to find Officer Amber on my front porch, flanked by two other officers. Two police cruisers were pulled up to the curb with their blue lights flashing. Mrs. Pritchard and Nell were next to my mailbox, cataloging every move.

"What's going on?" I asked Amber.

"I don't want any problems, McAllister. I'm just here to do my job."

"What are you talking about?"

Aunt Ginny and Sawyer came out from the kitchen. Georgina came halfway down the stairs, followed by Smitty with a drill in his hands.

"Poppy, what's going on?" Georgina asked.

Amber pushed past me to Aunt Ginny. "I'm so sorry, Mrs. Frankowski."

I was beginning to get very angry. "You'd better not be here for the reason I think you're here."

"Stand down, McAllister."

Sawyer could sense what was coming and started to cry.

Amber took out a pair of handcuffs and faced Aunt Ginny. "I have to place you under arrest for the murder of Brody Brandt."

The room was silent. Georgina rolled her eyes. "Well, that figures."

The blood drained from Aunt Ginny's face and she fainted.

I was stunned. How could this be happening? I was furious, and confused, and only had one thought. "Who is Brody Brandt?"

Chapter 15

Amber sat behind a brown metal desk in the processing room of the Cape May County Police Department. Officers milled about, some were at similar desks in the same olive-drab room, working on their respective computers. A boy of about twenty with greasy-looking black hair that hung in his eyes sat in front of one of the officers. He was wearing holey jeans and a dirty Metallica T-shirt and had one wrist handcuffed to a metal bench. He looked anything but repentant for his crime. He gave me a fight-the-power raised fist. I returned the same.

Amber sighed. "Brody Brandt won the prestigious Cape May County Humanitarian Award last summer for his work with at-risk youths. You could have read about him in the paper if you would get your head out of your butt long enough to care about anyone other than yourself."

"I didn't live here last summer, and stories about your local tractor-pulls and pie-eatin' contests don't exactly make the front page of the *Washington Post*."

Amber rolled her eyes with adept precision. "His secretary stated that she was dropping off some contracts at his home this morning, and found him lying dead in his bed. According to the crime lab, he was bludgeoned with something akin to a baseball bat. Officers on the scene reported no signs of a break-in, but the kitchen floor was covered with M&M's and the counter was littered with open takeout containers. It's her MO, McAllister."

"How could it be the same MO when Aunt Ginny has never killed anyone! Maybe he had a bunch of takeout containers lying around because he's a slob. Did you check to see if anything was taken?"

Amber thumbed through the incident report. "The victim lived alone, so there is no one to account for missing items."

"So, you're basing your entire case on the fact that the guy didn't clean up after himself?"

"The victim lived two-and-a-half blocks away from you, well within Mrs. Frankowski's zone."

"Aunt Ginny never left our street! And she only went to neighbors she actually knew. You searched our house, you checked under the trapdoor, where are the knickknacks? Where is the murder weapon? You've got nothing. You know Aunt Ginny didn't do this, Amber."

"So, you're a cop now? You think because you stumbled upon a killer once before that you know all there is about detective work? Is that it?"

"I'm saying, just think about this rationally. You know how this town likes to gossip. Tales of Aunt Ginny's nighttime raids have been told in every supermarket line and hair salon for days. It was in the *Cape May Star* yesterday morning. If someone wanted to frame Aunt Ginny, the paper gave it to them down to every detail."

"You've got quite an imagination, McAllister. I'm sorry this is happening to your aunt, but you'd better stay out of my way this time. Interfere with my case and

I'll have you in your old cell before you can say *Miranda rights*."

I fought the urge to punch Amber in the face. Mostly because the other cops in the room were eyeing me and I didn't want to make things worse for Aunt Ginny. I'd already posted bail, now I just wanted to get her home as soon as possible. Aunt Ginny had been through so much over the past few weeks, and she was old and frail. I was worried about what the stress of being in lockup would do to someone with her constitution.

Amber led me down the hall to the familiar holding cell I had spent a few hours in just a couple of months ago myself. Weak, old, frail Aunt Ginny was sitting on a bench with her sleeves rolled up, elbows on her knees, playing three-card monte and conning the other cell-mates out of their cigarettes and a pack of Juicy Fruit.

"Come on, follow the queen, ladies. Some of you should be good at this."

"Aunt Ginny?"

"Oh hey, Poppy. You want a piece of this?"

I shook my head and looked around at her cellmates, spotting a familiar face.

"Hey, girl, is this your aunt?"

"Hi, Bebe. You still here?"

"Naw, I was sprung the day after you. Just doing another tour."

"You've gotta learn to recognize the cops better, Bebe."

The caramel-colored inmate in hot pink short shorts, silver tube top and six-inch silver stilettos shrugged her shoulders and her Adam's apple bobbed up and down in her neck. "What can I say? I'm a sucker for a pretty face."

Aunt Ginny threw a med alert bracelet on the pile. "Put up or shut up, ladies."

Amber took a heavy ring of keys on a chain off her

belt and unlocked the cell. "You've got to get your aunt out of here before she forms a gang."

The other cellmates groaned as Aunt Ginny hustled them out of their few possessions. I took Aunt Ginny by the elbow and led her down the hall past the intake room. "Are you okay?"

"Yeah, but if I had more time I bet I could have won that drag queen's silver shoes."

"What would you do with size thirteen stilettos?"

"Show 'em off."

Sawyer was waiting in the car for us behind the police station. She handed me a paper cup of something warm from Gia's shop. "He made it special for you and said he would call you tonight to check in."

I took the cup and sipped. My almond-coconut latte. *He's so sweet.*

Aunt Ginny looked in the car window. "Anything for me?"

"Aren't you a little juiced up already there, Capone?"

Aunt Ginny cut her eyes at me and grunted.

Sawyer reached into the car and pulled out another paper cup. "Of course there's one for you, Aunt Ginny. Gia wouldn't have it any other way."

Aunt Ginny gave me a victorious smirk and took a slug of her coffee.

We arrived home to find Figaro moaning loudly in the foyer. Georgina threw the front door open before I could grab the knob. "Oh, thank God you're home, Poppy."

Aunt Ginny picked up Figaro. "I didn't know you cared so much, Georgina."

"What are you talking about? That infernal cat hasn't stopped howling since you were led out of here."

I sighed. "Georgina, really."

"What? Why do you have that tone with me? I'm not the criminal."

Sawyer, Aunt Ginny with Figaro, and I passed Georgina to sit in the sunroom to discuss our newest predicament.

Sawyer shook her head in disbelief. "How in the world could they think Aunt Ginny is capable of killing anyone?"

"I think we may be dealing with an opportunist," I said. "Someone who heard about the recent happenings here in the neighborhood, and decided to take advantage of Aunt Ginny's notoriety."

"Who would have time to plan something that quick? It was just in the paper yesterday morning."

"Maybe they heard the gossip around town about the robberies, and started forming a plan then."

"Have you ever met the man who was killed, Aunt Ginny?" Sawyer asked.

Aunt Ginny had a faraway look in her eyes. She shook her head. "I don't think so."

"It sounds like their evidence is circumstantial at best," I said. "They have no witnesses, no murder weapon, and no motive. What do you think, Aunt Ginny? You're being awfully quiet."

Aunt Ginny wouldn't look either of us in the eye. "What if I did it?"

"What do you mean?" I asked.

"I don't remember going to any of the neighbors' houses either. What if I went to this man's house and . . ." She trailed off and tears welled up in her eyes.

Sawyer put her hand on Aunt Ginny's knee. "There's no way you did this. It's not in your character."

I took Aunt Ginny's hand in mine. "Every house you went into, you were friends with the owners. They'd told you where the keys were in case of an emergency. You've been so worked up about strangers being in the house, I think your subconscious was hiding everyone's valuables to keep them safe. I don't believe for a minute that you hurt anyone."

Aunt Ginny wiped her cheek. "I know you're both just trying to help, and I love you for it, but I don't think I'll have a hairsbreadth of peace until I know for sure that I didn't kill that man. How could I live with myself if I find out I've done this?"

She was so pitiful and tiny, it was easy to forget that this was the woman who lived through the Great Depression, three major wars, five husbands, and the Newark race riots of the '60s. Back in the day, her friends called her the Scarlet Dragon.

Sawyer and I tried to come up with a plan to prove Aunt Ginny's innocence. Sawyer pulled out her phone and opened her Facebook account. "What if we start a social media campaign showing how the cops are trying to pin this on a little old lady who was sleepwalking?"

"That might embarrass them enough to look for other suspects at the very least."

"And I can try to find Brody Brandt's profiles to see what he's been posting and tweeting about. Maybe that will give us some leads for who he's been hanging out with."

"Check to see if he's posted anything about personal conflicts too. From what I've seen, people love to use Facebook as a passive-aggressive way to vent on the Internet."

Aunt Ginny sat quietly and rocked in her chair while petting Figaro. She ignored us while we talked, until she piped in with, "They sure have spruced up that jail cell from the seventies."

Um . . . say what now?

Before we could ask Aunt Ginny to expound upon that revelation, we were interrupted by a familiar bald little gnome. "Mrs. Frankowski, it is so good to see you back home again."

"Thank you, Smitty."

Smitty stood with his hat in his hands, and a timid look that we'd come to know as the forerunner to spilling bad news.

"Uh, while we're on the subject of problems, it seems that Georgina has hidden the waterfall sink for the Emperor Suite."

From down the hall we heard, "I'm trying to help you, Poppy!"

"Give him the sink, Georgina!"

From down the hall again, "I just think you're trying to be too trendy." Then Georgina stuck her head into the sunroom. "Stick to what you know . . . like beige."

"Georgina!"

"Fine!" Georgina stomped out of the room followed by a gloating Smitty.

"We have to get this figured out and clear your name so we can get the B and B off the ground before those two destroy it for good."

Figaro jumped down from Aunt Ginny's lap and she brushed enough hair off her slacks to make another cat. "What are we going to do? We don't have any money for a lawyer. And that first set of lodgers didn't go so hot."

Sawyer picked a tuft of fur off her suede skirt. "Maybe I can take some money out of the bookstore."

Aunt Ginny smacked Sawyer's hand. "Absolutely not, missy! Over my dead body."

"That's very generous, Sawyer, but no. I think we just need to find out who really killed Brody Brandt, so Aunt Ginny will be cleared. And I'll tell you what I'm going to do. I'm going to that house to see the crime scene for myself. The cops said it looked similar to the neighbors' houses after one of Aunt Ginny's raids, but I want to see it with my own eyes."

"Oh no, you are not!" Georgina stomped back in the room. "You are NOT breaking into a crime scene. Don't you remember what happened the last time?"

"Were you lurking in the hall?"

"I'm serious, Poppy."

"Georgina, I'm a grown woman. This is happening."

"Then I'm going with you."

"You're out of your mind, you know that?"

"I'm serious. No one is going to buy this house if they think a murderer lives here. As far as I'm concerned, this affects my investment. We need Ginny cleared, and fast."

"So, you only want to clear Aunt Ginny to flip the house?"

"I wouldn't say that's my only reason."

"Georgina, I can handle this on my own."

"I mean it, Poppy. If you think you're going into that house in the middle of the night, I'm coming along to keep you out of trouble."

"Who said anything about the middle of the night? It's not even five. No way . . ."

Smitty stood in the doorway with his giant, pleading cow eyes imploring me to get Georgina out from under his feet for a couple of hours.

"Fine. But you stay out of the way."

"You'll see that I'm right, Poppy."

I left the room and muttered under my breath, "Well then, that would be a first."

Chapter 16

I waited until the sun was setting, then googled the address for Brody Brandt. He lived two-and-a-half blocks down the beach. No way Aunt Ginny would sleepwalk that far to go to a random stranger's house. Georgina met me in the foyer dressed in black wool slacks, black cashmere sweater, black pumps, and black opera gloves.

"What, no black ski mask?"

She let out a heavy sigh as if she was thinking I was an idiot. "If we're going to break into someone's house, I want to be as inconspicuous as possible. Stick to the shadows and all."

"It's dinnertime. How are you going to skulk around in the shadows while people are coming home from work?"

Figaro came into the foyer, saw Georgina in her black camouflage, and walked over to rub up against her, leaving a wide swath of gray fur.

"Ack! Stay away from me, you pest. Poppy, your stupid cat always chooses the worst time to show affection."

Figaro sat on the step and gave himself a congratulatory

bath for a job well done. As I was shutting the door I gave him a reproachful look. "You're very sneaky, you know that?" A pair of innocent orange eyes blinked back.

I unlocked the car and hollered to Georgina, who was ducking behind a bush at the end of the sidewalk. "What are you doing?"

"Shhh! I'm trying to blend in. Why are you getting in the car?"

Just then, Mrs. Petricino came around the corner walking her toy Pomeranian, Thor.

Georgina froze like a statue.

Thor sniffed her shoe, which was peeking out from the bushes.

"Hiya, Poppy."

"Hello, Mrs. Petricino."

When they had passed us I said, "Because if we walk down there, everyone on this street will know exactly what we're doing, and I'd rather not announce it to the neighborhood."

Georgina looked around. "No one is watching us."

"Oh, trust me, they are. What happened to inconspicuous?"

"I was saving that for when we arrived at the house."

Oh, good plan.

I drove the car around the block and approached the victim's house from the ocean side. I parked in front of the Bagel Depot; its only customers this time of day were a couple of combative seagulls. I took a moment to listen to the sound of the surf crashing against the rocks of the jetty. Was there any sound more peaceful and relaxing than that? But then the breeze coming off the ocean blew my hair into a stringy mess, the salt air made my face feel sticky, and Georgina drove an icepick through my brain with her criticisms.

"This is why you don't get anything done, Poppy. We're supposed to be investigating a murder and you're lollygagging here, staring at the water."

Count to ten. Don't push her into traffic. "Let's get this over with."

We walked the rest of the block to Brody's house. From the sidewalk, I could see that there was yellow crime-scene tape across the front porch, and the front door appeared to be taped shut. There were no lights on inside the little white Cape Cod. We walked around to the backyard. Georgina got her heels stuck in the lawn and she had to call me back to lean on me while she extracted them. So much for discreet. The side door to the garage was unlocked. I pulled out the rubber kitchen gloves that I'd brought from home and snapped them on. I looked inside a few coffee cans that were lined up on a shelf by the door to the house until I found one with a key inside.

"What are you doing?" Georgina hissed.

"We're going in the house. I told you that at home."

"How did you know that key would be in there?"

"This is Cape May; people are more worried about tan lines and property taxes than getting robbed."

"Yeah, well, no one expects a sleepwalking old lady to crack them over the head with a bat either."

I threw Georgina a black look and jammed the key in the lock. "Listen, I learned the hard way, don't touch anything. Don't move anything. Don't leave any trace that we've been here. And most importantly, follow my lead. Don't go off on your own."

Georgina huffed. "I'm not an idiot, Poppy. I wore

the gloves." She straightened the seams running to her elbows.

"Yeah, well, if Renée Fleming is in here warming up, you'll be prepared."

We entered through the mudroom. A utility sink sat to one side, next to a washer and dryer. Overhead was a shelf holding a row of economy brand laundry detergents and cleaning supplies. A pair of dirty old sneakers sat on the floor next to a basketball.

The mudroom led into the kitchen. Georgina followed so closely behind me that she bumped into me with every step. "Georgina, give me a little space, will ya."

"You said stay close."

"I didn't say for you to hop on my back though."

"Well then, you should be more specific," Georgina hissed, then reached up and flicked on the kitchen light.

I flailed my arm out to flick it off as fast as possible. "What are you doing? Why don't you just call the neighbors and tell them we're here."

"How am I supposed to see anything?"

"Use your screen light on your cell phone."

While Georgina tried to figure out her apps, I got to look around. The kitchen was a hoarder's delight. The counter was covered with empty pizza boxes from Brother's, Chinese food cartons from Dragon House, Styrofoam containers from various local restaurants, and a couple of empty two-liter bottles of pop.

"Well, there's your proof right there that Aunt Ginny had nothing to do with this." I pointed to an unopened box of Twinkies on top of the microwave. "She loves those. If she was going to snack on anything, Twinkie wrappers would be all over the kitchen right now."

Georgina tiptoed around the room, holding her cell

phone out, leaning away from anything that looked dirty. "I think you're grasping at straws, Poppy. There's no telling what a sleepwalker would do under the influence of drugs. And where is the candy that was supposed to be on the floor?"

I looked in the trash can and saw what looked like a few pounds of M&M's. "The crime scene techs must have swept it up already."

"Look at his refrigerator door, Poppy."

"Brody must be the man in all these shots. Each picture is of him with a different kid."

"This one is at a graduation. This one looks like a medal ceremony of some kind."

"That one looks like he's camping with a whole group of them. They all look to be between fourteen and seventeen years old."

"Maybe he was a scout leader or something like that."

"I don't think so. No uniforms. Plus, it's both boys and girls. No, I think these must all be kids from his teen program."

In every picture, he looked so happy and proud. I found myself wanting to find his killer for his sake as much as to exonerate Aunt Ginny. I took one last look at the kitchen and found Georgina with her head in a cabinet and her butt in the air. Her cell phone near the ground.

"What are you looking at?"

"I'm looking for ants."

"Why?"

"Because a kitchen with this much food left out should be overrun with ants."

"Wow, that was really perceptive of you, Georgina. You know what else I don't see? Flies. This stuff hasn't been here long. I think it was staged."

I moved to the living room, where there was a blue corduroy sofa and a ship's wheel coffee table. One wall held a flat-screen TV and the other had a small desk with a lighthouse lamp and a laptop sitting on it. An enormous painting of a mermaid hung over the sofa, but the most fascinating thing about the room was that it was clean. Spotless.

Georgina crept in behind me. "Are we in the same house?"

I looked at the MP3 player plugged in on the end table. "This was definitely not a robbery interrupted. There are too many valuable things in this room that could have been taken."

Georgina looked around the room with her nose turned up. "If you say so."

The bedroom was sparse, just a small wooden nightstand with an alarm clock and table lamp, a matching dresser, and a queen bed. The bed was stripped of linens and pillows, probably at the crime lab right now. A dark brown stain made a Rorschach blot on the mattress. The room said nothing of the owner's personality unless Brody Brandt was quiet, plain, and boring, in which case it screamed his name.

"Do you see anything in here Georgina? . . . Georgina?"

I looked around. Georgina wasn't with me. I dared not yell for her in case someone overheard me. I was about to go look for her when I heard a horrifying sound. A toilet flushed. Georgina came out of the bathroom straightening her gloves. I stared in disbelief until she spoke to me.

"What? I had to go really bad."

"You might have left some of your DNA in there."

Georgina looked horrified. "I most certainly did not

leave DNA or anything else in there." She held up her hands in front of her. "I'm wearing gloves!"

Deep breath, Poppy. One. Two. Three. Four. Five. Okay.

The bedroom and bathroom turned up no new clues. Everything appeared to be in order. I don't know what I expected. A baseball bat covered in blood with a confession taped to it? I stopped by the desk again. There was a nearly full box of business cards that read, BRODY BRANDT, INVESTMENT BROKER, FREEMAN AND FURMAN, with the address and phone number. I took one from the box and slipped it into my pocket.

"Poppy, let's get out of here. This place gives me the creeps."

"You could have stayed home."

Georgina was indignant. "Someone had to back you up."

"Is that what you're doing over there in the corner, hiding behind that chair?"

"I'm being a lookout. And I would think you should be a little more thankful about it too."

"Ooooh-kay. Let's go."

My phone dinged and I pulled it out of my pocket to check the message. Someone had left a review for the Butterfly House on Yelp. My jaw dropped. One star. Bad neighborhood. No pancakes at breakfast. *It was a free weekend. Which couple could have done this? Or was it someone else?*

I cut my eyes at Georgina, who was studying her reflection in Brody's mirror. There was about to be a second murder in this house. I shoved my phone in my jeans and grumbled, "I'm ready."

Georgina practically ran from the house, but I was making sure everything was as we left it. I was feeling pretty satisfied with Aunt Ginny's innocence, but as I was putting the box of business cards back on the desk, I could see the outline of a shape in the dust. It was a little larger than the spread of my palm and shaped like a scallop shell. I ran my finger through the clearing and didn't leave a mark. Whatever was missing had been recently removed.

Oh no. Down to the last detail, it looked like Aunt Ginny had been here.

Chapter 17

I locked the house and replaced the key. Then I took off my gloves and shoved them in my pocket. Georgina walked tiptoe through the grass so as to not get her heels stuck again. I disposed of my gloves in the trash can at the Bagel Depot and got in the car.

"How do I turn my light off?" Georgina tapped her cell phone.

"What do you mean?"

"The screen. How do I get it to go back off?"

"It should just go out. Give me your phone. Georgina, what is this? Oh my God." I started to laugh.

"What? What is it?"

"You didn't have your screen on. You have thirty minutes of video recording yourself going through the house."

Georgina reached for the phone. "Give me that!"

I held it out of her reach. "You're making some hilarious faces. Look at how disgusted you were when you saw that mermaid painting."

"Poppy, give it back. Hurry up before I go into the bathroom."

"Oh God, you had it running in the bathroom." I

laughed again, but she looked embarrassed and I took pity on her. "Do you want me to delete it?"

"Yes."

"Okay, there. All gone." I handed it back to her and she tried to find her videos to see if I'd really deleted it like I said I would.

"It's not there, I promise." I drove us home and stopped at the curb with the car running.

"Aren't you coming in?"

"I have another stop to make. And for the love of God, please try to behave yourself in there, Georgina."

"I take offense to that, Poppy. When don't I behave with the utmost decorum?"

"You peed in the victim's house."

"That was an emergency."

"Earlier today you stapled Smitty's pants to the deck."

"How is that not behaving?"

"He was still wearing them."

"I wanted him to finish power washing."

"Well, leave him alone tonight and let him do his work. This project is taking too long as it is. Every time I turn around there's another emergency."

With a huff, Georgina got out of the car and delicately slammed the door. I could hear her calling for "Smutty" as soon as she turned on the porch light and it flickered and went out.

It was too late to go to the Freeman and Furman investment firm where Brody worked, but I had another idea. I pulled out my phone and googled the Cape May County Humanitarian Award. The news article stated that Brody Brandt, a Pennsylvania native, had been recognized for his work developing a program to keep at-risk youth busy through academic and community pursuits. That explained all the photos in his house.

The premise was that if they could keep their hands busy and expand their minds, they could keep off of drugs and stay out of trouble. He founded the Lower Township Teen Center two years ago. The center was awarded a grant from the chamber of commerce for their work with disadvantaged youth.

He sounds like a Boy Scout. Why would anyone want to kill him?

The article ended with the address for the Teen Center. I plugged the address into my phone nav and headed out.

The Teen Center was in a brown brick building between the library and the police department in the heart of a residential neighborhood known as the Villas. Even though it was dark out, there was a large basketball court that was well lit, and a concrete U-shaped ramp where kids were skateboarding between the buildings. The front lobby was painted lime green, and there was a bulletin board covered with notices about silent dance parties, *Pokémon Go* meet-up groups, and a Girls Who Code event. Jeez, all I did after school was homework and babysitting. Life was very different back in the '80s.

Down the hall was a bright lemon-yellow room filled with tables and chairs. Two vending machines were lined up against the back wall and a Ping-Pong table sat to the right. A group of kids sat around a table in total silence, tapping on their phones.

"Hi. I'm Poppy and I was looking for someone who would know Mr. Brandt."

The kids paused for a moment, staring wide-eyed and suspicious, then their fingers resumed tapping in a frenzy.

"I'm a friend. I'm trying to find out some information to help someone."

A girl of about fifteen with straight black hair and rectangular black glasses put her phone in her lap. "What about?"

I had not considered that news of Brody's untimely demise may not have reached his mentees yet, and I did not want to be the one to break it to them. "Does Mr. Brandt come here every day?"

One of the boys wearing jeans and a concert T-shirt for a group I've never heard of spoke up. "You a cop?"

"No, I bake gluten-free muffins and cookies for a coffee shop." Five sets of eyes lit up. "I could bring some in . . . in exchange for some information."

The girl with the rectangular black glasses asked, "Will the cookies be gluten-free? I can't be bribed without gluten."

"I'll make them full of gluten . . . and chocolate chips."

"Deal," another boy with curly blond hair said, "but the popo been all over this place."

"We told them, nobody here knows about no drugs. Brody wasn't dealing, man."

Drugs? That's new information. I set my purse down on a table and took a seat. "Do you know where the cops found the drugs?"

A black girl with her hair in an intricate tower of braids answered. "They found drugs in his house when they searched it after they . . . you know . . . found he was dead."

"Did you all know Brody was doing drugs?"

The boy in the concert T-shirt shook his head. "No way! Brody was clean. He had a policy against drugs."

The girl with the glasses said to the blond boy, "You know they planted them."

"Oh, straight up."

An Asian boy wearing a Manchester United jersey

spoke for the first time. "You can't trust 'em. Now they trying to shut us down."

"So bogus," the blond boy responded.

"I know a little something about that myself. I spent some time in jail a couple months ago for something I didn't do."

That got their attention. They had lots of questions, which I tried to be cool about. What was I accused of? Did I kill anyone? Did the cops rough me up? Did someone frame me?

"I was wondering the same things about Brody. Did he have any enemies that you know of? Anyone who would want to hurt him?"

The two girls started tapping furiously on their phones.

"If you know anything, it could really help find out who did this."

They nodded to each other in some secret teenage telepathy.

Braids spoke up. "There was a problem with Erika a few weeks ago. Her dad came in and threatened Brody, and said he should be locked up."

"Threatened him how?"

Concert-T answered me. "He said if Brody ever came near his daughter again he would kill him."

Braids continued, "Erika was Brody's favorite. He was trying to help her get a scholarship."

Glasses added, "He was really upset after that. Erika hasn't been around since."

"Do you know what the threat was all about?" I asked.

"We got the gist," Braids said. "Erika's father said that Brody should have his you-know-what cut off and shoved up his—"

I jumped in quickly. "Oh, I see."

The kids nodded their heads in accord.

"Do you know what Erika's father's name is?"

Glasses thought about it for a minute. "I don't know. I think Erika's last name is Lynch."

I sent the information to myself in an email, to follow up with Erika and her father later.

"Has anyone talked to Erika since the incident?"

Braids answered, "She won't see any of us. We told her it's not her fault."

Glasses nodded. "It was so unlike Brody. We just thought he had a special mentoring relationship with her. We had no idea that was going on."

The kids had no other information, and their attention span was exhausted, so I promised to bring cookies when I came back and I gave them my number if they thought of anything else. They promised to text. They were absorbed back into their phones before I was out of the room.

I headed back outside. A light wind rustled the dry leaves swirling around the parking lot. Something was making me feel uneasy, and I wanted to get in the car and lock the door as soon as possible. A movement to my right caught my attention. I looked up just in time to see a tall, skinny kid in a black hoodie disappear into the shadows. I didn't know what he'd been doing watching me, but I wanted to get as far away from the Teen Center as possible.

I returned home, where Fig waited for me by the front door. He tried to lead me to his food bowl, but I had another thing I needed to check on. I'd been uneasy since discovering there was an item missing from Brody's house. I didn't want to doubt Aunt Ginny, but I peeked in the liquor hidey hole, just in case.

Chapter 18

I spent the morning making brownies and muffins at Momma's for Gia's shop. I'd slept much better last night, having found Aunt Ginny's treasure trove still empty. Today I wanted to question Erika's father about his fight with the recently deceased. I googled Erika Lynch and came up with nothing, but there was a Jonathan Lynch on Eldredge Avenue in North Cape May. I cleaned up my station, waved goodbye to Momma, who answered by sticking out her tongue at me, and headed out.

The address took me to a two-story yellow house set back in a large yard on a shaded and deserted street. Somewhere down the block a dog was barking. I knocked on the door but there was no answer. I didn't even know if I had the right house, but I would have to come back tonight to try again.

It was too early for my afternoon meeting, so I killed some time sitting at Cape May Point, watching the seagulls and refereeing the numerous texts from Smitty and Georgina over the great light bulb debate of 2014. Sawyer sent me a text that Brody was a ghost. I thought she meant it as in he was haunting her, but apparently she meant that he didn't have a digital footprint. No Facebook, Instagram, Pinterest, LinkedIn, or Myspace accounts. He was the last holdout of the digital age.

I texted her back asking if she had time for a coffee date. Twenty minutes later I got a cryptic reply that she was busy and would call later. *Nice.*

At three o'clock I drove over to Cape May Court House, a neighborhood in the historic district. The investment firm took up three rooms of a two-story blue bungalow that had been divided into office space—two lawyers, a title company, Freeman and Furman, a hoagie shop, and a psychic palm reader. That's South Jersey zoning for you.

Freeman and Furman was on the second story behind a receptionist alcove. A small, mousy brunette sat behind a tiny wooden desk with an enormous fifty-line phone covered in buttons. It seemed a bit overkill given the size of the office. She had her head down on her desk and she was sobbing. A pile of used Kleenex littered the floor next to a wastebasket.

I cleared my throat. A pair of red eyes tried to focus in my direction.

"Hi, I called this morning about needing some investment advice."

The receptionist sat up and began tidying her work area. "I'm so sorry. I forgot that you were coming. Not that you aren't important to us . . . we've just had an office tragedy . . . a death." She snuffled loudly.

"I'm sorry, what happened?"

"One of our brokers died this past weekend. He was . . . murdered." Her face screwed up to a pinch and she crumpled into her chair.

I bent down to face her. "What's your name?"

She plucked a tissue and loudly blew her nose. "Judy."

"Can you tell me what happened, Judy?"

"He was a hero." She took a deep breath. "Now what will those kids do? Who could have done this?"

A loud "Ahem" from behind Judy startled us both.

A thin blonde in white fur booties, a white pencil skirt, and silk blouse stood in the doorway of one of the offices. "Can I help you?"

I stood and offered my hand. "Poppy McAllister. I have a three o'clock to discuss investment services."

The blonde narrowed her eyes at the receptionist. "Judy, why don't you take the rest of the day."

Judy rose limply, packed up her few belongings, and tore a corner off the flyer on her corkboard and shoved it into her pocket.

The blonde led me into a large room with a shiny cherrywood table surrounded by eight office chairs. A buffet with water bottles, a fancy new single-cup coffee-maker, and a stack of paper cups sat at the back of the room.

"I'm sorry about that. I'm afraid we've all had quite a shock today. I'm Kylie Furman, one of the partners here. Ken will be along in just a minute."

Kylie offered her hand and I shook it. A tall, thin man with a full beard joined us. If it weren't for his three-piece suit and paisley tie he would have looked more suited to sleeping in a cave and living off of twigs and berries than an investment office.

"Ken Freeman. Nice to meet you." He did not offer his hand, and if he really thought it was nice to meet me, he wasn't selling it. He flopped down at the head of the table and lay back in the big leather chair to stare at the ceiling.

For the next twenty minutes, I listened to Ken's half-hearted spiel about their services. I could tell his head wasn't in the game. Kylie kept biting her nails and stealing glances at him.

I finally got to the point of why I was really there. "I heard about your broker who was killed. Do you know what happened?"

Ken's nostrils flared and his beard bristled out like a puffer fish. "That is none of your business! If you're more interested in gossip, I suggest you find another investment firm!" He stormed out of the room, slamming the door behind him.

Kylie sighed deeply. "I'm so sorry for his outburst. We lost a great friend this weekend. Brody was a very important member of our team, and I think Ken is just trying to process."

"I'm sorry. I know losing someone you care about is very painful. What do you think happened? Was he having problems with anyone at work?"

Kylie shook her head. "Not at all. Brody was the best. We were about to make him partner." She choked up and her eyes filled with tears.

"About to make partner? Wow. So, I guess there was no one here who would try to hurt him?"

Kylie's face pinked and her eyes darted to the floor. "Perhaps it would be better if we reschedule."

She pulled a brochure out of a folder on the table. "Here, this lists our services and details the fees and exclusions. Why don't you take a look and give us a call when you're ready to sign?"

Before I could pick up the brochure, Kylie took me by the elbow and ushered me out with a bit more force than I felt appropriate for a business meeting.

On my way past Judy's desk I got a look at that flyer she'd ripped a piece from. It was for the Starfish Lounge happy hour, and the corner had been a coupon of sorts.

I took the stairs down to the street level and thought about the bizarre meeting. What was Ken so angry about? Why was Kylie so nervous whenever Brody was brought up? Judy seemed truly wrecked by Brody's death, and ready to talk. I'd really like to have a crack at questioning her. The only problem was that I had plans with Tim in an hour. This was really important. I couldn't let Aunt Ginny spend the rest of her life behind bars. I had to prioritize. Maybe there was a way to feed two cats with one fish, so to speak.

I took out my phone and called Tim.

"Hey, gorgeous."

"Hey, have you ever heard of the Starfish Lounge in the Villas?"

Silence. "The what?"

"The Starfish Lounge. It's down by the bay."

"Ahhh . . . why do you ask?"

"I have to *accidentally* run into someone who's going to happy hour, and I was wondering if we could move our date there."

"Uh-huh. Do I want to know what this is about?"

"Probably not, but I can fill you in later."

"Oh-kay. I guess we could do that. Where is it again?"

I texted him the address and promised to see him in a bit.

I really hoped Judy would give me something to work with, otherwise all I had was a few kids with a rumor. I'd never get Aunt Ginny cleared with that.

Chapter 19

What the Starfish Lounge lacked in class was only made worse with the putrid smell from the horseshoe crabs that had washed up from the bay's low tide. Weathered and gray, with few windows and fewer cars in the parking lot, the long, low box had a giant starfish in a net holding up a sign announcing HAPPY HOUR.

That seems overly optimistic.

The room was dark and sleazy with a smattering of tables around a stage in the back. A woman wearing a G-string and two poorly placed clusters of sequins gyrated on a pole to techno music. She was either in her forties or life had been cruel, or both. *Great. I invited Tim to a hoochie club full of half-naked women. As if I needed more reminders of my own measurements.*

"So, this is the Starfish." Tim put his arms around my shoulders from behind me. "I always wondered what this place was like."

I spun around to give him an apology for bringing him to this dive, but was interrupted when a waitress wearing a dress the size of a headband walked by carrying a tray of drinks. "Chef Tim! Hi!"

"Hey, Shel." Tim slid his eyes my way and had the

courtesy of having a flush of shame slide its way up the back of his neck.

"Really?"

"What? She comes in the bistro a lot with her husband."

"Uh-huh."

I spotted Judy sitting at the bar devouring a huge plate of potato skins.

"Come on, I see who I'm here to meet . . . Tim!"

"What?! I was listening."

"Wipe your chin, you're drooling."

The bartender asked Tim if he wanted his usual.

Tim cough-choked out a "Dude." He ordered us a couple of drinks and tried to look like he wasn't looking at the pole dancers.

I took the seat next to Judy. Her eyes were red and swollen, her expression held the vacant listlessness of someone who was all cried out. She had set up a framed five-by-seven photograph of herself and Brody sitting together.

"Hey, Judy, I hope you don't mind if we join you. I saw the flyer on your bulletin board. I'm so sorry about earlier. I hope I didn't get you into trouble with your boss."

"It doesn't matter. It will never be the same there again, now that *he's* gone."

I nodded toward the photograph. "Is that the two of you together?"

Judy picked it up and hugged it to herself. "This was taken at the office Christmas party last year."

"Were you and Brody a couple?" I asked.

Judy ducked her head. "No. Just friends. All of his free time was spent working with needy kids. Besides, I have my cats, and that's good . . . that's good."

"I have a cat too. His name is Sir Figaro Newton. Mostly I just call him Fig."

"Aww. I love that." Judy wiped a tear off her cheek.

I looked at the photo again. Brody was several inches taller and quite a few pounds heavier than Judy. He was solidly built, like someone who doesn't work out but has an active lifestyle.

"You were the one who found him this morning, weren't you?"

Tim blew his breath out, just now getting a hint of what he had gotten himself into. He spun around on the bar stool so his back was to the bar and he could look me and Judy in the eye while we talked. That stage must have been very distracting to him because his eyes kept swiveling up to the girls.

Judy furrowed her brows. "I realized he had forgotten to sign some contracts on Friday, and I didn't want to see him get into more trouble. So, I took the contracts to his house to have him sign and postdate them. When he didn't answer the door, I figured he'd left already to get down to the Teen Center with his kids. So I let myself in with the spare key to leave the contracts on the kitchen counter." She shook her head.

"Had you ever been to his place before?"

"No, but I knew right away something was wrong. Someone like Brody would never live that way. I thought maybe a raccoon had gotten in or an angry kid had vandalized his house. I was going to clean up for him. I never expected to find him there."

"What do you mean by you didn't want to see him in more trouble?"

"Ken and Kylie fired him. He didn't deserve it either. He was a hard worker. All the clients loved him. He handled some of our biggest accounts."

"I thought he was about to make partner?"

Judy laughed. "Are you kidding?"

Tim leaned in so Judy could hear him better. "You said he was fired?"

Judy nodded.

"What was that about?" Tim asked.

Judy's eyes flashed. "Lies! They had it in for Brody from the start."

I thought about Kylie and Ken and my meeting from that afternoon. They were both acting shifty, and Kylie outright lied to me.

"They said he was guilty, but I know he couldn't have done it. Not someone who gives his time to kids like that. He was a hero. A true humanitarian. No way would he stoop that low. You know the county just gave him an award."

Tim and I exchanged looks. Judy was wearing some rose-colored goggles.

"What exactly did Ken and Kylie say Brody was guilty of?"

Judy dunked a potato skin into a mountain of sour cream and shoveled it into her mouth. She seemed to be deep in thought while she chewed. "It's not like anything can happen to him now. A couple weeks ago, the auditors noticed there was money missing from some accounts. About a hundred thousand. All from Brody's clients. Ken and Kylie asked what he knew about it. Brody told them he didn't know where the money was, he didn't have anything to do with it."

"They didn't believe him?"

Judy choked. "Please. Who else were they going to accuse? He was like an only child standing in front of a broken vase. There was no one else in the room. I didn't handle the money. It's not fair. There was going to be a whole investigation, but now he's gone, so they'll just pin it on him and claim the loss on their insurance."

Tim signaled the bartender to bring Judy a cup of coffee. "But you don't think he did it."

Judy got a dreamy look in her eye. "I know he didn't do it. He had too much character."

Oh boy. "Did you know that the cops found drugs in his house?" I asked.

"First of all"—Judy picked up her fork and poked it at me—"I don't believe that for a minute. His whole life was about keeping kids off of drugs. I don't care what they found in his house, it wasn't his."

Tim leaned in to look around me. "Did this guy have any enemies outside of work? Anyone who would want to hurt him? Maybe an angry client?"

A busty half-naked dancer shook glitter all over Tim's lap and asked him if he'd want a private dance. He choked, from the sheer horror of being propositioned. Or it could have been because I gently pinched his arm and made him squirm. Either way, he couldn't answer, so I had to politely tell her, "I will cut you."

Judy was busy whispering sweet nothings to the photo of Brody, and hadn't acknowledged the question. I tried to get her attention again.

"Earth to Judy. Hey there. Did Brody have any enemies outside the office?"

Judy crammed another potato skin into her mouth and mumbled, "Not unless you count Kylie's lunatic boyfriend. He came in one day and went bat-poop crazy and accused Kylie of cheating on him with Brody. He said if Brody ever touched Kylie he would kill him. Then he punched a dent in my file cabinet and threw the old coffeepot out of the conference room window. It landed right on the psychic lady's Toyota."

Tim muttered, "I wonder if she saw that coming."

I jabbed him in the side. "Judy, do you know if Kylie's

boyfriend was right? Were she and Brody having an affair?"

"He wouldn't stoop so low to sleep with another man's woman. He was an angel. An angel with blond, curly hair. Hair the color of a bale of freshly rolled hay." Judy sighed.

"Uh-huh. Did you happen to catch the name of Kylie's boyfriend?"

Judy was nodding off. Her head bobbed, and her nose dipped into her sour cream.

"Hellooo, Judy."

"Oh, um, Ribbett, I think. Frank Ribbett, like a frog. It was embroidered on his uniform."

"What kind of uniform?"

"A blue one. I don't know, he looked greasy and smelled like oil."

Tim looked like he was trying to read the tramp stamp over one of the hoochie mommas' shorty shorts, and I was losing Judy's focus, so it was time to make my escape. I told Judy to call me if she thought of anything else and gave her my number. Tim paid the check and took one last look to the stage.

"That's it, let's go." I grabbed his arm and led him outside. "If I had known what kind of place this was, I would never have invited you here."

He laughed and put his arms around me. "Are you kidding? I vote Best. Date. Ever." He kissed me, and I felt warm and gooey, like cookies fresh from the oven.

We walked back to his car and he asked, "So, what was that all about? You aren't being accused of murder again, are you? That would be too much of a coincidence for anyone."

"It's not me this time, it's Aunt Ginny."

"Aunt Ginny? Who's she's supposed to have whacked?"

"His name was Brody Brandt and that hot mess in there was Judy, his secretary."

"I think Judy had a little crush on her boss," Tim mused.

"Don't you think it's strange that he was murdered right before they opened the investigation into embezzlement?"

Tim cocked his head and gave me a knowing look. "It is awfully convenient."

We both got into Tim's car and drove to El Queso in Del Haven. El Queso was a new restaurant for me. It hadn't existed when I was growing up here.

The ambiance was over-the-top and it took me a minute to take it all in. The walls were brightly painted stucco in shades of sand, turquoise, and pink. There must have been a hundred strands of Christmas lights crisscrossed back and forth over the ceiling. And if the health department ever closed them down, they could pick up a solid business selling off the piñatas.

"Wow. I've been to Mexico, and I've never seen anything like this."

Tim laughed. "I know. It looks like Tijuana exploded in here, but I know the chef and the food is really good."

I ordered a salad for dinner. Tim had an enchilada the size of a casserole for a family of eight. He ordered a refill on his tea and I considered stealing a forkful of cheese off his plate.

I filled him in on the doings at our house over the past couple of weeks. The sleepwalking, snacking, swiping trifecta and subsequent accusation and arrest. "I think Amber is gunning for Aunt Ginny because the method matches and the police can close the case quickly. Our mutual animosity doesn't hurt either."

"What would be Aunt Ginny's motive for killing this guy?"

"With sleepwalking, you don't need a motive. Aunt Ginny didn't have a motive for breaking into the neighbors' houses either."

"Maybe she was hungry because of that diet you have her on."

"That diet is her own fault; don't you feel sorry for her for that. She's the one who got me rooked into this Paleo thing in the first place."

I thought of Aunt Ginny having to forgo her favorite peanut butter and Twinkies at her age, and I softened. "Of course, she doesn't really have to do it with me anymore. It seems I'm going to be on it long term. But this does explain why she suddenly lost her appetite for breakfast. Anyway, news has been all over town about her midnight forays. Someone even tipped off the paper."

Tim sat quietly for a minute, as though he was thinking about whether or not to say something. Finally, he said, "How do you know she didn't do it?"

For a second I thought he was joking, but the look in his eyes said he was serious. "How can you think that?"

"How can you *not* think that? Aunt Ginny has always been crazy. Remember when she chased me with an axe?"

"She said be home by eleven."

"We were two minutes late! And how about when she caught that crow?"

"It was trying to steal her wind chimes."

"From inside the house?"

Tim was making some good points and I didn't appreciate it. "Even so, I don't believe she would ever commit murder, asleep or not."

Tim leaned back and crossed his arms over his flat stomach. His tanned, flat stomach. Where was I? Oh, right. I could tell that he thought I was in denial, but I still believed in Aunt Ginny.

He took some money out of his wallet and left it on the table. "How about we go for coffee Saturday night after my first seating? I can let my sous chef take over for the second."

The hair on the back of my neck stood up.

He continued, "There is a little place on the mall called La Dolce Vita. I bet you'd like it."

Gulp. "Where?"

He grinned wickedly and raised his eyebrows at me. "I think you know the place. I hear they have great muffins and a good-looking owner."

Worlds colliding. "Why do you want to go there?"

"I want to see where you work."

"I work in the kitchen in my house."

"And I want to see where they sell these muffins I keep hearing about."

"Riiiiight."

"Is there a problem with that? You don't want me meeting the other man in your life?"

There it is.

I tossed his words from the other day back to him. "No. We're adults. We're just keeping it light."

Chapter 20

Tim drove me back to the Starfish Lounge to pick up my car. He opened my door, and when I got out he pulled me close to him. "Remember in high school how we used to sneak away from Aunt Ginny and come up to the bay to make out?"

I giggled. "Yeah."

"Those were some of the best times of my life."

"Mine too."

He kissed me goodnight and I floated to my seat. He was still chuckling over my reaction when he pulled out of the parking lot.

How easy it would be to fall in love with him again. But I don't have time to focus on that right now. Aunt Ginny needs me to think of her first.

I didn't get anywhere with Brody's work, and Judy might not be the most unbiased witness. I checked the time and figured I'd see if Erika or her father were home yet. I drove up Bayshore and back to North Cape May.

There was a car parked out front and the light on the porch was lit. I could see shadows moving inside. I knocked, and a man opened the door. He was round and pink and looked to have the muscle mass of a canned ham. His short hair was heavily peppered with gray and stuck up on his head like a pincushion. A pair of blue sweatpants and a XXXL Flyers jersey clung to him for dear life.

"Can I help you?"

"Are you Jonathan Lynch?"

His eyes narrowed and his lips flattened into a straight line. "Who's asking?"

"My name's Poppy. I was—"

He started to close the door. "We aren't interested in Avon, Amway, or the Last Days Judgment."

I panicked. "No! I'm here about something else."

He folded his meaty arms across his jersey, and stared me down. "And that would be?"

I motioned to the Flyers logo. "Do you play?"

"A little."

"Roller or ice?"

"Roller. We have a pickup league that meets twice a week at Convention Hall. Is that it?"

"No, I wanted to ask about your daughter, Erika?"

He stepped outside. "Why? What has she done now?"

"Nothing . . . that I know of. I got her name from some kids down at the Teen Center."

His eyes were hard and black as plums. "She isn't going back there, and I told you people that pervert isn't allowed within fifty feet of my daughter or I'll have him arrested."

"By that pervert, do you mean Brody Brandt?"

Jonathan's nostrils flared and he took a step toward me. "I can't believe he would send you to my house after what he's done. I made myself very clear that if he came near Erika again, I would kill him."

I took a step backward.

"I'll make good on that promise. You tell that piece of—"

"You do know that Mr. Brandt is already dead, don't you?"

"What?"

"Someone killed him. That's why I'm here. To ask Erika if she knows anything that could help me find out what happened." *Like maybe her hostile father hit him over the head with a hockey stick.*

Jonathan's eyes darted around the yard. I wondered if he was assessing whether or not there were any witnesses about, so I took another step back.

"Are you with the police?"

"Well, no. Not exactly."

"So, you *are* with the Teen Center."

"Teen Center . . . ish. Why did you file a restraining order against Mr. Brandt?"

His ham fist clenched at his side. "Because he attacked my daughter. He was supposed to be helping those kids. He told Erika he could help her get into a good college, but it was all lies. He's using that Teen Center as a front to play out his sick fantasies. My poor baby barely got away from him before he forced himself on her!"

"Okay." I held my hands up in surrender. "Look, I'm just here to learn the truth. Nothing more."

He unclenched his fist, but his glower could still wither a cactus.

"Did you report Mr. Brandt to the police?"

"Oh, I wanted to, believe me. But my baby girl cried and begged me not to. She didn't want to go through more questioning with an investigation. I finally agreed that I would handle it without the police, but Erika is never allowed to go anywhere near that place again. I don't care if he's dead or not. I don't trust any of you people."

"I understand. I don't blame you. Do you think I could talk to Erika sometime? To ask her if she knows anyone else who may have experienced the same problem with Brody."

"No! Absolutely not. I don't want you harassing her. She needs to put this whole ugly ordeal behind her and move on with her life. Just leave!"

He stepped back into the house and started to close the door.

I sighed. *In for a penny, in for a pound.* "One more thing, Mr. Lynch?"

"What?"

"Where were you Monday night to Tuesday morning? You know, just in case I'm asked."

"It's none of your business, but I was flying in from Chicago. I have the boarding pass to prove it. Now I mean it. Stay away from us."

The door slammed shut.

Well, that could have gone better. He did seem surprised when I told him Brody was dead. Of course, that could have been practiced. That boarding pass would be a good alibi, if it exists. I wonder if a hockey stick does the same damage as a baseball bat if you hit someone over the head with it?

I walked back down the sidewalk to my car. I felt weird. The skin prickled on my neck. I looked back at the house and the upstairs curtain fluttered. For a moment, I thought I saw someone in the window, then they were gone. Maybe it was just my imagination.

Something about Mr. Lynch gave me the creeps. I got in my car and locked the door. How far would a father go to protect his daughter? Maybe Aunt Ginny's story in the paper gave him just the chance he needed.

Chapter 21

The sound of birds singing poured from my alarm clock and my eyes creaked open. I barely slept last night. I couldn't get Brody Brandt off my mind. Was he a hero, an embezzler, or a pervert? Who was this guy? I'd fallen asleep around four a.m. only to be shocked awake by the sound of Figaro wandering the halls and singing the song of his peoples. I threw a pillow at him to silence his moaning *merrrooooow merrrooooow*, but that only made him double his efforts.

Long past were the days of luxury where I could stay in bed till noon. I had too much going on right now. I crawled out of bed and tried a yoga flow. I dozed off for a minute or two in child's pose and abandoned the rest of the routine. *I'll try again tonight.* I showered and dressed and put on my makeup, just one layer today. I was too tired to try to impress anyone.

Downstairs I found Figaro curled up asleep in a sun-beam on the back of a chair in the front parlor. I leaned down and loudly sang, "'Swing low, sweet chariot. Coming for to carry me home.'" Which everyone knows is the cat equivalent to the midnight wails of *merrrooooow merrrooooow.*

Fig opened one disinterested eye, rolled over, and went back to sleep.

"Little punk."

"Who is?" Aunt Ginny breezed into the room wearing yellow chiffon and carrying a spray mister for her plants.

"Pavarotti here woke me up in the middle of the night."

Figaro stood, stretched, turned in a circle, and lay down in exactly the same position he'd started in.

Aunt Ginny misted her plants. "I think he misses you. You've been gone every morning, baking for the coffee shop. Shouldn't you be there now?"

"Not till this afternoon. I made enough to stretch two days. I have some work to do here on my laptop."

Smitty came through the room, followed by Georgina arguing about the electrical panel. Georgina was wearing overalls, a T-shirt, a hardhat, and a brand-new pair of construction-boot-stilettos.

"What the—?"

Smitty faced me, pink and breathless. "Oh, she's helping now. Yeah. Gonna supervise my installing a couple of outlets so . . . You know . . . It's a peach!"

Georgina hollered from across the room, "Get the lead out, Squatty! You're on the clock!"

Smitty's eyes bugged out, and he blew a raspberry.

Aunt Ginny was in a poke-the-bear kind of mood. "Well, you'd better go. You *are* on the clock, so . . ."

I mouthed, "I'm sorry."

Smitty grunted and followed Georgina out.

Aunt Ginny cackled devilishly to herself. "Ahhh, that was fun."

We went to the kitchen together for coffee and gluten-free maple pecan muffins that I nuked from the freezer. I called Amber to tell her about Jonathan Lynch's threat to kill Brody.

"I'm telling you, Amber, he was furious. If anyone has a motive to kill, it's a father whose daughter was molested."

"Why are you getting involved? This is an official police investigation, and you don't know what you're doing. Anything you mess up is punishable as obstruction. And you can believe I'll make sure you pay dearly." Amber hung up before I could give my customary smart-aleck reply.

"I wish she'd get the stick out of her butt."

Aunt Ginny poured each of us a second cup of coffee. "Some people have a hard time forgiving, even when they weren't intentionally wronged."

"I guess you're right. I didn't even get a chance to tell her about Frank Ribbett."

Smitty came around the corner looking over his shoulder. "I think I lost her."

"You know, it's a small house. You didn't disappear into a parking garage."

Aunt Ginny ignored us both. "Frank who?"

"Ribbett. Like a frog. He's Kylie's boyfriend. I can't find him on the Internet."

Smitty took a bottle of orange juice from the refrigerator. "That's because his name is Trippett. Frank Trippett. He works at Gleason's Garage over on Joplin in Rio Grande."

Aunt Ginny wrote the name down on a steno pad. "How did you know that?"

"It's where I take my truck for servicing."

"Well," I asked, "is he a nice guy? Could he be violent?"

Smitty shrugged. "I don't know. He can work wonders with a crankshaft."

"Squirrelly! Are you taking a break?" Georgina strutted in from the dining room.

Smitty put the orange juice back in the fridge. "Speaking of crankshafts."

Georgina had both her hands on her hips. "What are we paying you for?"

Smitty followed Georgina out, his head hanging low like a scolded child.

Aunt Ginny and I both laughed in the face of his misfortune.

I looked up the number to Gleason's Garage and called.

The phone rang several times before a gruff voice picked up. "Jimmy, so help me God, if this is you calling to harass me one more time about your piece of—"

I quickly interrupted. "I'm sorry, this is not Jimmy. I'm looking for Frank Trippett. Is he in?"

"Frank's off today, but he'll be in tomorrow at nine, unless he has a hangover, in which case he'll be in at eleven." Then a pause. "He'll probably be in at eleven." I made a note to visit him after twelve.

Sawyer called down from the front foyer. "Helloooo."

"We're in the kitchen."

Sawyer was gorgeous in tight white jeans, a wine-colored cashmere cowl-neck, and tan riding boots. Her supermodel good looks made me feel more schlubby the moment she floated into the kitchen. But then I was too tired to grouse this morning about what God had given me and Betty Crocker had perfected, so I moved on to acceptance faster than usual.

"Look what I found on the Internet." Sawyer handed me a printout. "Brody's obituary."

"That was fast."

"Evoy's Funeral Home don't mess around. Look at what I have circled."

"Brody Brandt is survived by a daughter, Christina Brandt, who lives in West Cape May and attends Atlantic Community College."

Aunt Ginny handed Sawyer a cup of coffee and sat at the banquette with us. "A daughter means an ex is somewhere in the picture."

"An ex always makes a good suspect," Sawyer said.

"You think she'll talk to us?" Aunt Ginny asked.

I googled Christina Brandt. "There's only one way to find out."

I picked up my cell and called the number. After a couple rings a woman answered.

"Junebug Consignments, Liz speaking."

"Oh, I'm sorry, I thought this was a residence."

"It is. I run a consignment shop out of the first floor. Who are you looking for?"

"Is Christina home?"

"Not yet, but I expect her anytime. Who should I say is calling?"

"Poppy McAllister. Would it be okay if I stop by the consignment shop today?"

"Sure, that's always okay. What are you looking for? Furs, furniture, or false eyelashes—I've got it all."

"Well, I run a bed-and-breakfast in Cape May, so I'm always on the lookout for quality antiques."

"Great. I'll get some pieces ready for you to look at when you get here."

We hung up, and I told Aunt Ginny and Sawyer, "Looks like I'm going to visit the daughter today. Do you want to tag along?"

"Oh, I can't." Sawyer frowned. "Julian called out sick and I have to get to the bookstore to open it."

"I feel like I haven't seen you in ages. What's going on with you?"

"I'm real busy right now in the bookstore. I'll try to get some time to hang out this weekend, okay?"

"All right." I wasn't convinced.

"What about you, Aunt Ginny? Want to come with?"

Smitty and Georgina bickered their way through the kitchen, picking up two muffins on the way to the back porch.

"How soon can we leave?"

Chapter 22

I handed Aunt Ginny my phone with the maps open and pulled away from the curb. "Here, you navigate."

"Are you sure I should be going with you? What if they find out I'm the prime suspect?"

"I say we don't mention that."

"Oh, that's a good idea. Turn left up here."

"So how are you doing with all this?"

"I've had better days. Nurse Tracy called this morning. Take the next right."

"What did she want?"

"Just to see how I was doing."

"Did she say anything about the police or the investigation?"

"Not a word, and I didn't bring it up. Too humiliating. Turn down that block there."

"Are you sleeping better?"

"I think so. That Rescue spray the witch doctor gave me is helping with my nerves."

"What's in it?"

"Mostly bourbon. I think I need a new bottle of it."

"Already? That was supposed to be a two-month supply."

"Are *you* home all day with Smitty and Georgina?"

"Okay, point taken."

"Over on the right. Yep, we're here."

"This isn't the consignment shop. It's Jingles ice cream parlor."

Aunt Ginny opened her car door. "I know. I want a milkshake before we go over there."

"Give me those directions!"

I waited for Aunt Ginny to come back with her peanut butter milkshake. She gave me a cocky smile full of false teeth, and we took off for Junebug Consignments, again. I drove along to the sound of her slurping. I'm pretty sure she was rubbing it in that I didn't have one.

Junebug Consignments was half junk-shop, half priceless antiques. An assortment of both littered the front porch and lawn. A big orange sign in the window announced SALE. I knew right away I had made a horrible mistake. Aunt Ginny's eyes were the size of half dollars, and I could see them spinning with cartoon spirals.

"Ooooooh. I'll just look around while you interrogate the witness."

"Maybe you should just wait here, Aunt Ginny."

The car door slammed shut and she was on the loose.

"Don't buy anything!"

"Can't hear you!"

A slender brunette in bright red glasses waved to me from the front porch. "Are you Poppy?"

"Yes, it's nice to meet you . . . Liz?"

"That's me."

"Are you Christina's roommate?"

Liz giggled. "No, I'm her mother."

"You are not. You look like you're in your twenties."

"Well, thank you. I was really young when I had her. Come on, why don't I show you around."

Liz's first floor was bursting like ripe snap peas, with two hundred years of history and charm. We walked room to room for about forty-five minutes, looking at the different pieces. She had a beautiful Eastlake carved walnut dresser with attached mirror that would be perfect for my Emperor Suite. I was asking about the price when Aunt Ginny popped her head in, carrying a gilded birdcage filled with plastic ivy.

"How much for this?"

"That's twenty-five," Liz answered.

Aunt Ginny disappeared like vapor in the wind.

"Um, Liz, I'm not just here to buy antiques."

"But you *are* going to buy some?"

"Yes. You can write up the two pieces here and I'll have my handyman come pick them up later."

"Oh good. Then what else can I do for you?"

"Well, I know it's not my place, but I heard about Christina's father's passing and I wanted to say that I'm so sorry."

Liz gave me an appraising look. "Are you a reporter or something?"

"No. I told you the truth on the phone. I run a bed-and-breakfast. I also bake gluten-free pastries for a coffee shop in Cape May."

Liz's eyes lit up. "You do? I have celiac disease."

"I have Hashimoto's."

"What is that?"

"It's a lot like celiac, only the thyroid is destroyed along with the digestive system."

"Aww. Going gluten-free was really hard for me. But now I have the hang of it. I made some gluten-free donuts this morning. You want to try them and give me your opinion?"

"I'd love to."

Aunt Ginny popped in with a stuffed bobcat. "How much is this?"

"That's thirty-six, but I'll knock off five if you get it with the birdcage."

"Sweet." Aunt Ginny vanished again.

Liz led me into the kitchen, where we had coffee and her homemade chocolate-frosted donuts.

"These are delicious. I'm going to have to buy me a donut pan to make them for the espresso bar."

"So, how did you know my ex?"

"To be honest, I've never met him. But I recently befriended some of the kids in his Teen Center, and I told them I'd try to find out what happened. Could I offer you some muffins or cookies in exchange for a little information?"

"Throw in a gluten-free chocolate cake and you have a deal."

Aunt Ginny popped in with a bronze statue of a horse and carriage. "What is this?"

"It's a clock. See the face there. The rider's crop moves up and down when you plug it in."

"How much?"

"That's fifty-two."

"Hmm, I'll think about it."

Aunt Ginny disappeared behind a bookcase.

Liz topped off my coffee and poured herself another cup. "This is a real shock for both of us. Christina came home from work and went straight up to her room again today. She's still refusing to come down to talk to anyone."

"Were Christina and her father close?"

Liz sighed and shook her head. "She had a difficult

relationship with her father. I got pregnant with her in high school, when Brody and I were young and stupid. He wasn't ready to be a father. He was absent for most of her life and I raised Christina by myself. Then Brody showed up one day and said he'd gotten his life together and wanted to have a relationship with her. By then she was a bitter teenager." Liz shrugged. "He had just started paying back child support a few months ago. He said he'd come into some money from an investment that had paid off. Christina's an adult now, but Brody said she could use the money for college tuition or a new car. She won't touch it. I've been holding it in a savings account for her."

"Did Brody have life insurance?"

"Not much. He'd just started putting money into a policy a couple of years ago as part of his newfound fiscal responsibility."

"Who's the beneficiary?"

"Christina. She's all the family he has."

"I met some of the kids down at the Teen Center and it sounds like Brody was a real inspiration to them. He was their mentor."

"Well, whatever you do, don't mention the Teen Center to Christina. She hates that place."

"Oh, how come?"

"She resented Brody starting the youth program. She said her father didn't have the time of day for her while she was growing up, but here he was bending over backwards for these kids he doesn't even know."

"I guess I can understand that. Did she ever meet any of them?"

"Not that I know of."

"The kids at the Teen Center said the cops found drugs in Brody's house. Do you think he could have had a drug problem?"

"I doubt it. Those days were behind him. Brody's been drug-free for years. But then again, anyone can relapse."

I made a mental note that Brody had at one time had a drug problem. The drugs the cops found might just be evidence after all. "Was Brody having any other problems that you knew about? Anything going on at the Teen Center maybe?"

Liz thought for a minute. "He had a problem with one of the boys a couple weeks back. The boy had started using again. Brody was especially close to him, so he was really broken up about it."

"Do you happen to have a name?"

Liz shook her head. "Uh-uh. Sorry. I just know Brody had to kick him out. Some of those kids are really bad news. The county sends them to Brody to see if he can rehabilitate them before they have to send them to juvie. At least they did. For a lot of those kids the Teen Center was their last chance." She bit down on her lip to keep it from quivering.

Aunt Ginny came in with a framed picture of a gnome wearing a bacon tuxedo, riding on the back of an owl. "Will you throw this in for free if I buy the clock?"

Liz narrowed her eyes at Aunt Ginny. "You sure know how to bargain. I'll throw it in, but you have to take it today before I change my mind."

"Deal!" Aunt Ginny fast-toddled out of the shop clutching her prize to her chest.

"That was nice of you."

Liz chuckled. "I would have been willing to pay her to take that off my hands."

"You've been so helpful, and I don't want to take too much of your time. Thank you so much. Please give

Christina my number if she wants to talk or can think
of anything else that could help."

"I will, and I'll call you if I see anything else that you
could use with that dresser."

I packed Aunt Ginny and all her ridiculous swag into
the car. "What in the world are you going to do with all
this junk?"

"Sell it at our yard sale in the spring."

"Are you kidding me?"

Aunt Ginny's eyes twinkled. "Just wait till Ethel sees
that carrot-baby figurine. Heee!"

Well, it brought her so much happiness, who was I to
say she couldn't have her bizarre trinkets. Judging from
the sixteen voice messages I'd racked up from home, I
hoped it would make whatever Smitty and Georgina
had waiting for us a little more bearable.

Before I pulled away from the curb, Liz ran after me.
"Hey, I did just think of something that could be important. I don't know why I didn't think of it before. I guess
it's because we were talking about the Teen Center."

"What is it?"

"A few months back, Brody had been doing private
counseling for a mystery kid outside of the Teen Center.
He had to keep his identity secret. I thought it sounded
kind of fishy, but we aren't together anymore so it was
really none of my business. Then one day he confided
in me that he regretted getting involved in it. He was
under a lot of pressure from the boy's family, and he
was really nervous about the whole thing."

"Do you know what kind of pressure?"

"I don't know anything more than I told you. He
wanted to keep me and Christina out of it. He only told
me in case something happened to him. And it looks
like something did."

Chapter 23

"Hold it to the right!"

"I am holding it to the right!"

"It's not level."

"You wouldn't know level if it spit in your eye!"

Smitty and Georgina were side by side on a ladder in the front foyer over the landing. Smitty had a drill in his hand, and Georgina towered over him, holding an antique silver chandelier. I could only assume they were trying to install it to replace the modern pendant from the Home Depot.

"Georgina, you know I'm paying workmen to do that."

"Oh, I sent them home."

I think my heart just stopped. Is this what it feels like when you're having a heart attack?

Aunt Ginny took out a tiny yellow canister and sprayed it into her mouth.

"So, you *do* have some Rescue Remedy left."

"I said I was low, not out."

"Georgina, why would you send the workers home? We are so far behind schedule already."

Georgina attached a chain to the light fixture. "If you want something done right . . ."

Smitty mouthed, "Help me!"

"Do you even know what you're doing?"

"Of course I do, Poppy."

Smitty shook his head no behind her.

Figaro watched from the steps, his whiskers twitching.

Aunt Ginny clucked her tongue. "Do you want to come to my room with me?"

Figaro jumped off the steps and started prancing down the hall in front of Aunt Ginny in the direction of her bedroom. I suspected he thought she was offering treats of some kind.

"Wait till you see the stuffed bobcat I bought."

Figaro paused with one foot in the air, looked back at Aunt Ginny, waited for her to catch up, then trotted forward until they both disappeared into the kitchen.

Georgina lost her balance on the ladder and Smitty dropped the drill to catch her. It clanged against the chandelier and one of the candlestick wells bent to the side.

Smitty grunted. "I can fix that."

I brought the rest of Aunt Ginny's items inside and put them in the mudroom until I knew where she wanted them. Georgina came in and took off her goggles.

"Where have you been all morning?"

"Aunt Ginny and I went to see someone who might have information about the deceased."

"Really, Poppy, don't you think you should let the police do their jobs? It's not like you have any training in detective work."

"The police officer in charge of this case has a grudge against me, so no, I don't trust her to be objective."

Georgina hassled me down the hall and up the stairs

to my room. "Well, I think you're being ridiculous. And while we're on the subject—"

"The subject of me being ridiculous?"

"I was talking to the handyman."

"Harassing the handyman."

"Listen, he says the house has good teeth."

"I think you mean good bones."

"Oh, that makes more sense. Anyway, with the unsavory element in the neighborhood, I think it would be in your best interest to finish the house and sell it. We could invest your money in some long-term annuities. I could have Paul draw up the papers for you."

"I don't need your broker drawing up anything and I'm not selling the house, Georgina. Besides, the only unsavory element to this neighborhood is the seagull mafia that ambush Curly's Fries. Why are you so intent on having me move back to Virginia?"

"You have a life in Virginia. We have all those committees that are depending on you to stuff their envelopes and organize their table settings. Maybe we can get you on the menu committee for the Waterford Historical Society, since you like to bake. What do you have here? You don't know these people. From what I've seen, there is a group of men who've been coming on to you. You know that can't be good, Poppy. A young widow, such as yourself. With your . . . attributes."

I stopped reading the email I had been skimming. Did she just say what I think she said? "Are you serious?"

"Well, you aren't exactly a supermodel, Poppy. I mean, be sensible. What else could these men want from you?"

"So, because I'm not thin, there is no way men could be interested in me?"

"I just think you need to be realistic. If you have

men chasing you, in your condition, maybe they're after something else."

I couldn't believe my ears. Where was a bucket of water when you needed to melt a witch?

"Like John's money." She went on, "Have you been telling these men about how much of your husband's money you've sunk into this long shot? Being an innkeeper? Maybe they want a piece of that."

I had to unclench my jaw and take some deep breaths before I could speak. "First of all, no one is after my money. Why is it so hard for you to believe someone could like me for me? For my personality, or my sense of humor. Maybe these men don't mind my size. Not all men are shallow and holding out for models."

Even as I was saying the words, I could feel the doubt bubbling to the surface. Why *did* Gia like me? He was so sexy. I'd seen the women flirting with him in his shop. Tim and I had a history, so maybe that wasn't as far-fetched. Still, how could I compete with pretty and perky Gigi? Maybe I was being a fool after all.

Georgina could smell my fear. She gave me a patronizing smile like she knew she had me right where she wanted me. "That's ridiculous. Men are only after one thing, and a grieving widow has no business giving it to them. You need to honor John's memory and protect his assets. I didn't go out of the house wearing anything other than black for a whole year after my Phillip died. It's your duty to mourn John for the appropriate time and stay faithful to him."

"Okay, Queen Victoria, back off. I'm not giving anything to anyone. I honor John's memory every day. He's been gone for almost nine months, and I will always love him. I was the one who took care of him when he was sick and stayed by his side right up to the end, so my mourning process started the day he was diagnosed. You have no right to question my faithfulness or my integrity. And my relationships are none of your business."

Georgina bristled. "Fine. Whatever you have to tell yourself. But you'll see. People will talk."

I looked around the room. "What people? Where are these people? No one is talking but you."

Georgina blew out another puff of annoyance, turned and stomped out of my room.

I sat on the edge of the bed, still shaking. How dare she. In a few short minutes she managed to call me fat, stupid, gullible, unfaithful, and a tramp. I had to send her home. Even when John and I were married I'd never had to endure this kind of psychological warfare day after day.

A heavy tear rolled down my cheek. Georgina had really picked at a scab on my heart. Maybe I was all of those things. Did I really deserve another chance at happiness? Was I just a fat fool?

I had to get away from this house. I grabbed my purse and ran down the stairs. Before I knew what I was doing, my subconscious sent me to my safe haven, baking.

Chapter 24

It was a lot later in the day than I normally worked in Momma's kitchen, and she let me know she didn't approve, waggling her angry attack eyebrows in my direction. Her kitchen staff were in full swing prepping for dinner. Pots of water were boiling, mountains of vegetables were being chopped, sauces were simmering, and casseroles were baking. Thank God the desserts were already finished and waiting on racks to be plated, so I wasn't going to be in anyone's way.

"Is it okay if I make a batch of cookies for the Teen Center? If it's not, I can come back in the morning."

Momma's mouth was set in a grim line. "Bah!" She waved me toward the pastry station, and resumed barking orders at the rest of her staff. "Marco, *mi portano gli gnocchi.*"

"*Sì*, Momma."

"*Mettere le lasagne al forno.*"

"*E fatto*, Momma."

"*Mescolare il minestrone.*"

I took out my storage box of ingredients and began to cream butter and sugar in the Hobart mixer. My hands were still shaking from the encounter with my devil-in-law. I focused on measuring out my dry ingredients and scraping vanilla beans until I could feel myself calming down. Baking was my therapy. Baking and eating. By the time I was ready to toss in the chocolate chips, I had to open another bag because someone had snuck in and eaten most of the first bag. Vandals! Okay, fine. It was me.

Gia appeared in the kitchen, calm and serene, like the eye of a hurricane. He was greeted to Momma's coos and the kitchen staff's calls of "hey-o!" I was immediately off-kilter, as the doubt monster Georgina had fed growled loudly in my ears. Gia came over to the pastry station and nuzzled my neck.

"*Mia bella*, mmm, you smell like chocolate."

"That's because I just ate a pound of it." *Oh my God, why did I say that?*

Gia chuckled and kissed my neck. "I like it. I was about to call you when I saw your car in the lot. Can you come over when you're finished? We have a surprise for you."

"A surprise? What is it?" I could hear my voice shaking from nerves. Thanks a lot, Georgina.

"You will see when you come over." Gia smiled in that mysterious way I hadn't yet figured out, and gave me a wink.

I finished my baking and cleaned up my station. Then I packed up two bags of chocolate chip oatmeal cookies for the Teen Center and waved goodbye to Momma and her line of cooks. Momma gave me her usual indecent response, but the line waved back and made "Ooooo" and kissy sounds. Momma glared at me and snapped at the line, who straightened up immediately and went back to prepping and sautéing.

What the heck was that about?

I walked in the front door of La Dolce Vita to find Gia's five-year-old son, Henry, bouncing from side to side, giggling. "We has a present for you."

I couldn't help but smile. He took my hand and led me to the back, where Gia was waiting. He was leaning against the counter with his arms folded. On the counter next to him stood a large wrapped box.

"It's a peacock!" Henry squealed.

Gia cocked his head toward Henry and put a finger to his lips.

"What is this?" I asked.

Henry giggled.

Karla came in and groaned.

"You'll have to open it to see." Gia arched an eyebrow.

I lifted the box, and beneath it was a brand-new KitchenAid professional-series mixer that had been custom painted to look like a beautiful peacock. It was gorgeous. I didn't know what to say.

"See! See!" Henry squealed again.

"I see it." I giggled. "This is for me?"

Gia's chest puffed. "For you. Do you approve? If you don't like the peacock I could get it painted to look like a chicken instead."

"No. It's perfect. I love it!"

Gia grinned. "*Bene.*"

"Daddy says you get a peacock because you're special."

Gia's neck flushed. "Okay, that's enough out of you. Time to go to home. Karla."

Henry's shoulders drooped. "But I want to stay with Poppy."

Karla laughed. "I don't know. I think Henry has a lot more to tell Poppy."

Gia turned Henry around to face Karla and gave her a look I couldn't see. "*Vai a casa.*"

Karla laughed.

"Bye, Henry."

Henry half turned and waved over his shoulder. "Bye, Poppy."

"Bye, Karla."

"Uh-huh."

Gia shushed them out the back door. When he came back he was rubbing the back of his neck and looked a little sheepish.

"So," I teased, "what was that about?"

"Kids. They say too much."

"Mm-hmm. Gia, this is so kind of you. I mean, it's just beautiful, but I couldn't possibly . . ."

I couldn't say any more because Gia's lips were on mine and he pulled me close against him. His kiss deepened and every single thought dropped out of my head and rolled out the door. I put my arms around his neck and gave in to him.

"Excuuuse me. Is anyone here?"

Gia moaned softly and pulled himself away. "I sent Karla home, now I have to cover the shop."

He looked into my eyes and the intensity of his gaze made my heart speed up. I leaned toward him again. If he only wanted one thing from me, like Georgina said, I might just be willing to give it to him.

He yelled over his shoulder, "I'll be right there." Then he turned to me and spoke softly. "I have to take care of this. Can you stay for a while? I miss you."

"I can stay for the rest of my life." Okay, maybe I didn't say that, but I would have agreed to anything right then. "I'm not going anywhere."

He led me out to the front, where he waited on a middle-aged lady with painted-on eyebrows, who looked like she'd been baptized in lemon juice. She held her lips in a tight circle so her nose stayed in a crinkle even when she spoke.

"I don't like coffee; do you have anything else?"

Then why are you here?

Gia was more courteous. "I can make you a hot chocolate or some tea?"

She pressed her lips tighter, as if deciding between a snake on a stick or a sack of spiders. "Well, I guess the hot tea will have to do."

"Certainly, ma'am."

Gia glanced my way and gave me a wink. He made the woman her tea, which she sniffed at, then returned her mouth to its unhappy pucker.

I couldn't wait for her to leave so we could maybe go back to where we were before she barged in with her sourpuss, but nope.

She paid her two dollars and nested at the nearest table to disapprovingly blow on her hot tea.

I sat on one of the bar stools and Gia made us iced Americanos.

"Are you sure you want me here so often while you're working?"

He leaned down closer to me. "I can't think of anything I want more."

Prunella cleared her throat loudly just in case we'd forgotten she was judging us from her perch.

After being hitched to Georgina's life for so long, I was practiced at ignoring pests. "I don't think your mother likes me."

Gia shrugged. "Momma doesn't like anyone."

"Did I do something to get on her bad side?"

"It's complicated."

Gia took out a clean rag and began to wipe down the counter. "How is Aunt Ginny doing?"

Okay, subject changed. I lowered my voice to keep some semblance of privacy. "Poor Aunt Ginny. I know she's innocent, but I can't tell if she's being set up or if this is just police department incompetence. After my visit to the victim's house, it's obvious that this wasn't a robbery interrupted."

Gia paused his cleaning. "You went in the victim's house?"

"Um . . . well . . . yeah."

"*Bella*, you have to be more careful. You just got your name cleared from the other mess."

"I know. But what would you do? What if your mother were being accused of murder?"

"My uncle Giacomo would sneak her out of the country on a fake passport with the olive oil distributor."

"Does he do that sort of thing a lot?"

"We don't talk about it. But I understand your point. Family first."

I wondered how much Uncle Giacomo charged for those services, and if he'd extend to me the family discount.

Gia put his rag in a bucket of sanitizer and pulled up the stool next to me. "Now, how do you know it wasn't a robbery gone bad?"

"For one thing, the victim was lying in bed, presumably asleep when he was hit on the head. And judging from the abundance of mess in the kitchen, the lack of it everywhere else in the house, and the M&M's that had been scattered all over the floor, I think someone planned to make it look like Aunt Ginny had been there sleepwalking."

Gia nodded. "So who is this guy who was killed?"

"I'm still trying to figure that out. The chamber of commerce gave him the humanitarian award and a grant for his youth program. His secretary seems to think he was the identical twin to Jesus, but his bosses fired him for embezzlement. His ex-wife said he was finally getting his life on track, but one of the parents from the Teen Center said he was a pervert who tried to molest his daughter. So, in short, I have no idea."

"Maybe he was all of those things. People are complicated. Even notorious gangsters can be good fathers."

"Are you trying to tell me something here?"

Gia shrugged. "Just making conversation."

"I just wish I could figure out a solid motive for murder. That would help narrow down the suspects. But this guy has as many adoring fans as he has enemies. And those kids he mentors have nothing but good things to say about him."

"You said he won money for his center?"

I nodded.

"Maybe we need to see who else was up for that award."

"A disgruntled charity? But why would you kill someone after the fact? It would be too late to get the money for yourself."

"Who knows why people do what they do. Greed is a powerful motivator."

"How would we find out who else was up for that award?"

"If you want, I can ask around. I have some connections."

I whispered, "Like, mob connections."

Gia's mouth twitched for a second, but he recovered. "I was thinking more about the chamber of commerce, but you're not far off."

"Oh."

Our prickly guest was finally finished being disappointed with her tea. She left her takeout cup on the table for someone else to clean up. The bell tinkled her exit.

I looked at my cell phone to see if I had any make-out time left and was sorely disappointed. "I'm afraid I have to go. I have to drop these cookies off at the Teen Center as a thank-you for some of the kids who talked with me the other night."

Gia pulled me close against him. "How would you feel about going to dinner with me this weekend?"

"I'd like that."

"Did you ever talk to your friend about us?"

"Hm?" *Talk to who? About what? Gia's eyes crinkle at the corners when he smiles.*

Gia couldn't hide the laughter in his voice. "I believe there is an old boyfriend in your life?"

Oh crap, that's right. "Uh . . . right. Tim. We did talk. In fact, he wants to bring me here for coffee one night. I hope that's okay."

Gia's eyes danced and he got that mysterious smile back. "Yes, of course that would be okay. I'll have to hit the gym before I'm sized up by the competition."

I could feel his muscles flex under his shirt. I giggled. *Competition.* "Competition for what?"

"For your heart, *bella.*"

Chapter 25

I parked under a street lamp. It was just turning dusk and I didn't know how long I would be. That same freaky vibe I got the last time I was here was back. The boy in the hoodie was watching me again from the edge of the woods. I shivered and quickened my pace.

I entered the lobby and a stout, matronly woman greeted me. She looked to be in her late fifties, but she had pink hair that was spiked up like Chef Anne Burrell, and funky silver cat-eye glasses she wore attached to a chain. She was wearing a T-shirt with words emblazoned across her ample midsection that said *Body by Pizza*. "Hey, what can I do for ya?"

I held up the bag of cookies I'd made at Momma's earlier. "I brought some cookies for the kids. I met a few of them Tuesday night and I told them I'd be back. My name's Poppy." I extended my hand. "I bake for La Dolce Vita."

She shook my hand. "Brenda. Dani told me a lady was here asking questions about Brody. Said you want to help find out who killed him. That must be you."

"Guilty. Which one is Dani?"

"Straight black hair, black fingernails."

"Oh, Dani's one of the girls. Okay, Glasses."

"You got it. I'm going to need you to sign in before I let you go back."

She handed me a clipboard with a list of signatures and times in and out. I signed my name while reading up through the list. Officer Amber had signed in Tuesday afternoon.

Brenda took the clipboard from me and eyed the bag of cookies. "So, did you find out anything?"

I opened the bag and held it out to her. "Would you like one?"

She reached in and pulled out three. "Don't mind if I do."

"Nothing definitive yet. Tell me, were you aware of any problems Brody may have been having with parents?"

Brenda munched on her cookie and nodded her head. "Jonathan Lynch."

"Can you tell me what happened?"

"He came in here one night screaming and cussing. Accused Brody of trying to rape his daughter, Erika. Brody was devastated. He wouldn't hurt a flea, let alone one of his kids. We lost some sizable private funding because of his accusation. I wanted to fight back, but Brody wouldn't go along with it. He didn't want another bad mark against Erika's reputation. Before I could try to convince him to clear his name, he was gone."

"So you don't think Brody attacked Erika?"

"There's no way. He thought the world of these kids. He would never hurt any of them."

"I heard he'd been working with Erika to get a scholarship."

Brenda finished chewing her last cookie, eyed the bag again, and nodded. "She's a gifted artist. Brody was working with her to enter some national contests that offer scholarships for art schools."

I tipped the bag her way. "Would you like another?"

"Thank you." She reached in and pulled out another cookie and examined it. "He loved mentoring these kids. It was his passion. He wanted to give them their best chance at success despite the circumstances that were stacked against them."

"What circumstances were stacked against Erika?"

"Well, I shouldn't be telling you this." Brenda looked down the hallway to see if anyone was within earshot. "Erika's mother killed herself a couple of years ago. Overdosed on Vicodin and Chardonnay. Erika was skipping school and failing most of her classes when the school counselor recommended she get involved with the Teen Center."

"That's terrible."

Brenda nodded and her eyes slid to the bag of cookies again.

"Has Erika been in since the blowup?"

"No one has seen her. It's sad. She was doing so well here."

"Other than Erika's father, was there anyone else whom Brody may have been on the outs with?"

Brenda thought for a minute, then looked at the bag in my hand.

I held it out to her. "You've been so helpful, why don't you keep these for yourself. I have another batch in my purse here."

"I couldn't . . . well . . . if you insist." Brenda gingerly took the bag and dove back in for another cookie. "All I've had to eat today is a salad and I'm starving."

I hear you on that, sister. I smiled.

Brenda finished her cookie. "Well, I know Brody wanted to reconnect with his daughter, Christina. She pretty much told him she never wanted to see him again after he won the humanitarian award for his work here."

"Why would she be so angry?"

Brenda thought while she chewed. "Brody wasn't always there for her. He wanted to make up for lost time with his daughter, but sometimes people cut you off and there's no way back."

I thought about Amber and how she'd been holding a grudge against me since high school. If she'd just let it go maybe she wouldn't be so intent on putting me in jail every time we spoke. "How about the charities? Was anyone put out that Brody received funding that maybe they thought they deserved?"

"Hmm. I don't know. They never said anything to us other than congratulations."

"Do you know who else was in the running for the award?"

"I did, but the short-term memory isn't what it used to be." Brenda tapped her temple. "Brody handled all that for us anyway."

I thanked Brenda and took the second bag of cookies back to the rec room, where the kids were congregating on their cell phones. They remembered me instantly. At least they remembered that I'd promised them food.

Blond boy jumped out of his seat the moment I walked into the room and put his hand out. "Whacha bring us?"

"Oatmeal chocolate chip cookies, as promised."

Glasses, who I now knew as Dani, put her hand in the bag, then pulled it out quickly like she'd been stung. "Wait, do these have gluten in them?"

"I made sure of it."

"Okay." She put her hand back in the bag and pulled out a cookie and smelled it. Like gluten has a smell.

Concert-T, whom Glasses told me goes by Jason, didn't say a word. Came over, took two cookies, gave me a big smile, returned to Ping-Pong. Teenagers.

Manchester told me his name was Eric, and was the first to ask about the investigation. "Did you find anything?"

"I'm still working on it. It will take some time, but I think I may have found a couple of suspects."

Braids, also known as Keisha, asked, "Oooh, who who?"

"I can't say anything yet, but I'm working on it. I want to clear my aunt as badly as you want to find out who killed your friend."

"Truth." Blond boy gave me a peace sign.

"Is Erika still in school?" I asked.

Keisha shook her head no. "I haven't seen her since the incident with her dad."

Jason, who was listening while playing Ping-Pong, served and said, "I think she dropped out."

Blond boy took another cookie. "I think she's in the work program."

"What's that?"

"She goes to work after lunch for school credit."

"Is that a thing?"

The kids all nodded their heads.

"Do you know where she works?"

Dani said, "During the day she works in an office answering phones, but at night she works at the funnel-cake stand on the Cape May boardwalk. She's probably there now."

Funnel cake. Why does it have to be funnel cake?

I thanked the kids and they *generously* offered to taste-test any cookies or brownies I made in the future before they were offered up for public consumption. To help me with quality control, of course. I told them I would come back with something for them to *evaluate* for me later. Concert-T Jason gave me a high five.

I thought of one more thing and stopped by Brenda's

desk on the way out. "Do you know anything about the boy who I keep seeing hovering around the edges of the parking lot?"

"Tall and skinny, wearing a hoodie?"

"That's the one."

Brenda sighed. "That would be Emilio. Brody had to kick him out for breaking the rules. He was so disappointed in him. You just can't help everyone."

I said goodbye and Brenda waved a cookie back and gave me a thumbs-up.

The sun had set, and the streetlights were coming to life, glowing like fireflies. I fast-walked to my car, chiding myself for my fear in a well-lit parking lot, when I heard a stick crack to my left. I jumped. Emilio was watching me from the bushes on the edge of the lot. *Why am I afraid? He's just a kid.*

I tried calling out to him. "Hey! Are you okay?"

He ran and disappeared into the woods.

He might be a kid, but his behavior is definitely threatening.

Chapter 26

"Poppy! Get up! We need to talk!"

I looked at the clock on my nightstand. It was 6:32 a.m. What could Georgina possibly want before seven in the morning?

"Poppy! I need you!"

I put my pillow over my head, but it didn't drown out the sound of Georgina banging on my bedroom door. I lifted the corner of my pillowcase and stuck my mouth out. "Georgina! Unless the house is on fire, I'll be down after I take my shower and get dressed."

Georgina yelled through my door again. "Really, Poppy, one would think you had nothing better to do, lying in bed all day like a rich widow."

I lay there fantasizing about winning the lottery so I could pay Georgina back her investment money and send her home to her cookie house in the woods. Eventually, I had to get my day started. I wanted to visit Frank Trippett at the garage after twelve, and I had some muffins and cookies to make at Mia Famiglia for the coffee shop.

I breezed through my morning yoga and cleansing

routine, dressed, and went down to the kitchen for some coffee. Figaro scared the bejeezus out of me when I came around the corner in the dark, and a set of orange eyes was looking up at me from down in the kitchen sink.

"Gah! What the devil are you doing in there?"

He didn't see the problem with his behavior. He blinked innocently, jumped out of the sink, and strolled leisurely over to his water bowl.

Aunt Ginny entered the kitchen wearing a pink sweater and poodle skirt with a white scarf tied around her neck. "Good morning."

"Are you going somewhere?"

"Like where?"

"I don't know. A costume party?"

"Why in the world would I be going to a costume party at seven thirty in the morning?"

"I just thought . . . the sock hop outfit and all."

Aunt Ginny shrugged. "Retro is making a comeback."

"I don't know if it's coming back from quite that far."

The doorbell rang as Aunt Ginny was about to make a point that only she would understand.

"Why don't I go get that," I said.

I opened the front door to find the nurse. "Oh, hi."

"Hi. I hope I'm not intruding. I'm Tracy, from Dr. Weingarten's office."

"I remember. Won't you come in?"

She blushed. "No, I can't. I just wanted to bring you this for Mrs. Frankowski." Tracy handed me a manila envelope.

"What is it?"

"The police came to the office and were asking questions. We all feel so bad about what's happened to Ginny, and we just want to help."

"That's very sweet of you."

She pointed to the envelope. "That's all the research

we can find on the drugs she was taking, clinical studies about sleepwalking and court cases where crimes were committed under the influence. I really hope it helps with her defense."

"I'm sure it will, thank you. Are you sure you don't want to come in and give it to her yourself?"

"I can't. I have patients waiting for me. Mr. Bressler bought himself a brace for carpal tunnel, and he's been chomping at the bit to come in and show it off." She turned and flounced down the steps. "But please tell her I said hello, and I'm rooting for her."

"I will." *That was sweet.* Maybe Aunt Ginny was right about going to her family doctor instead of the emergency room. Of course, I'm not going to tell her that.

I returned to the kitchen and handed Aunt Ginny the package.

"Who was at the door?"

"Nurse Tracy. She brought this for you."

Before we could open the envelope and check it out, Smitty stomped around the corner from the mudroom, mad as a hatter. "You won't believe what she's done now."

I stirred coconut cream into my coffee, then got comfortable at the table. "What's new?"

Smitty lifted one foot off the ground, his little bald head all pink with rage. "She filled my work boots with oatmeal!"

Georgina's giggle traveled around the corner, giving her presence away.

I willed myself not to smile, but my resolve broke with the squelch that oozed from Smitty's foot when he stomped it.

"It's not funny!"

I cleared my throat. "No, of course not. I'm sorry. Georgina!"

Georgina sidestepped into the kitchen. She was

head-to-toe in a winter-white Chanel pantsuit. Her hair was perfectly coiffed in the Jackie O bob. Her makeup meticulous. The only chink in her armor, the judgment in her eyes when she saw me dressed in my black yoga pants and faded Tweety Bird T-shirt.

"Poppy, you're finally awake. I wanted to talk with you about my bathroom door. It sticks."

"I think you need to clean Smitty's boots. Smitty, could you please take a look at Georgina's door for me today?"

Smitty saluted, then stomped over to Georgina, turned his hat around backwards, slanted his eyes, and stuck his teeth out. "Oh, so you fink you outtasmart me—you just big gnat in soup—go fry away."

Georgina turned red and poked him in the chest. "I told you to stop talking to me like that, it's offensive in ten different ways."

Smitty flapped his hands at his sides making hahhhh sounds and backed out of the room, his boots making fart noises as he went. Georgina followed him, poking and demanding he stop acting like a child. I was just glad to leave them to their own devices.

I put some fruit and coconut milk in the blender with chia seeds and flax seeds and made smoothies for the two of us.

Aunt Ginny looked through the contents of the envelope. "I think the DA is building a case against me."

I put straws in our smoothies and joined Aunt Ginny at the table. "To be honest, I don't think they're even looking for other suspects yet. But try not to worry, I have a couple of leads to follow up on today." I put my hand on top of Aunt Ginny's. "We'll figure this out. I'm going to rock around the clock."

Aunt Ginny smiled weakly.

"'Happy days are here again. Sunday, Monday, happy days.'"

She narrowed her eyes suspiciously.

"You won't be doing the 'Jailhouse Rock' on my watch."

Aunt Ginny rolled her eyes and pulled her hand out from under mine. "Where's my flyswatter?"

"What? Too far?"

The smile on her face was worth it.

Chapter 27

One batch of banana black-walnut Paleo muffins—check. One batch of Paleo pineapple upside-down cupcakes—check. One bowl of flour, boobytrapped by Momma to dump on my head when I started the Hobart mixer—check. It was gonna be one of those days.

I had a text from Gia saying he had news from his contact at the chamber of commerce, and to come over ASAP. I hurriedly cleaned up my station, and the cold station, and the dry goods storage, and the dish station. Because falling flour travels like a New England blizzard.

About forty minutes later, I took the deliveries through the front door of La Dolce Vita. Karla was working the register and serving pastries, while Gia was pulling the shots—um, literally—and making lattes. The whole room froze in their tracks when I showed up looking like the Ghost of Christmas Past. Karla took one look at me and lost it, but Gia took my hand and led me through the back and out the door to the parking lot, where he proceeded to swat me down with a dish towel.

"What happened, *mia bella?*"

"There was an incident."

"*Capisco.* You look like the Pillsbury dough lady."

"Not the most flattering icon."

"You are still beautiful."

Gia turned me to face him and tipped my chin up. He leaned down to kiss me, but we were interrupted by some obtrusive coughing. Karla said something in Italian, to which Gia answered sharply. He kissed my forehead. "Karla said there is a line forming for your muffins. Shake the flour out of your hair and come in, *bella.* I have news."

When the morning rush died down we had a chance to sit and talk.

"So, my friend in the chamber told me there were two other charities nominated for the humanitarian award last spring."

My God, his eyes are blue. What shade of blue is that? Robin's-egg? Summer sky?

"Each charity is governed by a board of directors."

When he says friend . . . does he mean female friend? Just how friendly is this friend?

"One was the Shore Animal Shelter and the other was South Jersey Hospice."

How pretty is this friend?

An amused smile broke across Gia's face, as though he could read my mind. "Are you listening?"

"Hmm? Yes. What?"

He breathed a little laugh to himself, then handed me a piece of scratch paper. "I've written down the names of the presidents of each board."

South Jersey Hospice: Glynnis Jackson
Shore Animal Shelter: Kenya Martin

"Do you really think one of these charities could

have been angry that Brody got the money for the Teen Center that they felt they deserved?"

"Maybe. But angry enough to kill him?" Gia shook his head. "I have a hard time believing that someone who rescues stray cats or helps the terminally ill would be that ruthless."

I checked my watch. "I'm going to Gleason's Garage this afternoon to try to charm Kylie Furman's boyfriend into giving me his alibi. I'll stop at these charities while I'm out."

"Why don't you come back when you're done and tell me how it went. We can have dinner together."

"I want to . . . but I feel like I should be with Aunt Ginny."

"Bring her with you."

"Really?"

"Of course. Wouldn't she like to get out of the house?"

I thought of Aunt Ginny in her poodle skirt and saddle shoes and smiled to myself. "I'll ask her."

The offices of South Jersey Hospice were in a cozy bungalow in West Cape May. The cheery waiting room was painted pale yellow with chintz overstuffed chairs and painted distressed-wood tables. A beautiful vase of yellow roses and white hydrangeas sat on the reception desk.

The CEO, Glynnis Jackson, an older woman who exuded style and grace from her white hair done in a sleek platinum bob to her flouncy black satin skirt and pink silk blouse, was able to give me a few minutes before her next appointment.

"So, what can I do for you, Ms. McAllister?"

"I'm doing research about the Cape May Humanitarian Award."

"I'm not sure I have much to offer you. I'm not on the committee for the award."

"No, but you were nominated for it last year."

"We've been blessed to be nominated a few times. It's a peer nomination process."

"What does that mean?"

"The businesses who are a part of the Lower Township Chamber of Commerce nominate local charities each year. We provide in-depth information to the chamber, such as our policies and procedures, testimonials, and financial information. The review board votes to narrow down the entries to three finalists and starts a campaign for the community to vote."

"How do people cast their votes?"

"Online and mail-in ballot. Voters have to register to prevent any one person or charity from flooding the ballot box and skewing the results unethically."

"And the winner gets an award?"

"A trophy and a cash donation."

"How much of a donation?"

"Last spring it was ten thousand dollars."

"Wow. Where does the money come from?"

"Mostly from chamber fund-raising events and community support. Why are you so interested? Do you have a charity you want to nominate?"

"I'm more interested in the last charity to win. Do you remember who that was?"

She thought for a minute, "I think it was one that did something with kids."

"It was the Teen Center in the Villas."

"That's right, I remember it was their first year to be nominated."

"Did you know the founder?"

"No, we've never met. I don't attend the chamber functions very often. I send one of our regular nurses to the networking events, but we work twenty-four hours a day, as you can imagine. There isn't a lot of time for self-promotion."

"Do you know who nominated you?"

"It's usually a family member that we've worked with. Hospice is a delicate ministry and families are in a fragile state when we're involved. People are so grateful to have help with their loved one's end-of-life care that we get many accolades just by word of mouth."

"Is there anyone at the hospice who would personally have anything to gain by winning the award or the grant money?"

"We all like the validation, if that's what you're asking, but we're a well-funded charity. I have a staff of twenty-four full-time nurses with a medical temp agency on call if we need short-time backup. A lot of what we do is covered by Medicare and some private insurance. We rely on donations and grant money to be able to provide for patients who don't have insurance."

"So, no one member of the charity keeps the donation, as a bonus maybe?"

"Heavens no. And if someone ever did, the auditors would catch it right away. We'd lose our tax-exempt status."

The receptionist knocked on the office door and told Mrs. Jackson that her next appointment had arrived. Glynnis excused herself, offering to meet with me again if I needed her. I thanked her and let myself out.

One down, one to go.

* * *

I had to drive into the Villas to find the Shore Animal Shelter. The shelter was in one of those low, aluminum-siding industrial-type buildings ubiquitous to South Jersey. It could be a health food store, swimming pool supplies, or a day care. You could never tell by appearance.

There were partitions outside in the back, made out of a twelve-foot-tall chain-link fence. Dogs in every shape, size, and color ran the maze of partitions, burning off restless energy. A barking chorus of hope hailed my arrival.

Inside, the shelter was a stark waiting room of green linoleum with a tall tan counter of off-white linoleum, and a few metal chairs. A bulletin board was covered in fliers advertising veterinary services and pet care classes. Whatever grant money these people got, it definitely didn't go to the decor.

Kenya was a young African-American woman, dressed in khakis and a green golf shirt with the animal shelter logo embroidered over the top pocket. She bounded into the room like a Labrador retriever, friendly and full of energy.

"Hi, it's so nice to meet you. Are you here for a dog, cat, or guinea pig today?"

"I hope I didn't give you false hopes. I'm not here to adopt. I'm looking for some information about the humanitarian award you were nominated for last spring."

"Oh. That's too bad. Well, come back to my office and let's chat."

Her office was at the end of the building, and we had to walk through many cages of small cats and dogs looking for someone to love them and take them home. *Smart strategy, Kenya.*

I had to be strong. It wouldn't take much for me to load five or six cats into the car and take them with me. We'd have to rename the B and B the Litterbox.

Kenya's office was small and cramped. Motivational posters featuring all manner of wildlife *hanging in there* and *being the leader of the pack* hung from one end of the office to the other. A wall calendar from Iams pet food sat on the desk.

"Have a seat."

From the only chair in her office I picked up a stack of new piddle pads for house training, but having nowhere to set them down, I placed them on my lap. I asked Kenya the same questions I'd asked Glynnis, and she relayed the same process for nomination. The main difference was the animal shelter's need for the grant money.

"We're a no-kill shelter. That means if we don't find homes for these little guys they live out their lives in here. Frankie, our Jack Russell terrier, has been here for seven years. Now he's our official mascot. Local government only provides so much in the way of financial support, and it barely covers the cost of room and board."

"Is this the first time you've been nominated for the humanitarian award?"

"Oh, no. We've been nominated many times. We have a lot of outreach programs, so we're well-known in the community. In fact, we won the award in 2013. See, here's my trophy."

She handed me a bronze statue of an angel holding up a star on a base shaped like a seashell. It was heavy, smooth, and could do some critical damage if you cracked someone over the head with it.

"So this is what the director gets when you win?"

"We all get one. Well, this and a check for the shelter. We used the grant money to expand our veterinary clinic to provide health care for our lodgers. Many of them come in with all kinds of problems—mange, fleas, infections. Our veterinarians donate their time, but medicine and labs cost money."

I handed the statue back to her. "You said *we all get one*. Who is *we all*?"

"All the officers get a trophy. This one's mine. I'm here all the time, so I keep mine in the office."

"Do you know who won this year's award?"

"I do. It was the new youth center. My cousin's kid has spent a lot of time in that program. It's done him a world of good."

"So you weren't upset that they got the money instead of you?"

"The youth center needs the money as badly as we do. I believe that when God closes a door, he opens a window. There will be other donations for us and they'll come at just the right time."

I thanked her for the meeting, and she walked me out. On the way toward the exit, I noticed a display of framed pictures hanging on one wall. They were photographs of successful adoptions and current residents looking for homes. In the center was a group photo of current board members, taken last spring. And there in the front row, standing next to Kenya, was none other than Brody's boss at Freeman and Furman.

"Isn't that Ken Freeman?"

"It is. He volunteers as our comptroller."

"What does a comptroller do?"

"He handles the money for the shelter."

"So, when things are tight, he'd be the first one to know about it?"

Kenya laughed good-naturedly, "I'm sure you're right."

"What kind of guy is he?"

"He's nice. Very . . ."

"Crunchy?"

Kenya laughed. "I was going to say very into nature, but I think crunchy is probably more accurate."

"You must trust him to let him handle the shelter's money."

"I do. Ken is a straight arrow. I can see how he's built his investment firm on the reputation of his integrity."

"Honesty means a lot to him?"

"It's his guiding principle. He only works with people who hold to the same code of honor."

"And all these people would have a statue like the one in your office?"

"Yep, every one of them."

Chapter 28

I had a bad feeling about Ken Freeman. Kenya said he valued integrity and honesty above all other things. Someone like that doesn't murder in cold blood. But it couldn't be a coincidence that the same person who fired Brody for embezzlement, was also on the board of a rival charity desperately in need of grant money. Of course, what kind of sicko kills someone because they were honored for helping kids in need? Maybe Gia was right and people aren't always who you think they are.

I drove down Fulling Mill Road into Rio Grande, heading for Gleason's Garage, and the car pulled itself into the Starbucks drive-through. I had mixed emotions about the car's decision to order a Frappuccino. Emotions like whether or not I was being disloyal to a sexy barista in Cape May, did I really need more caffeine this late in the day, and could I order a pumpkin spice cheesecake muffin without anyone finding out about it. I silenced these emotions with an iced Americano with two packets of stevia and a quarter cup of half-and-half. I only managed to break free from the muffin's lure by coming up with a plan for a gluten-free copycat in tomorrow's baking.

Cape May County had thumbed its nose at progress and preferred instead the bygone days of the mom-and-pop business. We're one of two states in the nation so afraid that you'll blow yourself up if you try to pump your own gas that we pay attendants to do it for you. We still have small businesses that elsewhere were bought out and replaced by big box stores, although I've heard rumors that there is a secret underground Sam Goody in the Pleasantville Mall if you know where to find it. They run the entire store on a Compaq with a dot matrix printer. For all of our chain-hating ways, our cornerstone was a Dunkin' Donuts. We're not animals.

Gleason's Garage was the equivalent of a Cold War–era Jiffy Lube. Men wearing oil-stained jumpsuits were either bent over engines or rolled under cars on dollies. The sound of the air drill competed with a weak radio playing Top 40 hits, and the smell of machine oil clung to the air. A greasy man with a cigarette hanging from his lower lip and the name *Toots* embroidered on his jumpsuit, asked me if I needed any help.

"I'm looking for Frank Trippett. Do I have the right place?"

Toots hollered "Frank!" over his shoulder and went back to his engine thingy.

Frank Trippett looked like the cover model for *Mechanic Monthly*. He was tall and lean and his jumpsuit strained over his pecs and biceps. He came from the back room wiping his hands on a red towel. "Yeah?"

"Poppy McAllister." I extended my hand.

Frank looked me up and down but did not take my offered hand.

"What can I do ya for, honey?"

"I wanted to ask you some questions about a man your girlfriend Kylie used to work with. Is there somewhere we can talk in private?"

Frank considered me for a minute, then hollered to

anyone listening, "I'm taking a ten." He led me out behind the garage to a wooden bench. The ground was littered with cigarette butts and crushed beer cans. A NO SMOKING sign was posted on the back of the building.

Frank pulled a cigarette out from behind his ear and lit it. "What's on your mind?"

"Did you hear that one of Kylie's coworkers, Brody Brandt, was killed this past weekend?"

He blew the smoke out the side of his mouth. "Kylie mentioned it."

"Did she happen to share any information with you about what might have happened to him?"

Frank took a long drag on his smoke. "That sounds like a question better asked of Kylie."

"She was very upset the other day when we spoke, and I really don't want to bother her again if I don't have to."

"Funny, I don't see a badge. Why should I tell you anything?" He gave me a patronizing smile.

"Kylie worked in the same office with Brody every day. He was fired just days before someone murdered him. That makes her a suspect. If she's innocent, any information you have could help clear her name." *Or better yet, incriminate her and get Aunt Ginny off the hot seat.*

"I don't know what I have to do with it."

"I was under the impression that you knew Mr. Brandt."

Frank shook his head. "Never met him."

"Never? I thought I was told that you and he had quite an argument a few weeks back."

Frank was a cool one. He didn't so much as flinch. He just leaned back against the bench and stretched his legs out. "Arguing ain't the same as meeting, now is it?"

"But you did threaten Mr. Brandt during that argument."

Frank smiled again, but it didn't reach his eyes. "Now who would tell you a thing like that?"

"I'm afraid the walls are thin in that old building. There were lots of offices where people overheard your fight. You told Brody you would kill him if he ever touched Kylie again. True?"

Frank took another long drag of his cigarette. "It was a misunderstanding. And the same busybody that's spreading rumors that I got into it with Brody should also be able to tell you that it was a one-time thing and happened ages ago. I had too much to drink, and I thought Kylie was cheating on me. She was always talking about this Brody guy she worked with, and his helping out a group of kids. I figured he was the guy. I'm not proud of it, but we worked it out."

Frank threw his cigarette butt in the dirt and ground it with the toe of his boot. He stood to go. "If we're done here."

"One more thing, Mr. Trippett. It would really help me out to know where you were the night Brody was killed. In case the police ask me."

He crossed his arms over his chest. "Depends on when it happened."

"Sometime between Monday night and early Tuesday morning."

"I was in bed. With Kylie. And yes, she will confirm that. I strongly recommend that you quit your nosing around, lady. Bad things happen to people who ask too many questions."

He strode back into the garage. He had a calm, relaxed manner, like someone who had nothing to hide. He was overconfident. But something about the way he carried himself set me on edge.

Chapter 29

"Come on, it'll be fun."

"I don't want to have fun. I want to sit in this house and be miserable."

"Aunt Ginny, Gia has invited us to come out for dinner. Don't you want to get out for a bit?"

"No! I don't want people seeing me and pointing *there goes the lunatic who robbed the neighborhood.*"

"No one is going to do that."

Georgina bustled into the kitchen clutching a red toolbox. "Don't be ridiculous, Poppy. I would do that. All my friends would do that."

Aunt Ginny jabbed her thumb at Georgina. "See!"

I sent Georgina a look that was meant to shush her. "I've met your friends, Georgina, and they're all stuck-up snobs."

"That's how I know they would point and gossip." Georgina hid the toolbox in the refrigerator behind some bagged salads.

I ignored Crazy Number 2 and turned my attention back to Crazy Number 1. "Aunt Ginny, please come with me. He invited you personally."

Georgina was suddenly in between us. "Who invited Ginny? Where are you going?"

Aunt Ginny fired on Georgina, "Poppy has a date tonight. With a good-looking man who wants to meet her family. What do you think of that?"

Georgina turned on me with hurt in her eyes. "Poppy, you promised. How could you?"

Before I could protest that I didn't promise anything of the sort, Smitty stormed into the kitchen after Georgina. "Woman! Where is my toolbox?"

Georgina offered a prim look and a shrug. "Why, whatever toolbox do you mean?"

Smitty started yanking cabinets and rearranging coffee mugs and frying pans. "You know exactly what toolbox, you old bat! Now where did you hide it?"

"Really, Spotty, you need to take better care of your things. No wonder this house is falling down around us."

Smitty turned purple and squirmy. "Falling down! Why you . . ."

Aunt Ginny took out her little yellow spray and gave herself a couple of squirts. "Let's go now."

Bella, come over to Momma's dining room. G
Gia had scrawled a note and left it at the end of the counter, under the chocolate syrup, behind a bag of espresso beans. Or, as I rather suspected, he left it out in the open and Karla repositioned it after he was gone, just to mess with me. Thankfully, he answered his text when I showed up at the espresso bar and didn't find him.

Aunt Ginny and I walked across the courtyard to the terra cotta dining room and waited for the hostess.

Aunt Ginny pointed to a table on the left side of

the dining room by the window. "It was just a few weeks ago that we sat under the trailing ivy and planned our strategy to prove you didn't kill the cheerleader."

I looked down at her and smiled. "I remember."

"*Bella!* You're here." Gia met us and enveloped first me, then Aunt Ginny, in hugs.

"Oh my, he's strong." Aunt Ginny whispered loud enough for the whole dining room to hear.

A hostess was led up to the podium by her lip piercing. She appeared at Gia's side and put her hand on his back. "These must be your guests we've been waiting for, Gia. I'll take you all to your table."

She took Gia's arm and led him back to the table where he had already been sitting. She held his chair out for him while she looked at him with puppy-dog eyes.

Gia came over first to Aunt Ginny and pulled out her chair, then did the same for me when she was seated.

Aunt Ginny whispered again. "He's got a nice butt."

I was mortified.

The hostess frowned, picked a chip off her blue nail polish, and tossed it on the floor. "Your waiter will be over in a minute." She leisurely strolled back to her station by the front door.

"Well, she was a delight," Aunt Ginny mused.

Gia put his hand on Aunt Ginny's. "I'm so glad you're here. You are very important to Poppy and she's very important to me, so I want us to be friends."

A shrill voice wafted through the room like an icepick in the brain.

"She wouldn't!"

A pair of Jimmy Choos clackity-clacked their way to our table. "Poppy. There you are. In your haste you must have forgotten me."

"Georgina, what are you doing here?"

Aunt Ginny rolled her eyes. "Did Smitty ever get his toolbox out of the fridge?"

Gia stood to welcome her.

Georgina ignored us both and took Gia's hand in hers. "I'm Poppy's mother-in-law. She was married for almost twenty years to my dear boy, John. He's only recently passed, you know."

I tried to disappear under the table, but Gia took it in stride. "I have heard so much about your late son. I'm sorry for your loss. Won't you join us?"

Aunt Ginny and I said in unison, "No!"

Georgina smiled. "Don't mind if I do." She settled herself into Gia's vacant chair, forcing him to sit across from me and between her and Aunt Ginny.

Georgina yelped, "Ow!" And glared at me.

Aunt Ginny muttered, "Oops. Restless legs syndrome."

Gia rested his face on his fist to cover his amusement, but the twinkle in his eyes gave him away.

If he even wants to do business with me after this it will be a miracle.

Three waiters arrived in unison, grinning and jabbing Gia with elbows and eyebrows. They fought over who filled our water glasses and who fluffed our napkins. Gia muttered something in Italian and jerked his head to send them away. First one, then another, then the third brought us a basket of bread.

"I think you have a fan club here," I said to Gia.

Momma poked her head out. *"Basta!"* She gave the waiters the evil eye and two of them scurried back to the kitchen. With a "Bah" and a wave of dismissal she waddled in after them.

"So, what's good?" Georgina purred as if she were an invited guest.

"The calamari is *perfetto*. The man-ah-cott is one of

Momma's specialties, or the linguine with pruh-zhoot is *mmph!* All the pasta is handmade and wonderful."

Okay, someone's a momma's boy.

Well, forget about ordering because food just started appearing from the kitchen. Bowl after bowl of pastas and casseroles and platters of meat smothered in sauces. Judging from the sounds of delight Gia was making, I suspected Momma was sending his favorite dishes.

Gia called a waiter over. "Please ask Momma for some pasta, *senza glutine* with Bolognese."

The waiter replied, "*Senza glutin-ah?*"

"*Sì.* Gluten-free."

He shrugged and took off, only to return a couple minutes later. "Momma ask for who?"

Gia nodded in my direction. "For the lady."

The waiter looked from me to Gia and an understanding passed between them. I believe it was similar to *as if Momma needs another reason not to like her,* but he returned to the kitchen anyway.

Georgina waved a piece of homemade bread in my face. "This may be the best thing I've ever eaten. Here, Poppy, you should try it. Oh, wait. Can you eat this on your diet?"

I took the bread basket from Georgina and moved it to the other side of the table.

Gia smiled sympathetically. "How did it go today?"

Georgina started, "Well, we got the hall bath recaulked and another coat of paint on the porch swing. Oh, you mean Poppy. Sorry. I'm just so used to eating with my son and Poppy, where they ask me about my day. I guess I got confused."

Aunt Ginny dropped her head in her hands and muttered, "And people say I'm the crazy one."

Dear God, I'm pretty sure that being with Georgina is going to kill me. And if I'm going to die tonight, please give me a sign so I can eat this bread and some lasagna before I go.

"It went . . . different than I expected."

"What happened?"

"For one thing, the charity people were both so nice and very helpful. It's hard to imagine either one of them behind the murder. I don't think the hospice board had a motive. They get plenty of money from insurance companies for the services they provide. They use grant money to help subsidize families who don't have private coverage for end-of-life care."

Aunt Ginny looked up from the plate of ravioli she was devouring. "You think a hospice would kill a rival charity owner in cold blood? Wouldn't that be counterintuitive for them?"

Gia nodded. "I agree. How about the other one? The animal shelter."

"Well, the director was very sweet. And I don't see any way she would ever be a part of a devious act. Her little office was wall-to-wall kitten posters."

Georgina patted her mouth with her napkin. "Cat people kill too, Poppy."

I ignored her. One of our trio of waiters brought my gluten-free pasta out on a silver tray and set it down with a flourish.

"Fooor the laaadyyy."

Gia shook his head and sighed. I thanked the waiter and went back to the day's recap. "The most interesting thing I discovered was that Brody's boss is on the board of directors for the animal shelter."

"Which one?" Aunt Ginny asked as she dumped a bowl of Parmesan on her pasta.

"Ken Freeman."

Georgina wound the pasta on her fork like it was trying to get away. "What are the odds that his boss would also be on the board of a charity?"

Gia handed Aunt Ginny the pepper grinder. "That seems too much of a coincidence to be ignored."

"I agree. Also, I found out that the humanitarian award is the big honking heavy statue of an angel holding a star over its head, and every board member of the winning charity, including Ken Freeman last year, receives one."

Aunt Ginny took a forkful of the gluten-free pasta from my plate. "I bet that could be used to shut someone's lights off for good."

"I was thinking the same thing."

Gia handed Aunt Ginny a bowl of sauce. "But what would be Freeman's motive? The Teen Center already had the grant money. Would he kill just for vengeance?"

"The whole rival charity angle seems a bit janky to me. But, Ken Freeman did fire Brody for embezzlement the Friday before he was murdered. What if Brody really did steal that money? Maybe that was enough to send Ken over the edge to take revenge for both offenses. A sort of misguided righteous justice."

Aunt Ginny took a forkful of manicotti off of Gia's plate. "Like killing two birds with one humanitarian award."

Gia's eyes widened when he saw the fork coming, but he was so tickled watching Aunt Ginny that he pushed his plate closer to her so she could have easier access.

I mouthed, "I'm sorry."

Gia grinned and gave me a wink.

Georgina started a choking fit that could only be quelled by one of our waiters pouring her another glass of wine.

Somewhere across the dining room, a couple tried

desperately to get a waiter to come to their table to refill their water, but they were all hovering around our table trying to blend in and look like they were not eavesdropping.

I went on. "Brody's secretary was adamant that there was no way he could have embezzled that money. She said it wasn't in his character."

Aunt Ginny peered at me over a forkful of Gia's manicotti. "Didn't Liz tell you he had come into money recently?"

"Well, yes."

"Then where did the money come from?"

"She said he got it from investing. He did work for an investment firm, so that isn't out of the question."

"Do you have any other suspects other than his boss and the girl's father?" Gia asked.

"There was an incident with Brody's other coworker, Kylie. Apparently, she has a very jealous boyfriend who showed up at work one day accusing Brody and Kylie of having an affair. I went to his workplace to talk to him this afternoon."

Gia ordered coffee for the table. "How'd that go?"

"He seemed charming, but with an undercurrent seething of hatred."

Aunt Ginny reached across the table and popped a *zeppole* into her mouth.

"Thing is," I said, "he says he was with Kylie all night and she'd back him up on that."

Aunt Ginny rubbed her stomach. "You're going to have to ask her."

Georgina waved an Italian donut in my face. "Poppy, aren't you having dessert? Dessert is your favorite."

I mentally tried to set Georgina's hair on fire. She saw my dark look and put the *zeppole* back on her plate.

For the rest of the evening we had coffee and spoke

about the espresso bar, and the bed-and-breakfast. Momma came out to see how her baby was doing. She patted his stomach and said he didn't eat enough. She watched me out of the corner of her eye and grunted. After kissing Gia's face a few times, she went back to her kitchen.

We stood to go and our comedy of waiters arrived instantly from just around the corner to pull out the ladies' chairs. There was lots of cheek kissing with Gia, and some kind of innuendo that made Gia blush and Georgina pout.

Gia gave me a chaste hug goodbye under Georgina's watchful scowl.

"Wish me luck," I told him. "I'm going to the board-walk to talk to Erika tonight."

Gia tucked a lock of my hair behind my ear. "You're smart, you don't need luck. Tell me all about it in the morning."

Georgina and Aunt Ginny piled into my car. I gave Georgina a questioning look through the rearview mirror.

"What? I had the little handyman drop me off earlier. You're my ride."

If I took her out to a field somewhere and left her, I wonder if she could find her way back home.

Chapter 30

I needed to get Aunt Ginny and Georgina home, then get over to the boardwalk to Erika's work before it closed, and I needed to do it without giving in to temptation and eating a plate of powdered sugar.

I can do this. I'm a grown woman. I'm eating healthy and taking care of myself. I've already had a splurge tonight with the gluten-free spaghetti—not exactly Paleo. I don't need to be bossed around by funnel cake. Be strong, Poppy.

The Cape May boardwalk was more than two hundred years old. Stretching only two miles along Beach Avenue, it's part weathered plank and part concrete. Officially called the Promenade, the younger generation called it the Boards.

The central point is Convention Hall, where we used to roller-skate as kids and Erika's dad played roller hockey. On either side are shops and arcades, the Fudge Kitchen and Morrow's Nut House. Erika worked down by one of the arcades. Since we lived around the corner, I parked at home, saw Aunt Ginny and Georgina inside, then walked over.

It was a bright and cold night down by the water. The wind coming off the ocean sliced right through me and I wished I'd worn a heavier coat. A smattering of people were on the boardwalk, a couple of die-hard tourists who'd heard how quiet the Cape May off-season could be, some coast guard recruits out for a frigid run, and a few locals working part-time jobs, wishing they'd made better life choices.

The funnel-cake stand was much like a neon shed with a window. It was covered in cardboard cutouts listing jelly toppings and flavors of soft serve. I knocked on the sliding glass and a teenage girl with greasy hair and a lack of ambition considered whether or not to alight from her stool and approach. She finally put her cell phone down and opened the glass. The smell of fried dough and chocolate sauce stung my resolve to abstain.

"Yeah?"

"Are you Erika Lynch?"

"Who wants to know?"

"I'm Poppy. Dani down at the Teen Center told me I could find you here. I hope that's okay."

She shrugged. "I got nothing to say." She started to close the window.

"Please. I just need a little help to save an elderly woman."

She considered me for a moment. "Save her from what?"

"She's being wrongfully accused of a crime. I just need to ask you a couple of questions."

"I can't hold the window open during working hours unless you buy something. My boss is watching me on the nanny cam." She rolled her eyes up to the corner above us.

"Are you sure I'd have to buy something? It's almost closing time, isn't it?"

She started to slide the window. "I've got the heater on."

"Can I get a glass of water?"

"It has to cost money."

"I don't suppose you have anything gluten-free, do you?"

"Uhh . . ."

"Do you know what gluten is?"

". . . no."

The smell was making my mouth water and I felt my resolve weakening.

"Gluten comes from grains. Look, I can't have anything in here."

The window started to close again.

"Okay, fine!" I could buy a healthy smoothie or a bottle of water, or a water ice to take home for Itty Bitty Smitty. Then I heard the words fly out of my mouth unsanctioned. "I'll have a funnel cake." *What?*

She took my five dollars and propped the window open. Then she took a plastic condiment bottle and squeezed the batter into the fryer in concentric circles. "What do you want to know?"

"I'm sorry for asking such a touchy question, but what happened between you and Mr. Brandt?"

"My dad says I'm not allowed to talk about that."

Great.

"I hear that you're a gifted artist."

"That's what they say."

"Was Mr. Brandt helping you apply for scholarships?"

Erika wouldn't meet my eyes. "Yep, he was."

"I don't want you to get into trouble with your dad, I just want to establish Mr. Brandt's character. Do you know if any other girls ever had a problem with him?"

She flipped my funnel cake over to fry the other side, but she still wouldn't look at me.

"Any of the other girls from the Teen Center, maybe?"

Erika blanched. She took the pillow of fried dough out of the oil, put it on the world's flimsiest paper plate, and dumped a mountain of powdered sugar on it, then chucked it through the window.

"Your dad said it happened at the Teen Center." I picked up my funnel cake and the wind blew powdered sugar all over my shirt and in my eyes. I managed to steal a bite of the crispy greasy sugar between coughs.

"Did you ever go to the police to report him?"

"My dad wanted me to."

"But you weren't up to it?"

She shook her head no.

"I understand that. I don't think anyone knows what they would do under those circumstances."

Erika shrugged.

"Do you think it would help if you had someone you could talk to about it? It doesn't have to be me, but I could help you find a counselor or—"

"No! Look." Erika spoke in a monotone. "I don't want anyone else to know. It's already gone too far. If I tell you what happened, will you promise not to say anything to anyone else?"

I took a deep breath before answering. "I will do my best."

"Brody told me to stay late to work on a scholarship application. When everyone else had left, he locked the door and turned out the lights. Then he grabbed me and forced me to kiss him while his hands groped me."

Ugh. My funnel cake now sat like a greasy rock on my heart. After hearing what this poor girl had gone through, I was ashamed that I was stuffing my face with pastry while I forced her to tell me about it. "That must have been awful, and you know it wasn't your fault."

"Whatever. I don't think I was his first victim, but at

least I'll be the last. End of story, now leave me alone."
She put her hand on the window and started to slide it.

"Listen, take my number. In case you need someone
to keep you company when your dad goes to Chicago
for work."

"What?"

"Chicago. Didn't your dad just fly back on the red-
eye last Monday night?"

"My dad hasn't been to Chicago in weeks. He was out
playing poker till two in the morning. He came home
in a pissy mood because he lost again."

"Oh, I must have misunderstood him."

"Yeah, I guess." She ran her hand through her greasy
hair. "I gotta turn off the fryer now, we're closing."

I gave her my number and she put it in her cell
phone and promised she'd text if she needed someone
to talk to. I dumped the rest of my plate of shame in the
nearest trash bin.

On my walk home, I thought about what Erika had
told me about Brody. I wouldn't blame Jonathan Lynch
if he'd killed him. If I had a daughter who was molested
I might do the same thing. But what was up with her
father not being in Chicago like he said he was? *Why
would he lie to me?*

My face started to itch and my pants were getting
tight. *Why do I do this to myself? I know I can't tolerate gluten
and sugar. Why don't I have any self-control?* The front of
my neck was starting to sting. Now my thyroid was
swelling. You'd think I'd be able to avoid food I react to,
so I'd feel better, but no. I just haaaad to have the
funnel cake. I should have at least had her wrap it up
for Georgina. If anyone deserves to get fat it's her.

I wallowed in my misery down the sidewalk and all
the way up to the porch steps until someone grabbed
me from behind. Fear coursed through me and my

heart began to race. I felt panic rise from the pit of my stomach and my funnel cake threatened to make a repeat appearance. I wanted to cry out for help but a hand clamped down over my mouth. I tried to scream, but it went nowhere. Everything in me roared *RUN!*

Chapter 31

I was dragged down into the hydrangeas. I tried to fight back. I flailed my arms around like a broken helicopter, but it was no use. I was powerless. I wriggled to my side, threw an elbow, and made contact with my assailant. I heard a loud "*Oomph!*" and I tried to crawl away.

A small voice croaked, "Please stop. I just need to talk to you."

I stopped struggling, if only to lull him into a false sense of security before I gave him a Warrior Two strike to the nose.

He let me go and I rolled to sit up. "Please. I didn't know any other way to contact you."

It was the skinny boy from the Teen Center.

"So you grab me from behind and pull me into the bushes? Are you out of your mind?"

His eyes were wide and his mouth hung slack. "I'm really good at making bad decisions."

"Ya think!" I scratched my neck where a couple small welts had broken out from my own bad judgment. The boy looked like a frightened possum. The hopelessness on his face caused me to feel sorry for him. I got up and went over to the porch swing and gathered myself. "Okay, what do you want to talk to me about?"

I got a better look at him once he was in the light and not covered by that enormous hoodie. He was shaped like a Blow Pop in size thirteen Chucks. Tall and very skinny with a perfectly round head too big for his body. He couldn't have been more than sixteen or seventeen years old.

I motioned for him to sit down in one of the rockers. "What's your name?"

"Emilio."

"I've seen you watching me."

"I didn't know if I could trust you."

"How do you know you can trust me now?"

"I don't, but I'm desperate. Keisha said you been coming in asking questions about Brody. I know stuff, but I don't have anyone who will believe me."

"Is that why you keep lurking around the Teen Center? You have information?"

He looked down at his shoes. "I've been banned from the TC."

"What'd you do?"

"I came in with a bag of hard candy."

"What's wrong with that?"

"Bro had a zero-T policy."

"Zero tolerance?"

Emilio nodded.

"For hard candy?"

Emilio nodded again.

"Why? Is it like a ruin-your-appetite-before-dinner kind of thing?"

Emilio narrowed his eyes. "Hard candy? Big H?"

I shook my head and shrugged.

"Heroin, lady. I came in with a bag of smack and Brody took it from me and kicked me out."

Well, don't I feel incredibly old now. Just where did I put my walker? "I see."

The porch light flicked on and off a couple of times. "What was that?"

"It's hard to say just yet." *I have my money on Georgina.*

Emilio shrugged. "Keisha said the cops found drugs at Brody's house. They were asking the others if he'd been dealing." Emilio jumped out of this rocker and began pacing. "It had to be mine."

"How are you so sure? Maybe Brody was doing the hard candy too." *Now I sound like an idiot.*

"No way, man, not after all he'd been through. Brody was my NA sponsor. He wasn't using again. He just got his seven-year medallion. He was helping me get clean and I blew it."

"Why would you buy drugs if you were trying to get clean?"

"I had a fight with my uncle Jack and he kicked me out. I tanked. I have self-destructive behavior. At least that's what Brody called it. You wouldn't understand."

I scratched my cheek and tried to breathe through the funnel cake tourniquet that had formed under my waistband. I nodded for Emilio to continue.

"I went to my dealer and bought a half piece. Brody says—said—that's what an addict does. No matter how bad they know it will ruin their lives, they still crave it. It has power over them."

My cell phone vibrated and I checked the screen. R U O K That's street slang for Are You okay? ~ Georgina.

I rolled my eyes on the inside. "Look, I get that. I really do." *More than you know.* "But why would you take it to the Teen Center if you knew it would get you kicked out?"

He placed his hands on top of his head and shook it. "I don't know, man. I guess I wasn't thinking. Maybe

I wanted Brody to find out. To see if he'd really kick me out."

"Well, mission accomplished."

Emilio nodded. "I had it coming."

My cell phone buzzed again. Is that a street thug? ~ Georgina.

I typed back I'm Fine. "Sorry. So how long had you been working with Brody?"

"Five months, since I was released. I did eight months in Johnstone. I got out early because they needed a bed. I had to sign an agreement to work the program and be accountable. Brody took me on and agreed to a mentorship plan. It was my last chance. My next strike I get charged as an adult."

"Your next strike for . . . buying drugs?"

"It's called possession. Don't you watch TV or anything?"

"Nobody gets arrested for possession on *Cake Boss*."

"What's *Cake Boss*?"

"It's like *Breaking Bad*, but with frosting."

Emilio nodded politely. "Hmph."

"So, Brody was helping you get your life in order."

"He was trying. After I'd been clean for a year we were going to get my record sealed so I could get a job after high school, maybe even go to community college, but I blew it."

"What do you mean, get your record sealed?"

"You know, so no one knows I've done time."

Brody the hero again. Was Brody Dr. Jekyll or Mr. Hyde? Could Emilio be lying about the drugs, to protect him? But why would you cover for a dead guy?

I heard a *tap tap tap* on the window. Then my phone buzzed again. I THINK I JUST SAW HIM ON TO CATCH A CRIMINAL. ~ Georgina

I typed back, **GO TO BED**. "Emilio, what do you know about Erika Lynch?"

"Erika?" He shoved his hands in his hoodie pockets. "Why do you want to know about her?"

"Something happened at the Teen Center, and I'm looking into it."

He shrugged. "Whatever."

"What kind of relationship did she and Brody have?"

Emilio punched the air. "Man, she be trifling."

"What? What's that?"

"Trifling, you know, she's shady. That girl's a stalker. Brody couldn't go anywhere without Erika magically showing up."

"Wasn't he working with her on scholarships?"

"Yeah, so?"

"Do you think everything was on the up-and-up with them?"

Emilio shrugged. "You ain't working on scholarships at ten a.m. at a man's work."

"She went to his office?"

"It was all over the Teen Center. Keisha said Brenda had to come pick her up and take her to school." He laughed to himself. "She had a serious rage fest after that. Serves her right."

"I gather that you're not a fan of Erika?"

Emilio looked out into the darkness. His eyes were sad and his voice soft. "Some people believe in second chances, and some don't." He shrugged. "Erika don't."

"Okay, do you know if Brody ever had any of the girls stay after the Teen Center closed? To keep working or anything?"

Emilio screwed up his mouth and shook his head. "I doubt it. He ran the nine p.m. NA meeting out of

St. Barnabas seven nights a week. He'd have to leave a few minutes early just to start the meeting on time."

"Hmm."

"So, do you think you can help me?"

"What is it you want me to do?"

"Tell the cops you got an anonymous tip that the drugs were from an unnamed source so they don't shut down the TC and destroy Brody's rep. They can't know it's me though . . . three strikes."

"I'll do what I can. But from now on, if you need to talk to me, just knock on the door."

"Thanks, lady."

"What will you do now?"

Emilio flipped his hood back up, covering his head. He swiped at his eyes. "I'm going to a meeting. A guy I used to work with said he could sponsor me . . . now that Brody is . . . gone. I don't know how I'll get along without him. He was like a brother." Emilio gave up a deep sigh. "For the first time in my life I believed in myself."

Emilio disappeared into the shadows. *How sad to be so young and have that many scars. I really hope he can get his life turned around.*

By now, Georgina probably had the house on high alert and everyone was worried about me. *I'd better go in and let them know I'm okay.* I tried the knob and . . . I was locked out. The blinking light on the alarm system said *Armed.*

Really? "Georgina!"

Chapter 32

I lay awake all night from revenge of the funnel cake. *I'm over forty years old. I shouldn't be bossed around by pastry. And yet, I still let myself be lured by the siren call of powdered sugar.* Figaro sensed my pain, didn't give a flip, lay on my stomach all night and rode out every wave of my discomfort with indifference.

Now I was dealing with day-after shame and eater's remorse. Determined not to spiral into a forbidden snack binge, I promised myself to get right back on the Paleo Diet Wagon . . . or at least the Caveman Wheel. Whatever applies.

I crawled out of bed and did my yoga flow while thinking about the past forty-eight hours.

Brody Brandt—hero, humanitarian, possible pervert, maybe drug addict, alleged embezzler. Love him or hate him, no one was on the fence.

I put myself together as best I could and headed downstairs. Aunt Ginny was flitting about the kitchen making a fruit salad. Smitty sat at the table drinking a cup of coffee and looking at a hardware store circular. They were far too relaxed.

"Where is Georgina?"

Smitty smiled wide. "Haven't seen the nut job."

I poured myself a cup and started to sit down just as the doorbell rang. "I'll go get it."

I spied two orange eyes peering out from the midst of a wandering Jew plant on the entry table.

That's not gonna end well.

The doorbell rang again before I could reach for the handle.

Good Lord, what's the rush?

Officer Amber stood in my doorway wearing her official police uniform. Her cruiser was parked in the driveway. I found myself choking back an egg of terror that hatched in my throat. "What do you want now?"

"McAllister. Is your aunt home?"

Aunt Ginny came down the hall drying her hands on her apron. "What is it?"

Amber stepped into the foyer. "Good morning, Mrs. Frankowski. I need to ask you a few follow-up questions. Could you come with me down to the station?"

"Am I being arrested?"

"No, this is just to go over your testimony again."

"Do I have to come right now? I have something on the stove."

The stove we don't have? I hoped Amber wouldn't come to the kitchen to check.

"Yes, I really need you to come right now."

Aunt Ginny began to wring her hands. "I have medicine I have to take in a couple of hours. You know I'm not well."

"It shouldn't take too long. I just have a few questions."

Aunt Ginny wrapped her arms around herself and started to sway back and forth. "Dear Jesus, give me strength. I don't think I can make it through this attack of the enemy!"

Amber leaned away from Aunt Ginny and eyed her curiously. "It's not really that serious, not yet."

I butted in, like I do. "If she isn't under arrest, why does she have to come to the station? Why can't you ask her your questions here?"

Aunt Ginny started to howl like she was in pain. Figaro dropped low to the floor and moaned.

Amber's eyes dilated and she took a step backwards. "Oh my God! Quiet down. Look, I have to show you some pictures on the station computer. That's all. Can I trust you to come in today on your own recognizance?"

I eyed Amber suspiciously. "She's not in trouble?"

Amber pointed a finger my way. "This is your doing. I just need to check some new testimonies against hers, but you've got her all wound up." Then to Aunt Ginny she said, "Just come down before eight p.m., okay, Mrs. Frankowski? That's when I get off my shift."

Aunt Ginny stopped howling and nodded.

Amber glared at me. "I'm going to hold you personally responsible for her getting to the station on time." She turned to go.

"Have you looked into Frank Trippett?"

Amber heaved a sigh. "You just can't help yourself, can you?"

I would not be deterred. "He's Kylie Furman's boyfriend. Apparently, he showed up at the victim's office and threatened him a few weeks back."

"What's your point?" Amber snapped.

"He was described by eyewitnesses as hostile. I met him the other day. Something about him feels malevolent. I don't trust him. Have you checked his alibi?"

Amber shook her head in disbelief. "If you don't butt out of my investigation, he won't be the only one who's hostile." Amber stormed away to her police car. She'd given nothing away.

I wasn't convinced. I returned to the kitchen, where Aunt Ginny was calmly drinking a cup of tea and reading the paper. A black cloud had descended. And when I say a black cloud, I mean a black cloud dressed in Marc Jacobs and wearing Chanel no. 5.

"Poppy, good, you weren't carried away by street thugs last night after all. I was concerned."

"You were so concerned you locked me out."

"Well, I had to protect the rest of us, didn't I? Besides, you looked like you could take him if push came to shove."

I considered that for a moment. *Was that another jab about my weight?* Georgina was getting more subtle with her insults as time went on. I had to get her out of here and soon.

"Oh, before I forget." Georgina pulled a pink card out of her pocket. "You had a phone call yesterday. Julie from Leeman and Furrier. She said it was very important."

"You mean Judy? From Freeman and Furman?"

"I don't know, I couldn't understand her. Girl talked like she had marbles in her mouth. Reminded me of a college roommate I had from Massachusetts. We called her Mumbles. Anyway, she said it was urgent."

I snatched the paper from Georgina's talons. "She told you yesterday that it was urgent and you're just now giving me this?"

"Well, I was very busy yesterday."

I left the room before I did something nefarious that Barbara Walters could talk about later. I went to my room and dialed the number on the card.

"Freeman and Furman, Judy here."

"It's Poppy. I just got your message."

"Oh good. I thought you may have forgotten about us."

"No, of course not. What's up?"

"I found something I think you need to see."

"Something like what?"

"It was hidden in Brody's desk, but I don't really understand it, so I don't know if I should show it to Ken and Kylie yet."

"And you want me to see it?"

"You're the only one who believed me that Brody was innocent. They fired him without having any proof. I don't want to show them this until I'm sure. Besides, you're a cat person. I trust you. Could you come today to take a look at it?"

"Absolutely. I'll meet you in thirty minutes."

"I'll be waiting."

I didn't know what Judy had found, but I sure wanted it to be proof that someone else had killed Brody. Was it too much to hope for a murder weapon and a signed confession?

Chapter 33

I parked at the curb in front of Freeman and Furman. A woman in long purple robes stood next to a black car with a dent in the hood, waving around some smoking branches. People were milling about, walking down the sidewalk, going into offices. No one else around seemed to notice anything out of the ordinary with the scene.

I walked up the stairs to the second floor. Before I could go into the office, I heard a *pssst* to my left. Judy was waving a pink scarf at me from the emergency exit.

"Get in here!" she whispered loudly.

I entered the creepy concrete stairwell to find Judy pacing nervously with her arms crossed over her chest like I had to do that one time I tried jogging. Next to her was a banker's box full of framed pictures of a young girl, a homemade clay ashtray probably made in school, a cactus plant, and other assorted office supplies. "Thank God you're here. They just got out of a partner meeting and it's only a matter of time before they come looking for me."

"What's going on outside?" I pointed in the direction of the curb.

Judy waved a hand in dismissal. "That's just Madame Zolda the psychic. She thinks her car is cursed or something."

"Why?"

"I don't know. I think someone broke into it last week and stole her good luck charm. Listen," she said in hurried, hushed tones, "forget about her. I was cleaning out Brody's desk yesterday morning, you know, to give his stuff to his daughter."

I looked down at the banker's box and the picture frames. "Are these all pictures of her?"

Judy whimpered. "That's Christina. He wanted to reconnect with her so badly. Now he won't have the chance."

"That's a shame. I met with Liz the other day and she said Christina is devastated by her father's death. I think she's regretting that decision now."

"Poor dear. If only she hadn't been so bitter and could have forgiven him for the mistakes he made when he was younger. We all do things we regret." Judy's body shuddered with a compressed sob. "Ken ordered me to clean out Brody's office so he could hire a new broker before tax season. I don't think he was even going to call the family to come get this stuff. I was going to drive over to Liz's consignment shop later, but since you know her, do you think you could take these to her? If I leave them here they might just end up in the dumpster."

"Of course, I can take them up for you. I owe her a cake anyway. Liz said that Brody had come into some money lately. Did he have any accounts that were doing particularly well?"

"He made a windfall for the Wintergate Corporation. They invested in some tech company that developed an app that tracks your heart rate and the early warning signs of heart attacks."

"Did he get a piece of their investment?"

"He made a commission, so yes. He got a nice check that month. Which I'm sure he spent on his Teen Center kids." She heaved a sigh, and her shoulders relaxed. "Anyway, here, I found this." She pulled a padded envelope out of her bra and shoved it into my hands.

"Oh, ah . . . okay." *That wasn't awkward at all.*

"It was taped to the bottom of Brody's center drawer."

I opened the clasp and peeked inside. The envelope was full of pages that had been printed off from an account. A yellow sticky note was stuck to the document with the words *I know* written on it. I fished in the envelope and pulled out a black flash drive.

"Do you think maybe Brody found the error in the books and he was going to turn this in?"

Or he hid it because it was incriminating. Why would you tape the proof that you were innocent to the bottom of your desk?

Before I could slide the document out of the envelope, I heard Ken's voice calling from the office. "Judy! Are you down there?"

Judy paled. "Quick, hide it!" she hissed. "If they know I gave you that I'll get fired."

I didn't have pockets or a purse, so I shoved it in my bra like Judy had done. *Ehhhhhck.* I cracked open the door to the hallway and saw Ken heading our way. I didn't want him to see the banker's box, so I did the only thing I could think of. I grabbed the cactus from Brody's things and jumped out into the hall in front of him.

"Hi there." I shoved my hand out and grabbed his

and began to shake it. "Remember me? I was here a few days ago to discuss your investment services."

"Err . . ."

"Can we talk for a minute?" I still had his hand and started to lead him back into the office.

Ken bristled. "Do you have an appointment?"

I gushed on, "No, but I brought you a plant for your office as a thank-you for our meeting the other day. Let's go put this on your desk and give it some water, shall we." I looked over my shoulder as I led him to the office door with his name on it. Judy slipped back in behind her desk and gave me a thumbs-up.

"And I just had to talk to you about the animal shelter."

We'd reached his office and I led him inside.

Ken rubbed his forehead, then looked around the room like he was surprised to find himself there. "What about the animal shelter?"

I put the cactus on his desk and poured some water on it from a bottle of Evian that was fresh from the mini-fridge. "Kenya's a friend of mine and she said your work with them has just been invaluable."

"She did?" He ran a hand through his beard. "I mean, I'm just the comptroller. She's the one who's hands-on with the daily operations."

"Well, now you're just being modest. Kenya said they couldn't run that place without you. You're a real hero."

Ken's chest puffed out and he rocked on his feet. "I do what I can. I think we should all strive to do good, and take care of the innocent ones who can't take care of themselves."

"She even has your picture on the Wall of Blessings, accepting your humanitarian award last year. That's the same award your deceased employee got this past spring, isn't it?"

"Ah, well . . ." He paused for a moment, then his eyes narrowed and he gave me a critical look.

Hmm, I may have overplayed my hand a bit.

His voice took on an accusatory tone. "What were you doing at the shelter? Were you spying on me? Is this about Brody?" His fist balled at his side and he took a step toward me. I took a step back toward his desk.

"What? No! Don't be ridiculous. I was looking for a pet—a cat. I mean I *have* a cat and I *want* to get him a friend . . . a little cat friend . . . to play with." I was nervous rambling and couldn't stop myself. "You know how much cats like to have other cats as friends. My little fella is lonely. So I went to Kenya . . . to adopt a cat . . . like you do."

He glared down at me with fire in his eyes, just breathing in and out.

"Can I see your award?" I squeaked.

"No!"

"Is that it there?" I pointed to a tall bronze statue of an angel on a scallop shell holding a star over its head.

His face flushed crimson and he lifted one arm and pointed to the door. "Get out!"

I lunged at the statue and grabbed it. This could be my only chance to examine it for dents or blood or something incriminating.

Ken stared frozen in disbelief.

Except for dust, it was in perfect condition. *How disappointing.*

"Do I have to call the police on you, lady?"

I put the statue back on the bookshelf in the dust outline it had come from, and started for the door.

"Your office could use a good cleaning. I know a service . . ."

"Out!"

"I'm just trying to help."

He pursued me at a menacing distance to be sure I was leaving.

Kylie stood in front of Judy at her desk.

Judy held the phone out to Kylie with one hand covering the mouthpiece. "He's left twenty-seven messages today. He's threatening to come in here."

Kylie vigorously shook her head no. "Please, tell him I'm not here." She ran back to her office.

Judy caught my eye and pointed to the phone. She mouthed, "Frank Ribbett," and stuck her tongue out.

Ken had one hand on my back and practically pushed me into the hall.

"You could do with some anger management classes," I offered as a helpful suggestion.

"If you so much as step one foot in here, I'm getting a restraining order issued against you!" He slammed the office door in my face.

Well, that could have gone better.

I returned to the stairwell and gathered up Brody's banker's box.

Out at the car, Madame Zolda was clutching a big pink rock and calling for her spirit guide. She didn't acknowledge me.

I put the banker's box in the trunk of my car. Suddenly I heard Ken yelling from the upstairs window. "And keep your stupid plant." He hurled the cactus and it landed on the windshield of Madame Zolda's car, breaking the glass and setting off the car alarm.

Madame Zolda looked at her broken windshield and her bottom lip started to quiver and her eyes teared up.

"That can't be good for business," I said.

She started to full-on bawl and I knew I had to make a quick escape before the cops came or a Patronus showed up. I didn't know which one would be more frightening.

I drove away and dialed Sawyer. I wanted to tell her about my run-in with Ken Freeman. Her phone went to voice mail . . . again. *Where is that girl? She hasn't answered any of my calls for days. I feel like she's hiding something from me.*

I headed toward the Garden State Parkway, and mulled over the conversation with Ken Freeman. That man had some serious rage issues. I could totally see him bashing Brody over the head. Heck, I could see him bashing Mother Teresa over the head if mildly provoked. I didn't get a confession or absolution out of him, but when I was in his office I did figure out why Kenya and his statues seemed so familiar. I had seen that scallop shell outline in the dust before. Brody had the same outline on his desk the day Georgina and I looked around his house. It looked like whoever whacked Brody stole his award, and maybe used that statue to do the deed.

Chapter 34

I pulled into the parking lot at the Teen Center. It was Saturday afternoon, so the place was full of activity. Skateboarders were riding the ramp in the back. A game of basketball was in full swing on the court and various kids were littered about the lawn and front walkway in different stages of electronic hypnosis.

I was here to talk to the girls to see if Brody had ever made inappropriate advances toward them like he had with Erika. It could open up the investigation into a whole new direction if I could prove Brody was attacking girls. I signed in at the front desk and said hello to Brenda.

"Did you bring any goodies today?"

"No, I'm afraid not. I had an emergency this morning and haven't done my baking yet. I can make some brownies and bring them early next week if you'd like."

Brenda shook her head. "No brownies. They're not allowed. Some kids tried to sneak pot brownies in once—now it's on the NO list."

"How about some butterscotch oatmeal crumble bars, then?"

"Ooh, they sound yummy."

"You got it. Hey, are Dani or Keisha around?"

"I haven't seen Keisha today, but Dani is in the computer lab."

She gave me directions down the hall and across from the Ping-Pong room I was in during my last visit.

The computer lab was a bright orange room with utilitarian fluorescent lights and a center desk in the back for a chaperone. Six long tables were set up in two rows. Several laptops were spaced apart, joined by cable spaghetti. A few boys were huddled in two rival groups, one on either side of a table, playing a video game against each other.

Dani sat in the front corner with another girl I hadn't met yet. She was a pretty strawberry blonde with a smattering of freckles across her nose. Dani looked up when I came in.

"Hi, Poppy. Did you bring more cookies?"

"I didn't today, but I've already talked to Brenda and I'll bring some cookie bars when I return."

Dani didn't look up from her laptop screen. "Hmm. Whatever it is, better bring two if Brenda knows about it. This is Clare."

Clare gave me an apologetic smile. "Brenda is usually on a diet and she gets hangry."

"I'll keep that in mind." I grinned. "Hey, I was wondering if I could ask you girls a very serious question about Brody."

Dani still didn't look up from what she was working on. "Sure, what is it?"

"Well, I was wondering if Brody had ever done anything inappropriate to you girls."

Dani and Clare blinked at me with wide eyes. Clare spoke. "Like what?"

"Well, you know, maybe touched you somewhere he

shouldn't or made you do anything you didn't want to—or wouldn't do in front of your grandmother."

The girls said in unison, "Ewwww."

Then Clare said, "Besides, my gran is a dirty old lady. She'd do way more than I'd be comfortable with."

"So, I take that as a no."

Dani folded her hands in her lap. "Brody never did anything like that to me. He always treated me with respect, like equals."

Clare nodded. "That's why so many of us came here. He was like, an adult, with like, adult rules and all. But you like, never felt like you were being looked down on, like you do at home or school. You know?"

"I'd really like your perspective on Brody and Erika's relationship."

Clare snickered. "What relationship? She had the same relationship we all had with Brody. He was our friend and mentor."

Dani added, "Well, actually, Erika was like Brody's biggest fan. Always 'Brody this and Brody that.' And I think Brody really got a kick out of that, 'cause he spent a lot of time with her."

"Do you think Brody could have taken advantage of her . . . enthusiasm?"

Dani cocked her head to the side. "If he did, then Emilio would have jumped him for it."

"Emilio? The boy who isn't allowed to come here anymore?"

"You know him?" Clare asked.

I remembered our run-in last night in the hydrangeas and rubbed my elbow where I'd jabbed him in self-defense. "We've met. Why would Emilio jump Brody because of Erika?"

"Emilio and Erika were dating up until a few weeks ago."

Dating? Neither one of them mentioned that little fact.

"He's not allowed here anymore 'cause he broke rule number one," Dani explained. "No drugs."

"Do you know if they're still dating?"

Clare shook her head no. "Erika broke up with Emilio a couple weeks before he was kicked out. He was really upset about it. I think it's what sent him over the edge."

"Why'd they break up? Do we know?"

"Emilio started using again. Erika was a hot mess, but she wouldn't be around drugs." Dani shook her head. "Not after her mom."

"So, Erika and Emilio are dating. Erika breaks up with Emilio because he starts using drugs again. Then Emilio gets kicked out of the Teen Center for possession?"

The girls both nodded, so I must have gotten that word right. "Then Erika's father comes in and threatens Brody for . . ."

Clare turned her palms up and finished my sentence. "For molesting her."

These kids don't miss anything. "Then Brody is murdered in his home."

Both girls nod.

"Do you think Emilio could have killed Brody for molesting Erika?"

The girls sat on the question for a minute, then Dani finally answered. "I think Emilio is capable of killing, especially if he's trippin'."

"What kind of relationship did Emilio have with Brody? Were they close?"

"Oh, def." Dani nodded. "Now that was someone

who got special attention too. Brody totally made Emilio his special project."

"Yeah. I kind of got the impression that E idolized Brody, didn't you?"

Dani nodded. "At least until he was kicked out. Then it all changed."

Clare looked out the window and shook her head. "It's a shame E had to go and screw it up."

"Have either of you girls ever been here at closing time?"

They both said yes.

"Did Brody ever ask you to stay late for anything? To keep working on a project or help him lock up?"

Clare's phone dinged and she picked it up. She typed while she answered me. "I don't remember Brody locking up. It's usually Brenda who closes."

Dani agreed with her. "Yeah. Brody usually leaves early."

"Has anyone else ever claimed to have been attacked by Brody?"

Dani was back on her laptop. "Not that I've ever heard."

I could see that I'd lost their attention, so it was time to go. "Thanks, girls. You've been a big help."

"Bye, Poppy."

"Bring us cookies."

I was back up at the front with Brenda.

"Leaving so soon?"

"I'm afraid so. I have a couple more stops to make and I have a sort of date tonight."

"A date, ooooh."

I grinned. "Hey, I was wondering, before Brody passed, who locked up at night?"

"I did. Why?"

"Did Brody ever stay late to lock up by himself?"

"A couple of times when I couldn't be here. But it was very rare. He had to leave early to get to a meeting."

"Do you remember who locked up the night Erika said Brody attacked her?"

Brenda gave me a sad smile. "Brody did. I had called out with a stomach flu. Believe me, if I had been the one to lock up, I would have nipped that story in the bud weeks ago."

"I was hoping. Also, someone told me you had to go pick Erika up and take her to school one day."

"Yeah. That's true."

"What was that all about?"

"Brody called me one morning from his day job. I was just in here doing some paperwork and getting some bills paid. Erika, bless her heart, skipped school to talk to him. When he was done counseling her, he called me to come take her to school so she wouldn't be marked absent."

"Do you know what she went there to talk to him about?"

"Brody never told me. But I know she was having some kind of crisis because her eyes were red from crying and she didn't speak to me the whole way to school."

"Hmm."

"Did you find the girls?" Brenda asked.

"Yes. They gave me a lot of good information. Like, did you know Emilio and Erika had been dating?"

Brenda took a drink from a can of Diet Dr Pepper. "Mm-hmm." She nodded.

"Was it serious?"

Brenda shrugged. "As serious as two teenagers can be."

"I spoke to Emilio last night. He thinks the drugs the

cops found at Brody's were the ones Brody confiscated from him."

"That would explain a lot."

"Did you ever report Emilio to the authorities?"

Brenda sighed. "No. When Brody found drugs on Emilio he was shattered. He'd been working to rehabilitate him for months. Kids come here from all kinds of backgrounds, some of them have been through the unthinkable. Brody worked with them to stay off drugs, make good life choices, further their education and live the best lives they could live. But at his core, his true passion was to help kids like Emilio who society had already written off. Whether it was to keep them out of prison or to help them restart their lives after incarceration, Brody would bend over backwards to give anyone a second chance."

"But this would have been Emilio's third strike."

Brenda nodded. "If we'd reported him he would have gone to jail. Brody hoped he'd regret it and make amends before we had to. I tried to get him to at least report the vandalism so we could claim it on our insurance policy, but he wouldn't do it. Brody didn't always see clearly when it came to helping these kids. He'd give to them at his own hurt. He said Emilio was acting out because he was in pain, and he'd eventually come around. When he did, we would have him work off the damage he'd done."

"Wait. What vandalism?"

"I thought you knew. Emilio showed up here in the middle of the night after he was expelled. He smashed a bunch of windows and a couple lights with a baseball bat. The security cameras picked up the whole thing. We had to spend some of our award money to replace the windows." She shook her head sadly. "We could really have used that money in the operating budget. It costs a lot just to turn the lights on here, and we rely on donations and government assistance to pay our overhead. Between the Lynch accusation and the report that drugs were found in Brody's house, we're in danger of losing all our funding."

"Where would you go if that happened?"

"Back to my old job at the detention center, I guess. I took a pay cut to work with Brody because I believe in this place. In the short time we've been here we've been able to help dozens of kids and bring hope to a lot of families."

"I wish I could help more," I said. "If there's anything I can do, please let me know."

"We have a party coming up. If we haven't been shut down, we could sure use some cookies."

I promised her I would provide whatever cookies or cupcakes they wanted when the time came for the party and said my goodbye. But on my way past the bulletin board I noticed a newspaper article. It had been covered up by another flyer that had been removed. "Brenda, what is this about?"

She looked out her cubicle window to where I was pointing. "That's the story the paper ran when Erika Lynch won first prize in the Cape May Art Show this past summer. Brody was so proud of her he put that up to remind everyone that good things happen when you work hard for them."

I looked closer at the image of Erika. She was holding a statue that looked like a man. He had his arms folded across his chest, his head was tilted slightly, and he was smiling. "What is this in her hand? Is that the award?"

Brenda came out of her office to look at the paper

on the board with me. "No, that's her entry. Erika's a sculptor. It's her tribute to her father."

"A sculptor? When you said artist, I'd assumed she painted." I read the caption. "'*One and Only*, in ceramic and mixed media.' Are you sure it's supposed to be her father?"

Brenda nodded. "If you read the article she says it is."

I read down the page. "She said, 'This is my tribute to my one and only, who has always been there for me.' She didn't specify it was her father. Besides, you've met him. Does this look like Jonathan Lynch to you?"

"Well . . . art is subjective."

"Do you have a picture of Brody around?"

"Of course."

Brenda rushed back to her cubicle and returned with a brochure for the Teen Center. On the back page was a photo of Brody next to some of the Teen Center kids. He was much stockier than the representation in the sculpture, but Erika had captured the contented smile on his face perfectly.

Brenda and I looked each other in the eye and she said, "Wow. I can't believe I never noticed that before."

Erika's tribute to her *one and only* was for Brody.

This new revelation only served to muddy the waters even more. It seemed that Erika may have idolized her mentor. The title of her tribute to him hints about a more intimate relationship than would be appropriate. Could Brody have taken advantage of Erika's vulnerability? And if that award-winning statue was made out of cast bronze, maybe I'd been wrong about the murder weapon after all.

Chapter 35

St. Barnabas was just a few blocks away from the Teen Center in the Villas. They should be having Mass in a few hours, and bingo sometime after that. I drove over to see if anyone might be around this time of day who would have worked with Brody. Maybe they could shed some light on his character for me.

The white brick building sat at an angle to Bayshore Road, giving passersby a beautiful view of its large stained-glass window and towering white steeple. A sign on the front lawn said COMMUNION WINE HAPPY HOUR 4 P.M.

There was a list of activities posted in the foyer. I scanned the list for anything pertaining to a twelve-step meeting, but found nothing. Luckily, I was approached by a man I assumed was a priest, judging from his black suit and white collar.

"Can I help you find your way, miss?"

"I was looking for someone who would know about the addiction meetings that are held here."

"I'm Father Brian, and I can help you with that. Do you need AA, NA, or SA?"

"What is SA?"

"Sexaholics Anonymous."

"Oh God no! Ah! I'm sorry! I mean I don't . . . I'm not . . . I'm here to find someone who might know someone I might know. But not for sex!"

"Whoa! Okay, settle down." Father Brian laughed. "Why don't you come in and have a seat, and you can start from the beginning."

We entered the large sanctuary full of statues and wooden pews facing the stained-glass apostles. I'd never been in a Catholic church before, so I did some discreet gawking before we sat down.

"It's a lot bigger on the inside, isn't it?" Father Brian smiled. "Now tell me what's going on."

"Okay. A friend of mine attends the NA meetings here. NA is Narcotics Anonymous, isn't it?"

Father Brian smiled and leaned back in his pew. "Well, it is, but anonymous meetings are anonymous for a reason."

"The person I'm looking for information about has recently passed away."

"Oh, of course. You want to know about Brody. He was a dear friend. He will surely be missed."

"I heard that Brody ran the Narcotics Anonymous meeting here."

Father Brian nodded. "Brody ran two meetings. The Monday through Saturday meeting at nine p.m., and the Sunday afternoon meeting at five."

"So, he was here every single day? What happened if he couldn't make it?"

"Three hundred sixty-five days a year. I stepped in for him a couple times when he couldn't be here, but that was very rare. He was totally committed to helping others. Besides, the group members were much more open to sharing with Brody, as you can imagine what with him being a former addict himself."

"Was he ever late to the meeting? Especially in the last couple of months?"

"I don't remember. We don't keep tabs on our volunteers quite to that level of severity."

"I have a friend who came to me looking for help the other night. Brody had been his sponsor. He's gotten himself into some trouble with drugs again, and he doesn't know where else to turn."

"Would your friend happen to be tall and skinny and fond of a hoodie?"

"He might be."

"Because he was just here last night. I know he fell off for a bit, but he has a new sponsor now. I think he's doing very well in the program. What are you concerned about?"

"Do priests follow the same rule of confidentiality as doctors?" I asked.

Father Brian cocked his head at an angle. "If you want this to be a confession, I am bound by silence."

"Okay, well, then I'm confessing that my friend has two strikes against him for drug possession."

"Okay."

"And he was caught with drugs by Brody, who confiscated them."

"Okay."

"Brody didn't report my friend, and the cops found the drugs in his home when they investigated his murder."

Father Brian's eyes flickered in acknowledgment, but he didn't interrupt.

"Now my friend wants to clear his mentor's name, but he can't go to the police because—"

Father Brian finished my sentence. "He already has two strikes."

I nodded.

"And your friend wants you to tell the police that the drugs weren't Brody's without telling them where they really came from?"

"That's exactly it."

"Okay, I think I have an idea that could help. There is an officer who attends Mass here every Saturday. Leave it to me."

"Really? Thank you."

"Of course. You can tell your friend that he can come talk to me anytime he wants. I'm no Brody, but I know someone even better." He looked up.

I smiled at Father Brian. "I will tell him."

"Now, do you still need to know where the meetings are?" He grinned.

"Do you have a twelve-step program for desserts?"

He patted his stomach. "Not yet, but if we did I would be the first one to sign up."

I was about to get in my car when a cute little VW Bug with Pennsylvania tags pulled in next to me and a familiar friend got out.

"Tracy?"

Tracy's head jerked at my voice. She twitched and fumbled her purse, spilling the contents on the ground. "Oh hi . . . uh . . . Poppy. Sorry, I'm such a klutz." She scrambled to scrape everything back in her pink bag and compose herself. "How is your aunt doing?"

I bent down to help her. "She has good days and bad days. We'll all be glad when this is over. What are you doing here?"

"One of my patients invited me to her support group, you know." She plucked at her scrubs. "Since I'm a nurse.

She thought her group would love my perspective. Her grandson goes to a teen center around here somewhere."

"Really, I've been there a few times. Who is her grandson?"

Tracy smoothed her hair back into place. "His name is Emilio."

"I know him."

"His gran has told me some about his life. Neither of his parents are in the picture. He's been in and out of juvie. He's had it rougher than most."

"It's hard to imagine some of the darker things that go on in our little town here, but I think Emilio is on the right track."

A shadow crossed over Tracy's eyes. "I wouldn't be too sure. You have to be very careful with addicts. Many of them are master manipulators. They can make you believe they've changed, and the minute your back is turned they're stealing money from your purse and cold medicine from your bathroom."

"I hadn't really thought about it that way. I've never had any drug abuse in my family." *Just insanity and mental illness.*

Tracy's eyes narrowed and her tone was sharp and bitter. "Then count yourself very lucky. It sounds like Emilio's caused his gran a lot of pain. You have no idea what that poor woman has been through. Drug and alcohol abuse can destroy a family. Sometimes the damage is so great there's no way back."

"You should call the Teen Center and see if you can give a talk there. I bet it would be well received. Ask for Brenda."

"I might do that, thanks. I better get inside before they think I'm not coming."

I tried to offer Tracy Brenda's contact information, but she jetted through the church door before I could find a pen. I drove home thinking about Emilio. How much do I know about him? He said he was trying to turn his life around, but I only had his word for it. Was it the truth, or was he manipulating me to get me to bail him out with the cops? I wanted to give him the benefit of the doubt. That's what Brody would do. I wonder how many times Brody was hurt by someone not quite ready to change. I was starting to see how he achieved hero status.

Chapter 36

I returned home to get ready for my date with Tim at Gia's coffee shop. *How in the world did I ever agree to this?*

I'd only had three boyfriends in my lifetime. Billy Ryder when I was in the first grade. He lived across the street from me and I told him we would have to get married before he could share my Popsicle. He agreed because I had a red, white, and blue Rocket Pop from the ice cream man. I divorced him when he refused to give me a bite of his blueberry frosted Pop-Tart a week later. Then there was Brent Johnson when I was in junior high. He was my boyfriend for a whole month on the bus until Alaina Bourne's boobs grew two cup sizes almost overnight. Then he was Alaina's boyfriend on the bus. And Tim Maxwell, my first love and former fiancé. We were together for three years until I got pregnant by someone else. All in all I'd say the best relationship of the three was Billy Ryder. He had a tree house in his yard, and he let me call the shots. I should have hung on to him.

My late husband was never my boyfriend, and our first date happened a year after we were married. That's a long story. Now here I was with two men interested in me at the same time. I was still waiting for someone to jump out and yell *You've been punked!* Girls like me don't have two men chasing them at the same time, do they? One man chasing me is like a unicorn spotting.

I ran up the porch steps and flung the door open. "I'm home!" There was a broken flowerpot and a pile of potting soil under the stand in the hall, and the wandering Jew plant had wandered off. *Hmph. Who could have seen that coming?* I grabbed the broom and dustpan and cleaned up Figaro's massacre, then hurried upstairs to change for my date.

Georgina met me at the top of steps with her rant of the day. "That little troll spackled my bathroom door shut!"

Down the hall I heard Smitty's Three Stooges "Whoop whoop whoop."

I took a deep breath to keep myself from laughing out loud. "Well, you did want him to work on it."

Georgina stomped her foot. "I wanted him to sand it!"

"You think maybe this is because of the oatmeal?"

"Poppy." Georgina leaned in and whispered, "I have to . . . you know."

"So go downstairs."

"Someone might hear me."

"Then use one of the other bathrooms. We have seven."

Georgina stomped down the hall to the sound of Smitty's snickering.

I went up the flight of steps to my room. Figaro was curled up on my bed, a few telltale purple leaves stuck to his fur. I picked them out and scratched under his chin. He stretched like a corkscrew. Belly up, top paws in one direction and bottom paws in the other.

"Why are you so naughty?"

He curled back up, opened an eye, and yawned before going back to sleep.

I quickly changed into a black leather skirt and black boots. Then I obsessed over the message I would send Gia if I showed up for my date with Tim looking better than I did when I came in with the muffins. I changed into jeans. Then back into the skirt. Then back into the jeans. I put on a green sweater. Changed into a black T-shirt. Then back to the sweater. I ran out of time to do my hair so I ran a brush through it and put it up in a clip. Then I changed back into the T-shirt. Then I touched up my makeup, changed back into the sweater, and ran down the stairs. My date had just pulled up to the curb, so I yelled to Aunt Ginny that I was going to the coffee shop with Tim and I'd be back later.

Tim had dressed up for the occasion. I reached up and straightened the collar on his crisp blue linen dress shirt. "You look extra handsome tonight. This wouldn't be a competition, would it?"

He gave a mischievous grin, then leaned down and kissed me. "Are you nervous?" he teased.

"Of course not," I lied. *I'm terrified. What if I blow it with both of them? That would serve me right. What if they make me choose? I barely know what I want today, let alone for my future. And who would I choose? I've barely spent any time with either one of them.*

"Are you sure? Because you look like you're going to be sick."

I gave Tim my best smile, which may or may not have made me look like a mental patient. We walked the few blocks over to La Dolce Vita in uncomfortable silence.

Gia was wiping down the bar when we arrived. He too was dressed uncharacteristically swanky for work on a Saturday night. The crease in his slacks was so sharp it could slice tomatoes. He didn't look at me when I came in. He was too busy locked in a stare-down with Tim. I could have set my hair on fire and neither one of them would have noticed me.

The main theme song from *The Good, the Bad and the Ugly* whistled from somewhere behind the espresso machine.

Gia's eyes held a vacant expression for just a flicker, then he shook his head and hollered over his shoulder. "Karla! *Ciò che è sbagliato con te?*"

The music went off and Karla's laugh floated to the front of the bar on the tension in the air.

I cleared my throat. "Tim, this is Gia. Gia, Tim."

I expected the men to shake hands, but instead they each gave a tense chin nod. Gia was the first to break out of the trance. "Welcome to my espresso bar."

"It's cute." Tim gave a smile that didn't reach his eyes. "I have a restaurant at the harbor. Maxine's Bistro. It seats two hundred. I think your little coffee shop could fit right in my back room."

Gia folded his arms across his chest, flexing his biceps, and leaned against the counter. "I prefer a smaller, more intimate affair."

Tim shifted his weight and looked around again. "Well, you do have smaller, for certain. It's a shame your business is so slow. Nowadays it's hard to make these little shops successful."

Oh good Lord. Just lock horns and get it over with already.

Gia gave him a tight-lipped smile. "Coffee is definitely much more popular in the morning, but defi that gives me more time to make love, at night, when a restaurant owner would be too busy."

Whoa, nobody's been making love.

Karla made a noise like "Mm-hmm!" and drew a one in the air with her finger.

Tim paled. "I'm glad Poppy has been helping you

bring in some new customers." Tim put an arm around my shoulders and yanked me against him. "I'd hate to see your business fail and for you to have to close up and leave town."

Gia smiled at me and we locked eyes. "Poppy has been the best thing to happen to me in a long time." Then he looked at Tim. "It must be hard for you, working in such a stressful environment without your own Poppy to assist you. No wonder you look so weak and tired."

Tim's arm stiffened.

I looked to Karla for help. She was leaning over the counter, enraptured. Her hands clasped together, her eyes moving back and forth like a referee at an underground cage match. She gave me a gleeful smile.

I cleared my throat again, and tried to get Tim to loosen his death grip on my shoulder. "Why don't we order some coffee and sit down. Gia has this wonderful seating area. I've often thought about sitting in here on rainy days, to read."

Karla pulled the pin on a comment, tossed it into the middle of the room, then stood back to watch the fallout. "You should bring a book with you, Poppy; you're already here every day. If Giampaolo had his way, you'd belong to him permanently."

Tim stumbled on the corner of the leather easy chair he was maneuvering past, and he fell into the seat.

Karla giggled at Gia's glare. "What? I mean as a business partner, of course."

Gia put his hand on his sister's shoulder, gave her a dirty look, and teasingly spun her away from us. "What would you like, *bella*? I'll give you anything."

I know he was asking for my coffee order, but whew! Such intensity in his eyes. My stomach did a little flip-flop.

Karla wasn't even a little deterred by her brother. She popped her head around the corner of the espresso machine again. "Why don't you make them some of the coffee cocktails you've been wanting to introduce for after hours?"

"That's a wonderful idea!" I raved. "That will bring a whole new customer base at night for dessert."

Tim folded his arms across his chest. "You know you need a liquor license for that. They can be really hard to get."

"I didn't think of that," I said.

Gia smiled that mysterious smile of his. "Already have one through Mia Famiglia. I just never thought about using it before."

Tim frowned.

"I got the idea from you, *bella*. You said the other day your truffle brownies would be perfect with raspberry liqueur in them."

Tim pulled my chair closer to his. "My girl has always had a gift when it comes to making up desserts. There was a time, back in the day, when she was going to be my pastry chef."

"You mean we were going to have our own restaurant together. Right?"

"Sure."

Karla poked her head over the counter. "Maybe it just wasn't the right time." Then she muttered under her breath, "Or the right partner."

Gia grinned again. "Now you sit, I will make you a couple of coffee cocktails that I have in mind." He left to make us the drinks, and I turned to Tim.

"Okay, you can relax your T. rex grip now. I think my shoulder is bruised."

"Sorry. Gigi told me he was good-looking, but I didn't realize . . ." He trailed off. "I should have worked out more today."

"Relax. You're perfect just the way you are. Are you

sure you want to stay? We could . . ." A shadow fluttered
across the front window. I normally wouldn't think anything of it, since we were on the mall facing other shops
and restaurants, and tourists were still milling about
enjoying the crisp autumn night. But I swore I heard a
fast-moving *click click click* move with the shadow.

"No, I want to stay. I haven't seen you in a few days.
Not since you took me to a strip club. Which was awe-
some." He was teasing me. That was a good sign that he
was relaxing. "I miss you, Mack."

"You haven't called me that in years."

Tim reached up and twisted a strand of my auburn
hair that had broken free of its clip. A plate of brownies
jutted between us. Karla held them there for a beat to
make a point before putting them on the table. "Some
of Poppy's Paleo truffle brownies to have with your
cocktails."

She turned to Tim. "They make a great team, don't
you think?" Then she scampered off.

Gia arrived with a tray and put a chilled rosy chocolate cocktail with a raspberry balanced on the edge of
the glass in front of me. "For my beauty here, a Raspberry Truffle. There's no dairy in it. Wait till you see
how it pairs with your brownie." Then he placed a
creamy concoction with three espresso beans floating
on top in front of Tim. "For you, a Wake-up Call."

Tim begrudgingly took a sip. "A little obvious maybe."

"Gia, this is amazing. The drink really brings out the
raspberry puree in the brownies."

Gia winked, and left us to our date. But he didn't
go far.

I gave Tim a bite of brownie with a sip of my cocktail.
"What do you think?"

He sighed. "I hate it, it's delicious. They do pair
beautifully and I can't believe this brownie is gluten-free."

I smiled. "And your drink?"

He shook his head. "Except for the innuendo, it's fantastic. I'd like the recipe, but I don't dare ask him."

"Want me to get it for you?"

"Yes, just not tonight. Let me leave with some dignity."

Karla began fastidiously sweeping the floor. Not the whole floor, mind you, just the floor under our feet. She jabbed at Tim a couple of times, then gasped. We followed her gaze to the front of the shop. There was a crazy person with her face smashed up against the front picture window. Her head was wrapped in a scarf and she was wearing giant sunglasses, but I'd recognize that crackpot anywhere.

Her head jerked back. The psychopath realized she'd been made, and clickity-clacked into the unsuspecting tourist next to her, apologized, and dove into the bushes.

I sighed.

"What are you thinking about?" Tim asked me.

"Just thinking about that movie *Psycho*."

"Speaking of psychos, did the police find anything out that will help Aunt Ginny?"

"No. I'm not sure they're trying really hard. She had to go over to the station today to answer some follow-up questions. I've tried to offer Amber some alternative suspects, but she isn't taking me seriously."

Tim covered my hand with his, but got knocked in the back of his chair by Karla furiously mopping a four-foot square of floor behind him.

Gia said something to her in Italian that she didn't like and she threw the mop behind the counter and stomped outside.

I filled Tim in about Emilio and Erika and the details of what I'd found out over the past couple of days, leaving out the bit about Gia helping me with the charity information. No need to light that match.

After the fourth time that I heard clickity-clackity sounds scurry by the front window, I knew I'd had enough. No blood was shed, no one ended up in the emergency room. It was a successful date.

I said goodbye to Gia, who gave me a very long, very intimate hug, and led Tim outside.

Tim pulled me into an embrace in front of the picture window. He leaned in and kissed me, but only for a moment, because Karla shot him in the face with a hose.

"Ach, sorry. I was watering the plants and it just got away from me."

Tim wiped his face with his hand and looked in the flowerpots. "There's only dirt in there!"

Karla gave him a beautiful smile. "The seeds are getting ready for next spring."

I took Tim's wet hand. "Why don't we head back to Aunt Ginny's."

We walked hand in hand past the other Victorian manor houses and bed-and-breakfasts. The mood was very different than it had been at the beginning of the night.

"Well, that Karla is definitely not team Tim, is she?"

I laughed. "Don't worry, she's not team Poppy either. I think she just loves the drama."

Tim spun me around to face him. "You know I'm crazy about you, don't you, Mack?"

My heart went to him. "I know. I'm crazy about you too."

He leaned in and kissed me and this time it was sincere and full of affection instead of marking his territory. When he broke contact he held me close and asked me, "What's going on?"

"Well, you said we were dating other people, so that's—"

"No. Not that. I mean over there at Aunt Ginny's. What's going on there?"

Down the block three police cruisers with lights flashing were pulling up in front of Aunt Ginny's house. "Oh my God!"

Chapter 37

I ran down the block, pulling Tim with me. All the lights were on inside the house. Figaro was sitting on the front porch, his body erect, his whiskers stiff, his tail twitching. Smitty sat next to him, his hat lying on the porch, forgotten. Police officers were searching the yard, the garage, and the neighbors' yards.

"Smitty! What's going on?"

Smitty was clearly upset. He opened his mouth to tell me, but Amber busted out of the front door onto the porch before he had a chance.

"McAllister! Where is your aunt? I told her to be at the station before eight, when I was supposed to get off. Now it's quarter past nine, and I had to come over here to collect her instead of going home and having a glass of wine."

"What do you mean, where is she? Isn't she inside?" I looked to Smitty.

He wrung his hands. "I haven't seen her all day. The cat won't even go in the house right now. I think he knows something is wrong."

"I don't understand. What do you mean, she hasn't

been here all day? Wasn't she here a couple of hours ago when I came home to get dressed?"

"No, she left this morning right after you did. She didn't tell me where she was going, just said not to wait up. I thought she was kidding since it was ten a.m. But she still hasn't returned."

I was stunned. The whole time I was getting ready for my date I thought she was watching television. She could be lying in a ditch somewhere, and I was off flirting and eating brownies.

Amber stepped to me. "I told you I was holding you responsible. Give me one good reason not to take you in for aiding and abetting, McAllister?"

I tried to be strong and put up a brave front, but my lip started to tremble. "I . . . I thought she was inside. What if she's been kidnapped? What if the killer got to her? What if she's . . ."

Tim put his arm around me. "Don't even go there."

"Who's been kidnapped?" Georgina appeared beside me, taking off the dark sunglasses and head scarf she'd used to disguise herself earlier. I was too distraught to point it out.

Smitty answered her. "Ginny is missing."

Georgina's hand shot up to her throat. "Oh God! Since when?"

"All day." Smitty dropped his face to his hands.

Tim nudged me. "Did she take any more of those sleeping pills? Could she be sleepwalking again?"

"No. There's no way. Even if she did, she wouldn't sleepwalk for hours."

Amber called in on her police radio that she had a missing suspect and requested a wider police search.

"Do we really need the manhunt?" I asked. "Can't we just wait and see if she turns up on her own?"

"I would, but the situation has changed."

"Changed how?"

"When I told her this morning to come down to the station, it was because we had a few new reports of break-ins and missing items. The victims don't live near you and the reports don't come from credible sources. So, we figured they were coming from attention seekers and opportunists. I wanted to show Mrs. Frankowski some photos to see if she knew any of the alleged victims."

"Okay, so what changed?"

"As of this evening, an eyewitness has come forward who identified Aunt Ginny leaving the victim's house the night of the murder."

My chest constricted, and my breath came ragged and shallow.

Georgina stepped in and asked the question that wouldn't form on my lips. "When you say identified, do you mean they know Ginny, and they said they saw her specifically?"

"No, they described an elderly woman, slightly stooped, with bright red hair in a beehive style, wearing a pink track suit and leaving the victim's house carrying a rolling pin at two a.m. on the night in question. We showed them a lineup of photographs and they ID'd Mrs. Frankowski."

Smitty blew out a pent-up breath. "I thought that had to be done in person. You do it by pictures now?"

"The photographs are preliminary. I was coming tonight to take her in for a lineup. That's when I discovered that she was missing. This doesn't look good, McAllister. Everything about this confirms that your aunt is guilty."

Fear was being replaced with panic and a burst of adrenaline. I jumped to my feet. "I don't care what it looks like. I know Aunt Ginny is innocent. Instead of calling the police force down on her, why don't you call the hospitals and make sure she hasn't been in an accident, or worse." I grabbed my purse and headed for my car.

Amber's face reddened with irritation. "Get back here, McAllister. You're not leaving my sight."

"I'm going to look for Aunt Ginny. I'm not just waiting here while she could be out there hurt and scared."

Tim followed me. "Then I'm going with you. I'll drive."

I put my hand up. "You know what would make me feel better? If you went in your car and checked out the emergency room and urgent care. We could cover more ground and find her a lot faster if we split up."

"Whatever you need, I'm here for you." Tim gave me a quick peck.

Smitty jumped up. "Where do you want me to go?"

"Smitty, you go to the beach, boardwalk, grocery store—then call me."

Smitty saluted. "You got it, boss."

Tim and Smitty drove off in their vehicles and I started for mine again.

Amber spoke like she was scolding a disobedient child. "You aren't in any condition to be operating a vehicle. For once in your life, leave it to those who know what they're doing."

"You can't stop me, Amber."

Amber reached for her handcuffs.

"I'll go with her." Georgina stepped between me and Officer Airhead. "I'll keep her safe."

Amber wrote something down in her flip book, then tore it out. She handed it to Georgina. "This is my cell. Call me hourly until you find her."

Georgina nodded.

I had started the car and was about to leave them standing there. Aunt Ginny needed me.

Georgina grabbed the door handle and jerked it open. She flopped into the front seat as I took off with the passenger door closing by the force of my determination.

I'm coming, Aunt Ginny. Hold on.

Chapter 38

"I had one job. Take care of my aunt. That was it. I just had to keep her safe, and I failed."

I was driving up and down random streets of Cape May with tears in my eyes, and I didn't care who saw me. My heart was sick. Nothing else mattered right now but finding her.

Georgina was trying to comfort me and be encouraging. "Maybe Ginny is off on one of her wild activities. You know you can't control her."

"Sure she's a handful. She's determined to squeeze every drop of excitement out of her golden years and live to the extreme, but she's also well up in years. What's a minor accident or illness at my age could easily lead her to a stroke or heart attack that she'd never recover from."

Georgina patted my arm. "We're going to find her. I'm sure there's a logical explanation. She's probably at a friend's house."

The tears were streaming down my face and my nose was running. I wiped my eyes with my sleeve.

I can't lose her. She's all the family I have left in the world. If only I hadn't wasted so much time numbed out in front of the television when I could have been with her. I didn't have a great plan, and I couldn't seem to focus on making one. I was spinning out.

"I don't know where I'm going." I banged the steering wheel with the palm of my hand.

Georgina handed me a tissue from her purse. "Why don't we call your friend. The one with the boy name. Maybe she's heard from Ginny."

I pulled over and blew my nose. I dialed Sawyer's number on my cell. *Please pick up this time.*

"Hello?"

My voice broke with a surge of fear. "Sawyer?"

"Oh God, honey, what's wrong?"

"Aunt Ginny is missing and the police are looking for her. Is she there with you?"

Sawyer gasped. I could hear the quiver in her voice. "No. She's not here. I haven't seen her. Where are you now? I'll come join you and we can look for her together."

"I'm just a few blocks away, I'll come pick you up."

Five minutes later, I screeched to a stop in front of Sawyer's condo. She was waiting in the parking lot holding two bottled iced coffees and a box of Kleenex. Sawyer jumped in the back seat and offered me my pick. I took the coffee. I didn't read the ingredients. I couldn't have cared any less about my diet than I did right then. I popped it open and chugged.

Sawyer offered the other coffee to Georgina, who politely declined. "Have you checked any of Aunt Ginny's old haunts?"

I shook my head no.

"How about the fire department? I think they have bingo tonight."

"That's a good idea." Georgina patted my arm again. "Let's go there."

I took off for Cape May Station One, while Georgina filled Sawyer in on the drama with Amber.

I pulled into the parking lot of the big white building. The three bay doors for the ambulance, pumper, and ladder trucks were all open—ready in case a fire broke out. A sign was posted on the front door. THIS IS A SMOKE-FREE FACILITY. Even for Bingo.

They were using the auxiliary room since the dining hall was still undergoing repairs from another ill-fated bingo night a few weeks earlier. The less said about that, the better.

I quickly looked for Aunt Ginny, up and down the rows of tables in the brightly lit hall. You would think her purple hair would make her easy to spot, but apparently a lot of these ladies got their hair done at Vo-Tech Beauty School.

"Poppy! Over here!"

I followed the voice to Mrs. Dodson and her daughter Charlotte. I rushed to their table to ask if Aunt Ginny had been there.

Mrs. Dodson was one of Aunt Ginny's best friends and coconspirators. Fleshy and jowly, her head slightly tilted back, her lips pursed in the modicum of proper British gravity. She offered me some of her contraband cookies she'd sneaked in. "I haven't seen Ginny tonight. Why?"

"She's missing, and I'm afraid she could be hurt or worse."

"Are you sure she isn't sleepwalking again?"

"She's not on that medicine anymore, and she's been gone all day."

Charlotte asked her mother, "Do you think she took off because she's being accused of murdering Brody Brandt?"

Mrs. Dodson replied, "Not Ginny. The Scarlet Dragon doesn't back down from anything."

"Okay, well, if you see her, please call me right away." I wrote my number on one of their used bingo cards.

Mrs. Dodson stood, and grabbed her cane and her purse. "Play my cards, Charlotte."

"Ma! Where you going?"

"Don't give me lip, missy. I'm going to help find Ginny."

"But Ma! It's getting late. What about your hypertension?"

Mrs. Dodson snatched her tin of cookies from the table. "I'll take a pill. Come, Poppy."

I called back to Charlotte, "I'll keep an eye on her."

Mrs. Dodson climbed into the back seat of my Toyota and greeted Sawyer. Sawyer introduced her to Georgina.

Mrs. Dodson offered everyone some of her cookies. "Have you tried the Senior Center? I think there's a class of some kind tonight."

"On my way." I took off for the Senior Center and said a prayer that Aunt Ginny would be there.

"Great juniper! What is in these cookies?" Georgina began to fan herself.

Sawyer wheezed and took a slug of her iced coffee.

Mrs. Dodson replied with a reserved pompousness. "The secret is a good stiff shot of Irish whiskey."

Sawyer choked. "That's more than a shot."

I hoped we wouldn't get pulled over. I'd be forced to take a Breathalyzer just from the second-hand fumes in the car.

"It's good for the constitution. Here"—Mrs. Dodson held the tin out to Georgina again—"you look like you could use another."

Georgina held her hand up to wave her off, but reconsidered and helped herself to two more.

Mrs. Dodson put the lid back on the tin of cookies. "Now what's this business with the humanitarian all about?"

Sawyer filled Mrs. Dodson in on the details so far, including the new information about the eyewitness.

"Could it have been in self-defense?" Mrs. Dodson asked.

"What do you mean?" I asked.

"Well, I know Ginny would never hurt anyone unprovoked, but if attacked first, well. That's another kettle of fish."

"No. I'm afraid not. Mr. Brandt was lying in bed when he was hit with the murder weapon. There was blood all over the mattress and none on the floor."

"I didn't see that when we were in the house," Georgina said.

"You were in the bathroom."

Georgina popped her third whiskey ball in her mouth, and looked out the window.

"Well, if you ask me"—Mrs. Dodson tilted her chin up and half closed her eyes—"it was one of them hooligans who were always hanging around his house that done it."

"What hooligans?" Sawyer asked.

"You know I don't like to tell tales," Mrs. Dodson cautioned. "But Myrtle Pickler, who attends my quilting club, told us that Philomena Crawson, who lives across the street from Mr. Humanitarian himself, said that Brody Brandt is one shady character."

"Shady how?" Georgina asked.

"Well. His neighbors had to start a Neighborhood Watch program just to keep an eye on him."

Sawyer's phone chimed and she checked it. "Just on him?"

Mrs. Dodson gave her a knowing look. "He was the only one selling drugs to teenagers out of his house."

I pulled into the Senior Center parking lot and parked half in the spot and half up on the curb. I looked in the rearview mirror at Mrs. Dodson. "How do you know he was selling drugs?"

"That many hooligans would only be about for one reason." Mrs. Dodson tapped her nose with her finger. "Philomena suspects he was using the Teen Center as a front for his drug-lord operation." Mrs. Dodson pursed her lips and nodded sagely.

I jumped out of the car and so did Sawyer. We ran down the sidewalk into the redbrick building and followed the sounds down the hall to the activity room. The seniors were busy kneading dough while a young lady at the front of the room demonstrated how to work an electric pasta cutter. A little white-haired man doubled over a walker on tennis balls was having some trouble. "Help! Help! I got my necktie stuck in the roller!" The young lady rushed over to unwind him from the machinery.

"What are you girls doing here?" Thelma Davis was at one of the long tables in the pasta class. Short and plump, her old lady hairdo was tinted just slightly pink. She was dressed in a pink sweat suit that had been bedazzled with a giant flamingo. She'd apparently gone rogue in the pasta class, and had decided to make a necklace and rings out of her dough instead of vermicelli.

"Mrs. Davis, have you seen or heard from Aunt Ginny?"

She shook her head, "No. I don't think so. Not today anyway."

Sawyer took over. "Aunt Ginny is missing and we're checking all the places she would normally go."

Mrs. Davis peeled her dough jewelry off. "Do you think she might be out sleepwalking again?"

"She's not on that medicine anymore, and she's been gone all day," Sawyer repeated.

Mrs. Davis grabbed a pink pocketbook off the shelf. "I'm coming with you."

"Hey! That's my purse." Another little old lady wearing an apron that said *Hot Stuff Coming Through* cried out to Mrs. Davis in alarm.

"Sorry." Mrs. Davis replaced the pink purse and picked up a blue one next to it. "This one must be mine." She checked the room to see if anyone else would claim it. The room was silent. "Okay, let's go."

We piled back into my Toyota, and the ladies all said hello. Mrs. Davis was introduced to Georgina. She then had a couple of Mrs. Dodson's whiskey balls. So did Georgina.

Sawyer was trapped in the back in a geriatric sandwich between Mrs. Dodson and Mrs. Davis. If I did find Aunt Ginny, how would I fit her in the car? One problem at a time.

Mrs. Davis offered up the suggestion, "Why don't we check the bowling alley? There's that new senior league Ginny may have joined. I think they're playing tonight."

I took off toward Wildwood for the Bowling Lounge with my search posse. The gnawing fear in my stomach grew with each disappointment. Maybe the bowling alley would bring me some relief. I checked my phone. No messages from Smitty or Tim. They hadn't found her either. I caught a snippet of conversation between the gals in the back.

"Then he was accused of molesting that poor girl," Mrs. Dodson said. "Myrtle Pickler said the father wants the girl to see a professional therapist over the matter. But she won't go."

"I never trusted that Erika Lynch. She dresses way too hotsy totsy for my taste." Mrs. Davis had taken out her crochet needles and yarn from her purse and was working on an afghan. "I wouldn't believe a word that comes out of her mouth."

"Well, innocent until proven otherwise. That's what I always say." Mrs. Dodson nodded. "But if you ask me, he's guilty as sin."

I got a text from Smitty. Aunt Ginny was not at the beach down from our house, the boardwalk, or the Acme market. He'd also tried Cape May Point and various frozen-custard stands. He was going to show her picture around to some of the local shops to see if anyone had seen her, but so far, she was a ghost. Aunt Ginny was gone, girl.

Chapter 39

The Bowling Lounge was a fifty-two-lane bowler's paradise. I don't think it had been updated since the '50s. The neon sign showed a ball rolling toward a tower of pins and striking. Sawyer was wedged in, so Georgina jumped out of the car to go in with me. From the lobby we could smell the rental shoes, lane wax, and Ellio's frozen pizza cooking in the oven.

There was a sign by the register that said NO OPEN BOWLING. The lanes were all reserved for leagues until midnight. I asked the guy working the shoe rentals if he could page someone for us.

"Would Ginny Frank-ow-ski, please come to the shoe rental desk. Ginny Frank-ow-ski."

I drummed my fingers on the desk while scanning for Aunt Ginny. "Do you see her?"

Georgina answered, "Not yet."

A hefty older black woman wearing a bright yellow bowling shirt shuffled up to the desk. "Poppy? I thought that was you."

"Mother Gibson." I let out a sigh of relief. "Is Aunt Ginny here with you?"

"No, child. I'm here with my church's senior league,

Livin' on Spare Time." She showed me the team logo on the back of her shirt. "We're playing the Bowl Movements tonight. I haven't seen Ginny. Is she lost?"

"Well, I don't know. She's missing." I started to tear up again.

"Do you think she could be out sleepwalking again?"

Georgina answered, "She isn't on that medicine anymore, and she's been gone all day."

Mother Gibson thought about that. "Well, that's not good, child. The police are gonna think this proves she's guilty."

"They already think that." Georgina swayed.

"Thank you, Mother Gibson, we're going to keep looking."

"Well now, hold on a minute. I'ma get my sweater and my smokes, and I'ma go with you."

She returned with her belongings and we went out to my car.

"Oh. I'm so sorry. I don't know what I was thinking. I already have a car full with the other ladies, and I don't have any more room, I'm afraid."

Mother Gibson looked around. "Come on. We'll take the church van. The team will be playing for a couple more hours and they won't even miss it." She opened the door and the keys were hanging in the ignition.

I tried to protest, but it was falling on deaf ears. These ladies knew what they wanted, and right now they all wanted to move over to the Brethren of the Guiding Light's blue church van.

I took the keys from Mother Gibson because I wanted to live long enough to rescue Aunt Ginny, and other than Sawyer I might have been the only driving candidate who didn't have cataracts and night blindness.

The ladies piled in. Georgina headed to the back so Sawyer could sit up front with me. Hellos and introductions went all around, followed by Mrs. Dodson's whiskey cookies.

Sawyer suggested we check the clubs since we were already in Wildwood. "Aunt Ginny likes dancing, doesn't she?"

"I know just the club to check too." I headed toward Caliente, a salsa club, and prayed that God wouldn't smite me for taking the church van someplace so seedy.

Tim called to tell me he didn't find Aunt Ginny at the hospital or any of the urgent care facilities. "No one has seen her all day. Where do you want me to go next?"

"I don't know. It's already past ten. Most places are closed now."

"You know what, I'll call some of the chefs I know to see if she was spotted in any of their restaurants tonight."

"Thanks, Tim. I'll talk to you soon." I clicked off the phone and caught up with the conversation in the back.

Mrs. Dodson and Mrs. Davis brought Mother Gibson up to speed with the investigation and the Hunt for Red Octogenarian. Sawyer and Georgina filled in any missing details.

Mother Gibson took out a cigarette. "I bet it was an inside job. You know, someone in that teenager center."

Mrs. Davis grabbed the cigarette and threw it out the window. "Don't you even think about lighting up in this van, Lila. These whiskey balls are ninety percent alcohol. If you light that match you could blow us to kingdom come."

Mother Gibson went on without skipping a beat. "What I can't figure out is why. What reason would those kids have for killing him?"

"Especially since he was the one supplying them with drugs," Mrs. Dodson said. "But you didn't hear that from me."

Mother Gibson went on. "I heard their teenager hangout was about to be shut down."

Sawyer turned around in her seat to better see the group of informants in the back. "Shut down? Why?"

"They were about to lose their funding because the director was caught in a compromising position with one of the girls."

Mrs. Davis chimed in. "I bet it was that Erika Lynch. I told you that girl was up to no good."

Mrs. Dodson tutted in judgment. "I hear tell his daughter won't have anything to do with him either. He abandoned her when she was a baby."

Georgina joined the biddies. "Well, who could blame her? Hit me with another of those whiskey balls, Edith. Poppy, are you doing okay up there? Do you need anything?"

"I'm hanging in." I put the van into park and opened my door. "We're at the salsa club. I'll go in and check for Aunt Ginny."

Mrs. Dodson flung her door open. "I'll come with you. I need to stretch my legs."

The club was bright and loud. A neon sign in the parking lot flashed a dancing margarita and promised that EVERY NIGHT IS LADIES NIGHT. A wave of laughter spilled out into the parking lot on the beat of the bongo drums.

The place was shoulder to shoulder at the bar, and a conga line was dancing around the room. I tried to spot my feisty little old lady in the crowd, but it was no use. There were too many people. It was Saturday night, and Saturday night at the shore was made for clubbing.

"Look, there, the conga line."

My eyes darted up and down the line of dancers. "Where? Is it Aunt Ginny?"

"No, but it's someone who might know where she is."

Mrs. Dodson trudged through the crowd, cane first, up to the front of the conga line. A tall, silver-haired man wearing tight black tuxedo pants and a red silk ruffled shirt open to the waist was the engine. It was none other than Mr. Shake Your Boom-Boom Ricardo, himself.

"Mr. Ricardo," Mrs. Dodson went on. "We are looking for a woman."

"Aren't we all?" Mr. Ricardo kicked his hip out. "Hey!"

I stepped in. "Mr. Ricardo, do you remember me? I'm Ginny Frankowski's niece?" We had to move backwards to the beat to keep facing him.

Mr. Ricardo kept leading the conga line while talking. "Ah yes, of course. How is Ginny? I keep telling her to run away with me. Hey!"

"Well, that's just it. We can't find her. We were hoping you might know where she is."

Mr. Ricardo stopped in his tracks and broke out of the conga line. They kept moving around the room without him. "Ginny is missing? My little red hen?"

Mrs. Dodson grabbed his hand. "Do you know where she is, man? We're running out of time."

"Are you sure she isn't sleepwalking again?"

Mrs. Dodson sighed. "She isn't on that medicine anymore, and she's been gone all day."

"Mr. Ricardo, we've been looking for well over an hour, and we still have no idea where she could be. Do you have any ideas?"

"I may have one. Come on."

Mr. Ricardo took me by the wrist and led me outside. "Where's your car?"

I took him to the church van, where he climbed over a couple of ladies and sat between Mrs. Davis and Georgina. He gave them each a big smile. "Hellooo, ladies. Do I smell whiskey?"

Mrs. Dodson pulled out her cookies and they did another round. Georgina giggled when they came to her.

"What is your idea, Mr. Ricardo?"

Mr. Ricardo had one arm around Mrs. Davis and one around Georgina. "About what?"

I felt the hopelessness rising up from deep within me. "For finding Aunt Ginny."

"Oh, right. Ginny and I often go to the Court House Diner after dancing. She loves their red velvet pancakes."

"Court House Diner. Okay." I put the van into drive and we were off again. Although I feared it was just another fruitless lap of a very long wild-goose chase.

Sawyer rubbed my shoulder. "We'll find her."

I looked in the rearview mirror. I was starting to suspect my occupants thought I was driving a party bus.

"Poppy, honey, do the police have any other suspects?" Mother Gibson called up from the back.

I glanced in the rearview mirror. "I don't know that they are looking for other suspects, but I know Mr. Brandt had trouble at work with one of his bosses, and the other one of his bosses had a jealous boyfriend who may have threatened him."

"Oooh, tell me more about that." Mrs. Davis crocheted another row on her blanket.

I filled them in about Judy and Ken, about the embezzlement charge and the charity angle. And about Kylie and her boyfriend, Frank Trippett.

"Wait," Mrs. Davis interrupted. "Frank Trippett who works as a mechanic?"

"Yes, do you know him?"

"I know of him. I know he used to be married to Helen Sheer's daughter, Olivia."

Mrs. Dodson groaned. "That scoundrel? I didn't know that was his name, but I've heard Helen talk about him often enough."

Sawyer turned in her seat to face the back of the van again. "What do you know about him, Mrs. Davis?"

"Well"—Mrs. Davis's crochet needles moved in time to her words—"I know he put Olivia in the hospital a few times. Once he broke three of her ribs because dinner was cold when he got home. She was finally able to divorce him, but she had to move out to the Midwest to keep him from finding her."

Mrs. Dodson added, "Helen gets twelve cards a year from the girl. One for every holiday in every month. Their whole life was turned upside-down by that wicked man."

Sawyer turned back to me. "If Frank Trippett was abusive to his first wife, he's probably abusive to Kylie."

"And if he's that violent," I said, "I bet he'd be capable of killing out of jealousy."

We pulled into the Court House Diner parking lot. I was about to go into the old-fashioned diner with its black-and-white checkered linoleum floor and table-top jukeboxes, when I saw a familiar pair walking toward the car next to us. I rolled down the window. "Mr. and Mrs. Sheinberg, what are you doing all the way out here?"

I hadn't seen them since I'd had to apologize for Aunt Ginny stealing Mrs. Sheinberg's rooster pot holder.

Mrs. Sheinberg was small and stooped from years of working hunched over in her family's Jewish bakery. She had beady black eyes that noticed everything. "Hiya, bubula, what's this you're doin'? You chaperoning an old-fogey field trip?" She snickered to herself.

Mr. Sheinberg was tanned and wrinkled, with a nose too big for his face and a fluffy tuft of white hair on the top of his head like he was always having a 1980s sort of hair day. He reminded me of a Silkie chicken. He looked in the window and saw Mr. Ricardo in the midst of the ladies. "Uh-oh. Rooster in the hen house!"

Mr. Ricardo replied, "Hey-yo!"

Mr. Sheinberg answered my earlier question. "Pancakes." He jutted his thumb at Mrs. Sheinberg. "This one loves the chocolate chip pancakes. She could eat a longshoreman under the table."

Mrs. Sheinberg smacked his arm. "He don't know. You here for the pancakes too?"

"No, I'm looking for Aunt Ginny. She's missing."

"Uh-oh." Mr. Sheinberg scrunched his mouth up. "She isn't on the lam, is she?"

"Are you sure she isn't sleepwalking again?" Mrs. Sheinberg asked.

To which the whole van said in unison, "She doesn't take that medicine anymore, and she's been gone all day."

Mrs. Sheinberg took a step back. "Oh. Okay. Not sleepwalking then."

Mr. Sheinberg pointed to the diner. "Well, she isn't in there, is she, pook?"

Mrs. Sheinberg shook her head. "Uh-uh. We'd a seen her if she was. And we were there, like, what?" She looked at Mr. Sheinberg.

"An hour."

"Yeah, an hour so . . ."

"All right, thank you. Drive safe going home."

"You too, bubula. Be careful with that band of meshugas you got there."

"I will, Mrs. Sheinberg, thank you."

I addressed my little troupe of helpers. "Well, I'm out of ideas. Where else do you think we should look?"

The van was silent for a minute. Then Mr. Ricardo asked, "Wait, who are we looking for?"

Mrs. Dodson leaned forward and informed him, "We are looking for Ginny, you old fool."

Sawyer and I shook our heads.

So I made a decision. "We should probably get the van back before the church people notice it's gone and report it stolen."

From the back of the van there came a chorus of *awws*. Then someone suggested we look for Aunt Ginny at the Chippendales-style male strip club, Sausage King. I couldn't prove it, but I was sure that suggestion came from Georgina, who was drinking her twelfth whiskey ball. Everyone vigorously agreed except Mr. Ricardo, who tried to make the point that those men weren't real dancers. To which Mrs. Davis asked, "Oh, do they dance too?"

I feared that I was losing control when I was saved by a call from Itty Bitty Smitty.

"She's home!"

"Thank God, are you sure?"

"Yep. She's right here. I stopped in just to check, thinking maybe she'd come back home, and there she was. Just sitting on the couch petting the cat."

I moved the phone away from my mouth and told the van, "Aunt Ginny is home!" A cheer went up. I told Smitty, "Don't call Amber yet, I'm on my way."

"You got it, boss. Nyuck-nyuck-nyuck."

I hung up the phone and put the van in drive. I was heading back to Wildwood to start unloading crazies.

"So, about that nudie club?" Mother Gibson wanted to know.

"I'm sorry, but I've got to get home to Aunt Ginny and find out what happened today. Plus there is this matter of the eyewitness to deal with."

Everyone was disappointed to have the evening cut short. Well, everyone who was liquored up on whiskey cookies, that is. I was so relieved I started to cry again.

"I tell you what," Sawyer suggested. "Let me take you and Georgina to get your car so you can get home. Then I'll drop everyone else off. I can get a ride home from the bowling alley."

"Who are you going to get to pick you up from Wildwood?"

"Don't you worry about that. I have someone."

I didn't have the emotional strength to disagree, so I let Sawyer return me and Georgina to the Senior Center. I got out of the van and Mrs. Davis said to me, "This was fun. We should do it again sometime."

Mrs. Dodson added, "Only maybe the next time without the missing person or murder investigations."

Everyone agreed that that would be best.

Georgina stumbled over to the wrong car and tried to open the passenger door. "I shink ish locked."

I held my key up and hit the lock button so my car chirped from two doors down.

Georgina tried to get in again. "Noishnot working."

I chirped the lock again. "Try it now."

Georgina tried pulling the door harder.

I laughed and let out some of the tension I'd been carrying. I was so relieved that Aunt Ginny was alive and safe. I had to catch my breath and calm my emotions. Because now that I wasn't afraid anymore, I was going to go home and kill her myself.

Chapter 40

"Atlantic City!"

Aunt Ginny paused in her petting of Figaro when she realized the tone of my voice was not casual.

"What is wrong with you?! Do you have any idea how much trouble you're in?"

"What?" Aunt Ginny shrugged. "What's the big deal? I saw the senior bus trip to the casinos listed in the *Shoppee*. It sounded like fun. I was back by midnight."

I paced back and forth in front of the little redhead-now-purple-head, who was dressed in a silver sequined tank top that had a dirty word monogrammed in velvet on the front.

"And why are you wearing a shirt with that word on it?"

"When I bought it, I thought it said *slots*."

Smitty and Georgina sat on the sofa behind me, silent, watching.

"Do you know how bad you had me worried? How could you pull something like this? What were you thinking? You couldn't leave a note?"

"Do you want me to answer any of these questions?"

"No! I thought you were kidnapped by Brody Brandt's killer. Or lying dead in a ditch somewhere. And Amber. Oh! Don't get me started about Amber. She's on her way over here right now. She told you to come down to the police station today before eight. How could you blow her off like that?"

"I didn't feel like going."

"Well, you're going now, missy. And there's not a thing I can do to stop it. What do you have to say for yourself?"

"I saw a Barbra Streisand impersonator who was fabulous. You'd never guess it was a man."

I was speechless. After all I'd been through over the past few hours and this was the best answer she could come up with. Blue flashing lights peppered the front-room curtains. Thankfully, the sirens were silent.

Georgina let Amber in while I glared menacingly at Aunt Ginny sitting in the armchair calmly petting Figaro. "Pleash come in, Offisher Fenton."

Amber was wearing plain clothes and her blond hair was hanging past her shoulders, out of her usual austere bun. "I'm officially off duty, but I told dispatch to call me when Mrs. Frankowski returned. I wanted to take her in personally." Amber addressed Aunt Ginny directly. "I heard you had yourself a little excursion today."

Aunt Ginny shrugged. "I guess so."

Amber spoke in calm tones like she was addressing a jumper. "Didn't I tell you to come down to the station by eight p.m.? It's now after midnight. What's your excuse for that?"

"Caesars Palace had all-you-can-eat crab legs for $1.99."

Smitty and Georgina groaned from behind me.

Amber shook her head and took a pair of handcuffs from her back pocket. "All right, Mrs. Frankowski. Let's get this over with."

I was still furious, but I didn't want to see Aunt Ginny led out like a common perp on TV. "Do you have to put those on her?"

"She's proven that she's a flight risk. Come to the station first thing in the morning and I'll let you know where we stand."

Amber led Aunt Ginny out the door and into the back of her waiting cruiser.

Aunt Ginny's eyes never left mine as they pulled away. My heart broke for the second time today.

Chapter 41

"How could you arrest her? When we were in the fifth grade, before you got too good for me, you came to my slumber party, and she stayed up with us all night telling us ghost stories and teaching us how to braid. That is the same woman you took out of my house last night in handcuffs. She may have used some bad judgment yesterday, but you know she didn't kill anyone."

Amber tapped a pen on her desk. "She didn't give me a choice. I gave her more latitude than I'm technically allowed. As far as the DA is concerned, if this eyewitness positively IDs her, they are ready to prosecute."

Another officer led a small, thin man out of the back room. He was well dressed in a slick purple suit with tightly tapered pants and a gray tie. The officer thanked the man and told him if they needed anything else they would contact him. The man was escorted to the door, then the officer came over to Amber and handed her a slip of paper.

"I'll be right back. Stay here."

Amber disappeared through the door to the back of the station with the other officer.

Stay here? Right. I shot out of my seat and ran after the man who had just left the building.

"Excuse me, sir."

He stopped and turned around. "Yes? I thought I was free to go."

I took him by the arm of his purple jacket and led him to the side of the building, away from the front door. "I just have one more question for you. You were the eyewitness that was brought in to identify the old lady accused of murder, right?"

"I thought that was supposed to be confidential."

"It is. I'm the police stenographer, I was listening in over the intercom and my uh . . . recording machine broke down during the lineup."

"Really. I didn't know it was being recorded."

"We do it all the time for our records. So the officers can refer to it later to make their case. Standard operating procedure. You know."

"If I had known I would have enunciated better."

"You were perfect."

He blushed. "Well, what do you need me to do? Do I need to come in again?"

"No. I just need to go over your testimony with you to be sure I got it all right." I pulled out a little steno pad from my purse and flipped to the page that had my grocery list. "Can you please repeat exactly what you saw the night of the murder?"

"Like I said, it was about two a.m. I was out walking my bichon, Marmalade. She gets an upset tummy. Too much stress from living with Mother. We're getting our own place soon."

Coffee, strawberries, coconut oil. "Okay, so far I have what you said."

"I was walking past Mr. Brandt's house and I saw an old woman come out of his door holding a rolling pin covered in what I thought at the time was pie filling. FYI—not. Eww."

"What made you think it was an old woman?"

"Because she was small and hunched over. And she shuffled when she walked, like she was used to a walker." He hunched himself over and shuffled in a circle.

"And what was she wearing?"

"Don't you have this written down?" He peered over the edge of my steno book.

"Yes." I held my notebook closer to my chest to keep him from seeing the words *chocolate chips.* "I need to hear it from you to confirm it."

"Okay, she was wearing a magenta track suit, the silky nylon kind from the nineties. And her hair was bright red. I noticed because someone with that color hair has no business wearing bright pink, you know what I mean?"

I nodded. "How was her hair styled? Were you able to see it?"

"A typical old lady 'do, done up like a swirl on her head. You know, B-52's 'Love Shack' style."

"And what shade of red? Did it look like mine?"

"No, it was much lighter with a touch of pink." He held his hand to the side of his mouth and leaned in. "Somebody's been to Vo-Tech."

"Did you ever see her face?"

"Nope."

"By any chance, was she eating?"

"How would I know? I just saw her shuffle out of the house and look around."

"Did you see which way she went after that?"

"Sorry, no. Marmalade did her poo-poos and I was busy cleaning it up when the lady disappeared."

"Then where did you go?"

He put his hand on his chest. "Marmalade and I went home."

"Which way do you live?"

"I live down the street toward Decatur, two blocks from the beach."

Okay, that's toward our house. "And when you took Marmalade home, you never saw the lady on the other side of the street or in front of you."

He took a step back. "Well, no. My gosh, you know, I didn't."

"So she couldn't have walked down the road toward your house?"

"You're right. She had to have gone toward the beach or I would have seen her."

I'm sure the ocean would make a perfect place to wash off a murder weapon. "Thank you."

"No, thank *you*. I'm so glad you asked me that. It's amazing the things you can remember." He gave himself a little hug. "Don't forget to call me if you need anything else. Especially if the trial is going to be on TV and you want me and Marmalade to testify."

"We'll let you know."

I watched him get in his orange Prius and pull out of the lot. He gave me a little finger wave as he drove off.

So, either Amber's star witness was a big fat liar itching to start a reality show career, or someone put on a vintage track suit and a wig to impersonate a certain little old lady and frame her for murder. That would rule out both Ken Freeman and Jonathan Lynch. Unless of course the impersonator was an accomplice to the killer. Hmm, that's a thought.

"McAllister, are you back there?"

"Ahhh, yeah. I was just getting some air." I stuffed my notebook back into my purse and rushed toward the front of the police station before Amber came back to find me.

Amber was on the front steps of the police station with her arms crossed and her police sunglasses hiding her eyes. Aunt Ginny was not with her. "I need you to be calm. There's been a development."

Chapter 42

"If you go outside of your permitted zone you will set off the alarm." Amber snapped the band in place on Aunt Ginny's ankle and locked it. "I had to call in a few favors to get your confinement moved from a holding cell to your house, so don't let me down and run off again."

We were in the front parlor, where Amber was fitting Aunt Ginny with a tracking monitor. Figaro was sniffing the black plastic band tentatively. He gave the red flashing light a swipe with his paw. Amber reached down to pet him on the top of his head, and he recoiled like she was poisonous, which made Aunt Ginny snicker under her breath.

Amber's police radio crackled to life. She turned her head and clicked the button to speak. "Affirmative, front room to the left."

A team of officers strode into the house. The one at the front handed Amber an official document. She looked it over and handed it to me.

"You've seen one of these before, it's a warrant giving us access to search the premises." Amber motioned for the officers to get started.

"Just so I'm clear," I asked, "what are the charges?"

"She's being placed on house arrest pending her trial. I hear the DA is pushing for involuntary manslaughter. All you can do now is pray that some evidence surfaces that points away from her."

"I appreciate the captain's latitude with us, Amber."

Amber stood and checked the monitor's tracking app on her phone. "Don't think for a minute it was a personal favor to you. I was able to pull some strings citing her age and health concerns."

Aunt Ginny grunted and looked away.

"But you're in charge of making sure that she stays put until her trial. If she runs off again, I'll have to keep her in county lockup." Amber looked at Aunt Ginny. "And no one wants that, Mrs. Frankowski."

Aunt Ginny shook her foot to see what would happen. "How am I supposed to take a bath with this thing on my leg?"

"It can get wet, it's waterproof. You just can't leave your allowed zone."

"And what is my allowed zone?"

"About three thousand feet. Roughly the size of your yard."

Aunt Ginny looked at her anklet and frowned.

Thirty minutes later, the search team came back through the house, finishing their quest. They left with a couple of rolling pins, including my brand-new French one I'd just bought from the chef supply store with Tim. They also had a couple of thick wooden rods, followed by Georgina protesting.

"Hey, those are my custom-made cedar boot trees. They cost me a small fortune."

Amber made some notes in her flip book and snapped it shut. "I'm done here. If anything new turns up, call me. Remember to stay in your zone, Mrs. Frankowski."

Amber went to the front door and took one last look into the parlor at Aunt Ginny sitting placidly on the love seat, shaking her foot. Then she said to me, "You do a terrible job of keeping her safe."

"It's not my fault. Containing her is like wrestling a baby cheetah. Before you can blink an eye she's into something else."

Amber's mouth twitched. She cleared her throat and put on her sunglasses, then turned and walked out the front door.

I went back to the parlor with Aunt Ginny. We stared at each other for a minute. We both sighed.

Aunt Ginny stood and stretched. "I'm going to go take a little nap. The cot in the jail cell left a lot to be desired in the way of comfort. I didn't get a wink all night."

"Okay. If you need anything, just holler."

"I will." Figaro the traitor trotted off after her.

Amber is right, as much as I hate admitting it to myself. I have to do a better job protecting Aunt Ginny. I don't know how much time she has left. I want her to have fun, but I don't want to see her get hurt. I have to figure out who really killed Brody Brandt before Aunt Ginny gets convicted for it, and time is quickly running out.

My cell phone rang. It was Amber.

"McAllister, what is your aunt doing?! I haven't even gone around the block yet!"

"She's taking a nap."

"Really? Do you have her in your sights?"

"Well, no, I . . ."

"She is setting off her anklet. Go see what she's doing now!"

I hurried down the hall, through the kitchen to Aunt Ginny's bedroom. "I don't see how that's possible." I flung open the bedroom door. Aunt Ginny was sitting in the middle of her bed with a screwdriver, an ice pick, a pair of pliers, and a meat tenderizer mallet, trying to pry the lock on her tracking anklet.

"Aunt Ginny!"

"What?"

"Knock it off! You're setting off your alarm!"

Aunt Ginny threw down the screwdriver and flung herself onto her back on the bed. "Argh!"

I tried to calm my voice on the phone. "False alarm, everything is fine. Nothing to worry about here."

"Make sure it stays that way!" *Click.*

I looked back at Aunt Ginny drilling holes in her ceiling with her eyes. I could hear the gears moving in her head, concocting another plan. "Look, Lindsay Lohan, you leave that anklet alone or they're gonna haul you out of here. County jail doesn't have the Game Show Network—I would know."

Aunt Ginny flung herself on her side away from me.

I was afraid to leave the house, so over the course of the next few hours I made phone calls, and checked on Aunt Ginny. I called Gia and my midnight posse who had helped me search for her, and told them Aunt Ginny was officially charged and under house arrest.

Then I checked on Aunt Ginny, who was in the corner of the yard playing the hokeypokey and sticking her foot through the fence, trying to see how far she could go before she would activate her anklet.

Then I addressed the police who showed up because her alarm was going off.

So apparently her range was about two feet from the edge of the neighbor's yard. On all sides. Which I now knew because she pulled the same stunt three more times. Once when she was "in the potty," once when she was "doing laundry," and once when she was "watching TV" and I was in the bathroom.

"Why are you doing this?"

"Research."

"What kind of research?"

"They're getting slower."

"Are you testing police response times?"

"I can't answer that."

"Why not?"

"It's called plausible de-ni-a-bility."

"I'm exhausted. Could you just give it a rest, for God's sake?"

Aunt Ginny looked contrite. She sighed. "I'm sorry. I know I've put you through a lot over the past couple of days. Why don't I make us some coffee and we can go over the plan my lawyer sent over?"

"That would be good. Thank you."

Aunt Ginny went to make us some coffee, and I called Tim.

"Hey, gorgeous, what's happening?"

"I just wanted to thank you again for last night. I don't know what I would have done without your help in checking the hospitals and urgent care facilities for me."

"Of course. I'll always be there for you, you know that. What happened with Aunt Ginny after Amber took her in?"

"She's been formally charged with murder."

He sighed. "I was afraid it would come to that."

"I still think she's innocent."

"I think you need to face the facts, Mack. She may not be."

I was angrily defending her honor when there was a knock at the door. A police officer had Aunt Ginny by the arm. She was wearing a wet suit and a baseball hat, and carrying a croquet mallet.

"What the . . . ? Tim, I gotta go."

"We pulled her over at the end of the street, ma'am."

"What are you doing?"

Aunt Ginny rolled her shoulders back. "I was going to the community center pool to play water polo."

I was dumbfounded. "You can't. Why would you . . ."

Aunt Ginny lifted her foot up. "She said it was water-proof."

"She also said you can't leave the yard."

Aunt Ginny stormed back to her room. "You never let me have any fun!"

I apologized to the officers and promised to try to do better. They didn't seem to believe me, and a patrol car sat in front of my house for the remainder of the day.

Georgina stayed blissfully out of the way most of the day. I suspected a cookie hangover.

Figaro followed Aunt Ginny back and forth, fascinated. He knew something was up, he could feel it in the energy riding on the air. He liked this new show and didn't want to miss an episode.

Meanwhile, Aunt Ginny fidgeted and whined. She paced the floor and complained. "I'm old. I could die any day now."

"You won't."

"I shouldn't be locked up like this. I'm not an animal."

"It's temporary."

"I-I can't breathe. My chest is getting tight . . ."

"No, it isn't. Sit down."

Aunt Ginny flopped in her easy chair in front of the television. She pouted for a couple of minutes, regrouping. "I'll give you a hundred dollars if you let me go to the movies."

"Show me the hundred."

"Gah!"

There was a knock at the front door. I looked at Aunt Ginny.

"What? It isn't me this time. I'm right here."

I stood to get the door, then stopped. I turned back to Aunt Ginny, who had leaned forward in her chair to get up. She was hovering over the seat trying to look nonchalant. "What?"

"Come with me."

"I don't wanna."

"Do it anyway. I don't trust you by yourself."

I took her hand and together we walked to the front door. It was Sawyer, and she'd brought the old biddies with her. Sawyer enveloped Aunt Ginny in a hug. "I'm so sorry. I heard about the house arrest, and I thought you could use some company tonight to support you."

Aunt Ginny teared up. I teared up. Sawyer sobbed. Then the old biddies came in and wanted to see the anklet.

The rest of the night passed a little easier, thanks to the distraction that Sawyer provided, and the peach schnapps that Mrs. Dodson brought in her bingo bag. Georgina heard her new best friends were in the house and bearing gifts, so she pulled herself away from her room to join the party.

It was almost one a.m. before the ladies wore down. Sawyer and I could barely keep our eyes open, but Aunt Ginny and "the girls" were playing their fifth round of rummy.

"Sawyer, thank you. You saved me tonight."

Sawyer waved her hand. "It was nothing. I can't imagine what you're going through. Is there anything else I can do?"

"Well, I have to get some work done tomorrow morning and I can't take my eyes off of her for a minute. Could you come babysit for a while?"

"Sure. I have someone in the bookstore who can cover for me tomorrow morning. Piece of cake."

"You know she's going to try to get over on you and sneak out."

"She'll be fine. Aunt Ginny loves me. She won't give me any trouble."

I smiled and nodded. "Sure, let's go with that."

Chapter 43

The next morning, I let a bleary-eyed Sawyer in to help keep an eye on the Gangsta Granny.

"How'd it go last night?"

I sighed. "The schnapps helped. She didn't try to escape until around five a.m."

"Is that why there's an Officer Birkwell in front of the mailbox?"

"He had the pleasure of frisking her, to fish her spare car keys out of her bloomers this morning."

"That explains his sour mood."

Sawyer and I had coffee and blueberry streusel bars made with cassava flour for breakfast, while Aunt Ginny was still in bed—I hoped.

Smitty came through the kitchen whistling a tune, and grabbed one of the Paleo pastries.

"Where is my range, Smitty? I've been nuking stuff from the coffee shop for almost two weeks."

Smitty poured himself a cup of coffee and groaned. "I'll call again this morning. The last I heard it was in Sheboygan."

I put my cup down hard on the table and gave Smitty a look.

He gave me a lopsided frown. "Paperwork error—theirs! Not mine."

"Please see what you can do."

Smitty saluted. "You got it, boss." Then he peeked out onto the side porch for Georgina.

"You don't have to worry. The Queen has taken a spa day. Said she was stressed out and needed some pampering."

Smitty gave me a deadpan look. "I don't know what we will do without her today." He left to enjoy his morning and look as though he was working hard while accomplishing very little.

I asked Sawyer a question that had been on my mind for several days. "What's been going on with you?"

Sawyer shifted uncomfortably in her seat. "What do you mean?"

"Well, I hardly see you unless there's an emergency. Granted there have been a lot of emergencies lately."

Sawyer shrugged. "I've been around."

"Are you mad at me?"

"What? No! Don't be ridiculous."

"You rarely answer your phone."

"It's not you . . . it's . . . I've been busy."

I waited for her to go on.

"I don't want you to judge me."

"When do I ever judge you?"

"Well, you don't. But you might."

"I promise to try to keep my opinion to myself."

Sawyer didn't look convinced. "I'm not ready to talk about it yet, but maybe soon."

Aunt Ginny slogged in from her bedroom. "Mornin' Thelma, Louise. What commotion are you cookin' up this dismal day?"

Sawyer beamed her a big smile. "I'm here to keep you company this morning."

Aunt Ginny grinned much like the Grinch when he planned to ruin Christmas. "Today is looking up after all."

"Behave yourself, Aunt Ginny. I have to go make some muffins at the restaurant this morning."

"I always behave myself."

Sawyer choked on her blueberry bar.

"Uh-huh. Well, behave like someone else then. Someone old who likes to sit around all day and knit."

Aunt Ginny waved her hand at me. "Pssshhh."

I checked the time on my phone. "Okay, I've got to get my day started. You two have fun. Or rather, Sawyer, have fun. Aunt Ginny, nap a lot."

I heard Sawyer trying to make plans for inside activities like puzzles and board games with Aunt Ginny as I headed up the stairs to my room. I did my yoga. At least I tried. I was under so much stress that I was a lot tighter than usual, so I couldn't quite get the positions right. I took my shower and got ready for my day. As I was hanging up my clothes, the envelope Judy had given me two days ago fell out of my blouse.

I had forgotten all about that, with the search for Aunt Ginny and the arrest and all. I opened the clasp and removed the documents and the flash drive.

The folder contained printed sheets with a Post-it note stuck to the top page that said *I know!* The pages were account transactions with Brody listed as the broker.

They were all moderate debits, from $5,000 to $10,000. The combined total was $100,000. All debits from different client accounts over the course of three months, but they were all deposited into the same account for

Wit'sec Industries. The last transaction was dated a week before Brody was murdered. I googled Wit'sec Industries. It didn't exist. The only thing that came up was the federal government's Witness Protection Program.

My phone rang. It was Officer Amber. "Her alarm is going off, McAllister!"

I hollered downstairs, "Sawyer!"

Sawyer hollered from the kitchen, "Aunt Ginny!"

Aunt Ginny hollered from the yard outside my window, "Fine!"

Then there was the sound of doors slamming and feet stomping.

"Sorry, Amber."

She hung up.

"Well, goodbye to you too." *Whatever.*

I plugged the flash drive into my laptop. There were two files. One was a backup file from the server, and the other was titled Screenshots. I tried to open the backup file but I didn't have the software installed to run it, so I clicked on the Screenshots folder. Inside were pictures of the same printouts I had before me. Only instead of Brody's name listed as the initiating broker, Kylie's was recorded. The file was dated three weeks earlier than the hard copies, and the file path on the screen showed that the pictures were taken from the backup logs.

When John was alive, I did some part-time work for his law firm. Mostly receptionist and admin duties. It was part of my job to run the backups on the server every night. Once I clicked on an innocent link while doing completely work-related tasks. Okay fine, I was buying a pair of shoes. The link hid a virus and it brought our entire network down. The IT department had to restore all our data from the backup tapes.

Judging from the dates on these printouts, I'd say

Kylie made these transactions, and later changed the name in the file to implicate Brody. Only she never cleared out the backup files from the server. Brody must have discovered what was going on and found the proof that he was innocent. But why would he sit on it? Why tape it to the bottom of his desk instead of going to Ken and saying *Look what I found*?

I picked up the papers again and flipped through them. They weren't all ledger sheets. The last page was from the Teen Center. It was a student file for M. Huber. M. Huber enrolled in the Teen Center program last January and graduated with forty hours of community service in April. What is so special about that? Maybe this was sitting on Brody's desk and he accidentally scooped it up with the ledger printouts. I know I've done that. You lose your personal property tax bill and later find it in the folder with your veterinary records.

I put the Teen Center document on top of the stack. I'd return it to Brenda when I saw her later. But now, I had to talk to Judy. I saved the information to my hard drive just in case I would need it later as part of Aunt Ginny's defense. Then I took out the flash drive and put all the items back in the folder while I called the office.

"Freeman and Furman, Judy speaking."

"Judy, it's Poppy."

Judy started whispering into the receiver. "Hi, did you look at the papers?"

I whispered back, "I did, and I think you're right. Something doesn't add up." *Why am I whispering?* "I think we need to show this to Ken. Could I come in this morning and—?"

Judy cut me off. "No way. You can't come back here. Ken was furious the other day. He said to call the police if you even step foot in the building."

"Well, that's not fair. What if I want a hoagie from the deli?"

"I suggest wearing a disguise."

"Then I guess I'll have to give you the papers and you can show them to Ken."

"What? Me? I don't know what I'm looking at. I only know that Brody had those papers to prove he didn't steal any money."

Ah, Judy, ever the optimist.

"I need you to do the talking, Poppy. We need to come up with a way to get you in front of Ken without him going berserk and poking your eyes out."

"Yes, that would be preferable."

"How about your boyfriend? Could he do it?"

"I can ask him."

"Good. I'll put an appointment for a Mr. Nesbitt down on the schedule for two o'clock this afternoon. That's right after Ken returns from lunch. He'll be in a better mood after he has his green smoothie."

"His what?"

"You know, spinach, kale, algae. That sort of thing. He drinks it every day."

"Eww. That must be why he's so angry all the time."

Judy laughed, then remembered she was supposed to be whispering. "Two o'clock. Remember, your boyfriend's name is Mr. Nesbitt."

"I'll tell him."

I was running late to Momma's for the baking, but I knew what I had here was important. If Kylie killed Brody to cover up her embezzlement, this could be the evidence that got the anklet off of Aunt Ginny.

Speaking of the resident convict, I wondered how things were going downstairs.

Sawyer was sitting in the library texting someone, and smiling to herself.

"Where's Aunt Ginny?"

"She said she was going to her room to knit."

"Knit?"

Sawyer's eyes grew big as revelation dawned on her. "Oh no. Not again."

Before we could rush around looking for her, there was a slow knock at the front door. It was Officer Birkwell with Aunt Ginny. Aunt Ginny was wearing overalls, Smitty's work boots, Georgina's hard hat, and dark glasses. She was covered head to toe in mud. Officer Birkwell had his hand on Aunt Ginny's shoulder and a very weary look on his face.

"What happened?" I asked.

Aunt Ginny replied, "I don't want to talk about it." She shrugged out of the officer's grasp and stormed off to her room.

When she was out of earshot, Officer Birkwell said, "I caught her army-crawling through the back garden while hiding under a laundry basket."

"I am so sorry. Can I make it up to you by bringing some fresh baked cookies home in a few hours?"

He gave me a weary smile. "I won't say no."

Chapter 44

I said a prayer, and against my better judgment left Sawyer in charge of Aunt Ginny. I called Tim from the car and asked if he could help me with Freeman and Furman this afternoon.

"Oh. I, ah, I can't today."

"Too busy with the bistro?"

"Um, no. I promised Gigi I'd go with her up to the Blue Claw to source out some crabs."

"Oh."

"Can we do it tomorrow?"

"I'm not sure it can wait, but don't worry about me. I'll figure something out."

"Are you sure?"

"Yeah . . . Yeah . . . It's fine."

"Okay, thanks, Mack. Let's have a date later in the week. You pick."

"Sure. I'll check my schedule."

Hmph, Gigi. I guess that's what it means to be just keeping it light. I'll bet Gigi isn't keeping it light.

Now what am I gonna do? I don't want to throw one of my girlfriends to Ken Freeman. He has killer *written all over him. That dude needs anger management classes like nobody's business. I should check with Father Brian to see if there's a meeting for that at St. Barnabas.*

No time to obsess. I had to get some work done today. I walked into the kitchen at Momma's. She was hand-rolling fresh pasta on a floured worktable. The bouquet of smells from the fresh basil and oregano she was rolling between the sheets of dough transported me back to one summer in Tuscany with John.

"Good morning, Mrs. Larusso."

She came up to me and spoke low and rambly in Italian. I'm not positive, but I think she was casting a spell.

I gave her a nervous hand pat to the shoulder. "I hope you're having a nice day."

She jumped like I'd used a Taser on her. She jabbed a stubby flour-encased finger at my clavicle and a white cloud wafted up from my shoulder. "Bah!"

"Okay. I'm gonna go make some cookies and coffee cake bars now."

Momma breathed like a bull getting ready to charge.

"All right then. I'm going." I backed away and over to the pastry station.

Momma went back to kneading dough like Chuck Norris.

Gia had left me a note pinned up on the Hobart.

Bella, come over as soon as you are finished. I have a big surprise for you. XXX.

XXX? As in super sexy XXX? Oooh. No wonder Momma gave me the evil eye. With my luck, she just put a hex on me to prevent Italian men from kissing me.

I got my ingredients sorted for a pan of crumb cake and a full sheet of butterscotch-oatmeal crumble bars. One recipe for breakfast, and one recipe for dessert. While I measured, and creamed, and folded, I wondered what Gia's surprise could be. He just gave me that beautiful custom-painted KitchenAid stand mixer. I hadn't even brought it home yet. I definitely didn't want to bring it in here to Momma's kitchen.

I glanced back at Momma and gave a timid smile. She growled something that sounded very similar to "*burstarici* into *flameos*." *Okay then.*

I was far too worried about Aunt Ginny trying to escape house arrest to allow myself to get upset by Gia's smother today. Yeah, I said smother.

If his surprise was XXX rated, well, I don't think I'm ready for that. I haven't dated in over twenty years. I hear that there is a lot of waxing that happens nowadays, and I don't want to scare anyone. Besides, all we've done is kiss a few times. Despite Tim's declaration of *Let's keep it loose and see other people*, I still felt weird kissing both men. I'd lived with the stigma of being a cheater for most of my life. And let me tell you, everyone judges a cheater. The entire country music genre is built on the shame of the cheatin' heart. Although the thought of Tim out with Gigi today was easing my pain a bit.

Ding ding ding.

Oh my God, it's Aunt Ginny's anklet. Oh no, wait. That's the timer. I took the pan of crumb cake out of the oven and set it on the rack to cool.

One of Momma's line cooks entered the kitchen. "What smells delicious? Is that cinnamon cake?"

Momma gave him her patented stink eye. "*Andarsane!*"

He didn't break stride, just pivoted and walked back out.

I got a text from Sawyer.

Where do you keep your Vaseline?

Why?

No reason.

Look in AGs medicine cabinet.

Got it.

I would find out what that was all about later, I supposed. I took the butterscotch-oatmeal bars out of the
oven, set them to cool on the rack, and cleaned up my
station.

Twenty minutes later, I was wrestling my conscience,
and my nerves, as I crossed the cobblestones to the
coffee shop. Gia was standing at the counter completely
naked, wearing only an apron. Okay, that didn't really
happen but a girl can dream, can't she?

Gia was waiting on two young women in painted-on
jeans who were shamelessly flirting with him. He
poured on the charm. I stood back and watched the
spectacle while dealing with a tidal wave of body envy.

One of the girls wanted to put her phone number in
Gia's cell. He apologized and said it wasn't with him. So
she dug through her bag for a pen. Coming up empty,
she turned and asked me for a pen.

I handed her mine. My eyes met Gia's and he gave
me a conspiratorial wink. The pretty little size two wrote
her number on Gia's hand, then handed the pen back
and said, "Thank you, ma'am."

I did my best old lady voice. "That's okay, dearie, just
drop the hickey in my bag. My arthritis is acting up som-
p'in fierce and I can't grip anythin' jus' now."

"Oh, okay, sure thing." She politely returned the pen
to my purse, oblivious to my sarcasm.

When they'd left, Gia shook his head and chuckled.
"Were you doing Aunt Ginny?"

"What'd ya think?"

"I think you're evil."

"So they say."

He locked the front door and turned the sign to CLOSED. "Come. I have a surprise for you in the kitchen."

I tried to swallow the lump in my throat, but it wouldn't budge. "You do?"

"Yes, and get ready, it's a big one."

I took a deep breath.

"I wanted to give it to you the other day, but it wasn't up yet."

Oh God.

He spun around and covered my eyes with one hand. With the other, he led me into the room. "Are you ready?"

"Ah . . . well, the thing is . . . Oh. It's a double oven."

It was a totally different kind of sexy from the one I thought I was being offered. Gia had installed a cobalt-blue forty-eight-inch Viking dual fuel range. "It's stunning."

I moved closer and rubbed my hands down the side. I checked out the ovens, and the proofing drawer. "It's beautiful. You're going to love having this."

Gia grinned. "Not me, *bella*, this is for you."

"For me? How?"

"Now you can do all the baking for the shop right here. You don't have to go to Momma's anymore."

I flung my arms around his neck and kissed him. "That may be the best news I've had in weeks."

Gia held me close. "You don't mind doing the baking here instead of your home? Until your own oven shows up. It should show up eventually, right?"

"I don't know, the last I heard it was stranded somewhere in the Midwest. Baking here will make deliveries much easier and I won't have to cart ingredients back and forth from my house."

Gia kissed me. "I'm so glad you like it. Karla said you would resent me trying to force you to be here every day."

"What's that now?"

He stuffed his hands in his pockets. "She, ah. She said if you wanted to be here more often you would be. That if I tried to trick you with this"—he pointed his elbow toward the oven—"that you would resent me pressuring you."

I tried not to smile. "Are you trying to trick me?"

He shrugged. "I wouldn't say trick."

"What would you say?"

"I would say I'm sweetening the deal."

I wondered how much of this was prompted by the admission that I had another man in my life. "I see. What if it didn't work? What if I didn't want to come in every day to bake?"

His eyes looked like a sad cow's. "That would be fine. I can't make you."

"Okay, now that's just pitiful."

Gia's face broke into a grin and he was back to his sexy old self. He pulled me close. "So, you don't mind?"

"I'm very excited to come here and bake every day for the near future."

"Good." Gia kissed me and I wrapped my arms around his neck. The kiss deepened and I forgot all about Aunt Ginny's attempts to pry off her anklet. "Do you want to stay awhile, and take the new oven out for her first spin?"

"I'd love to, but I have to find someone to help me with a covert operation."

"*Mia bella*, what are you getting into now?"

I pulled the folder out of my bag and showed Gia the printouts. He pulled out a pair of reading glasses and slid them on.

I thought it was impossible for him to get any more attractive, but I was wrong.

Gia smiled. "Go on."

I took a steadying breath. "The flash drive shows that

it was Kylie who actually moved the money, not Brody. The funds were deposited into what I think is a bogus account."

"What is *bogus*?"

I giggled. "It means fake. I don't think the company listed actually exists. I need to get someone to confront Ken Freeman and show him the backup files."

Gia paged through the ledgers. "How is this connected to Aunt Ginny's arrest?"

"Brody was accused of embezzling thousands of dollars of clients' money. He was fired for it, but he was murdered before the auditors could start an official investigation. I've been looking at Ken this whole time, thinking he might have killed Brody for damaging his firm's reputation of integrity, or even possibly out of anger that the Teen Center won the grant that Ken felt the animal shelter deserved."

Gia's head bobbed. "People have killed for less."

"And this guy has some serious anger issues. But here we clearly have files that implicate Kylie in the embezzlement. Now I'm wondering if I've been wrong about Ken all along. If Kylie was robbing clients, and framing Brody, she might have killed him to cover it up."

"Because the dead can't prove their innocence."

"Exactly."

Gia took off his glasses and put them away. He paced the length of the kitchen and back, thinking. "Is it possible that these people stole the money together, and killed Brody to cover it up?"

"An eyewitness did claim to have seen someone resembling Aunt Ginny coming out of the victim's house the night of the murder. It's possible that we're looking for a killer and an accomplice."

"So, what do you need me to do?"

"You're going to help me?"

Gia shrugged. "This is no problem. I'll call Karla to cover the shop."

I breathed a sigh of relief. "That would mean so much to me. This guy is seriously full of rage every time I see him. You need to be careful in there."

Gia flexed his pecs. "I've been working out."

Oh my, the room is spinning. I'm hearing music.

"*Bella. Bella.* Your phone is ringing."

"Oh . . . hello."

"McAllister!"

"I'm on my way." I clicked off. "I have to go to the escape room. Aunt Ginny is wreaking havoc with her anklet again."

"What is this escape room?"

"My house. Aunt Ginny has already beaten it several times. I'll explain when I come back to get you at one thirty."

"I'll be right here waiting for you."

I rushed home. Officer Birkwell was standing guard at the front door. His lips were set in a grim line. I handed him a bag of butterscotch-oatmeal bars as a peace offering. His shoulders heaved as he took a deep breath. "Thank you. Good luck in there."

I steeled myself for what was to come. Sawyer and Aunt Ginny were sitting side by side on the couch in terse silence. Sawyer gave me a strained smile. Figaro sat on the piano bench, his eyes alert and his whiskers twitching.

"Everything okay in here?"

They both answered me. "Yes, sure. Everything's fine."

"Why is Aunt Ginny covered in blue paint?"

Aunt Ginny wouldn't make eye contact. "I don't want to talk about it."

"Oh-kay."

Sawyer stood up and grabbed her purse. On her way past me she said, "I was wrong. You're a saint." And she shot out the door with a bang.

It looks like I would have to get Aunt Ginny a new babysitter for the afternoon shift, and I needed to find someone fast. My two o'clock meeting was rapidly approaching. If I was lucky, I could put an end to this whole mess this afternoon.

Chapter 45

"Thank you for coming on such short notice." Kim was one of my best friends from high school, and the most flamboyant and daring of our group.

She took off her military jacket revealing a Hello Kitty T-shirt over striped leggings. "It's no trouble. I wish I had known sooner what you were going through. I could have helped you look for Aunt Ginny. Rick works nights now, so I'm home all alone with the iguana."

I tilted my head in Aunt Ginny's direction. "She's been very difficult to control. Sawyer may not talk to me again for days."

Kim chuckled. "I'm sure we'll be fine. Isn't that right, Mrs. Frankowski?"

Aunt Ginny sat on the couch with her arms crossed. She scowled at Kim. "What's that going down your shoulder?"

"I just came from Island Tattoo. It's a cherry blossom branch and hummingbirds. Why are you covered in blue?"

"Paint grenade. What did you do to your hair?"

"Chameleon dye. It changes colors in the sunlight. I see you went with the purple."

"Vo-Tech."

Aunt Ginny and Kim gave each other an appraising chin nod.

"Okay, well, you two have fun." I took Kim aside and said, "Don't let her out of your sight. Whatever she says she is going to do, don't believe her."

Kim nodded. "Okay."

Aunt Ginny stuck her tongue out at me.

Down at the mailbox, Officer Birkwell was debriefing Officer Consuelos at the changing of the guard. I said goodbye for the night to the former, and apologized in advance to the latter. Then I headed back over to the Washington Street Mall to pick up my partner in crime.

"We'll take my car, *bella.*"

"Are you sure? Mine is right here."

Gia furrowed his eyebrows. "I am a man. The man drives the car for the lady."

I laughed. Then stopped. "Oh, you're not kidding."

"*Bella.* If you drive me around I will be *zimbello.*"

"What does that mean?"

"Everyone will laugh."

"Okay, vanity thy name is Giampaolo. Where is your car?"

Gia grinned. "Come with me."

He took me around the block to a pay lot. He gathered the key from the attendant and led me to the back, where his car was encased in a giant blue car-shaped sock. He pulled the sock off, revealing a gorgeous silver convertible.

"Wow. What is this?"

He gave me a look like I was either crazy or blind. "It's a Spider."

"A Spider?"

"*Sì*. Alfa Romeo Spider. From Italy." He wiggled his eyebrows.

I felt like James Bond on a secret mission in the passenger seat. I gave Gia directions, but failed to mention that we didn't need to break the sound barrier to get there on time. "You know the speed limit on the Parkway is sixty-five."

"That's just a suggestion."

"I'm not sure that it is."

Gia gave me a wink and sped up.

We arrived at Freeman and Furman about five minutes faster than mathematically possible. I tried to flatten down my Tina Turner hair, and I felt around to make sure all my parts were where they were supposed to be.

"You want me to do that?" Gia offered.

I giggled. "You just focus on what you are supposed to say to Ken Freeman."

"Okay, but if you change your mind . . ."

I handed him the Bluetooth earpiece, and we tested the connection on my phone. "I'm going to listen from the stairwell. Here is the folder with the flash drive and the documents."

Gia tapped the earpiece and gave me a thumbs-up.

We headed into the building, passing Madame Zolda. She was dressed in a blue caftan and turban. Several long necklaces made out of crystal beads were hanging around her neck and arms. She went around in a circle under the PSYCHIC READINGS wooden sign in the yard, lighting candles. Muttering in spooky tones, she reminded me of Ursula the sea witch taking the Little Mermaid's voice.

We made momentary eye contact, and she paused in

her ritual. An owl came out of nowhere and flew right into the wooden sign, knocking it to the ground. Her eyes flew at me. I pushed Gia on the back and we rushed into the building before she made a scene.

From my hiding spot in the stairwell, I heard Gia introduce himself to Judy as Mr. Nesbitt, here for his meeting.

Judy's voice came over the phone loud and clear. "Wow. *You're* Mr. Nesbitt?"

"That's right. *I'm* Mr. Nesbitt. Why are you circling me like this?"

"You're just. Wow. I gotta find out where Poppy hangs out."

"Is Mr. Freeman ready for me?"

"Oh, yeah. I'll take you into the conference room."

A moment of silence followed by Gia. "Don't you want to lead the way?"

"No, I'm going to follow you. It's just through that door over there. Lord have mercy."

I heard Gia let out a quiet chuckle to himself.

"Right in here, Mr. Nesbitt."

"Thank you." Then after a couple minutes, "Shouldn't you go tell Mr. Freeman I'm here?"

"Right. I should probably do that."

Gia whispered into the Bluetooth, "I thought she was going to sit in my lap for a minute."

I stifled a giggle.

"Hi. Ken Freeman. Nice to meet you."

"Likewise."

"Judy was a little vague about the reason for the appointment. Do you have some investments you want me to take over, or are you starting a new portfolio?"

"Actually, I'm here as part of a private investigation into the murder of your coworker Brody Brandt. I have something you need to see involving the charges of embezzlement."

I could hear the shuffling of papers. Then Ken's voice. "What is this?"

"These documents implicate Mr. Brandt as the agent moving the funds into this account. But we've done some digging, and we don't think this is a genuine account. We believe it is . . . bogus."

I smiled to myself at Gia's use of his new word.

"I absolutely agree," Ken said. "The only thing my investigator can find under Wit'sec is the Witness Protection Program. I think Brody set up a fake account and was funneling client investments to it."

"Have you followed the account number here to see where the money went?"

"I've tried, but it's tied to an offshore account for this Wit'sec Industries. I haven't been able to get any information on it at all. We need to get that money back to our clients. We have an umbrella policy that will cover our losses if we can't recover the funds, but my reputation will be ruined forever. My auditors have checked into Brody's U.S. accounts and they can't find a link or a trail anywhere."

Ken sounded truly distressed about his clients' money. Maybe he wasn't in on it with Kylie after all.

Gia continued. "That may be because of this. These are backup files dated three weeks before Mr. Brandt was killed."

Ken hollered, and I had to move the phone away from my ear. "Judy! Bring my laptop!"

There was a moment of silence while they waited for Judy. I was so busy concentrating on my phone that I never heard her sneak up behind me.

"You! This is all your fault!"

Madame Zolda grabbed my shoulder and jerked me around.

I covered the phone with my hand. "Shhhhh!"

She poked at me with a white crystal shard. "Why are you here?"

I whispered and cut my eyes toward Judy's desk in the office. "Please go away. This is important."

"You keep coming here and bringing your dark energy."

"Please leave me alone before someone hears you."

Madame Zolda raised her voice. "No! You have a black aura around you. You are the harbinger of death."

I tried to find the mute button on my phone but the psychic was shaking me. "Look, lady, I will talk to you in a minute, now please be quiet until I am finished here."

Madame Zolda's eyes rolled back in her head and she started to wave back and forth. "You will be cursed for what you have done to Madame Zolda."

"I haven't done anything!"

"Madame Zolda sees all. Destruction and misery will follow you all the days of your life."

"Okay, you're twenty years too late. Now, please, this is important."

"Everywhere you go, for the rest of your life, you will find nothing but death."

I rifled through my pockets. "I will give you twenty-two, twenty-seven dollars to go away."

Madame Zolda started screeching, "Yip yip yip yip yip!"

Ken Freeman flung open the door to the stairwell. "What the devil!"

Madame Zolda grabbed the twenty-seven dollars from my hand and took off down the stairs. "And you owe me a new sign, lady."

I hollered after her, "I don't control the owls."

Gia crossed his arms and leaned against the door-jamb. "Poppy is the one who discovered the truth for you, Mr. Freeman."

Ken glowered at me. "Well, come on then."

Chapter 46

I was force-marched to the conference room where Kylie had joined Ken and Gia. She was in tears, slunk down in an office chair. Her face was blotchy and her nose was running.

Ken placed his hands on the table and leaned down toward Kylie. "All I want to know is why. Why did you do this?"

"I'm sorry. I know it's no excuse, but I'm desperate." Kylie looked from Ken to Gia to me. "I have to get out of here before he kills me."

Ken asked, "Who?"

I answered for Kylie. "Frank Trippett, her boyfriend."

Kylie started crying harder. "You don't understand. He's violent. I never know who will come home at the end of the day. Sometimes he brings me roses, and other times . . . If dinner isn't to his liking, or he doesn't like my tone . . ."

"What happened the day he accused you and Brody of having an affair?" I asked.

Kylie wiped her nose on her sleeve. "In here, he made a scene. He threatened Brody to stay away from me. He punched a file cabinet and generally made a fool of himself. At home, he burned me with cigarettes and called me a whore." She lifted her blond hair to reveal a few round scars on the back of her neck.

Ken was ashen. "Why didn't you tell me what was going on?"

Kylie sobbed. "I'm ashamed."

Judy ran in from the hall with a box of tissues. She ran to Kylie and put an arm around her. "You aren't the one who should be ashamed. That monster is."

I wanted desperately to help Kylie, but I needed to clear Aunt Ginny first, so I had to bring the conversation back. "So you skimmed the money and framed Brody for it?"

Kylie's body shuddered with the anguish of one weighed down with utter hopelessness. "I didn't know it would be discovered so soon. I thought I'd be in Iceland before the auditors' review. By my absence you would have figured out that I was the one who borrowed the money from our clients. I was going to try to pay you back one day. I never meant for Brody to get fired."

"Did you kill Mr. Brandt to throw the auditors off?" Gia asked.

"What? No. I didn't kill anyone." She looked around the room. "I'm not a violent person. I just want to run away and hide. I never would have hurt Brody; he was my friend. I've been living with so much shame over what I've done to him, how I changed the records to blame him for the transfers. He tried to get me to leave Frank after that day. He even offered me five thousand dollars to help me make a fresh start."

"Why didn't you take it?" Gia asked.

Kylie shuddered. "If Frank ever found me, and found out another man had given me the money to get away, Brody and I would both be dead."

Gia and I looked at each other.

"Where was Frank the night Brody was killed?" I asked.

"At the bar with his friends. Like every other night. He told me you were looking into Brody's murder and if you asked, I was to say he was with me all night, or he would dislocate my shoulder again."

I winced. "Do you think Frank killed Brody?"

"I wouldn't doubt it. Frank has a violent temper, especially when he drinks, and he always drinks. I can't say for sure that he did it, but I can't say that he didn't either. All I know is that I was home alone when it happened."

Ken covered his face with his hands like he was trying to wash away the grief that sat before him. When he looked up he said, "Kylie, I really am sorry about this. I will do everything I can to help you. But if the insurance company or the auditors find out that I knew you stole that money and I didn't fire you, they'll put me away for insurance fraud."

Kylie sniffled. "I understand."

A police officer appeared in the doorway of the conference room. Kylie started to cry again. She was joined by Judy, who was crying with her now. After getting statements from all of us, the officer took Kylie into protective custody.

Only the three of us remained in the conference room. A heavy silence hung in the air.

Gia swiveled his chair toward Ken. "When did you call the police? We never left this room."

"One of the officers is on the board of directors at the animal shelter. I texted him and told him what was going on and asked him to send someone over." Ken pointed a finger at me. "That's why you wanted to see my humanitarian award, isn't it? You thought I killed Brody."

I answered him frankly. "I'm still not sure that you didn't."

Ken bristled. "What would make you think that?"

"Well, you thought he was stealing from you, didn't you?"

"Yes."

"You probably assumed that he was using the money for drugs."

Ken sat back in his chair and gave me a sideways look. "Why would I think that?"

"Because of his history with drug abuse."

Ken stared openmouthed.

Gia asked him, "You do know that he was an addict, don't you?"

Ken stammered, "Wh—I—it didn't come up on his background check. His record was clean. Are you sure?"

I nodded my head. "Yes, I'm positive."

"I wouldn't have hired him had I known. The auditors would never have allowed that."

"Then why do you have such a chip on your shoulder every time his name is brought up?" I asked.

Ken ran his fingers through his beard. "Because he lied to a lot of people."

"About what?"

Ken was avoiding eye contact. "I'm not at liberty to say."

"Why not? You can't hurt him now."

Ken shifted in his seat. "I found something. I can't tell you what it was, because I promised Brody I would never speak of it. He may be gone, but a lot of people could still be hurt if the information got out."

"Unless you know something about who killed him, you have my word that I won't tarnish his reputation."

"All I will tell you is this. A few months ago, a woman stormed into the office demanding to see Brody. He took her into the conference room, but we could all hear her screaming, *How could you do something like this! You are going to get us shut down. After everything we worked for, how could you jeopardize it like this?* She threatened to blow the whistle on him if he ever did whatever it was again. He pleaded with the lady to let it go. He said it was for the good of the Teen Center, and he promised it would never happen again.

"A couple of days later, we had the toner changed in the copier. The machine recalibrated and spit out the last ten pages that had been saved in its memory. I found a document with Brody's name on it, that he shouldn't have had. I knew it had influenced the humanitarian award committee, and I figured out that it was what that lady had been so upset about."

"What was on the document?"

"You'd have to ask the woman."

"When you say *woman*, do you mean a young girl who looked like she was skipping first period? Dirty blond hair?"

"No, this was a big gal, with spiky pink hair."

"Really? You're sure about that?"

Ken cocked an eyebrow. "That's not a look you easily forget."

Judy appeared and knocked on the open conference room door. "I'm so sorry to interrupt, Mr. Freeman, your four o'clock is here."

Ken promised that he would call *Gia* if he learned any new information that could help us find Brody's killer. I guess he was still holding a grudge against me about that cactus.

The Psychic Readings sign was still lying on the ground. The owl was dazed and wobbly. His foot was stuck in the center of the P in psychic.

I climbed into Gia's prized Spider for my breakneck ride home, and as I was snapping my seat belt into place, an eerie feeling drew my attention to my right. There, through a crack in the blinds of the first-floor office, a pair of piercing eyes watched me, unblinking. Like the eyes of God over Long Island. It sent a chill up my spine and gave me the oddest feeling. I never wanted to come here again.

Chapter 47

When I pulled up in front of the house, Officer Consuelos was nowhere to be seen. *That's strange. Maybe they pulled Aunt Ginny's detail because they caught the real killer and she's no longer on house arrest.*

I opened the door and Kim called out, "Did you find her?"

"Aw, not again!"

Kim was sitting on the couch in the sunroom, her face the shade of her pink Hello Kitty T-shirt.

"I may have underestimated your aunt's level of determination to break out of here."

"How long has she been gone?"

"Fifteen minutes, maybe. She said she was going to take an aspirin for a headache. The cat started to howl and roll around like it was hurt, so I was distracted trying to figure out what was wrong with it. The next thing I knew, Officer Consuelos came in and said her anklet was going off."

Figaro was standing guard in the hall outside the kitchen. He stretched and rubbed up against my legs.

"So, this time she used an accomplice."

Figaro froze.

"No Friskies treats for you, one week."

He blinked, and flopped over.

Kim paced back and forth across the hall from the sunroom to the kitchen and back. "I watched her very carefully. Didn't fall for any of the excuses. I kept her distracted with game shows. I don't know how she planned it all out."

"I think she's been running drills in her head for years in case something like this ever happened."

The front door swung open and Officer Consuelos had Aunt Ginny by the elbow. He was joined by another officer whom I hadn't seen before.

Aunt Ginny was wearing flippers and carrying a surfboard. She shrugged out of the officer's grasp and marched down the hall. "Commie pigs!"

"Where was she this time?"

Officer Consuelos finished making a note in his flip book. "She was at the end of the block trying to hitch-hike to Higbee Beach."

Kim chuckled. "That would explain why she didn't take her bathing suit."

Officer Consuelo's eyebrows shot into his police hat. "You know it's not a nude beach anymore. Not since 1999."

Kim smiled. "I'm willing to bet Aunt Ginny doesn't know that."

"I'm willing to bet she does, and doesn't care," I said. "She'd have been stripped down before you could call it in to the station."

"I can hear you!" Aunt Ginny hollered from down the hall. "This anklet didn't make me deaf."

Officer Consuelos responded on his police radio that the package was delivered, and resumed his post outside the front door.

Kim gathered her military jacket and her purse. "I hope you got some good information today."

"I didn't get a confession from the killer. Just another wild lead to run down."

"I'm sorry." Kim hugged me. "Call me if you need me again." Kim looked down at Figaro lying on his back, staring blankly at her with his tongue hanging out the side of his mouth. "But, you know, not for a couple of days, okay?"

I found Aunt Ginny in the kitchen. "How was your day?"

She gave me a dirty look. "The doctor's office called. I missed my follow-up appointment."

"What did you tell them?"

"That I was being held prisoner on house arrest, and wouldn't likely make it in anytime soon."

"I see."

Georgina breezed in smelling of lavender, peppermint, and cucumber.

"I feel like I'm a brand-new woman." Georgina spun in a circle.

"That would be great," I muttered under my breath.

Georgina put her Coach purse on the hall table and took her sunglasses off. "So what did you do today?"

"Same thing I do every day. Make some muffins. Question a perp. Get a hex put on me by a sheisty psychic."

Georgina blinked a couple of times. "Did you see the muffin man?"

"The muffin man?"

"Yes, the muffin man."

"Yes, I saw the muffin man. Who lives on Drury Lane?"

Georgina shook her head. "What are you talking about?"

"What are *you* talking about?"

Georgina put her hand up to her forehead. "I need

to go lie down. Eight hours of pampering undone by five minutes of conversation with you."

I giggled to myself. Georgina was too easy. I went into the kitchen to toss myself a quick salad. I wanted to go to the Teen Center in a couple of hours and ask Brenda about what Ken said today. She had to be the woman who blew up at Brody in his office. How many other large, spiky-pink-haired ladies could there be in Cape May? I had to hear her side of the story. I never suspected that Brenda could be the killer, but maybe I'd missed something big.

Aunt Ginny came from her bedroom. "I want to order a pizza."

"Okay, order a pizza."

"You don't mind?"

"Of course not. You're having a rough time right now. You get whatever you want."

"In that case, I'll get a side of garlic butter to go with it." Aunt Ginny picked up the receiver of her ancient phone on the wall.

"You know that anklet is butter-proof."

"Oh. Then never mind."

With her pizza ordered we sat together at the table. She looked tired. All her crafty ways were taking it out of her. "Why are you so hell-bent on escaping house arrest?"

"I don't have much time left and I don't want to spend it in a women's prison."

"I'm doing the best I can to find the real killer, I promise."

"I know that. But ever since Amber put this doohickey on my foot, I hear a clock ticking down the minutes of my freedom." Aunt Ginny started to tear up.

I moved to her side of the banquette and put my arm around her. "Even if you were to go to prison, I won't stop looking for ways to set you free. We had a good day today. Gia and I were able to cross Ken and Kylie off the suspect list. We had to add Brenda, and Frank Trippett just rocketed to the top, but I think it's still progress."

Aunt Ginny blew her nose in a hanky she pulled from inside her bra. "So, you spent the day with the sexy Italian. Good. That's also progress."

As if someone turned on a diva-alert beacon in the sky, Georgina pounced into the kitchen. "You what? I asked you if you were with the muffin man."

"Is that what you were talking about?"

"Poppy, you knew that's what I meant."

Aunt Ginny rolled her eyes. "Georgina, no one knows what the devil you're talking about half the time."

Georgina tapped her foot in time to my rising blood pressure. "You know how I feel about you spending so much time with other men, Poppy."

"Yes, and I also know that you're unreasonable and it's none of your business."

Aunt Ginny stiffened her spine. "Well, I'm thrilled that she's spending so much time with that lovely man. You would have her remain a widow for the rest of her life, Georgina, but I want her to be happily married again someday."

Georgina's hands flew up to her hips. Her face turned crimson. "Poppy has no business getting married again. She wasn't that great a wife the first time around. She can barely take care of herself."

In times like this, it's interesting to note that when I cross the threshold from irritated, to angry, to what I feel right now, I don't yell or scream. I get quieter. And I was very, very quiet. "What do you mean, I wasn't a good wife to John?"

Smitty walked into the kitchen, overheard the conversation, grunted, and made a quick retreat.

"First of all, you tricked him into marrying you by pretending to be pregnant. And you're bad with money. Never taking my advice on what to properly invest in. You make decisions on a whim, like this ridiculous inn you're trying to run here. You've sunk all of John's money into this place."

"Georgina, hear me now, because I won't ever be saying this to you again. I was pregnant. And I lost my baby. And if you ever bring my pregnancy into doubt again, it will be the last time we speak."

Georgina paled, but she remained silent.

Aunt Ginny stayed next to me, unmoving like a soldier at arms. I could feel the strength rolling off of her like the swell of the tide.

"And as to how I am with my money—and I do mean *my* money—not John's money. I built a life with my husband and we shared everything equally. When he died, the insurance money became mine. I never wanted to be in a position of collecting it, but here I am. How he ever let you put our assets in trust so you could dole them out to me based on your whims, I'll never understand."

Georgina's voice came out stiff and arrogant. "I'm only trying to help you, Poppy. You don't know how to take care of a house or bills."

"How do you know how I am with money? Who do you think paid the bills and ran our house for twenty years?"

Georgina stamped her foot and blew her breath out of her nose like a bull who just spied a red cape. "If John could hear you now, he would be so ashamed. Talking to your mother-in-law like this. Spending money, cavorting with strange men. You dishonor him."

Did you hear that sound? That was it. That was the sound of a camel's spine fracturing under the mountain of straw Georgina had been shoveling on me for years. As the fury skyrocketed through me, a tense calm descended, and my voice was just above a whisper. "You have no right. John isn't here. He's dead. And the only thing good about that is that you aren't my mother-in-law anymore. As far as I'm concerned, you're just a minority stake in a business agreement."

Georgina sucked in a lungful of air.

"I think it would be best if you gather your things and head home to Waterford. Tonight. I can't talk to you. I can't even look at you. I'll get a loan to pay you back your investment so we can be done here, once and for all."

Chapter 48

I needed to be anywhere but here. I felt like a pot of spaghetti boiling over. Georgina had stomped off to pack her bags, and I had the restless energy that needed a good punching bag.

Aunt Ginny patted my arm. "She's only lashing out because she's hurt."

"I thought you were on my side."

"I'm always on your side. It's just that Georgina said some very hurtful things, and I know that she upset you."

I opened the refrigerator and freezer, hoping a cake or some ice cream had magically materialized. "She's been saying hurtful things for twenty years. Why should now be any different?"

"I think she's insecure. Insecure people can be very ugly when they're trying to protect themselves."

"Protect herself from what? I didn't attack her."

Aunt Ginny handed me the peanut butter and a spoon. "Well, I don't know. But she feels threatened about something. I think in her own way she was trying to get your attention. Maybe her abrasiveness is a cry for help."

I shoveled a mound of peanut butter into my mouth. "Om arye somen nker ot onaday."

Aunt Ginny got herself a spoon. "You're right. Maybe it is a cry for someone to knock her out one of these days."

Smitty peeked into the kitchen with his hat in his hand. "I'm, ah, going to take her to a hotel and drop her off for the night."

"Whatever."

Smitty ducked his head and put his hat on.

The front door closed a couple minutes later, and I breathed a sigh of relief. I had to get control of myself. I needed to get my head back to the critical task at hand.

I called another dear friend from my youth—it looked like I was cashing in all my chips in one week—and asked Connie if she could keep an eye on Aunt Ginny while I ran an errand. She was gracious enough to leave her husband and two girls, and come over to help me out for a while.

Twenty minutes later, her husband, Mike, dropped her off, and I got hugs from him and the girls. "Thank you so much for coming, Connie."

"It's no problem. Mike's taking Sabrina to cheerleading practice at the high school and Emmilee has a lesson tonight, so he was already doing his rounds."

Emmilee came in with Connie to show me her new fluffy unicorn.

"Nice. What's his name?"

"It's a her, and her name is Poppy."

"You named her Poppy?"

"Yes, 'cause she's so fluffy."

Mike spun Emmilee around and nudged her toward the door. "Okay, that's enough. We got to get you a Happy Meal and drop Bean off. Say goodbye to Mommy."

"Bye, Mommy and Poppy."

Connie patted Emmi affectionately. "Bye, liddybit. Have fun at ballet."

Once we were alone, Connie hugged me hello. "I think she means because your hair is so fluffy and pretty."

"Uh-huh. I've had worse said about me in just the past hour, so it's all good."

I caught my friend up on the events over the past couple of weeks.

"I already know. Kim told me all about it this afternoon over coffee. I've been expecting your call."

"Whatever you do, don't give Aunt Ginny an inch. She'll be out the door and on her way to Reno faster than you can go pee."

Connie ran a hand through her pixie-cut brown hair. "I met Officer Consuelos on the way in. He warned me not to fall for any emergency cries for help over vermin."

"I believe he was burned by that excuse this afternoon."

"Don't worry. I came prepared. I have a secret weapon." Connie patted her leather tote bag. "Fingers crossed. You just go do what you need to do."

I thanked her and grabbed the bags of butterscotch-oatmeal crumble bars I'd made hours ago at Momma's—my farewell visit—oh happy day.

I rage-drove into the Villas. Good thing it was the off-season. Less chance of hitting a tourist trying to find the bay, to catch the sunset while struggling to ride a bicycle they hadn't dusted off in twenty years. And I was in a tourist-hitting mood.

I walked into the Teen Center with the bag of bars hanging from my hand. Three kids swarmed me and the bars evaporated like a sweater to a family of moths.

Brenda was poring over a stack of bills while drinking a Diet Coke. "I heard the stampede when you came in. How's it going?"

"It's good." I pulled a wrapped package out of my purse. "I saved you a bar."

She perked up at the news. "You're my hero."

"Hey, I found out something today that I wanted to run by you."

"Shoot."

"Brody's old boss told me that a woman showed up in his office one day and they had quite a knock-down, drag-out."

Brenda's face pinked up to match her hair. She took a gulp of her Diet Coke.

"Was that by any chance you?"

"Did Brody's boss hear what the fight was about?"

"He heard enough. He said the woman accused Brody of doing something underhanded that could put the Teen Center in jeopardy."

Brenda sighed. "What will you do with this information?"

"That depends. If it isn't related to the murder investigation, I'll keep it to myself."

Brenda held two hands up. "Okay. You got me. I went to Brody's office and ripped him a new one. I discovered something that could destroy everything we've worked for, and it could have sent him to jail."

"Oh God. What was it?"

"I'm embarrassed to say, and now that Brody's gone, I don't want to speak ill of the dead and ruin all the good he's done."

"I understand. Why don't you just tell me what you found."

"Brody had intake papers and community-service records for Michael Huber."

Oh right. I reached into my purse and pulled out the letter that had been stuck under Brody's desk with the financial records. I peeled off the Post-it that had the words *I know* scrawled on it. "This M. Huber?"

Brenda paled. "Where did you get that?"

"It was in some stuff Brody had at work. I thought it was filed there by accident."

Brenda came out of her little office and pulled me by the elbow down the hall. She took me into a storage closet full of cleaning supplies, toner cartridges, and computer paper, and shut the door behind us. She snatched the letter from me.

"Oh, jeez. I found this one day when I was cleaning out the files. I almost left it on Brody's desk so he would have to come to me to explain, but the more I stewed over it the angrier I got. So I drove over to his work to confront him. If anyone finds out about this, we'll be shut down. He's done a lot of good in the community. I would hate to see one mistake ruin all that."

I looked at the letter in her shaking hand. "I feel like I'm missing something. What does Michael Huber have to do with Brody being disgraced?"

"This is a page from Michael's file. It shows forty hours of community service that he worked off while he was part of the program. And it says that he successfully completed alcohol awareness classes."

"Right?"

"Michael never came here."

"What?"

"Brody took a 'donation' of fifteen thousand dollars and received a nod to the humanitarian award committee from the mayor in exchange for signing off on his son's community service records, saying that Michael attended the program, when he didn't."

"Why would Brody do that?"

"Our money had run out and we were about three days away from being shut down. Brody said that Mayor Huber approached him asking for help. He wanted his son to get private counseling instead of attending a twelve-step program."

"Counseling for what?"

"Alcohol abuse. The boy had been sentenced to forty hours of community service for an underage drunk-and-disorderly charge."

"I've never heard of that."

"He was at a high school party—parents out of town—lots of jocks, you know the sort. The neighbors called the police and they raided. The kids scattered, but Michael didn't get away fast enough."

"He was arrested."

"This was his first offense, and a minor one at that. But someone wanted to make an example of him. Probably because of this new transparency-in-politics movement started by Congressman Clark."

"Okay, so Michael was sent to the Teen Center in lieu of juvenile detention?"

"Only the mayor felt it was a family issue that should be handled at home. He said his son didn't have any addiction and he didn't want him mixing in with the kind of kids who come here."

Brenda rolled her eyes and I responded with a shared look of disdain.

"I gather that it's a crime to sign off on community service hours that don't happen?"

"It's a Class D felony. Brody could have been fined thousands of dollars—or worse, he could have gone to jail. And he knew better. He should never have gone along with something like this. If this had been discovered, the county would have pulled our funding, private donations would dry up, and the whole program could have been destroyed."

"So, Brody cheated to win the humanitarian award?"

"No. We won fairly. He committed fraud to get nominated. When I found this"—she shook the paper—"I blew a gasket."

"Who else knows about this?"

"Only the boy's father, Mayor Huber. And he has his own motivation to keep this under wraps."

"I would guess so. So only the mayor and Brody knew about this until you discovered the paperwork. Then you went to Freeman and Furman to confront him?"

Brenda slumped down on an upturned bucket. "He regretted making the deal with the mayor from the start. He wanted to help these kids so badly. The humanitarian award hadn't even been on our radar, so fifteen thousand dollars plus the possible award money was like winning the lottery. He said he was blinded by the thought of how many kids we could save."

"What did you-all spend the money on?"

"Rent, a lot of late utility payments, and the computer lab. The computers are monitored twenty-four hours a day. We hold classes teaching basic programming and network security. Although every time I walk in there they seem to be playing *World of Warcraft*."

A familiar boy in a hoodie opened the closet door and almost dropped the box he was carrying.

Brenda shot to her feet. "Holy schmagoly!"

"Uh, sorry."

"Emilio? Hi! You're back?" I asked.

"Yeah." A stunned Emilio put the box on the shelf and hugged me. "Thank you for what you and Father Brian did. The cops know the drugs were confiscated from a kid, but they don't know it was me. I'm in the clear. And now Brody don't look bad either."

Brenda folded Michael Huber's document into a tiny rectangle. "Well, I don't see any mouse in here. Let's head back to my desk up front."

Emilio picked up his box and took it with him.

Brenda walked down the hall trying to appear unconcerned, but she twisted the document in her hands. "Brody wanted Emilio to be brought back when he made things right, and now he has."

I guess two old ladies in a closet didn't seem out of the ordinary to Emilio. He chatted amiably about his late mentor. "Brody always said that no matter what you done, it's not too late to change. That's why he worked with screw-ups like me. He don't want to see us make the same mistakes he did. Now I'm volunteering here every day to work off the damage I done when I hit bottom and trashed the place."

"You've been given another chance," I said. "Don't waste it."

"I won't. I'm a week away from getting my thirty-day chip."

"Good for you."

Emilio grinned. He set the package down on Brenda's desk.

"So what's in the box?"

Emilio took out a bronze sculpture of a smiling man.

"Isn't that Erika's piece?"

"Yeah. Brody was going to place it in the trophy case to surprise her. He had a sign made special for it. Before there was all the drama. I found it stashed in the bottom of the activity-room closet."

I took the plaque in my hand. It was inscribed: "For Erika. You've always been like a daughter to me. You are capable of remarkable things. We are so proud of you. Reach for the stars."

"It's beautiful. So, Erika was like a daughter to him?"

Brenda took the statue in her hands. "We got word this morning that she's been offered a full scholarship to the New York Academy of Art. Brody and I had planned to throw a party to celebrate her achievements if she got in. I guess that's not going to happen now. Erika's dad won't even allow her on the parking lot."

"Why don't you let me try to talk to her one more time? I have to discuss something with her father anyway." *Like why he lied about being in Chicago.*

Emilio put the statue and the plaque back in the box and handed it to me. "That would be great if you could get her to agree to it. She can be really stubborn when she has a chip on her shoulder. I've been on the wrong side of that before."

Erika's story was starting to smell like the bay at low tide. I just had a feeling in my bones that she wasn't being entirely truthful. One thing that became clear over the past week was that even the nicest people are capable of heinous crimes when they're desperate.

I had no problem believing that a father could kill his daughter's molester. But, as messed up as it would be, what if Erika and Brody had been in a misguided relationship that ended badly? Could Erika have killed Brody in a jealous rage? Could she have convinced her father to kill Brody to defend her honor? I had to get back over to the Lynch house tomorrow. Maybe the plaque Brody had inscribed for Erika would encourage her to be more forthcoming with the details.

I returned home expecting a legion of police dealing with Aunt Ginny's latest Houdini act, but I was pleasantly surprised. Aunt Ginny and Connie were relaxing on the sofa in the sunroom, watching TV. There was a mostly empty bottle of bourbon on the coffee table next to two shot glasses.

Connie lit up when I entered the room. "There she is."

Followed by Aunt Ginny. "Hiya, Poppy Blossom. Did ya catch the killer yet?"

Aunt Ginny's cheeks were flushed and her eyes were glassy. "No, not yet. Still working on it. Whacha doin'?"

"Watching *Cops*. Connie made up the best game."

Connie grinned. "Secret weapon."

Aunt Ginny picked up a shot glass. "We drink every time a shirtless redneck is arrested or a perp says *That isn't mine.*"

Connie laughed. "We eat a handful of pretzels every time they let the police dog off its leash."

"Ooh, it's back on aaaand . . . shirtless redneck!" Connie poured a shot and they both took a drink.

God bless Connie.

"Do you need me to call you a taxi?"

Connie swayed to her feet. "No, Mike is on his way. I texted him when I heard you park. I hope tonight was a success."

"I don't know if *success* is the word I'd use. I seem to be running to the end of a lot of leads and I'm no further along than when I started."

Aunt Ginny hoorayed and took a shot.

Connie watched her with a smile on her face. "Well, keep trying. We're all pulling for you."

"While you're at it, send up a couple of prayers. Tomorrow I have to face off with a wife beater and let him know that he has no alibi."

Chapter 49

It was six o'clock in the morning and Figaro was pitching himself a hissy. He was standing on his hind legs looking out my bedroom window, growling and spitting for all he was worth. I pushed the curtain aside and saw nothing down in our yard. Fig started pacing like a caged lion. I grabbed my bathrobe. "All right. Let's go see what has you so worked up."

He led me down the front staircase to the front door, pausing every few yards to be sure I was following. Then he stood on his hind legs and swatted at the doorknob.

"Where was this level of ingenuity when I locked myself out last week?" I opened the door and Fig darted onto the porch. His fur stood up down the center of his back and his tail bristled like a bottle brush. Broken eggshells created a minefield all along the lavender-painted boards. Egg whites tracked slime trails like giant slugs, and congealed yolks were scattered like the house had chicken pox. Figaro tried to sniff at each one, his dainty paws making sure to avoid any unpleasantness.

I, however, trudged into the thick of it, slipping

only once on a slime trail. From the yard I had a better vantage of the vandalism, and it made matters much, much worse. In addition to the barrage of nature's AA bombs, someone had spray-painted *MURDERER* in bright red paint on the front of the porch steps.

Who would do this? Could it be Georgina, lashing out because I sent her away? Frank Trippett? He would surely know that Kylie was fired and arrested by now. Although egging the house really didn't seem his style. And how would he know Aunt Ginny had been arrested or that this is where we live? Emilio knows where we live. And he has vandalized before, but he really seemed like he was turning a corner and getting his life together again. Of course, someone else from the Teen Center could have tipped off Erika that I was coming to talk to her again. Those kids could text the Constitution in thirty seconds using just emojis.

I went back in the house to fetch my cell phone and call Smitty. I wanted him to know what he was in for with the porch. Smitty had just left me a voice mail that he was calling out sick today. *Well, that's just great.*

I quickly changed into some workout clothes and grabbed a mop, a bucket of water, and some sponges. I took some pictures of the carnage just in case I would be questioned later, and spent the better part of the morning scrubbing red paint and jumbo eggs off my newly painted, now freshly ruined, lilac porch slats.

Aunt Ginny poked her head out the front door around seven thirty. "What happened out here?"

"Just some kids playing pranks."

"I see Figaro is helping by chasing that butterfly."

"He is nothing if not vigilant."

"Well, I'm going back to bed."

"Is that code for I'm going to shimmy down the drainpipe and make a break for Tijuana?"

"No. I don't feel well. I think I have a touch of the flu."

"Is it the real flu or the Wild Turkey bourbon flu?"

Aunt Ginny waved her hand at me in dismissal and disappeared back into the house.

Once I got the porch finished and got myself cleaned up, I had to call in a babysitter for today. I called Sawyer, who didn't answer. Kim had an appointment. Connie had to work. I was out of options. And desperate. Aunt Ginny could easily escape from any one of the neighbors. She was far too sophisticated for the biddies. Only one name came to mind, and no way was I that desperate. Not after how she'd treated me in high school. *Come on now, Poppy. Didn't we learn our lesson here a few weeks ago? It's time to put the past behind us and give people another chance.*

You know how sometimes you have an idea that you know is a bad one, but you just can't think of a better one? You know this is going to blow up in your face, but you don't know how to stop it. I was having one of those ideas right now. And its name was Joanne Junk.

"Joanne? Hi."

"Who is this?"

"Um, it's Poppy McAllister." *Click.*

Redial. "Joanne, don't hang up." *Click.*

Sigh. Redial.

"What do you want!"

"I am in desperate need of a favor. Are you still working the dinner shift at Menz's?"

"Yeah, so what?"

"So, you don't need to go to work until this afternoon, right?"

"Where is this going, poo face?"

Poo face. Oh good. We've descended to first grade name-calling. "I need someone to come . . . house-sit for a few hours."

"House-sit? Why?"

Deep breath and dive in. "My Aunt Ginny is on house arrest, and I need someone to come sit with her to make sure she doesn't escape."

Silence. "Is this a trick?"

"No. I really need someone to stay here for the day."

"Why are you asking me? Why not one of your lesbian friends?"

I knew this was a mistake. "The girls, who are *not* lesbians, can't make it today. And I haven't lived back in Cape May but a few weeks, so I haven't really made any new friends yet."

"Well, that's not surprising. You can be really abrasive."

I blinked a couple of times and checked my pulse to see if that last comment had killed me. "So, what do you say? Just for a few hours?"

"Fine. Text me the address. And I expect to get paid by the hour."

"Fine. I'll see you soon."

God help me.

Fifteen minutes later, Joanne Junk showed up in a red pickup sporting a KEEP HONKING—I'M RELOADING bumper sticker. She was a big gal. Beefy from years of field hockey and beer in a can. She was wearing a Phillies T-shirt and XL gray sweatpants with the word *Juicy* written over the butt. She was carrying a brown paper grocery sack. "So, this is your place, huh?"

"Yes, or rather it's Aunt Ginny's. What's in the bag? You didn't need to bring lunch. You can help yourself to whatever you want here."

"It's not lunch, you idiot. It's my knitting."

"You knit?"

Joanne scrunched her eyes down and took on a mocking voice. "Yes, I knit. You got something to say about that?"

"No. There's just an irony here that I can't go into right now."

"Whatever. Let's get this over with."

I showed her around the house and introduced her to Officer Birkwell when he showed up for his morning punishment. I left my number and got the heck out of there before she could change her mind.

Now that I wasn't carting ingredients back and forth, I walked over to Gia's shop. He broke out into a big smile when I came in through the back door.

"Coffee first?" He winked.

"Coffee always." I slumped down on a bar stool. *He may as well learn now that I am not a morning person.*

He started to pull a shot to make my coconut almond latte. "So, do you have everything you need to do the baking here?"

"I'll have to bring my rack with me."

Gia's eyes traveled south from my mouth, and his eyebrows went up.

I felt my cheeks heat up. "My baker's rack. For cooling."

He clicked his tongue and shook his head in mock disappointment.

"Are you sure you want me baking here every day? I might get in your way."

Gia folded his arms across his chest and leaned against the counter, giving me an appraising look. "You still don't know?"

"Know what?"

Gia grinned and shook his head.

"Don't give me puzzles first thing in the morning. I can't think yet."

"Not yet, *bella*." He went back to frothing my milk.

"Not yet what?"

Gia gave me a wink. He placed the latte in front of me on the counter. "Now drink."

He didn't have to tell me that twice.

I spent the rest of the morning flirting, I mean baking. I made Gia two sets of muffins, two kinds of cookies, and a pan of brownies. I even had time to make Liz's gluten-free chocolate cake. It's amazing how much baking you can get done when you're not in a hostile work environment and someone keeps you in a constant supply of coffee.

"I never thought I would say this, but there is a point where I've had too much coffee, and I hit that mark an hour ago."

Gia laughed. "I sold a record number of muffins and brownies today. I think the smells coming from the kitchen are enticing people who only come in for coffee."

"That's good. I was hoping that would happen."

"Are you finished for the day?"

"Yes, I have to follow up on a lead I got from Kylie before she was arrested, so I'm revisiting Frank Trippett."

"Be careful, *bella*. I don't like the sound of this *teppista*."

I stifled a giggle. "And what exactly is a *tep-i-sta*?"

Gia thought for a moment, then took out his phone and typed something into it. "Is, how you say, *hood-lum*."

I put my hand on his arm. "Okay, I'll be careful of the hoodlum."

Gia grinned and grabbed my wrist. He pulled me tight against him and suffocated me with a bear hug and a kiss.

When he let me go and I turned around to pick up the cake, he swatted me on the rear. My jaw dropped and I jerked my head around to look at him. He had one eyebrow quirked and a smile that dared me to play-fight back. But I knew if I didn't get out of there fast the whole day would be spent fooling around. And I mean that literally.

I fast-walked home on my caffeine buzz to put the cake in the fridge before going to Gleason's Garage. I found Aunt Ginny in the front yard with Joanne. Aunt Ginny was walking the perimeter of the yard and Joanne was following behind, taking notes on a legal pad. Figaro was crouched in the grass, ready to pounce on Joanne's untied shoelace.

"What are y'all doing?"

They answered in unison. "Nothin'."

So I left them to it and asked Officer Birkwell, stationed at the garden gate, "What's going on over there?"

He rolled his eyes. "They're working together to see if Mrs. Frankowski's rights are being violated by her anklet zone being smaller than her property line."

"Oh good Lord. Is this going to be a problem for you?"

"Not so far. It's been easier having her occupied with something other than fleeing the scene."

I took one more look at the trio before going inside and storing the cake in the refrigerator. Having second thoughts, I took it back out and stuffed it in a box in the laundry room. I wrote *Kale* on the box in red marker to hide it from Aunt Ginny, then put it back in the laundry room on the counter.

Out in the yard I heard Joanne. "AAHH! Stupid cat! What are you doing?"

I chuckled to myself. I was almost sorry I had to leave them. I'd love to see what else Figaro had planned. But if I was going to talk to Frank Trippett and stop in at the Lynch house after school, I had to get a move on. I had a suspicion that one of them may have egged our house this morning, and before the day was over I wanted them to know that I knew.

Chapter 50

It was just after one at Gleason's Garage. Most of the mechanics were out back eating lunch and killing themselves slowly with cigarettes. I found Frank Trippett bent over the engine of a Jaguar, muttering a colorful strain of profanity.

"Excuse me, Mr. Trippett?"

Frank's head jerked up and he hurled a menacing growl my way. "What!"

Frank had a mean look in his eye, like he would like to kick a puppy, and he smelled like a brewery. I kept my voice calm and light. I'd be darned if I let him see any fear in me. "I'm sorry to disturb you, I wanted to ask about Kylie."

Frank's eyebrows dug into his forehead and his lips pressed together so tight they disappeared. "You know damn well Kylie is in police custody. Probably because of you, nosing around where you don't belong."

"I spoke to her yesterday, like you told me to."

"I never told you to talk to her."

"You did, actually. You told me you were with Kylie the night of Brody's murder. You said to ask her about your alibi. And I did."

Frank folded his arms across his chest with an arrogant smile. "And she confirmed it."

"No, actually she said she was home alone all night."

I've had a shortage of pleasure in my life. But wiping that smug look off of Frank Trippett's face, and seeing his shock when I said Kylie denied his alibi, will always be in my top ten moments. "She said you were out drinking with your friends like you do every night."

"I don't believe you. She would know better—"

I cut him off. "Than to defy you? To stand up to you? Because you're just a bully, Frank. A common, lowlife bully. And I think you killed Brody Brandt. Not because you were jealous, but because you're controlling, and you knew Kylie would be better off with someone like him. Isn't that right?"

Frank picked up a crowbar and took a step toward me. "You fat cow. Who do you think you are, coming in here and threatening me? I warned you the other day to butt out. Some of you gals just don't know your place."

"What are you going to do with that?" I tried to control the nerves in my voice, but even I heard a slight tremble. "All your coworkers are right outside. Someone will hear you." *And my bloodcurdling screams if you try to hit me with that.*

Frank smiled smugly. He turned on the air drill. It's high-pitched *whirrdddtt* reverberated off of the aluminum walls of the garage. *Okay, checkmate.*

"What'd you tell the cops?"

"I told them everything," I lied. *Although in retrospect that probably would have been a better idea than barging in here armed with just a pocketbook and some sass.* I took a step backwards and fumbled in my purse for my phone. Frank torqued the air drill with one hand and raised the crowbar over his head with the other. I looked behind me for a path of escape, but Frank had driven me to a corner. I picked up a wrench and prepared to fight back when a gunshot cracked through the garage.

Frank dropped the crowbar and raised his hands over his head.

Officer Amber stood in the garage bay door with two officers and six mechanics flanking her. She had her gun raised to the sky, where she'd fired off the shot. "Frank Trippett, you're under arrest for the armed robbery of the Wawa on Route 9."

"And the murder of Brody Brandt," I added.

Amber shook her head. "Nope. Not the murder of Brody Brandt. We have Frank here on the security camera robbing the Wawa at gunpoint, two a.m. the night Mr. Brandt was killed."

Frank called me a couple more names that I didn't care to repeat. The two officers spun Frank around and cuffed him, then led him out while reading him his Miranda rights.

I pleaded with Amber. "But maybe he did both. We don't know the exact time Brody was killed."

"We know close enough to narrow the window. There is no way Mr. Trippett could have committed both crimes."

"But . . . but you saw he was about to attack me with a crowbar, didn't you?"

"A lot of people probably feel that way. It doesn't make them murderers."

"But this one is violent. He beats up his girlfriend."

"I know. Who do you think tipped us off? Ms. Furman gave us the names and places of Frank's usual crew, and we were able to match him to the Wawa job."

"So you're absolutely certain he's not the killer?"

"At least not Brody's killer. Frank has a long rap sheet full of violence and petty theft. We'll run his fingerprints through the network and see what else pops up. In the meantime, what is someone who was warned not to get involved in a police investigation doing questioning potential suspects?"

My mouth went dry. "I was just bringing my car in for service."

"Then why was he about to slug you?"

"We disagreed on the price."

"Uh-huh. Get out of here, McAllister. Don't let me find you anywhere near this case again or I might not be able to find my gun so quickly the next time."

I stormed out to my car and slammed the door. *What is it gonna take to get someone other than a McAllister arrested for murder in this town?* I grabbed my cell phone out of my purse. *Sure, there you are, now.* I was riding on too much caffeine and adrenaline, and it had to burn up somewhere. I dialed Sawyer, who did not answer, again. *That's it. I'm going over there to find out what's going on with her once and for all.*

I may have broken a few traffic laws driving back into Cape May. I would have to apologize to Gia for my hypocrisy later. I went straight to Sawyer's bookstore. Through the Looking Glass was on the mall, a few doors down from Momma's restaurant.

I parked in the back, fed the meter, walked around, and threw open the front door, ready to call down fire and brimstone on somebody.

There was Sawyer. Standing behind her register. Fluffing the skirt on an Angelina Ballerina. Not a care in the world. Her eyes met mine and her hand froze like her expression.

"Sawyer. Is your phone broke?"

I watched her swallow, and her eyes slid to the stockroom door.

"What's going on? You've been hot and cold with me for days."

I didn't need her to answer. The good-looking answer sashayed into the room carrying a stack of *Nancy Drew*s. "Hey, Poppy, what's up?"

Sawyer examined a piece of fuzz on her slacks to avoid my gaze.

"Kurt. Shouldn't you be tending bar at the Ugly Mug or propositioning a co-ed somewhere?"

"Poppy!" Sawyer shot me a shocked expression and took the books from her ex-husband and placed them behind the counter.

I couldn't get over the gall of her tone. "You're surprised with me? He put you through hell your entire marriage. The only reason I came to Cape May was to support you in case we ran into him at the reunion with his flavor of the week. And we did!"

"It's not what you think. Kurt is just helping out because his hours were cut back at the bar."

Kurt was your average Cape May beach bum. He'd broken the threshold of his forties without ever having to work a morning shift in his life. He could live out the rest of his days underground, and his tan still wouldn't fade. I don't think he owned a shirt with buttons on it, but he could charm the pants off of a soccer mom before she had to be back for snack time to hand out the oranges.

He ran a hand through his short blond hair. "This tourist season was slower than usual. People just aren't coming here as much with the economy bad, so we had to make some cutbacks at the Mug."

"You're paying him? He hasn't even paid your alimony yet."

Kurt took a step closer. "Poppy, I know you care about Biscuit here, and I was a terrible husband to her. I'm just trying to make a few things right, that's all."

Sawyer turned pleading eyes to me. "He's just here

to help me with a few repairs, and some restocking. It's not like I'm sleeping with him."

"Then you're the only one."

Sawyer bit her bottom lip to keep it from quivering. "People can change, Poppy."

"Beyoncé couldn't change this fast. Your divorce was just finalized a few weeks ago."

Kurt shoved his hands in his pockets. "You don't gotta believe me, but I'm not out to hurt anyone. I'm just trying to turn my life around, and make something out of myself before it's too late. Sawyer was helping me make some cash so I could take a couple of night classes."

I was still fuming. I couldn't stand to see Sawyer hurt, and every encounter with Kurt left her broken. But after all the time I've spent trying to figure out who Brody Brandt was, maybe some of his sympathy for the downtrodden was wearing off on me. I wanted to believe Kurt. I just didn't. But I was willing to try for Sawyer's sake.

I put my arms around Sawyer and she hugged me back. I whispered in her ear, "Please guard your heart this time. He always has had a way of worming back in there."

She whispered back, "I know. I just don't want to hate him anymore."

Kurt gave us both an awkward grin. "Group hug?"

We both said, "No!"

"Okay, just asking."

Sawyer pulled back to look me in the eyes. "Are we okay?"

"You and I are okay." I looked at Kurt. "You and I are not."

Kurt held his hands up in surrender. "Okay, okay. I get it. Some people can hold a grudge for a lifetime."

"A lifetime! You brought a stripper to our high school reunion less than two months ago."

"Fair point."

Sawyer took me by the arm. "Let's go sit in the Queen of Hearts room and you can tell me what's going on with the investigation. How is Aunt Ginny holding up?"

"You'll never believe who is watching her right now."

"Who?"

"Joanne Junk."

"No way!"

"I have to pay her ten dollars an hour to do it, but yeah."

"Well, don't that beat all."

"I just came from Frank Trippett's work, where Amber arrested him for another crime. One that absolves him of Brody Brandt's murder."

"Oh no."

"And I'm running out of suspects."

Kurt came in with a stack of books to load the romance section shelves.

I said, "Kurt, do you have to do this section now?"

He looked at me over his shoulder. "Yeah. I can't hear you from the mysteries."

Sawyer tsk-tsk'd, then turned back to me. "Have you found out who might have had a motive? I mean Brody Brandt was a hero around here. Helping all those kids. Getting them off the streets. The county just gave him that award. I just can't imagine who would want to hurt him."

Kurt slid a couple more books on the shelf and moved down a row. "Someone who wasn't doing as good as him, and didn't think he deserved it."

"What?"

Kurt continued to shelve books. "You know how it is. People just hate to see anything good happen to their enemies. They want them to wallow in misery their whole life so they get what they deserve." Kurt tossed me a glance over his shoulder. "I think you know what I'm talking about."

I felt the heat creep up to my ears.

He went back to shelving books. "Nobody's perfect. Everyone's hurt someone at some point. And no one wants to see the guy that wrecked their life become the town hero and get an award for it."

"Oh my God, Sawyer. He's right. This whole time we've been looking at Brody's present. We should have been looking into his past."

Chapter 51

The sun was low in the sky over North Cape May. Soon the clouds would be pink and gold, and a chill would ride in on the ocean breeze. I had a very small window to talk to Erika Lynch before I had to get home to relieve Joanne. Luck was on my side this afternoon, and Jonathan's car was parked at the curb. Two for one.

The front door was open and the television was on, playing *Say Yes to the Dress.* No one was in the living room, but I could smell hot dogs and macaroni-and-cheese cooking. *I miss being seventeen.* I knocked on the screen door.

Erika came around the corner out of the kitchen. She halted when she saw me. "You again!"

I held up the box I'd gotten from Emilio. "I brought you something."

Jonathan rumbled down the stairs like an avalanche. "What are you doing here? I thought I told you to stay away."

Erika put her hand on his arm. "Wait, Daddy."

Jonathan looked at Erika. "What is it, kitten?"

Erika looked at me. "What's in the box?"

"If you let me in, I'll show you."

Erika opened the screen door, all the while keeping her eye on the box in my hands. Jonathan still had not lost his bluster, even if his daughter had taken some of its force away. "This better be something important."

I set the box on the coffee table and pulled out Erika's statue. "Does this look familiar?"

Her eyes lit up and she tenderly took the sculpture from my hands. "Where did you find it?"

"Emilio found it in the Teen Center."

She started to tear up. "I thought I'd lost it forever." She dropped down to the couch and cradled the sculpture in her arms.

Jonathan sat in a chair across from her. "It's beautiful, baby. That's why they gave you a scholarship to that school." He turned to me. "New York Academy of Art—full ride. My girl's got more talent in her pinky toe than you or I will ever have."

Jonathan watched Erika with so much love in his eyes that it must've destroyed him when she came home and told him Brody had molested her. "I heard. Congratulations. I have something else for you too."

She brushed a tear from her eye before it could break free.

I pulled the plaque out of the box and handed it to her. "He was going to present it to you at a special ceremony to show you how proud they all were."

Erika read the plaque and she started to weep.

Jonathan took the plaque from her hands and his face reddened a darker shade than it naturally was. "How dare you bring this—"

"Daddy. No."

"He hurt you, baby. And I won't have these people—"

"I lied." Erika was sobbing now.

Jonathan's expression froze. His lips moved but

no words came out until he said, "What do you mean, you lied?"

"I made it all up." Erika spoke through sobs. "He never touched me. I was in love with him, and I threw myself at him. The one night he had to lock up, I stayed late and told him how I felt. I tried to kiss him and he was horrified."

Jonathan's eyes misted up.

"He turned me down. I was humiliated. I wanted to hurt him as much as he hurt me. So I told you he molested me for revenge. I wanted you to be angry for me. Only you went down there and threatened him, and made it worse. Now everyone knows what I said. And they think he's a predator and he's not. I'm the predator." Erika crumpled to a heap on the couch, clutching her sculpture of Brody.

Jonathan went to his daughter and pulled her into his arms. "It's okay, baby. It's okay. We all make mistakes. We'll get through this."

Erika sobbed. "And now he's gone. I can't even tell him how sorry I am."

"I'm sure he knows." Jonathan smoothed her hair down. He looked at me and said very softly, "I'm sorry I threatened you."

"You don't owe me an apology. Any father who loves his daughter as much as you do would have done the same thing."

Jonathan tipped his head up to the ceiling and wiped his nose with his hand. "I don't know about that. I . . . may have done something awful."

"What do you mean?"

Erika sat up and wiped her face with her shirt. "What did you do, Daddy?"

"I thought he hurt you, baby. And you wouldn't let me go to the police."

I took a deep breath. This could be it.

Jonathan looked from Erika to me. "Look, this is a family issue. I appreciate all you've done for us but . . ."

Erika said, "Just tell her. This whole time she's only been trying to help."

Jonathan took a deep breath and let it out slowly. "After Erika told me what happened, I broke into his house and planted a plastic sandwich baggie full of pot."

Erika's jaw dropped open.

Jonathan nodded. "Then I called the police to report him. I was trying to get him shut down so he couldn't hurt anyone else. If I couldn't get him sent to jail for attempted rape, I thought maybe I could get him arrested for having drugs."

Not likely from a little baggie of pot. "When did this happen?"

Jonathan swallowed hard. "The night he was killed. But he wasn't home when I was there. I bought the drugs from a kid I always see hanging out at the 7-Eleven. Scruffy-looking white kid, full of pimples. Then I drove over to Brody's address and let myself in with a key I found in a coffee can in the garage."

"Okay, so far I'm with you."

"I looked around for a place to stick the drugs. Then I saw it. His stupid humanitarian award there on the desk in the living room. That dumb angel statue, mocking me. I set the pot right next to it and got out of there."

"Do you know what time that was?"

"It was nine. I knew he'd be at his NA meeting then."

"How did you know that?" I asked.

Erika took a shuddering breath. "We all knew Brody's schedule. He never missed a meeting if he could help it."

"Where did you go after that?"

"I was pissed. And a little nervous that I would get caught for planting the drugs. So I went over to my cousin Jimmy's house to drink beer and lose at poker. Jimmy drove me home sometime around two."

"That's true," Erika said. "I can vouch for him."

Jonathan patted her back. "So can Jimmy. And three other guys."

"Why did you tell me you were in Chicago?"

"To get you off my back. I don't know you."

"Okay, well that's true."

"I've made a lot of mistakes since my wife died. Some days I struggle to keep my head above water. My wife really did a number on us when she overdosed on painkillers. A friend of mine suggested Erika and I start going to Nar-Anon meetings at St. Barnabas."

"What is Nar-Anon?"

"It's a support group for family members of addicts."

"I didn't know there was such a thing."

"Drug abuse doesn't just ruin the addict's life, it hurts the whole family. I really wasn't thinking clearly when I planted the drugs. I just knew my baby was hurting."

Erika's lip trembled. "I've done so many things I regret. I wish I could erase the past year and have a do-over."

"I know how you feel," I said.

"I . . . I'm sorry. But I egged your house and painted *murderer* on your porch."

Jonathan reared back. "Erika. Why would you do that?"

"Because when I heard that Brody was dead, I thought that you killed him, Daddy. Because of what I'd said." Erika started to cry again. "And I didn't want you to go to jail. I can't lose you too."

"How did you know where I live? And what made you

think to target me? I never told you who was accused of the murder."

"Dani and Keisha figured out that it was your aunt who was arrested. And I got Emilio to give me your address. Of course, I lied to him to get it. I told him I needed your help." Erika turned pleading eyes on me. "You can turn me in if you want to, but you don't have to tell the police my dad planted that little bag of weed, do you?"

"I'm not turning anyone in. I've cleaned up the porch. There's no lasting damage. And I won't tell the police about the drugs unless they ask." *And they won't ask.*

The Lynches seemed mollified with that answer.

"So, while I'm here, could I ask you something else? What do you know about Brody's past?"

A brief flicker of pain showed behind Erika's eyes. "Like what?"

"Did anything happen with him that stands out? Did he do anything or make any enemies who might want to hurt him today?"

Erika thought about it for a minute. "Maybe. I don't know anything specific, but he probably made some enemies back in the days when he used to deal."

"Deal?"

Erika nodded. "Drugs."

"Brody was a drug dealer?"

Erika shrugged. "You have to get drugs to do drugs. And there's only a couple ways to get drugs. Spend money or trade services. When guys trade services it's usually by being a middleman."

Where has this information been for the past two weeks?

Erika continued, "You know who would know for sure? Brody's ex-wife. They used to do it together. If he made any enemies, she would know. Heck, she could even be one. He didn't exactly do right by her."

Thank God I had a ready excuse to go visit Liz tomorrow. I had that banker's box of Brody's items and her chocolate cake.

I thanked Erika and her father for the information. Before I left, I told them about the party the Teen Center wanted to throw for Erika to celebrate her scholarship.

She teared up again. "I don't know if I can go there. I'm so ashamed."

"Emilio told me that Brody was the king of second chances. I think he'd want you to be there."

Erika smiled and hugged her sculpture tightly. "I'll think about it."

Jonathan walked me to my car. A very different send-off than the last time I'd been here. He asked me, "When you came here tonight, how did you know Erika's story wasn't true? How did you know she wasn't molested?"

"I wasn't sure. Not until Erika told the whole story. It did seem out of character for him, though. Everything in Brody's life pointed to making amends. He wanted to restore the relationship with his daughter most of all, but she wasn't ready. Erika was like a surrogate daughter to him. And you don't make a pass at the girl you think of as a daughter."

I drove home thinking about my encounter with the Lynches, father and daughter. Erika lashed out at Brody because she felt rejected. The hurt and anger made her say a lot of horrible things that she would regret for the rest of her life. My mind went to Georgina and our fight, but I squashed that thought back down. I wasn't ready to understand or forgive her yet.

I parked and said hello to Officer Consuelos, then let myself in. Aunt Ginny and Joanne were on the couch in the sunroom watching *Wheel of Fortune* and eating Liz's chocolate cake.

Joanne hefted herself off the couch. "It's about time!"

Not the worst greeting I've ever received from Joanne.

"Nice try, hiding it in a box of kale." Aunt Ginny gave me a fork salute.

"How'd you find it?"

"It was Joanne's idea."

Joanne was getting her bag of knitting and her jacket. "I told Virginia, there's no way you baked all day and had nothing to show for it. And judging from the size of your thighs, you're not exactly a kale eater."

I paid Joanne and sent her on her merry way before I was tempted to shove her cake in her little troll face. Besides, I had to be nice. I might need another favor sometime. Like tomorrow when I returned to the ex-wife who might have found a way to make up for all that missing alimony.

Chapter 52

"I'm going stir-crazy in this house. I have to get out."

Aunt Ginny woke up pre-cranked, and nothing could calm her anxiety. I tried reason. "It's only been three days."

"I'm not putting my life on hold any longer. I'm old. I don't have much time left."

I tried bribery. "If you behave yourself today, I'll bring you some egg rolls from Dragon House."

"If I want egg rolls I should be allowed to go down to Wildwood and get them myself! Did we wake up in North Korea this morning? Where are my rights!"

I tried threats. "Do you want Officer Amber to put you in a cell?"

"I will take that little blond know-it-all over my knee if she even thinks about taking me in."

And finally, I resorted to trickery. "Here, hold my cell phone for me for a minute."

"What's this? What's your doohickey doin'?"

"Oh that, it's a game. It's called Candy Crush. I forgot I left that on."

"How's it work?"

"Like this, see."

"Oooh. That looks fun. Let me try."

"Sure. I'll be right back."

Well, that should hold her for a couple hours.

I pulled the banker's box of Brody's items out of the mudroom, where I'd stashed it the other day. I hoped to find something that would give me a clue about Brody's past. It was full of framed school photographs of Christina, Father's Day cards, a couple drawings of a big stick figure with blond hair and a little stick figure with brown braids, holding hands. That must be Christina and Brody. In the bottom, I found a clay ashtray with *Best Dad* scrawled on the front. The bottom had the year. She must have been in first or second grade.

It was just a few items, but they had obviously meant the world to him, and my heart could barely hold the sadness of it all.

I put the box in the trunk of my car. I wouldn't have a cake to deliver, but I had to talk to Liz about Brody's past. This wasn't something that could wait. All I needed now was a babysitter. I could beg Sawyer again, but it might be too soon for that. She was still dealing with PTSD from the other day. I went back in to the kitchen, where Aunt Ginny was oblivious to everything but the screen of my phone, and picked up the landline. I could try Joanne, but I was getting low on cash.

A pitiful figure wrapped in a gray pashmina that matched her downcast eyes quietly slinked into the kitchen.

"Georgina. What are you still doing here?"

"I want to talk to you."

"About what?"

"The other day we both said some things we regret ."

"I don't regret anything."

Georgina unwrapped herself and sat down at the kitchen table across from Aunt Ginny.

Oh, so you're staying?

"You're moving on with your life, and I have to make peace with that." She sighed. "And I'm sorry I said you were a bad wife. You were a wonderful wife, and John adored you. I was just trying to scare you away from getting involved in a new relationship."

"Why would you do that?"

"Well, I know I can be a bit heavy-handed once in a while."

Was Hitler unpleasant once in a while? "Go on."

"It's just that . . ." Georgina's eyes teared up. She looked out the window toward the porch swing. "You're all I have left . . . and you're leaving me behind."

"What are you talking about?"

Georgina wiped a tear away from her eye before it could ruin her mascara. "Phillip's gone. John's gone. And if . . . when . . . you get remarried, you'll be gone. I don't want to be alone."

"Where am I going?"

"With your new family. You won't be my daughter-in-law anymore. I'll never see you again. All our fun times will be over."

Where was I for these fun times?

"You're just . . . you're the only daughter I'll ever have."

Her lip quivered, and more tears forced their way over the layers of Maybelline.

I took a good, hard look at Georgina. She was small. And vulnerable. And for the first time, she looked sincere. My heart swelled with pity for her, even if my head battled against it. In the end, pity won.

"Georgina, you won't have to be alone. Even if I were to remarry, not that I'm planning on it, you will always be a part of my life." That was a hard truth to swallow. I had to take a deep breath and let it out to regroup. "Just like John will always be a part of me, you and I will always be family."

She relaxed her shoulders, and her face brightened. "Why don't you call me Mom?"

Whoa. "Baby steps."

Aunt Ginny looked up from my phone. "How long has Georgina been here?"

"About six levels."

"Is she staying?"

"That's up to her."

Georgina smiled. "I'll have Squiggy bring in my bags."

Smitty is going to kill me. "You could really do me a favor today."

"Sure. What is it?"

"I have to run an errand. Could you stay with Aunt Ginny and keep her out of trouble?"

"I can try."

"That's all anyone can do."

Chapter 53

I drove over to Liz's consignment shop with Brody's belongings. I really didn't want Liz to be guilty. I liked her. But people can do strange things when their emotions get away from them. Some people will plan for years before they make their move to get revenge. Just look at Georgina. She's made my life hell for twenty years. If that's how she treats those she loves, imagine how she'd treat her enemies.

Liz answered the door wearing a fluffy red sweater and Levi's. "Hi. How does the vintage Eastlake look in the guest room?"

"It's gorgeous. That will go a long way to make a statement with our guests when we officially open in the spring."

"What's in the box?"

"Do you know Brody's secretary, Judy?"

"We've never met, but I've talked to her on the phone a couple of times. Apparently, Brody could walk on water."

"That's definitely Judy. Well, these were Brody's things that he had at the office. She thought maybe you and Christina would like to have them."

Liz's eyes softened. She took the box from me. "Come on in. I'll make us some tea."

A young girl of about twenty was sitting at the table eating a bowl of Cocoa Puffs. She had her father's face but her mother's brown hair and hazel eyes. "You must be Christina. I'm Poppy."

She gave me a timid smile. "Hi."

"I've heard so much about you. How are you doing?"

"A little better."

"That's good."

Liz and Christina went through the box reminiscing, oohing and giggling over each item.

Christina pulled out the "Best Dad" ashtray and her lip started to quiver. Her voice caught in her throat as she said, "Thank you for bringing me these."

"Of course. I'm sure your father would have wanted you to have them."

Liz put the items back in the box and handed it to Christina. "Why don't you take these up to your room, honey? And let me and Poppy chat."

When Christina was gone, Liz sat down with our mugs of tea. "We have to go clean out his house this week. It's going to be so hard on her."

"Maybe it will make her feel closer to him in some way, and bring some closure."

"I sure hope so. She's been miserable. Have you found out anything yet about what happened?"

"Well, I've run into a few brick walls. In fact, that's part of why I'm here."

"Oh?"

Please be innocent, Liz. "How did yours and Brody's relationship end?"

"The same way most relationships end. With lots of name-calling and tears and hurt feelings. But we eventually got over it. I think as we matured we both realized that we were equally guilty, and equally innocent."

"What do you mean?"

"We were seventeen. We didn't know what the heck we were doing. How can you expect two teenagers to make a marriage work? Marriage is hard for grounded adults. With us, you throw in a baby and some drugs— we were doomed."

"Did you ever want to kill him?"

"All the flippin' time. Love and hate are two sides of the same coin. And every day was a toss-up between heads and tails with us. We just couldn't make it work, but I know I will love him until the day I die."

"Last night I learned that Brody used to sell drugs."

"That's how we met. Brody was my dealer."

"I thought you met in high school."

"We did. I used to buy coke from him twice a week after seventh period. Then one day we started partying together. A year later we had Christina."

"Where did you go to high school? West Philly?"

She laughed. "In a small town in Pennsylvania. Middle-class white people are the largest group of drug buyers in the country. Life in the suburbs is that boring. I used to spend my babysitting money on coke every week to help me get all my homework done."

"My God, Liz. I would have never guessed. You and Brody must have made some enemies in those days. Is there anyone you can think of who would want to kill him? Maybe his drug supplier? Or a disgruntled buyer?"

"Doubtful. The only things that get you on the outs with your base are stealing or squealing, and Brody never did either. Now the *family* of a client. That's another story. They never blame the user for seeking a score. They blame the dealer, as if he lured their precious baby into a back alley and forced them to do blow."

This conversation was sounding more and more like a prison interview in a movie, not a chat over tea with a small-town mom. "Are there any angry family members who might be harboring a grudge against Brody?"

She closed her eyes for a moment, and when she opened them they were glassy and full of pain. "There was one, but it was almost twenty-five years ago. Surely they would have moved on by now."

"I don't know, Liz, there is no statute of limitations on grief."

Liz hesitated. "You have to understand, Brody was a good guy. A jock. He wasn't exactly your Colombian drug lord. He only started selling drugs to keep himself in supply. One day he sold a gram of coke to a new kid at school. He didn't know the guy from Adam, had never met him before, but his eyes were flashing dollar signs, so he didn't ask any questions."

Liz picked up her tea with shaking hands and took a sip from her mug. "We found out later that the boy had never done drugs before. He was only thirteen. He was just trying to make an impression on some older kids at a party. He OD'd and died."

"Oh my God, Liz."

"Brody was very lucky that he was tried as a minor, because he was only sentenced to ten months in juvie. He turned eighteen on the inside. He bounced around aimlessly for a few years after he was released. That's when I called it quits and got out. I had Christina to protect. I broke ties from Brody and got clean. That boy's death was a real wake-up call. But Brody couldn't get over the pain of being responsible for it. He never dealt again, but he bottomed out on heroin."

"I can't even imagine what he went through, or the boy's family."

"It was big news in our small town, and so many people were angry when Brody was released. They wanted him to rot in jail forever. The boy's death sparked community outrage that trickled over to me and Christina. It's why we moved away. Follow me." Liz got up and walked into a small sitting room off the kitchen. She got a picture off of the shelf and handed it to me. "This was taken right after I got pregnant. I'm not even showing yet. The boy overdosed in my seventh month."

The picture was of a young Liz and Brody standing in front of their high school. Liz was carrying a stack of books and Brody had his arm around her. They were looking at each other and laughing at some now-forgotten joke.

The name of the high school in block letters on the building caught my attention and made the skin on my scalp prickle. "Where did you go to school?"

"Harmony, Pennsylvania. See, you can just make out the name Harmony High right there in the picture."

My heart dropped within my chest. "Liz, what was the name of the boy who died, quick!"

"Ah . . . ah . . . Justin. Justin Rhodes. Why?"

"Did he have any sisters?"

"One. She was a lot younger than him. Tina, I think. No, Tracy."

An image flashed in my memory just like the photograph I held in my hands. I thought she was just being extra nice, but maybe she was checking up on Aunt Ginny the whole time. "Liz, can I use your phone, please?"

Liz handed me her cell. "Yes, of course."

I dialed my own cell phone. My voice mail came on.

I tried it again. Same thing. Either Aunt Ginny was hitting *ignore* or the battery was dead from playing Candy Crush. No one answered the home phone either. Georgina wouldn't pick up. Smitty wouldn't pick up. *What is going on over there?*

I handed Liz her phone and the picture. "I've got to go!"

"What is it? What's going on?"

"I know who killed Brody. And I know why they're trying to frame my aunt for it."

Chapter 54

I rushed home, my hands shaking so hard I thought the engine was seizing up in my Toyota. I threw the car in park and left it running, passed Officer Birkwell, who raised an eyebrow, tore into the house, passed the library where Smitty and Georgina were locked in an embrace. *What the*—*!* I would have to wrap my brain around that later. There was no time right now.

I ran up to my room to my laptop and googled the article about Harmony, Pennsylvania, and Justin Rhodes. I found what I was looking for and printed the page. I grabbed the paper and tore back down the stairs, hopping over Figaro at the halfway point.

Aunt Ginny was coming down the hall. "What has gotten into you?"

"I figured it out. I should have suspected sooner, but I thought she was just doing her job. Stay here! Don't let anyone in before I get back."

The drive to Dr. Weingarten's office in North Cape May didn't take long. I would have liked more time to prepare what to say, but instead I had to focus on breathing. I could feel a full-blown panic attack coming on, and I needed to be cool right now. I looked at the clock on my dash. There was always the chance that she wouldn't be there. If all the patients were gone for the day, they could have closed early. If Yolanda was back from maternity leave, she could have gone to her next assignment. I could be too late.

I pulled into the crushed-clamshell parking lot. Nurse Tracy was just locking the front door. She glanced up and we made eye contact. Her hand froze on the doorknob. She knew I knew. I threw the car door open while she frantically jammed the key back in the lock and shimmied it around, then flung the door open and ran back inside. But I was too quick for her to lock me out. I threw my hip against the door and pinned her between it and the waiting room wall.

"I know what you did, Tracy!"

"You don't know anything!"

With surprising strength, she pushed the door back against me. I jumped into the waiting room and faced her, one on one. "After all these weeks of you checking on Aunt Ginny and offering advice." I held out the printout of Justin Rhodes's death for her to see.

She stood there, her chest heaving from exertion. "So how'd you figure it out?"

"Brody's ex-wife told me about your brother's overdose. When I learned that Brody was from Harmony, Pennsylvania, I remembered the logo on your scrubs. *Nurses Do It in Harmony.* That was the final piece."

"Did Brody's ex-wife tell you who was responsible for my brother's death?"

"She told me Brody sold him the drugs that he OD'd on."

"Justin would never have died if Brody hadn't been pushing cocaine on kids. And then my family finds out that Cape May gave that scumbag the humanitarian award." Tracy's fists were curled tight at her sides. "Are you kidding me? They may as well have spit in my mother's face. My parents' lives were destroyed that day. They wanted to die right along with him. My mother hasn't left the house since I was seven years old. Can you imagine the pain she has had to live with, watching them bury her son? And you people wrote in the paper that he was a hero."

Tracy looked toward the back of the office, where I knew there was a fire exit on the side of the building. She took a step toward it and I shifted my weight in the same direction.

"I can't imagine what your family has been through. No one should ever have to go through the horror of losing a child. But does killing Brody make your brother's death any less painful? Now he has a daughter in pain just like you were, and she hasn't done anything wrong."

"You think I don't know that? Her life was ruined the day her father decided to play around with drugs. Why do you think I go to Nar-Anon meetings? I try to help people like her whose families' bad decisions have caused them so much pain." Tracy took a step toward the reception desk. "Every day I see patients whose lives have been destroyed by drugs. Their bodies are twisted with pain, their minds damaged from continual abuse. And we let the delinquents that supplied them the poison walk free. I took this assignment for a chance to get close to Brody, to tell him how he destroyed my family, and see if he had any remorse at all. Waiting for the opportunity to give him the punishment he deserved that the justice system mucked up the first time around. I've dedicated my whole life as a nurse to help people like your aunt. Are you really going to take that away from me? For a killer?"

Tracy made a dash through the door, back toward

the exam rooms. I caught her and wedged her up against the reception desk.

"But you framed my aunt for the murder. What kind of sick person sends an elderly widow to prison to cover up her own crime?"

Tracy pushed back against me and got her foot up against my knee. "Your aunt came in here with that crazy story about her sleepwalking and breaking in to her neighbors' houses. I looked up your address online and saw that you were only a couple of blocks away from where he lived. I couldn't pass up my best chance. I feel bad about your aunt, but she's old, and she'll have a good defense because of the sleeping pills. Why do you think I gave her all the research she'd need to defend herself?"

"If you didn't want her to go away for your crime, you wouldn't have put on the red wig and tracksuit when you killed him."

"I had to make it look legit, in case someone saw me. You wouldn't believe how nosy the neighbors are. I hear them gossiping in the waiting room every day. These old people know more about what's going on in this town than the local news."

I grabbed Tracy's wrist and pulled her around to where her back was in front of me. "I can't let you do it. Not to Aunt Ginny." I didn't know if it was all the yoga or pure rage, but I had Tracy pinned. Only I didn't know what to do next. I didn't have my phone to call for help. I looked around the reception desk for the office phone. I tried to pull Tracy with me so I could get close enough to reach the receiver. I never saw her reach into her purse and pull out the statue. Tracy's arm came up and she hit me hard on the side of the head with Brody's humanitarian award.

My vision dimmed and I went fuzzy. Suddenly the

floor was beneath my knees. It wasn't supposed to be there.

Tracy backed up to the fire exit. "I really thought after what you went through a few months ago that you would stay out of the police spotlight and leave this alone. You were just accused of murder yourself. You know how small towns have long memories. Some people still think you're guilty."

"So, you're going to run now? You won't be able to hide from the cops. They'll be all over you when I tell them what I know."

"Whose story do you think the police will believe? Mine, that you broke in here looking for drugs because you were distraught over your elderly aunt killing the town hero, and I whacked you in self-defense? Or yours, that two people in your family have now been framed for murder? Cops don't like coincidences."

Blood was running from the side of my head, stinging my eye. It was hot and sticky and smelled like copper. If I didn't do something now, I would pass out and Tracy would kill me without a fight. I knew my last chance was to lunge at her and hope I could knock her down and get that statue away from her.

I made eye contact with my good eye and shifted my weight. Before I could push off, the fire door flew open and slammed into Tracy. She hit her head against the cinder-block wall and crumpled into a heap. Aunt Ginny, followed by Georgina, burst in through the opening, ready for a fight.

I looked at Georgina. "You're supposed to be baby-sitting."

Georgina's hands flew up to her hips and she made a loud *tsk!* "You left your laptop on. She checked your browser history and figured out where you were going. Keeping her home was not happening."

The front door to the office cracked in half as two police officers kicked it down. Amber stepped through and said from the top of the hall, "Mrs. Frankowski, what part of house arrest don't you understand?"

Aunt Ginny pointed at Tracy on the floor. "I already took out the perp. You're zero for two. You know, you're not so good at this."

Amber let out a heavy sigh and reached for her police radio. "Officer Fenton taking a 10-7od-Frankowski. Out." Amber turned and walked back through the now shattered front door. One of other the two officers cuffed Tracy's still form and called it in for transport.

I asked the other, "What's a 10-7od-Frankowski?"

"A 10-7od is a police call for I'm off duty, personal time. Frankowski is a code our precinct has adopted, meaning I'm going for a drink and to lie down for a while."

"I understand completely."

Epilogue

"All our full-time chambermaids are assigned. This late in the year we are pretty short staffed."

I held my cell phone away from my bandaged temple while I checked on the pan of macaron shells in the oven at Gia's shop. It was my twelfth batch, and if this one didn't turn out I might just throw the whole pan in the back alley. "I know it's last-minute, but I would be so grateful if you could come up with someone. I just don't have the time to run the kitchen, and administrative duties, plus do all the cleaning. My bed-and-breakfast already didn't get off to a good start. Moving forward, I need to make a really good impression on guests, to bolster our reviews."

"Well, I hesitate to offer this. But you did say you were desperate."

"I'll take anything."

"I have a part-timer, Ermintrude Galbraith. She usually cleans off-season vacant properties with no one in residence."

"When can she start?"

"I can send her this afternoon for an interview."

"If you've vetted her, the interview is just a formality. I'm sure we'll love her."

There was a pause. "The interview is Mrs. Galbraith's requirement to see if she is willing to work with you."

This time there was a pause on my end. "Oh. Okay, that's fine too."

We made plans for a two o'clock interview and I ended the call. I removed the sheet pan from the oven and threw the hateful almond discs on the counter.

"Every single batch is wrong! Overmixed, under-mixed, cracked, no feet, hollow. Why do the French have to make everything so complicated!"

Gia was not able to hide his amusement from his position by the walk-in refrigerator. "Calm down, fiery red-head. You'll get it. You are so talented I have no doubt that you'll conquer the 'pretentious pastries,' as you call them. Besides, the dining room is full of people with their fingers crossed for this to be another batch of uglies."

On cue, Henry trotted in. "Did they work? Can we have more pis-nash—pis-smash . . ."

He'd been trying all morning to say *pistachio.* "Keep at it. I want to see where this ends up."

Henry giggled.

Gia tousled Henry's hair. "Say pee-stock-ee-o."

Henry rolled his eyes. "You sound like Nonna."

Be careful with that name. If you say it two more times she might appear, and I'll start having nightmares again. I picked up my pastry bag and filled some of the shells with chocolate-orange ganache, then I filled a few with Henry's favorite pistachio while Henry wiggled his butt and hopped around the kitchen trying to say *pistachio* some more.

Sawyer popped into the kitchen. "Did that batch turn out?"

"Nope."

Followed by Kurt. "Oh good. Somebody hogged that last plate and I only got two."

Sawyer punched Kurt on the arm. "I did not hog them. And you had six!"

"Did I?"

I still wasn't happy with Sawyer's newfound tolerance for Kurt. I didn't trust him any more than I could fit into a size five. Why she insisted on forgiving and trying to help him was beyond me. People like Sawyer and Brody always saw the good in people. I'm not as generous.

Gia put the finished macarons on a tray. "They may not look perfect yet, *bella*, but they taste *delizioso*."

Karla poked her head in the kitchen doorway. "Hey, you got customers out here."

Gia left to tend the espresso machine. I lifted the tray and offered Karla a macaron.

Karla recoiled like I'd offered her a tub of lard with a spoon. "Eww. No way. You don't eat carbs and look like this."

Sawyer reached for the plate. "I'll have hers. Being skinny is overrated."

And that's why Sawyer is my best friend.

Two batches of shells in the trash later, I cleaned up my mess and kissed Gia goodbye. "I have to get home to interview a potential chambermaid. I'll see you tonight at dinner."

Gia pulled me close for a deeper kiss, then handed me a coconut-almond latte he'd made me to go. "I can't wait."

I walked home while going over the chaos of the past

couple of days in my head. Aunt Ginny was officially off house arrest as of this morning. She was probably halfway to Vegas by now. Liz had called the police station after I left the other day and filled them in on the history between Brody and Tracy. Amber was on her way to question Tracy when Aunt Ginny's anklet alarm went off. Tracy tried to plead temporary insanity to get her case thrown out, but since she'd had over twenty years to plan the murder of Brody Brandt, the judge wasn't buying her story. She was being held in county lockup pending her trial. I should tell her to say hi to Bebe for me the next time Bebe comes around.

Kylie Furman turned over her offshore account information to the auditors. With the money back in the clients' accounts, Ken Freeman dropped the embezzlement charges. Kylie was able to provide evidence linking Frank Trippett to three more crimes in exchange for witness protection relocation. She may not be living it up in Iceland, but it looks like her Wit'sec plan worked after all.

I'd been over my conversation with Georgina so many times I had it memorized. I never would have guessed that her pushy, overbearing demeanor was a cover for insecurity. Don't get me wrong, she hadn't changed any; she was still Georgina. But now when I looked at her I tried to see past her crunchy exterior to find the soft nougat center that just wanted to be loved and included.

No one that I'd met in the past couple of weeks was black or white. Everyone was shades of gray. Not to be confused with another kind of shades of gray. Although they might be that too, I mean I don't know them that well. But each one had a side they showed the public, while the real them was a lot more complex. Liz appeared to be a typical South Jersey single mom, and she had helped her ex-husband sell drugs. Jonathan Lynch was putting up a fierce grizzly-bear front, but when his daughter was involved, he was really just a big teddy bear. And Kylie Furman—who would ever have guessed that such a beautiful and intelligent businesswoman would be hiding abuse or devising a plan to disappear? Of course Brody Brandt was the biggest surprise. I wasn't sure which version of him would turn out to be real. Town hero or shady drug addict. In the end it was a little of both. You never know what you're willing to do when you're desperate. I guess we're all a tangled mess.

Georgina met me at the door. "There's a scary old lady prowling around upstairs who says she's here to inspect the house."

Someone should tell her we're over our limit on scary old ladies. "Already? She's twenty minutes early."

"What's she doing here?"

"She's interviewing for the position of chamber-maid."

"So you're still planning on staying then?"

Smitty hollered from on top of a ladder in the library. "Woman! I thought we talked about that!"

Georgina hollered back. "I was just making sure." Then to me she said, "Well, if you insist on staying in this godforsaken hellhole, I'll just have to make the best of it."

"That's the spirit." I set my purse down on the table in the foyer. "Georgina, you'll be back before you know it for Thanksgiving."

"I guess I can bring a few things and stay awhile."

My heart stopped beating. So this is what it feels like to be dying.

"Aren't you going to say how excited you are to hear that?" Georgina asked.

"There are no words to express how I feel about that."

Georgina took that as a compliment and went to boss Smitty around some more. "You are doing such a good job up there, Smutty. That ceiling medallion looks almost like new. You missed a spot."

I found Aunt Ginny at the dining room table drinking a cup of coffee. "How does it feel to be free?"

"Happier'n a possum eatin' a sweet tater."

"So . . . pretty excited then."

Aunt Ginny grinned.

"Brenda called this morning. Jonathan Lynch dropped off a donation of ten thousand dollars with an apology for the damage done to Brody's program."

"That will go a long way to smooth ruffled feathers."

"Guess what they want to do with it?"

"Go to Disney World?"

"No."

"Build a racetrack?"

"No."

"Put on a Michael Jackson concert?"

"Um . . . We may need to catch you up on the news. No, they want to expand their kitchen for culinary lessons. Brenda wants to offer more life skills and trade classes. Some of the older kids in the program have been kicked out of school. This is a chance for them to learn a skill that will help them find employment."

"That sounds like a winner. Are you going to teach the classes?"

"A few. I told her I would volunteer my time in our off-season. Tonight I have to deliver cookies for Erika Lynch's scholarship party."

"So she's going for it?"

"Yep. Emilio convinced her to own it, and move past it."

"I'm so glad."

"Me too. And, since you've been cooped up in this house for a week, how about I take you with me tonight. It will be your first sanctioned trip out of the house."

"Not tonight. I'm kind of tired. I thought I would stay in and read a book."

Are you kidding me, old lady? I narrowed my eyes at Aunt Ginny. "You've tried to escape for a week. Officer Birkwell had to go on administrative leave."

Aunt Ginny hid behind her coffee cup, grinning to herself.

Georgina marched into the dining room, followed by a stern matron in a starched white apron over a steel-gray uniform. The woman appeared to be about an hour past retirement age. Figaro slinked in behind them.

I shot to my feet to introduce myself. "You must be Mrs. Galbraith. It's a pleasure to meet you."

"Sit."

Oh, okay. I dropped back into my chair. I felt fifteen again and I had been sent to the principal's office.

"All of you."

Georgina took the seat across from me. She looked as intimidated as I felt.

Smitty was going to join us, but heard Mrs. Galbraith dressing us down and with a "Nyahh-ahh," he was back out the door.

"First of all," Mrs. Galbraith went on, "I do not work Sundays. Sunday is the Lord's day and I treat it as such. If you have any check-ins or -outs you will be on your own."

"I'm sure that—"

She cut me off. "Second. My hours are eleven to three. If your lodgers have not gotten their belongings out by eleven on check-out day, you will be cleaning the room yourselves."

I sat quietly, waiting for number three.

Figaro jumped up on the table and sat in front of Mrs. Galbraith, baiting her. We all held our breath.

"I do not like cats. I do not appreciate them in my kitchen or my dining area."

Figaro walked to the middle of the table and flopped down. Then, raising his back leg, gave Mrs. Galbraith full view of the bathing ritual of his hindquarters.

The blood drained from Mrs. Galbraith's face. Georgina covered her mouth with her hand while her eyes remained on Fig. I was too stunned to move. He knew better. This was a blatant challenge of Mrs. Galbraith's authority.

"The cat will have to go."

"The cat stays." Aunt Ginny was the only one not terrified of the domineering woman in front of us. "He's my emotional-support companion cat. His orange vest is around here somewhere."

Figaro twisted back to look at Aunt Ginny with much the same expression we all had for Aunt Ginny in that moment.

Mrs. Galbraith breathed out long and slow, like a tire with a slow leak. "Fine. One last thing." She pulled something from her apron pocket and dropped it on the table. It was Georgina's diamond tennis bracelet. "I found this in the second-bedroom floor vent."

Georgina picked it up. "My bracelet. I thought it was gone forever."

"How in the world did it get in there?" I asked Georgina.

Mrs. Galbraith clasped her hands behind her back. "I imagine the person who had been wearing it was lying on the floor listening through the vent when the clasp broke."

Georgina flushed crimson. "Why would you think something crazy like that?"

"Because you can hear every word spoken from the kitchen through that vent."

Aunt Ginny and I looked through the dining-room door to the kitchen ceiling.

Georgina dropped the bracelet into her pocket. "Well, I wouldn't know about that."

Mrs. Galbraith paced the length of the table. "If you agree to my terms, I will draw up a contract."

Georgina came alive when it was our turn in the negotiation. She stood to her feet and straightened her white blazer over her blue slacks. "I have a few things I'd like to add."

Mrs. Galbraith raised a hand to stop Georgina. "Absolutely not. I will only take direction and concerns from the primary, Mrs. McAllister."

Georgina's eyes nearly popped out of her head.

I jumped to my feet and thrust my hand out. "You're hired."

I was getting my cookies together for the Teen Center later that day when I got a phone call from Tim. "Hi."

"Hey, gorgeous. I have a proposition for you."

"I'm being propositioned. Oooohh."

Tim laughed. "I can issue any kind of proposition you're interested in. But right now, I wanted to know if you'd be willing to help me out—since you're finished with your police investigation," he said dryly.

"Sure, help you with what?"

"I know you're really busy these days with all the time you spend baking at the coffee shop."

"Uh-huh."

"But, would you have time to be on my team when we compete at Restaurant Week?"

"You want me to cook with you?"

"Yeah, if you're okay with that. I'd still be the head chef, but you could be a line chef under Gigi."

"Gigi?"

"Yeah, we're combining efforts this year and she's going to be my sous chef."

"So, she'll be second-in-command?"

"Right."

"And I'll answer to her?"

"Well, you'll answer to both of us."

Oh goody. I looked outside to see if hell was freezing over. "Send me the information and I'll get back to you."

"It's not for a few weeks, but I hope you'll say yes, Mack. I miss you."

"Way to make it harder for me to say no."

"That was the idea. And, hey, let's go to coffee later."

"Anyplace in particular?"

"Yeah, Starbucks."

"Chicken."

I had just hung up with Tim when Smitty hollered from down the hall. "Poppy!"

"What?"

"The range is here."

"It's about time."

Please turn the page
for recipes from Poppy's kitchen!

PALEO ESPRESSO BROWNIES

4 large eggs
1 cup coconut sugar
1 cup honey
*8 ounces melted butter or coconut oil
1¼ cups cocoa, sifted
1 scraped vanilla bean
½ cup tapioca starch
½ teaspoon sea salt
1 shot espresso (Use 1 teaspoon of coffee extract
    or ¼ cup coffee if you don't have espresso.)
pinch cayenne
1 package allergy friendly chocolate chips (or
    1½ cups of chopped dark chocolate chunks)

*Use coconut oil if you are a Paleo purist. They now make coconut oil that has no taste, so it won't influence the flavor of the brownies.

Preheat the oven to 300° F. Butter and flour (or use baker's spray containing oil and flour) an 8-inch square pan (or line the pan with parchment paper).

In a mixer fitted with a whisk attachment, beat the eggs at medium speed until fluffy and light yellow. Add sugar and honey. Beat until well combined.

Add remaining ingredients, and mix to combine.

Pour the batter into the prepared 8-inch square pan and bake for 45 minutes.

Check for doneness with the tried-and-true toothpick method: a toothpick inserted into the center of the pan should come out clean. Remove to a rack to cool. Resist the temptation to cut into it until it's mostly cool.

GLUTEN-FREE
BLUEBERRY BUTTERMILK MUFFINS

3½ cups one-to-one gluten-free flour mix, such as
    Bob's Red Mill
1½ cups granulated sugar
4½ teaspoons baking powder
1 teaspoon baking soda
1 teaspoon kosher salt
2 cups buttermilk, shaken
¼ pound (1 stick) unsalted butter, melted and
    cooled
1½ teaspoons grated lemon zest
2 extra-large eggs, lightly beaten
2 cups fresh blueberries (2 half-pints)
½ cup sliced almonds
Sanding sugar

Preheat the oven to 400° F. Line muffin tins with paper
liners.

Sift the flour, sugar, baking powder, baking soda, and
salt into a large bowl and mix together. In a separate
bowl, mix together the buttermilk, butter, lemon zest,
and eggs.

Make a hole in the center of the dry ingredients and
pour the wet ingredients into the dry ingredients. Mix
with a fork just until blended.

Fold the blueberries into the batter. Don't overmix!
Scoop the batter into the prepared cups, filling them
almost full.

Sprinkle with sliced almonds and sanding sugar.

Bake the muffins for 20 minutes, until golden brown.

Recipe makes 2 dozen muffins.

PALEO CHOCOLATE-ORANGE MUFFINS

1 cup coconut sugar
⅓ cup + 1 tablespoon melted coconut oil
6 tablespoons unsweetened cocoa powder
6 tablespoons HOT water
2 eggs
2 teaspoons vanilla extract
⅓ cup almond flour*
⅓ cup tapioca flour*
1 cup cassava flour*
2 teaspoons baking powder
¾ teaspoon baking soda
¼ teaspoon salt
3 tablespoons orange zest
¾ cup vanilla or plain coconut or almond yogurt
    (or sour cream for a non-Paleo version)
1 bag allergy-free chocolate chips

*For a non-Paleo version, 1⅔ cups gluten-free one-to-one flour may be substituted for the almond, tapioca, and cassava flours.

Optional Glaze

Make a glaze using ½ cup powdered sugar, 1 tablespoon orange zest, and add enough juice from the zested oranges to make a thin paste. Drizzle over the muffins when they're cool.

Preheat oven to 400° F. Line a standard-size muffin tin with liners; set aside.

In a large mixing bowl or the bowl of a stand mixer, combine the sugar and oil. Beat on high for 2 minutes. Combine the cocoa and the hot water in a small bowl and whisk until a smooth paste forms. Add to the sugar and oil, beat for 1 minute. Add the eggs, vanilla, and orange zest. Mix until combined.

In a separate mixing bowl, whisk together the flours, baking powder, baking soda, and salt. Gradually alternate adding the dry ingredients and the yogurt to the large mixing bowl. Mix well.

Using a spatula, fold in 1 cup of the chocolate chips.

Using a large scoop, fill each liner. Sprinkle the remaining ⅓-cup chocolate chips on top and gently press into the batter. Place in the oven to bake for 7 minutes at 400° F, then reduce the heat to 350° F and continue baking for 10–12 more minutes, until a toothpick comes out clean (except for melted chocolate chips). You may have to poke them a couple of times to get a good spot.

Remove from the oven and allow to cool in the pan for 5 minutes before transferring to a wire rack to cool completely. Drizzle with the orange glaze if desired.

Makes 1 dozen muffins.

PALEO BANANA-WALNUT MUFFINS

3 or 4 large ripe bananas (1⅔ cups mashed)
3 eggs, room temperature

3 tablespoons coconut oil, melted
1 teaspoon vanilla extract
⅓ cup almond butter
⅓ cup coconut flour
1 teaspoon ground cinnamon
¾ teaspoon baking soda
¾ teaspoon baking powder
½ teaspoon sea salt
1 cup toasted walnuts, chopped

Preheat the oven to 350° F. Line a muffin tin with paper liners or grease with coconut oil.

In a large bowl or mixer, whip the bananas until mashed. Add eggs, coconut oil, vanilla extract, and the almond butter until fully combined.

In a separate bowl, sift the coconut flour, cinnamon, baking soda, baking powder, and salt together. Add to the wet ingredients and mix well. Fold in the walnuts.

Divide the batter between the prepared muffin tins.

Bake in the preheated oven for about 16–19 minutes. A toothpick inserted into the center of a muffin should come out clean.

Remove from the oven and allow to cool on a wire rack for about 10 minutes. Flip out onto a cooling rack to finish cooling or you'll have soggy bottoms.

Makes 1 dozen muffins.

GLUTEN-FREE
HONEY MAPLE PECAN SHORTBREAD

This shortbread recipe is fabulous by itself or as a pie crust. With the addition of the pecan topping these become pecan pie bars.

¾ cup cassava flour
¾ cup one-to-one gluten-free flour blend
¾ cup almond flour (this really gives the shortbread a crumbly texture)
1 cup sugar
1 cup *good* softened butter (Butter is the big flavor here. Substituting coconut oil or anything else will not make shortbread. The better the butter, the better the shortbread.)
3 vanilla beans, scraped (or 2 tablespoons vanilla extract)
Pinch of sea salt
Pinch of nutmeg (optional)

Maple Pecan Topping

2 eggs
½ cup sugar
½ cup pure maple syrup
1 cup chopped pecans

Preheat an oven to 350° F.

Line a 9 x 13-inch baking dish with parchment, making sure the parchment comes up the sides of the dish.

Combine the butter and sugar in a mixer. Mix until fluffy. Add salt, vanilla, and nutmeg if desired.

Add in the flours and beat until a dough has formed. Press into a parchment-lined 9 x 13-inch baking dish, and prick with a fork.

Bake the shortbread in the preheated oven until golden brown, about 20 minutes. While the shortbread is baking, beat the eggs in a saucepan along with ½ cup sugar, ½ cup maple syrup, and 1 cup pecans. Let mixture come to a gentle boil. Cook for 5 minutes. Pour the hot pecan mixture over the hot crust, and return to the oven. Continue baking until firm, 12 to 15 minutes. Remove from the oven and let cool. Lift the shortbread out by the parchment paper and cut into pieces. I like to cut the bars into rectangles then cut those rectangles into triangles.

GLUTEN-FREE BUTTERSCOTCH–OATMEAL BARS

Bars

> 1¼ cups one-to-one gluten-free flour
> 2 cups gluten-free quick-cooking oatmeal
> ½ teaspoon baking soda
> ½ teaspoon salt
> ¾ cup butterscotch chips
> 16 tablespoons (2 sticks) browned butter
>   (I'll explain below)
> 1 cup packed dark brown sugar
> 1 large egg
> 2 teaspoons vanilla extract

Crumble Topping

> ½ cup (1 stick) unsalted butter, melted
> 1 cup gluten-free flour

¾ cup gluten-free rolled oats
½ cup granulated sugar
¼ cup light brown sugar, packed
pinch salt

Glaze

¼ cup butterscotch chips
4 tablespoons dark brown sugar
2 tablespoons cream
½ teaspoon salt

Preheat the oven to 350° F and adjust an oven rack to the middle position. Line a 9 x 13-inch baking dish with parchment, making sure the parchment comes up the sides of the dish.

In a medium bowl, whisk together the gluten-free flour, oats, baking soda, and salt.

Place the ¾ cup butterscotch chips in a large bowl.

In a small saucepan, melt the butter over medium heat and let the butter cook until golden brown in color, about 10 minutes, taking care not to burn.

Pour the hot butter over half the butterscotch chips and whisk together until melted and smooth. Whisk in the brown sugar until combined. Whisk in the egg and vanilla. Stir in the flour mixture, just until incorporated.

Scrape the batter into the prepared pan and smooth the top, spreading the batter evenly to the edges. Bake the bars until a toothpick inserted into the center comes out with just a few moist crumbs, about 16–18 minutes.

While the bars bake, place the ¼ cup butterscotch chips, brown sugar, water, and salt in a small microwave-safe bowl. Microwave the mixture until melted and smooth, about 2 minutes on 50 percent power. Whisk to combine well.

Drizzle the glaze over the warm bars. Let the bars cool completely in the pan. Remove the bars from the pan using the parchment overhang and cut into squares. Serve.

Please turn the page for an exciting sneak peek of
Libby Klein's next Poppy McAllister mystery,

RESTAURANT WEEKS ARE MURDER,

coming soon wherever print and eBooks are sold!

"I don't care how good Dr. Oz says it is, I'm not eating vegan cheese." Aunt Ginny took the last stuffed pheasant off the Frasier Fir, wrapped it in tissue paper, and placed it in an old Woolworth's hatbox to store until next Christmas.

I put the lid on the box of antique nutcrackers and placed it by the doorway for my handyman, Itty Bitty Smitty, to store in the attic the next time he was here to fiddle with his perpetual chore list. "But Aunt Ginny, you haven't even tried it yet. It's made from cashews."

Aunt Ginny stuck her tongue out. "That might just be the most disgusting thing I've ever heard. I'd rather eat the plastic it's wrapped in."

Figaro made himself his usual nuisance and batted a sparkly red and gold ornament from a low branch across the floor and chased it out into the foyer.

"Come on. You said you'd do this diet with me. You know how much better I've been feeling since I went Paleo four months ago."

"Yeah, I know. Everybody knows. Because you won't stop talking about it. I've never heard anyone go on so much about gluten, inflammation, and free-range vegetables in my whole life. Back in my day you ate what you wanted and got old gracefully. You never complained that you were bloated, or your brain was foggy."

I rolled my eyes to myself. If Aunt Ginny didn't spend the better part of each day grousing about her aches and pains her jaw would atrophy, and she'd need physical therapy. I picked up the three boxes of Belgian chocolates that she had received for Christmas from her "Secret Santa." I suspected Aunt Ginny's "Secret Santa" was a little redhead in her eighties with a penchant for caramels. "Where would you like these, Saint Nick?"

Aunt Ginny snatched the boxes from my hand. "I'll put them in my room with that bottle of Amaretto that mysteriously showed up under the tree."

I threw my hands up. "It's a Christmas miracle!" I followed the trail of glitter down the hall to the kitchen where I found a gold sparkly Figaro peeking at me with one eye, the other side of his body hiding behind the trash can. I checked the time. Thirty minutes till the event of a lifetime, working side by side with Tim, my ex-fiancé, as his pastry chef in a real professional kitchen. Just thinking about it made my scalp tingle. "Come on, Liberace, let's brush you out before I'm dealing with something gold and sparkly in the litter box."

I plopped down on the floor in the sunroom and ran a brush through Figaro's black smoke fur. He hummed like a Harley, his copper eyes slitty like two winter crescent moons reflecting on the Atlantic.

Aunt Ginny waved a pair of bright orange leather hands at me from the doorway. "What should I do with Georgina's present? These must have cost your mother-in-law a fortune, but who in their right mind needs Italian calfskin car gloves just for driving five minutes to the beauty parlor once a week? And why in the world did she get this gaudy shade of orange?"

My eyes flicked up to the pumpkin-colored swirls atop of Aunt Ginny's head. "I think she got them to . . . match." I smiled.

Aunt Ginny narrowed her eyes. "Well then you take them, they match your hair too smarty pants."

"Hey, don't blame me for Georgina's gaudy taste. At least you didn't get a custom monogrammed barbecue brand to sear your initials onto your steaks. I can't even re-gift that."

Aunt Ginny sat in her rocker and wound a ball of twinkle lights into a hive for me to figure out next Christmas. "I'm glad things are going better between the two of you. Especially since it looks like she'll be visiting regularly now that she and You-Know-Who are an item."

We gave each other a look and shook our heads. The memory of Georgina locked in a passionate embrace with a certain little bald handyman was a disturbing image.

Figaro swatted my hand and tried to bite me, signaling the grooming event was over. I took the ball of lights Aunt Ginny had painstakingly knotted up and put them in another storage bin.

I hiked up my skinny jeans, which were drooping over my hips. I giggled to myself. I hadn't worn anything that could be classified as too big since I played dress-up in Aunt Ginny's petticoats when I was six.

I boxed up the penguin mafia and the Nativity Scene, which somehow always managed to merge into one display, and checked the time on my phone again. Ten more minutes.

Aunt Ginny toddled around the corner heaving a

giant light up gingerbread house for the stack. "Is it time?"

"Almost." I grinned and took the Sweetie Shoppe from her.

"You've been bouncing around here like a grasshopper on a hot pavement."

"I can't help it, I feel like my fairy godmother finally showed up and said you're going to an all-you-can-eat pie buffet, and everything has negative calories. I've waited my whole life for this day. I thought I had greater odds of fitting into a size seven again."

Aunt Ginny put a papery hand on my arm. "I know how much this means to you, Poppy Blossom. I wish you had just gone to culinary school instead of that fancy college. I want you to slow down and enjoy every minute of it. Even working with Gigi."

I groaned. The thought of Gigi, Tim's cute little incessantly perky mentee, was irritating enough to blister a melon. "I will. I'm not going to let Gigi get to me this time. I feel like my life is finally taking a good turn. Like I'm going to make something out of myself after all. If I had a beret, I'd throw it in the air."

Aunt Ginny cocked her head. "You've made plenty out of your life. What do you call the Butterfly House? You've turned this old Victorian into a beautiful bed-and-breakfast."

I taped up a box and glanced at the chipped crown molding and the scuffed baseboards. "We're almost there. We've had a rocky start, but I think in the spring we'll be ready to officially open for guests. If I can ever get Smitty here to finish up."

Aunt Ginny crossed her arms. "Thank God for the off-season. Lord Jesus help us come Easter."

I took one last look around. Christmas was packed away for another year. It was time to turn some daydreams into reality. Today I become a chef, even it if was for only a week. I looked at my phone again.

"It's time." I gave Aunt Ginny another hug. "I'll see you in a few hours after the Meet and Greet."

A shaking rumble to our left caused me to pause and listen. "Did you hear that?" It happened again.

Aunt Ginny let out a loud sigh and pointed to the box by my feet. It was moving.

I ripped the tape off and Figaro popped out like a deranged jack-in-the-box covered in tinsel.

"This is why Pastry Chef Pierre Hermé doesn't have a cat."

Connect with Us

Visit us online at
KensingtonBooks.com
to read more from your favorite authors, see books
by series, view reading group guides, and more.

for sneak peeks, chances to win books and prize packs,
and to share your thoughts with other readers.

facebook.com/kensingtonpublishing
twitter.com/kensingtonbooks

Tell us what you think!

To share your thoughts, submit a review,
or sign up for our eNewsletters, please visit:
KensingtonBooks.com/TellUs.